THE ADVENTURE
OF THE BUSTS OF
EVA PERÓN

THE ADVENTURE OF THE BUSTS OF EVA PERÓN

Carlos Gamerro

Translated by Ian Barnett
in collaboration with the author

LONDON · NEW YORK

First published in English translation in 2015 by And Other Stories
London – New York
www.andotherstories.org

First published as *La aventura de los bustos de Eva* in 2004 by Grupo Editorial
Norma, Buenos Aires, Argentina
© Carlos Gamerro 2004, 2011, 2012

English-language translation © Ian Barnett 2015

ISBN 9781908276506
eBook ISBN 9781908276513

A catalogue record for this book is available from the British Library.

This book has been selected to receive financial assistance from
English PEN's 'PEN Translates!' programme, supported by Arts
Council England. English PEN exists to promote literature and our
understanding of it, to uphold writers' freedoms around the world,
to campaign against the persecution and imprisonment of writers
for stating their views, and to promote the friendly co-operation
of writers and the free exchange of ideas. www.englishpen.org

Supported by the National Lottery through Arts Council England.

Supported using public funding by
ARTS COUNCIL
ENGLAND

CONTENTS

PROLOGUE

The day Ernesto Marroné returned home from the Los Ceibales Country Club after a splendid afternoon's golf and discovered the poster of Che Guevara hanging on his teenage son's bedroom wall, he knew the time had come to tell the truth about his guerrilla past.

Not that this had been a secret kept under lock and key: his wife had, of course, been partially privy to it – after all, they were already married at the time, and something of that magnitude was harder to hide than an extra-marital affair – but, far from attempting to pry, Mabel had always clipped his timid attempts at confession with a curt 'I'd rather not know'. His in-laws, and to a lesser extent his parents, were aware of something; just how much he'd never dared find out. And at the office, of course, it was an open secret. Who hadn't heard of Marroné's rise through the ranks of the Montoneros, the far-left Peronist guerrilla force, who had taken hostage no less than his company's president, Sr Fausto Tamerlán? But his children had, for better or worse, been spared this knowledge – until today.

That's how it is, thought Marroné with a sigh as he unknotted the laces of his Jack Nicklaus golf shoes; there's no escaping the past. No matter how far you run, sooner or later it catches up with you – with all of us. Because, far from being an exception, Marroné's story was emblematic of a whole generation – a generation now striving to erase the traces of a shameful past with the same diligence it had once devoted to building a utopian future. Who then would dare to point the finger at him, who to cast the first stone? Take this very place, no need to look any further: how many of the current occupants of these beautiful houses half-hidden among leafy groves had, in the past, with the same hand that now gracefully swung a Slazenger, taken up arms against privileges far less unjust than those they now enjoyed?

The hot shower restored the warmth driven from his body by the June cold and the bitter memories, and strengthened his purpose: the time had come for his son to know the truth. He wouldn't even discuss it with Mabel beforehand as he usually did, in case she challenged his decision and weakened his resolve. A couple could walk the path of life blithely avoiding silent corners and wisely passing closed doors. But a son was different. To a son, the secret, the silence, the indifference of a father was a message, a command, perhaps even a curse, all the more insidious for having gone unsaid. Perhaps if this had concerned his daughter Cynthia, Daddy's pampered princess, he could have left it for a future date. What could she know, when only yesterday her Barbie games and today her hairdos, weekend discos, diets and innocent flirting with boys her own age and background occupied all the free time her studies at the Country Club school afforded her? If it was true that in those days the impetuous advance of the guerrilla movement had added thousands of women to its ranks, it was equally true that today any such possibility was well and truly dead. With boys, however, you could never be sure. They always went for them first, taking advantage of their idealism, their romantic yearnings for adventure, their worship of risk for risk's sake; of all that energy that was so much easier to detonate than to channel and conduct along the ordered circuits of society. He had faith in his son: he was a brilliant young man, 'fated to succeed', a born leader and true friend, and most of all he had a noble heart. But it was precisely these qualities – what was best in him – that made him easy prey to the siren song of the violent and impatient. Marroné knew better than anyone. Hadn't they succeeded with him? How could he believe then that his son was safe?

Dressed now in his casuals, which he would wear until bedtime, he passed the open door of his son's room and came, once again, face to face with the sharp, black and white outlines – no shades of grey – of the Che Guevara poster. His eyes looked into the intense, defiant ones of his all-too-famous compatriot, but, unlike other times, this time he met his gaze. 'It might have worked with me,' he said to him, 'but you won't have it so easy with my son. Because he's not alone; he has me. And I . . . I know you all too well.' Marroné felt a stab of pain in his chest on thinking about how many lives could have been saved if only parents had spoken to their children in time. 'We never realised,' they'd say later as if they'd never received the warning that flashed from the romantic revolutionary's fiery eyes on hundreds of walls, in hundreds of children's rooms. A whole generation had sacrificed itself on the altar of dubious idols – a generation of which he, Marroné, was a survivor. But what had he survived for if not to tell his story, and in the telling to prevent it being repeated and lay the unquiet ghosts of the past to rest in the slumber of the grave?

Now wasn't the time though: Tommy was out, just finishing his rugby training at the San Isidro Athletics Club, and by the time he got home his mother and sister would be back from their usual Sunday evening shopping spree at the mall, and their presence might encroach on the privacy a father-and-son talk demanded. Tomorrow, like every Monday when Ernesto and Tomás Marroné drove the seventy kilometres of freeway separating him from the office block in Puerto Madero and his son from the university, would be the time to talk it over at their ease. And, in the meantime, he'd have all night to think about what to say.

One thing worried him above all else.

Would he be believed? Could his son, could anyone looking at the Ernesto Marroné of today believe that he, the financial manager of the most powerful construction and real estate conglomerate in Argentina, had once crouched in the lawless shadows of clandestinity and declared himself the enemy of the very society that now sheltered him? That he had not only raised his voice, but taken up arms against so-called injustices which his intervention had in any case only helped to aggravate?

Ernesto Marroné didn't get a wink of sleep that night.

He lay there wide awake, hands folded behind his head, eyes fixed on the ceiling where the streetlights shining through the tree branches cast shadows of phantasmagorical crucifixions, and let the memories flood back. There, as on a blank screen, he watched the film of his rebellious past from beginning to end – a film that, for him at least, had begun sixteen years ago, the afternoon he was first summoned to the basement of the building on Paseo Colón – to the subterranean office complex that the company's president had christened with the poetic, Valkyrian name 'The Nibelheim', but which all his employees had more familiarly christened 'Tamerlán's Bunker'.

1

THE FINGER OF TAMERLÁN

'Sr Tamerlán's kidnappers have set new demands, Sr Marroné.'

Seated on the other side of the desk, Marroné slid his eyes over the polished cranium of Govianus the accountant, who rarely looked up, preferring instead to follow the vague gestures with which his own languid hands accompanied the conversation. Within hours of the news of Sr Tamerlán's kidnapping by the Montoneros, Govianus had taken possession of both the imposing metal desk – which looked for all the world like an over-turned safe – and the immense sealed vault in which it lay. From here he had, for the last six months, directed all the negotiations, in close liaison with the victim's family, yet in all that time he still hadn't grown into the place. The room was too big for him, the desk was too big for him, even the gold fountain pen with the monogram 'FT' finely engraved on its base looked too big between his fingers. A dwarf – that was what Govianus the accountant reminded Marroné of: a bald, bespectacled dwarf usurping the dominions of a giant.

'What do they want now? More money?'

'If only, Marroné, if only. I sometimes regret the fact that kidnappings in this country aren't performed by the Mafia. At least with them you know where you are; we speak the same language. But all this nonsense about improving the conditions of our workers – always the workers, mind you; the office staff be damned, as if we didn't suffer too – all this welcoming like lords the delegates that yesterday we spurned like dogs, all this dishing out of food in the shanties . . . Give me a break! You know what they want now? You know the latest thing they've come up with? They want us to put a bust of Eva Perón in each of our offices. Even in this one! Can you think of anything more absurd?'

Marroné didn't answer, as he was already mentally totting up the number of busts needed to meet the new demand. Eighth floor: the 'Valhalla', the meeting room and two other offices; seventh floor: nine offices, a hallway . . .

'The hallways too?'

'What do I know? You'd better include them, can't be too careful. Maybe they want them in the bathrooms as well, so she can watch us whip it out. I'm telling you, Marroné, I'm at the end of my tether. First Sr Fuchs – may he rest in peace – now Sr Tamerlán . . . Are we the only company in the country with presidents to kidnap? These boys ought to practise a more effective system, like crop rotation . . . They have it in for us, I reckon. Rather unfair considering our staff are 100 per cent Argentine. Fuchs had been a citizen for years and Sr Tamerlán has lived here since he was ten. No need to remind you that he arrived on the 17th of October 1945 of all days . . . But these boys don't know a thing about history. Oh well. Just so long as they don't take it into their heads to torch us, the way they do the foreign companies . . . '

Clearly Govianus the accountant needed to get this off his chest, and Marroné instantly recalled Principle Four of the 'Six Ways to Make People Like You' listed in Dale Carnegie's

How to Win Friends and Influence People: 'Be a good listener. Encourage others to talk about themselves.'

'But you and your family have very tight security, don't you?'

'Regrettably. Do you know what it's like having guards in your living room from dusk till dawn? One of them never flushes. They're taking over the house bit by bit. Now they've commandeered the remote control. Think about it. *The Mod Squad, Police Woman, Starsky & Hutch* . . . I only get a break on matchdays. My wife and I had to buy ourselves a telly set for the bedroom. And no one dares ring the bell any more. The other day they pulled a gun on the soda-man and had him drink a squirt from each of the siphons he was delivering. In case they were trying to poison me, they explained later. You could hear the belch all the way to Burzaco. But my problems are insignificant next to Sr Tamerlán's. Time is running out, Marroné. It's been six months. The kidnappers are losing their patience. Look.'

Govianus was holding out a rectangular stainless-steel box, the kind used to sterilise and store hypodermics in, coated with a thin film of frost. Marroné took it. It was ice-cold to the touch, as if it had just been taken out of the freezer.

'Open it, open it.'

Marroné tried, but his fingers kept on slipping on the frost and the steel wouldn't yield. Eventually he managed to work a nail into the groove and lifted the lid. The moment he laid eyes on the contents he let out a yell and flung them in the air.

'A finger! It's a finger!'

'Of course it's a finger, Marroné! It's Sr Tamerlán's finger! Thank your lucky stars its owner isn't around to see the way you treat it. Well don't just stand there gawping. Help me find it!'

They had to crawl about among electricity and phone cables, chair legs and wheels, to find the two halves of the box and its grim contents. Marroné was unfortunate enough to find the finger. It was livid, mottled with yellow and grey, and the nail, despite being neatly manicured ('as if deliberately spruced up for its big day' was the gruesome thought Marroné's mind whispered in his ear) had a menacing air about it, like one of those amulets made out of animal claws. He looked around queasily for something to pick it up with and, when Govianus looked away, he pulled a plastic bag out of the waste-paper basket, slid his hand in and bagged it like a dog turd. Through the plastic the cold of the dead flesh played up and down his spine like a xylophone. Carefully he replaced the finger in its hollow of cotton wool and returned the box to the surface of the desk. An incisive question flashed across his brain.

'Can we be sure it's Sr Tamerlán's finger?'

'It's tested positive with police forensics, which I needn't tell you is no guarantee in this country. But I daresay all of us in this company know that finger well. Correct me if I'm wrong, Sr Marroné.'

Govianus had tilted his head slightly and lowered his glasses to the bridge of his nose, his naked eyes staring at Marroné over the frames as if daring him to disagree. He wasn't wrong of course. Until that moment Marroné had not truly been aware of the degree of savagery or fanaticism of the men they were up against. Cutting off Sr Tamerlán's index finger was like cutting off Samson's hair, Cleopatra's nose, Caruso's tongue or Pelé's legs; like kicking Perón's teeth in or castrating Casanova. These men were capable of anything! Nothing was sacred to them! They were no doubt aware of the profound significance that Sr Tamerlán's finger held for all the employees in his company, and by mutilating him they had struck right at its innermost core. There had been no better-guarded secret in the company, yet they had uncovered it. But then again it was common knowledge that the subversives had infiltrated the government, the trade unions, even the army. Why should *they* be the exception? They're everywhere, thought Marroné with a shudder; you never really know who you're talking to. While Govianus answered a phone call, Marroné let his gaze rest on the once vital finger that had until recently ruled their lives and now lay inert in its steel sarcophagus, and for an instant his eyes welled with tears. It was the same one, no doubt about it. How could he have been in any doubt? He remembered the exact day he had made its acquaintance, together with the man it was still attached to, because it was, amongst other things, the very day that marked the onset of the inveterate constipation that had afflicted him ever since: the day Sr Tamerlán had interviewed him in person and offered him the post of head of procurement, which he still held. That meeting had changed his life, had had a profound effect on him. Thanks to his MBA in Marketing from Stanford and certain family contacts he had sailed comfortably through the pre-selection process, but it was common knowledge in the business world that the final requirement for joining any of the companies in the Tamerlán Group was a personal private interview with the great man himself. It was rumoured that, when it came to selecting management staff for his companies he had an infallible method for separating the wheat from the chaff, though none of the applicants – successful or otherwise – had wanted to divulge what it consisted in: a tacit pact of silence that only deepened the mystery and added grist to the mill of rumour and speculation. It was known that, after the kidnapping and death of Sr Fuchs, Sr Tamerlán had completely restructured the company, secretly sifting through the entire management staff, orchestrating rises and falls, and removing those whose loyalty to the new president was not what it should be, in order to create many a vacancy like the one Marroné had aspired to.

The week before the interview he had spent in eager anticipation of the meeting, which would mark a watershed in his life – if, that is, all went smoothly; if he could say the right thing at the right time, sit back and let Sr Tamerlán take the floor, smile a lot, offer condolences for the demise of his late partner, try to strike the proper balance between sincerity and formality. He could think of nothing else: each and every night of that interminable week he had bombarded his wife at dinner with stories of the mythical Tamerlán; he would dandle his son on his knees, and instead of 'horsey-horsey', would come out with 'tam-tam-Tamerlán'; and in bed, before going to sleep, he and his wife would get embroiled in all kinds of monomaniacal speculation about the traps Sr Tamerlán might set him at the ever-so-mysterious interview, which he sought to pre-empt by reading and rereading Warren P Jonas's *Are You Ready for Your Job Interview?*, until the pages dropped out. It was rumoured that many who had smoothly negotiated the hurdles of Rorschach, handwriting, psychological and a battery of other tests bit the dust on this final strait, Marroné would remark, fairly quaking with the thrill of it. And far from getting bored, his wife would feed the flames with newspaper and magazine cuttings about Sr Tamerlán. And, at night, in the breaks afforded them by the boy's night terrors, they made love with an ardour unknown even in their early days – although, as often happened in moments of great anxiety, Marroné usually came early. But once, almost without trying, he must have got a hole-in-one, for, exactly nine months later Mabel gave birth to little Cynthia, and when he first clapped eyes on her, Marroné thought he could make out the unmistakeable traces of Sr Tamerlán's features in the little girl's, as if at the delicate moment of conception the mental image that never left his head had been imprinted on the malleable surface of her cells.

In those fraught days not even such releases of tension would allow Marroné to sleep: he would spend the rest of the night awake, running through all the possible variations of his impending conversation with the great company man, planning strategies and evaluating possible scenarios and outcomes. The most important thing – the real trick – was to stay off the beaten track, to dare to innovate – to be, in a word, creative. There could be nothing more tedious for a restless man of genius like Sr Tamerlán than the tawdry routine of a job interview. But this one Marroné would make unforgettable. He would seize the initiative from the off: for instance, he would find something in the office to praise sincerely – a picture, an antique lamp, the wood panelling – as had James Adamson, president of the Superior Seating Company, in his interview with Mr Eastman, as he had read in *How to Win Friends and Influence People*. Sr Tamerlán's stern face would immediately light up and he would go on to tell him the history of the object in question: 'It has been in my family for generations. My father, at the start of the Great War . . . ' The conversation would at once assume a relaxed, informal tone: with jubilation they would discover common interests, like big-game hunting or Wagnerian opera – interests that, if truth be told, had recently been acquired by Marroné after acquainting himself with Sr Tamerlán's tastes, through reading old issues of sporting magazines and listening to *The Valkyrie* till he dropped. Won over by the open smile and sincere interest of his aspiring head of procurement, Sr Tamerlán would gradually lower his guard and confess his most intimate fears: of not being the efficient storm pilot his fleet of companies needed to navigate the unpredictable climes of the national economy; of not being able to compete with the ghost of his late partner and predecessor in the efficient handling of the intricate conglomerate; or – prophetically – of becoming the victim of an attack by the very people who had kidnapped and murdered his partner. By degrees the conversation would shift from the personal to the managerial: one by one Marroné would drop in suggestions on how to streamline the company's management, taking the precaution to pass these off as ideas of Sr Tamerlán's own, which he, Marroné, was merely plucking from the air and making *explicit*, as recommended in Raymond Schneck's *Sit Your Boss on Your Knees*. On the spot he would be offered the post of marketing manager, which he had secretly longed for, with the promise of the vice presidency, which Sr Tamerlán's rise to the presidency had left vacant, glimmering almost within reach like a ring on a merry-go-round – at which moment Marroné's fantasy reached the dizzying summit of this stairway of imaginary questions and answers, and dropped him back on the twin realities of the as-yet-unconsummated meeting and the scorching bed, on which he feverishly tossed this way and that, buffeted by the elbows of his sleeping wife, until the cogs and gears of his desires and fantasies meshed again, and Marroné's mind once more started the laborious ascent of the seemingly endless spiral staircase of his waking dreams. His brain glowed like a lump of burning coal, and he turned the pillow over and over in futile attempts to cool his head. The ironies of fate: his innards had him running to the bathroom that week at all times of day and, as D-Day approached, at night too, as if they knew such irresponsible freedom would end for ever upon the fateful day of the feared and longed-for interview.

Which did not take place in the as yet non-existent bunker – in those days a mere archive and storage space in the basement – but at the antipole of the building, under the bulging dome of amber crystal that crowned the stately turn-of-the-century construction's upper floor, baptised by Sr Tamerlán himself with the poetic name 'Valhalla'.

Sr Tamerlán's desk, an imposing mahogany catafalque, was placed precisely beneath the crystal dome and, being a sunny day, Marroné was met on entering by the sight of his future employer submerged in a nimbus of golden light that isolated him from the surrounding atmosphere, as if he inhabited a reality of a different order and as if the desk, the objects strewn about it and the man himself sitting erect on his curved-armed throne were made of a more refined material, of gold and light.

'That desk . . . ' Marroné began his well-rehearsed routine.

'Drop the pants, please.'

Sr Tamerlán had spoken without looking at him, without even looking up from the folder he had been leafing through – a bid for tender perhaps – and on hearing this unusual request, Marroné's eyes scoured the enormous room in case the words had been intended for someone else and he was about to make a fool of himself. No, they were the only ones there. Marroné undid the buckle, loosened his belt, then the inside button of his James Smart trousers. As they were a wide fit he had no trouble pulling them over his shoes, except for the left heel, which got caught, forcing him to hop briefly on one leg. He folded them carefully, but having nowhere to put them, he hung them over his bent arm. His underpants, however, were worn and cheap-looking, and he was glad his shirt tails hid them from view.

'Those too,' said Sr Tamerlán without so much as a glance, as if taking it for granted that Marroné's initial response would be dictated by modesty.

Marroné obeyed, recalling at that instant an enigmatic phrase attributed to Sr Tamerlán by a reliable source: 'Anyone who wants a career with us has to wear the company's underpants.' It was no doubt a reference to whatever it was that was about to happen. Sr Tamerlán closed the folder, rose from his chair, rounded the desk and walked towards him with his hands clasped behind his back, looking him up and down. For a moment Marroné feared Sr Tamerlán would open his mouth and examine his gums. Outside the enchanted circle of light Sr Tamerlán might pass for an ordinary human being, until he fixed his eyes on yours. Then, what the yellow light had softened leapt at you like a dog loosed from its muzzle: two eyes as blue as icebergs, and as hard. But it was only when Marroné looked down at his hands that sheer terror enabled him to wrest back the words that his surprise had taken from him: with his left hand Sr Tamerlán was pulling a proctologist's rubber finger-stall over his right index finger.

'I've already had the medical,' stammered the terrified Marroné.

'Don't be stupid, Marroné, or I'll regret hiring you before I do. It isn't your prostate I'm worried about, let alone your haemorrhoids; in fact, all my most efficient executives have them: makes them edgier, more aggressive. Like ulcers. No, Marroné, it's a different part of you I want to reach. Move forward a few steps, please. That's it. Now rest both hands on the desk. Put those down there. Have no fear, we'll give them back to you on your way out.'

Marroné deposited pants and underpants on the glassy wooden surface. The warmth of the golden light caressed his face and the back of his hands, and its brightness made him half-shut his eyes. Through the cracks he managed to see what Sr Tamerlán had been flicking through. It wasn't a bid for tender as he had first supposed but a magazine called *Queen Studs*. A naked, hairless hunk stared out from the cover with come-hither eyes, one slack hand draped casually over his crotch. As if both ends of his body were connected by a single taut thread, Marroné's pupils dilated as fast as his sphincter contracted to a full stop.

'As you must surely know, Marroné, physicians and philosophers have for centuries been searching for the physical seat of the soul. Pythagoras, for example, contended that the soul is air or, put another way, breath – which led him to locate it in the lungs; Democritus would complete the idea with an intricate atomistic lucubration to explain why the soul doesn't come out of our mouths every time we exhale. The Stoics fluctuated between placing it in the heart or the head, but they agreed that it then extended through the body in seven polyp-like tentacles that informed our five senses, our speech and our organs of generation; from there it was but a short step, taken by Sir Thomas Browne amongst others, to the notion that the soul is handed down to the child in the father's seed, and thence to its relocation in the balls. The mystical, theosophical or spiritualist traditions, on the other hand, usually favour the cardiac zone; *The Upanishads* situate it beautifully in a small chamber in the shape of a lotus-flower at the very centre of the heart. The Assyrians, however, located it in the liver. Stupid race. They deserved to die out for that if for nothing else. Then there were those who spoke of several souls, such as the Egyptians, who counted seven, distributed around the body; whilst Plato, always thrifty where material reality was concerned, cut them down to three: the rational, located in the head; the thumetic or spirited, in the chest; and the appetitive, between the diaphragm and the navel. Now, with that last one he really hit the post. Descartes, on the other hand, went completely the other way: he claimed the soul was housed in the pineal gland, this being the only single rather than dual structure of the brain and sense organs; which is why some have tried to link it with the third eye of the Buddhists – the eye of the soul.

'This last notion, though essentially wrong, would eventually help me to see the truth. As you can see, many of the scholars, poets and thinkers in the history of East and West have devoted their days and nights to pondering or even scientifically investigating this tricky point. What a bunch of incompetent cocksuckers! Five thousand years of culture and I always end up having to do it myself! Still. All that effort may not have been in vain; the truth is sometimes nothing more than the qualitative leap forward that springs from an accumulation of blunders. Yes, Marroné. The third eye – the eye of the soul – does exist, hidden within us, waiting to be awakened; just not in the middle of your forehead. So where is it? With due modesty I think I can safely say that I have solved the riddle. Legs a little wider, please.'

Marroné felt the first, tentative contact between his buttocks, then an increase in pressure as the rubber surface began to work its way inside. All the words hoarded over the last week completely evaporated from his mind. At that moment, had someone asked him his name, he couldn't have answered with any certainty.

'It was pretty obvious, though the answer lay not in anatomy, but in language. Why do you think they always talk about the "seat" of the soul? Why do you think the phrases "save your soul" and "save your arse" are so closely alloyed? Why do you think we say "I can't be arsed" to express flat refusal? Didn't it ever strike you as odd that we locate the seat of integrity not in the head or the heart, but a fair bit lower down? And what, Marroné, is the organ of our integrity but the soul? That's why when your soul won't bend, your arse won't budge. As long as you own your arse, you own your self. That's why if you're going to work for me, there's one thing you need to be very clear about. In this company we applaud freethinking, creativity and imagination; you're free to have your own ideas and feelings, but your arse is ours. We aren't asking much. We can't get into your head, true, but we can get into your arse. And once we're in, we give you the freedom to think whatever you like. That orifice is our most sensitive organ for perceiving errors, and there's no better antidote for idiotic leanings towards independence or rebellion than a nicely puckered arse. From now on, Marroné, when you're in any doubt, consult your arse and it'll tell you what to do. Remember: your arse is your best friend.'

While he spoke, Sr Tamerlán kept his finger still but rigid. Once his monologue was over, he began to withdraw it, and that was perhaps the most humiliating moment for Ernesto Marroné, when by reflex his sphincter contracted on Sr Tamerlán's finger as if he were trying to keep it there just a little bit longer. It was the final proof, if any were needed, that Sr Tamerlán was right: Marroné could no longer call his arse his own. But the stupefied blank that the removal of Sr Tamerlán's finger had left in his mind was not to be filled by such elaborate sentiments as offence or humiliation, not even when, terminating the interview, Sr Tamerlán tossed the used finger-stall into the waste-paper basket like a spent condom.

'I expect great things of you, Marroné. Be here for work first thing on Monday.'

As he left, he thought he caught ill-concealed smiles in every glance, stifled laughter behind his back, and, that night, when his wife, eczematous with impatience, asked him the moment he walked in through the door, 'And? How did it go? Did you meet him? Did you meet Sr Tamerlán?', Marroné opened his mouth to speak and stood there staring until he found the words to deny all personal contact with the great company man. 'I got the job,' was all he managed to say.

'So? Think you can do it?' The weary voice of Govianus the accountant, who had finished his telephone conversation, brought him back with a thud from dome to basement, from glaring past to murky present. He cast around as if the eye of his mind had also to grow accustomed to the change of light. If the top-floor office and its vicinity to the heavens, its blinding light and bracing wind blowing in from the river, had always conjured for Marroné a majestic galleon in full sail, this office, with the unflagging ultramarine and emerald green of its windowless walls, the fish-tank lighting of its fluorescent tubes, the armoured metal furnishings and the refrigerated air descending motionlessly from the vents in the ceiling, resembled nothing so much as a submerged submarine in wartime. And wartime it undoubtedly was when proud men like Sr Tamerlán, accustomed to leading the nation's economic destiny from the prow, were forced to dig lairs and hide underground like hunted animals. Construction work on the bunker had been completed shortly after Marroné joined the firm, and the engineer and labourers Sr Tamerlán had imported had been flown back to the USSR: only the big man himself would be privy to the secrets of its construction. But the office they now found themselves in was just the tip of the iceberg, the semi-public space of a much vaster subterranean complex: some hidden point of the mute surfaces surrounding Marroné concealed the entrance to the secret chambers that only a handful of the elect had seen, though rumours circulated in the company about the treasure accumulated in the vault, enough to buy wills ('arses,' his mind corrected) and to finance acts of sabotage; about the communication equipment powerful enough to jam all the radio and television sets in the country and commandeer the airwaves; about the power plant with supplies for several months, the weapons and explosives depot, the larders and freezers overflowing with the choicest produce of five continents; and especially about the executive bed-rooms, entirely covered with mirrors, and complete with rotating waterbeds, jacuzzis and fat catalogues of products from the ports of Northern Europe and the Far East. The bunker could accommodate the company's top executives, and their sexual partners of choice, male or female (wives and children were strictly banned as counter-effective to the ruthless exercise of power). If a communist revolution was ever victorious in Argentina, capitalism could hole up here and hold out for months. Months! Ha! Sr Tamerlán had been kidnapped in broad daylight by the guerrillas before he was able to see his super-sophisticated lair completed, and maybe now, locked away in dungeons more primitive, dug by his captors, he would be reflecting on the vanity of the insatiable human longing for security.

'All we have to do is contact our usual supplier and place an urgent order,' answered Marroné. 'No big deal. That's why I'm head of procurement, isn't it? But as you know . . . '

'Please, Marroné, not that again. You know all promo-tions are frozen until Sr Tamerlán gets back. Help me rescue our president and I promise you that, when all this is over, I will speak to him myself in person about your promotion to marketing and sales.'

'When all this is over,' Marroné mentally retorted to the unmannerly Govianus, who, without waiting for him to go out, had plunged his nose back into his paperwork, 'I may not need a middleman to speak to Sr Tamerlán and ask him for what he'll no longer be able to refuse.' As he waited for the lift to take him back to his office on the sixth floor, he looked up at the model of the Monument to the Descamisado, which stood in the lobby: sheer forehead, shirt unbuttoned to the waist, right hand on chest, left clenched in a sinewy fist. The monument had been commissioned during the golden years of the first Peronist government and, at a purported 137 metres, was intended to be the tallest in the world. But by the time Perón fell from power in 1955 the building work hadn't even started, and the model was shunted discreetly to the basement where it gathered dust until Perón's return to power two years ago, when they had decided to move it into the lobby. Instinctively Marroné adopted his plebeian counterpart's posture of Herculean determination, as befitting someone who has heard destiny knocking on his door. This, he said to himself, was the opportunity he had so longed for to prove to Sr Tamerlán his personal devotion, to show him he wasn't just another employee ('Just another arsehole,' the devious side of his mind said in a whisper that the saner side dismissed with a mental grimace) and to join the inner circle of Tartars, as Sr Tamerlán had taken to calling his personal guard of samurai executives. 'The arrival of those busts, Marroné,' he would say when it was all over, the two of them lounging in the plush white armchairs of his living room (a living room he could relax in, thanks to Mabel's collection of magazine cuttings, as comfortably as in his own), each warming a glass of cognac in their cupped hands, 'was providential. They'd already pronounced my sentence, the murder weapon of the chosen one was already pointing at my temple – they draw lots, Marroné, such is their bloodlust that they will fight each other for the privilege. But tell me something . . . The idea of concealing a transmitter in the sample bust, was it really the police's or . . . ? Of course. I knew it. What is a man like you doing vegetating in procurement? Marketing? Don't be modest, man. Look, I need to recover, have some time to myself, travel the world in the company of my darling wife. And Govianus, we can agree, much as we acknowledge his efforts over these last few months, isn't the man for the job . . . He lacks fibre, grit, *drive* . . . If it had been down to him, I wouldn't have enough fingers left to warm this glass. Besides, Ernesto – mind if I call you Ernesto? – I needn't tell you that the doors of this house are always open to you. So my daughter Clara won't feel so alone while we're away, will you, Clara, darling?'

By the time the lift reached the sixth floor it was the day of his wedding to Clara Tamerlán and the bubble of his imagination burst with the rarefaction of the reality around it: Sr Tamerlán had no daughter, and Marroné was already married. But despite his right hemisphere's natural tendency to such tangential flights of fancy, it didn't escape the notice of his more sober left side that this wasn't the time for dreaming but for living up to the name of executive and executing.

'Busts? Of Evita? No, what problem could there be?' the jolly voice of the owner of the Sansimón Plasterworks, the company's main supplier, answered him good-naturedly. 'A few years ago it would have been a different story, but these days . . . They're going like hot cakes. How many did you say? No, not that many in stock, but I'll have them run off for you before you can say "Evita Perón". Why don't you drop round first thing tomorrow and I'll show you the different models. Will you be wanting some of the Governor too?'

After hanging up, Marroné gazed out of the window of his deserted office at the crawling columns of vehicles as they drained from the city centre, and indulged in two more flights of fancy: the short version, in which he passed himself off as a member of the guerrilla to rescue Sr Tamerlán and fled with him through the slums at night, carrying him through a hail of zinging bullets; and the longer version, in which beneath Govianus's unimpeachable mask he discovered a guerrilla leader who had infiltrated the company years ago and bled it to swell the coffers of subversion. Knowing he had been exposed, Govianus holed up in the bunker and asked Marroné – named sole negotiator by mutual agreement of the parties – for a plane to take him and several political prisoners to Cuba in exchange for Sr Tamerlán's release; in the end, realising the game was up, he bit the cyanide pill carried by every subversive and died in Marroné's arms, but not before revealing Sr Tamerlán's whereabouts and whispering his final message. 'Been in their power for years. Wasn't all my doing. Took me to the Soviet Union, had me brainwashed. In death I can be the man I used to be: Ulrico Govianus, accountant, loyal servant to the company and its president and director general. Sr Tamerlán's finger it's . . . in the freezer, in the bunker, third shelf down, under the beefburgers,' Govianus would reveal before breathing his last, his penchant for the prosaic breaking the spell of Marroné's second daydream. But it wasn't just Govianus's impertinent coda that brought him back to reality: a distant voice that seemed to reach him from his innermost being was calling to him, as if hesitating before the gates of his consciousness, and as it became more audible, the initial chill that had gripped his body on seeing the severed finger gradually thawed to a warm and pleasant inner glow. The sensation was unmistakeable, but so many months had passed since he had felt it with such intensity that it was like bumping into an old friend you never expected to see again. At once incredulous and grateful, with the hypnotic certainty of a dream, he pulled out a half-read copy of *The Corporate Samurai* and the key to the executive bathroom from the second drawer of his desk, and stepped out of his office and into the corridor.

His deep-seated constipation had accompanied him like a faithful dog ever since he had started working at the company. No sooner was the post of head of procurement his than his intestines, as if unbeknownst to their owner, had turned against him and tangled themselves into a perverse Gordian knot that he could only cut with the aid of powerful laxatives. It was a problem of timing more than anything, but also of setting, and ultimately of that rare commodity in the life of the efficient executive: relaxation. It was getting harder and harder in the morning to find the necessary peace and quiet: his wife wouldn't let him use their en suite bathroom because the smell would, she claimed, pervade her morning ablutions; and the children's bathroom was prey to all-important needs – use by their son, a change of nappies, toothbrushes, medicines, nebulisers – rendering any prospect of relaxation utopian. Last, the downstairs guest *toilette* was besieged by the fervent Doña Ema, the enormous maid who, advised by Sra Marroné of her husband's early-morning needs, had immediately decided, with her impregnable common sense, that it was merely a naughty habit and purposely chose that time to clean it or, if Marroné did manage to evade her vigilant eye and take cover within, she would decide to wax the floor outside and charge at the bolted door, first with the waxing cloth, and then – her coup de grâce – the wailing floor-polisher, until he gave up. But if going to the toilet at home had become a mission nigh on impossible, things weren't much better at the office. Rarely was there time amid the daily rush to enjoy that much-needed oasis of peace and quiet, and anyway, Marroné was incapable of feeling at home in the toilet without a book in his hands – not only to make the most of his time, but because a pleasant and instructive read had the virtue of soothing him and steering his performance to a successful outcome; what's more, he felt embarrassed at the thought that some employee or colleague – especially if it was a woman – should see him entering or leaving the bathroom with reading matter, and although he had perfected a posture of camouflage to that effect, which involved wedging the book under his armpit and cleaving his arm to his side in order to conceal it from prying eyes, the average size of books on management made any dissimulation unviable. Hence the office was far from ideal.

But this time things were different: in spite of its immaculate hardback binding, *The Corporate Samurai* was a pocket edition, and Marroné could walk the empty corridors with utter impunity. And although he crossed paths with no one on the short walk, it was with a sense of triumph that, once the bathroom door was closed and bolted, he sat down on the toilet seat and opened the volume at the bookmarked page.

The Corporate Samurai belonged to a select minority of texts that had successfully applied the principles of millenary oriental wisdom to the modern art of management: titles like Dwight D Connoly's *The Art of Competition*, adapted from Sun Tzu's celebrated *The Art of War*; or *The Tao of Management* by Dean Tesola, who brought the immemorial wisdom of Laozi to the conference table of a modern corporation. True, *The Corporate Samurai* lacked the astonishing relevance of the former and the philosophical depth of the latter, and sometimes lapsed into mere pedestrian substitution, mechanically replacing 'samurai' with 'executive' and 'battle' with 'competition', giving rise to entire paragraphs such as: 'When the company enters into competition the executive must camp out day and night in the office, developing competitive strategies without a moment's rest. It is necessary for employees of all ranks to dig any ditches, strongholds or outposts needed to protect the company from enemy attack and prevent them invading their markets and making off with their clientele.' But it also contained paragraphs that could be described as sublime, such as its majestic opening, which Marroné always reread before embarking on the rest of the book: 'What every executive must have constantly in mind, night and day, is that they will die. Death is their goal, their north, their main occupation.' Marroné had meditated long and hard on this astonishing idea, which he had first taken for a rather melodramatic variant of the executive's maxim 'Go to work every day expecting to be fired', but subsequently, after reading further, had discovered a deeper meaning. For a samurai executive, following the Way of the Executive involved subordinating personal achievements and goals to a higher end: the good of the company, the honour or, as in his case, the very life of its president. European or American readers of *The Corporate Samurai* were lucky enough to be able to take the phrase figuratively, but in this antipodean reality the idea of death was no metaphor for demotion or dismissal, but a palpable and concrete possibility; nor was the battlefield merely that of commercial competition, but also that of the streets where modern executives had to fight it out day and night against bombs, machine-gunnings and kidnappings. Nonetheless, the essential virtues of *The Corporate Samurai* were its accessibility and reader-friendliness, and Marroné, who knew from experience that the effort of disentangling the meaning of a complicated text might prolong rather than facilitate the task he was engaged in, started to read:

> Though the Way of the Executive first and foremost entails developing the qualities of strength and efficiency, he who develops only in these respects shall reach no further than becoming a rustic executive of little consequence. Therefore, even a lower-ranking executive will do well to try his hand at music – clumsy though he may be – at painting or literature or some other art, albeit in moderation. For he who becomes completely absorbed in it and neglects his professional duties shall turn soft of body and mind, and lose his martial qualities to become a self-absorbed, second-rate artist. If one should grow too passionate about an art, it is easy to behave like some bright and witty chatterer in the company of your serious and reserved fellow samurai. This may be amusing in terms of social life, but it is an attitude that does not befit the Way of the Executive.

At this point a number 3 interrupted the flow of the text and Marroné, who was always extremely punctilious when it came to footnotes, skipped to the bottom of the page to read the note in question:

3. Although modern western executives have not adopted the tea ceremony practised by samurai knights, they have developed other forms of professional and social contact. Golf, for example, has been highly popular with company people since the days of the big tycoons. Hence, the executive who wishes to progress in the world of business must at least be familiar with the correct way of gaining access to the golf course, and know how to choose his clubs and keep score correctly, for which it is recommended that he take a few lessons from a pro. The golf club is a most suitable place to close deals and forge personal relationships, far from the distractions of the office, and the spirit of golf, properly cultivated, can do much to sweeten the Way of the Executive.

Accompanying the downward motion of his eyes, as if a blockage had finally been removed, Marroné's innards voided themselves placidly in one, and he closed the book and gave a sigh of relief. He hadn't had such a good bowel movement since he'd started working at the company, he told himself, contemplating the profuse fruit of his belly while doing up his trousers and reaching for the flush button. There could only be one explanation for it: something deep inside him, something the meaning of which he wasn't yet able to unravel, had loosened when he had set eyes on the mortal remains of what had in life been Sr Tamerlán's index finger. Leaving the bathroom and advancing down the corridor with the buoyant stride of a moon-walker, Marroné felt like a new man, as if – how else could he put it? – his soul had returned to his body, and not without a secret frisson of impishness he smiled to himself: maybe the Montoneros had ended up doing him a favour after all.

2

MARRONÉ BY MARRONÉ

To offset the day's highs with an unquestionable low he was forced to share the lift to the car park with Aldo Cáceres Grey, the executive usurping the chair that Marroné yearned with all his heart and soul to sit in: marketing and sales at Tamerlán & Sons. Cáceres Grey was a perfect specimen of an endangered species: the high-born executive who owes his post less to his curriculum vitae than to his pedigree, and more to his golfing handicap than to his academic scores. Sr Tamerlán wasn't in the business of hiring fops on the strength of their double-barrelled surnames, but as one of the surnames also happened to be his wife's, and as his little nephew was only a minor pain, and his assistant manager obsessively efficient but a social liability, the balance between the demands of business and those of high society might appear quite sensible. But for Marroné, whose head teemed with new ideas fresh from the US, Cáceres Grey was nothing but a bar to the company's progress, an obstruction blocking the new thinking that was changing the face of business across the world. And to cap it all his rival had had the cheek to bang Mariana, the twenty-year-old secretary that Marroné, hobbled by scruple and guilt, had timidly, almost cryptically, been wooing all spring. Screwing your colleague's secretary violated the executive's tacit droit de seigneur over his subordinates and was nothing short of an act of war, a gauntlet thrown in his face. Marroné had taken it up, unbeknownst to Cáceres Grey, and had secretly been choosing his weapons ever since. Which didn't stop him answering his rival's condescending smile with a frank and open one, as recommended in *How to Win Friends and Influence People*.

'Well? Are the tower blocks selling or aren't they?' he asked with a toothy grin.

'There's a sucker born every minute. Hey . . . What about Uncle? Any news?'

'Who?' asked Marroné, knowing perfectly well that Cáceres Grey was referring to Sr Tamerlán, but feigning ignorance to parry what he saw as an obscene exhibition of kinship.

'Come on, don't be silly. If you've been called to the bunker, it can't have been to talk about the price of airbricks.'

'Oh. You meant Sr Tamerlán's kidnapping. No, we didn't discuss the subject,' he lied, with a thrill of private delight. So word had already got round of his descent into The Nibelheim. If this busybody only knew . . . he couldn't even suspect the extent to which Marroné was not only in the know but in the core, the nerve centre . . . at the very helm.

'Auntie is out of her mind; visiting her's an ordeal. And my two little cousins aren't far behind. We try to give them support, you know, over the phone; but there comes a point when you don't know what to say. If you ask me, they've already offed him. They don't usually keep them this long. Remember the head of Fiat?'

He gave Cáceres Grey a non-committal smile. Why bother telling him that he, Marroné, had irrefutable evidence to the contrary? Though, now that he came to think about it, the arrival of the finger didn't prove Sr Tamerlán was still alive. The latest hard evidence – the customary photograph with that day's newspaper – was over a month old, and while it wasn't the standard pose (Sr Tamerlán had turned round at the last moment to show himself wiping his backside with it), the still visible headlines had left no room for doubt. But, on the other hand, he could easily have been executed since the photo was taken and kept in the freezer to be chopped up like a chicken and the chunks posted in instalments. No, they wouldn't do that, he corrected himself; he'd be a lot harder to cut up frozen; they'd have chopped him up beforehand.

'It must be hard for her . . . ' Marroné began.

'That's the least of our worries. The trouble is she's out of control. Uncle used to keep her in check, you know, and now there's no one to stop her. Only the other day she was being interviewed for *Gente* magazine, and she tried to mount the photographer. He asked her to lie on the conjugal bed, you know, to hit just the right tear-jerking note, and she says she got all misty-eyed and next thing she knew . . . I know six months is a long time, but what are staff for? You have to watch your step with journalists. They'll publish anything.'

Marroné didn't know what to say, and it galled him all the more. It was another of Cáceres Grey's famous put-downs: from his position of privilege as a member of the Family he revelled in disclosing embarrassing private details and talking with over-familiarity about people his colleagues were obliged to refer to with the utmost ceremoniousness.

They got out of the lift at the car park and, after bidding each other farewell with formal courtesy – Marroné sincere and emphatic, extending his sinewy right hand in a virile American handshake; Cáceres Grey with Parisian nonchalance and a hint of irony, his slack hand floating palm down as if he were expecting a subject's kiss – they each headed for their cars: Cáceres Grey to his orange '68 Mustang Coupé; Marroné to his champagne-coloured Peugeot 504. Before he got in, Cáceres Grey shouted to Marroné over the roof of his car:

'Be a good chap and remind Mariana to call me tomorrow!'

The phrase hadn't finished ricocheting around the bare cement columns and walls before Cáceres Grey slammed the door and started his engine, and for a split second Marroné yearned with every fibre of his being for a gelignite blast to blow him out of existence for ever, before reminding himself that at that distance it would catch him too, and the last thing he wanted was to share another journey with his hated enemy, even if it was to the Hereafter. Marroné was more cautious: as he had been taught on the survival course (given by a retired French colonel and Algerian War veteran) he examined the locks to see if they showed signs of having been forced or displayed traces of plastic explosive, inside or out. Once – he still shuddered to remember – he had discovered the feared pink gunk inside the lock but, after the alarm and evacuation of the building, it had been identified by bomb-disposal experts as 'masticated Bazooka bubble gum', and for several weeks Marroné was the butt of his colleagues' jokes: they would offer him chewing gum at all times of day, or blow bubbles and burst them in his presence – all except Cáceres Grey, who was unusually attentive and understanding with him, congratulating him on his sense of responsibility and so confirming Marroné's suspicions about the authorship of this unforgivable prank. He then checked under the chassis, kneeling on his handkerchief to protect his trousers, and on getting up he said a quick Our Father and slid the key into the lock. Nothing. Once inside he examined the wiring and, opening the hood, got out again to check the engine: everything seemed to be where it should be. Even so, before starting the engine, he said two Our Fathers one after the other – first in English, then in Spanish – and gave a sigh of relief when the friendly purring of the Peugeot's motor told him he had won another victory against death.

It was the same issue with this routine check as when he took his books to the toilet: he was embarrassed to be seen, particularly since, with the violence of the times, Tamerlán's Tartars had apparently adopted a philosophy resembling the one expressed in *The Corporate Samurai*. Whenever two of them went down to the car park together, they would make a whole ceremony out of the simple act of leaving work in their cars, with remarks like 'See you in the celestial spa' or 'Tamerlán or death' and then counting 'One, two, three!' before whirling their keys like sabres and plunging them into the locks of their cars. After exaggerated laughter (and private sighs of relief) they repeated the burlesque ceremony by starting up their engines, and at no time – they would have seen it as an unpardonable breach of the warrior's code – did they lower themselves to following the safety procedure, even though they knew that what was at stake wasn't just their own physical integrity, but their colleagues', and – if the bomb was big enough – the entire building's.

They'd even given the game a name: 'Montonero Roulette'. Marroné knew that there was little or nothing of the bushido code and a good deal of the most vulgar and pedestrian Latin American machismo in all this horsing around but, incapable of withstanding peer pressure, in the presence of a colleague he would affect identical behaviour, so, if he had to go down to the car park with one of them, he would delay his departure with petty excuses – stopping the lift on the pretext of talking to someone, claiming to have forgotten important papers, or as a last resort the infallible 'What a bloody fool, I've left my car keys upstairs' so he could go through his procedure later, safe from sarcastic glances. As of today he would have to take more precautions than ever, for, as a key player in the negotiations, he was now a target for the assassins: his name might at that very instant be passing from mouth to mouth at a meeting of the Montoneros' Central Committee: 'Marroné? Marroné? What do we know about him? Bring me all you've got on Ernesto Marroné.'

Before leaving, he waved to the car park attendant, whose name, in spite of his supposed adherence to Dale Carnegie's Third Way to Make People Like You ('Remember that a person's name is to that person the sweetest and most important sound in any language'), Marroné could never remember. Most of his colleagues not only didn't make the effort, but would consider it demeaning to recall the name of such a lowly subordinate, but Marroné was mindful of the exemplary case of Andrew Carnegie, the author's father, who was able to call all his workers by their Christian names, and in all his years in charge of the steelworks he wasn't troubled by a single strike. It crossed his mind to ask the man his name and jot it down in the notebook he always carried with him for just that purpose, but that would be tantamount to admitting he'd forgotten it: he'd be offending rather than making himself liked, which only defeated his purpose. And then . . . what if he was a mole planted by the Montoneros and Marroné's impertinent question only aroused his suspicion? It didn't seem very likely: the man had been working at the company for years and was too dark for a guerrilla; but that was no guarantee either. In the inexorably spiralling violence even the poor had begun taking up arms against the rich, and the most unlikely of people, with unimpeachable service records, were daily being won over to the subversives' side, becoming willing accomplices or merely useful idiots in their service. When simple persuasion failed, it was supplemented with death threats against their person or against their families, or the slow drip of ideological indoctrination, which by accumulation could culminate in a total brainwashing. Difficult times indeed.

His thoughts grew less sombre as the Peugeot surged up the exit ramp and emerged from the fluorescent light into the radiance of the summer afternoon, to join the double column of cars that crawled with rush-hour sluggishness along the side-lanes. This was the most vulnerable part of his journey and, in spite of the suffocating heat, he kept the windows firmly closed: while one eye checked the rear-view mirrors to make sure he wasn't being followed by 'rovers' from the guerrilla, the other was intent on the pedestrians, who, with Argentinian contempt for white lines and red lights, kept materialising between the trunks of the tipa trees and recklessly darting between the moving cars. 'If some person srows zemselves in front of ze car,' he heard the idiosyncratic Spanish of Colonel Bigeard, 'do not stop.

Run zem over and let ze Legal Department take care of it. Iz easier to escape a trial zan a kidnap.' After an accidental detour via Balcarce, he managed to get into the safer central lanes and exceed walking pace, until, on reaching Alem, the traffic opened up like spray squirting from the nozzle of a hosepipe, and Marroné could wind down the window and let the wind dry his sweat-drenched face. Seven thirty-five. If everything went well, he'd be home by eight, he told himself, relaxing and automatically turning the stereo on to listen to the B-side of *The Socratic Pitch*: 'Once the dialectic moment of your presentation is over, and your formerly sceptical listener has become an ardent "yes-man" for your proposals, it is time for the midwife to step in. *The Socratic Pitch* will teach you the art of . . . ' As the tape reeled out its litany, which he knew almost by heart, having listened to it twice a day for almost thirty days (side A on the outward leg, side B on the return as recommended by the enclosed booklet), he amused himself with the familiar beauty spots along the way that glowed with the almost spiritual raking light of the golden hour: the majestic tree-covered slope of the Plaza San Martín; the stately Kavanagh Building and the brand-new Sheraton Hotel, symbols the one of past splendour, the other of future prosperity; the French grace of the Palais de Glace and the virile archaism of Antoine Bourdelle's Monument to Alvear, flanked by the four alle-gorical figures of Victory, Strength, Eloquence and Liberty; the imposing Graeco-Roman façade of the Law Faculty; the Asiatic splendour of the Assyrian column and its towering bulls; and the galactic curves of the Municipal Planetarium . . . Paseo Colón and Avenida Libertador, he was fond of saying, were the spinal column of a better Buenos Aires, one that no Porteño need be ashamed of: a city every bit the equal of the great capitals of Europe and America, the axis of a better, more desirable country; and whenever he had to play chaperone to foreign visitors, it was with delight that he faced the challenge of plotting routes that joined up all the beauty spots without passing any of the eyesores (in daylight at least, which was when they might create a worse impression), and he found nothing more reward- ing of his efforts than the spontaneous exclamation of an important foreign executive or businessman: 'This doesn't look like South America at all!' Ah well, he said to himself, pressing the stop button and interrupting Socrates in full swing – just for today he could take a break and indulge in his own thoughts. For it had not escaped Marroné's notice that he was facing a decisive turning point, one that – with hindsight – would divide not only his career but his life into a before and an after. Until today, he ventured to himself as he savoured the idea, he had merely been living; today perhaps he was beginning to write his autobiography.

'How did Marroné become Marroné? That's a good ques- tion. There are moments in the career of every top execu- tive . . . They're things you sometimes can't put on your CV, but they're precisely the kind of things that make everyone want to read your CV. This is one of the golden rules of what I earlier called "the marketing of the self". Let me give you an example: when, thanks to my forceful yet sensitive han- dling of negotiations, I managed to rescue Fausto Tamerlán from the clutches of Marxist terrorism, I was no more than a "junior executive" fresh from the United States. True, I had brought back with me an MBA in Marketing from Stanford and a battery of innovative ideas, but I was no more than a cog – necessary perhaps, but replaceable – in a complex commercial machine. My coolness, calmness and collectedness, and above all my leadership abilities, proven in those dark hours when the whole future of the company hung in the balance, were the making of me. From that moment on, I became in all but name the CEO of Tamerlán & Sons, as it was called in those days. Sr Tamerlán's prolonged captivity, coupled with the tortures inflicted on him – which included mutilation – had left physical and mental scars that kept him from anything more than nominal leadership, and that vacuum had to be filled by a providential man full of new ideas and the will to implement them. The now world-famous Marroné & Tamerlán Ltd had until those days been no more than a family enterprise, in the most limited sense of the word, and one that had never known bracing exposure to the elements of healthy competition, having grown up in the shadow of a nanny state, which, by the way, it will soon be time to wean ourselves off permanently.' Marroné raced ahead with his autobiography, sticking close in language and style to the ones he so loved to read – those of Henry Ford, Alfred P Sloan, Thomas Watson Jr and Lester Luchessi – and dictating it to an imaginary listener who sat there, cassette recorder in hand, in the empty passenger seat. He liked to imagine himself dictating it because, as he now set about explaining to his attentive scribe (a ghost writer who had at first accepted the assignment just for the cash, but who, all agog, was now receiving a veritable masterclass in leadership and – why not? – in life too), the only executives who can afford the time to write their biography themselves have either retired or failed. Marroné now drove under the General Paz flyover and entered the suburbs, the docility of his Peugeot 504 and the wind, which barely ruffled his gel-slicked hair, intoxicating him as if he were breathing the air of high mountain tops, and spurring him on with his autobiography, which he had tentatively titled *Marroné by Marroné*: 'My family spared no expense when it came to securing a first-class education for me, which I received at the exclusive and expensive St Andrew's College in Buenos Aires, from where I graduated in 1964 with the honour of having obtained the coveted turquoise- and brown-striped prefects' tie and the captain's badge of the Dodds House rugby team. My time at St Andrew's bequeathed me many gifts, such as my sound command of the English language, which has led to many a foreign businessman expressing disbelief when I confess to being Argentinian; a solid humanist background in the best British tradition; and the essential school spirit, which in the world of business translates into donning the company jersey . . . ' ('Underpants,' whispered the sly side of his mind once again, and he mentally swatted away the intrusive word) ' . . . but I learnt two essential things that marked my subsequent career: I learnt to command and I learnt to obey.

'I learnt to obey, to let myself be guided,' he explained now to an audience not of one but of hundreds, the cassette recorder turned microphone, and the inside of his Peugeot grown to the proportions of the immense St Andrew's assembly hall, decked out in homage to its favourite son, Ernesto Marroné, who had acquiesced to afford them a few hours of his precious time to deliver a lecture on leadership that would later be published in full in the school magazine, *The Thistle*. 'To let myself be guided by my teachers and coaches,' he continued, smiling encouragingly at the front rows,

where the serried ranks of his old teachers sat – a few still
active, others now retired but expressly invited for the occasion – and following the recommendations of *How to Develop
Self-Confidence and Influence People by Public Speaking*, by – who
else? – Dale Carnegie, his eyes rested for a second on each
of them in turn: Mr Adams; Mrs Halley; Mrs McCarthy; Mrs
Oxford, who used to force him, retching, to finish his milk
in the dining hall; Sra Polino; Sra Regamor; Mr Guinness;
Wójcik the Pole; the PE teachers Mr Trollope, Osvaldo Lamas
and Willy Speakeasy; Uve; Sapa; El Pollo; Mr Peters; the fearsome Sr Macera, who had humiliated him before the whole
class and then flunked him in Anatomy . . . 'And by learning to obey, I learnt to command, to be a leader. What is a
leader?' asked Marroné in the theatre of his mind while his
body handled the wheel and pedals of his Peugeot, respected
traffic signals and dodged neighbouring cars. 'The wise
leader does not push to make things happen, but allows the
process to unfold on its own. The leader teaches by example
rather than by lecturing others on how they ought to be.
Bosses are appointed; leaders are chosen by their peers,'
he thought, stringing together a series of phrases from
The Tao of Leadership, now casting his eyes over the faces of
some of his former schoolmates: 'Slim' Sörensen; Ramiro
Agüero, who used to call him 'sissy' at break-time in primary
school; Alberto Regamor, the brainiac who had won the Dux
Medal and whose features Marroné's memory insisted on
confusing with those of the hated Cáceres Grey; and many
others; but his satisfaction was complete when he spotted
the unmistakeable, neatly trimmed ginger hair of Paddy
Donovan, his high-school hero, who, on meeting his gaze,
smiled back, his teeth whiter-than-white, and raised both

thumbs approvingly. And beyond the guests and familiar faces, their heads bobbing expectantly on a sea of dark-blue blazers with their thistle-flanked badges bearing the motto '*Sic itur ad astra*', stood the future leaders of Argentina, and there in their midst, bursting with pride, was little Tommy . . .

As he pulled down the garage door, Marroné remembered the disposable nappies his wife, beleaguered by the chronic shortage of supplies, had asked him to pick up at any price. He had promised to look for some near the office, but being by nature somewhat prone to distraction – 'the Achilles heel of creative thinkers', the specialist literature called it – and to losing himself in reveries, he had clean forgotten. As Mabel would never in a million years pass up the opportunity to make a scene if he dared to come home empty-handed, he pushed the creaking wooden door back up in order to go and raid the supermarket on Avenida Libertador, before he remembered that it was 'Closed for Refurbishment', the usual euphemism for 'Blown Up by the Montoneros' (or the ERP, who knows). He thought of trying the duty chemist's, but he'd left his newspaper at the office and his mission to retrieve the one from indoors and get out again without being seen was aborted by little Tommy's vigilance, who, alerted by the noise of the gate or perhaps the car, intercepted him on the ground-floor landing with his strident demand of 'Tweeties! Tweeties!' – which, of course, his father had forgotten to pick up, along with the nappies. To the abject confession of his empty hands little Tommy's mouth responded with an O of incredulity that instantly narrowed to a ∞ of incessant wailing, which inevitably brought Mabel running. 'I bet you've forgotten the nappies too,' she spat at him in greeting, at which the 'Hello darling' that Marroné had at the ready barely managed to escape his throat, strangled and squeezed dry of any genuine emotion. 'I was just going to check the paper for a chemist's,' he said, adopting a decisive tone, but Mabel was ready with her answer and fired at him: 'Haven't you heard there's-a-shor-tage, Ernesto? The chemist's haven't even got aspirins in stock!' 'Of course I have. You seem to forget that I'm the head of procurement for one of the leading comp . . . ' he began in an offended tone, but realised too late that he'd put the ball just where she wanted him to (Mabel always beat him at tennis). 'You might be head of procurement at the office, but at home you can't even pick up a lousy chocolate bar,' she snapped as little Tommy, seeing his position defended, redoubled his bawling, and Marroné felt the tension running up and down his body in thick, indignant waves of pure stress; with the stoic fatalism of the serial somatiser, he knew that that night he would suffer from heartburn and insomnia, and it was with a supreme effort of self-control that he stopped himself from screaming in his wife's face: 'The life of a very important man is in my hands and you're banging on to me about candy bars!' But he couldn't do this without jeopardising the whole operation, and so he turned once again to the pages of *How to Win Friends and Influence People*, to be precise, to the chapter entitled 'If You're Wrong, Admit It' from the section 'How to Win People to Your Way of Thinking', which advised: 'Say about yourself all the derogatory things you know the other person is thinking or wants to say or intends to say – and say them before that person has a chance to say them.'

'You're right, my darling,' said Marroné through jaws clenched as tight as a hydraulic press. 'You deserve a better husband than me. All that effort you make morning, noon and night, running the house, and I can't even remember one little errand you ask me to do . . . ' As his tongue waded laboriously through the viscous insincerity of his words, Mabel's features gradually lost their tautness, as if each admission of guilt loosened one of the threads that tensed it, and very soon she was the one coming to his defence: 'Well, Ernesto, I wouldn't go that far, I mean we've got enough to last till the weekend' ('Then why did you kick up such a fuss about it, you bitch!') 'and you, Tommy, be quiet will you, your daddy's had a long day at the office, come here, I've got some sweeties for you upstairs . . . ' and Marroné, now certain of victory, allowed himself to add a ginger 'First thing tomorrow I'll pop out to the supermarket in La Lucila', only for Mabel to reply: 'No, no, you're always in a dreadful hurry when you leave, I don't want you doing anything to add to your stress. I'll have Doña Ema pick some up for me at the weekend, they have everything in the shanties you know, never go short of anything. We'll soon be resorting to cloth nappies out here and *they're* spoilt for choice – course they resell what the government gives them, so Doña Ema tells me. Cynthia's just woken up, can you believe it? Like she knows you're home. Want to go up and see her?'

At dinner, which consisted of a starter of boiled ham and Russian salad, a main course of *milanesas* and mash, and a dessert of crème caramel and *dulce de leche*, Mabel gave him the latest update on little Cynthia's latest escapades, encouraged by her husband's studied posture of the absorbed listener. Knowing how to listen, after all, was one of the secrets of success in business and private life, for Principle Six ('How to Make People Like You Instantly') reminds us that even if you happen to be President of the Republic, the person you are talking to is a hundred times more interested in themselves, in their petty needs and problems, than in you and your great ones. What everyone ultimately wants is to feel important, and listening with attention was an infallible way of satisfying that basic need, Marroné was repeating to himself, when Mabel suddenly blurted out:

'Is anything wrong? You've hardly said a word since we started eating.'

'I was listening carefully,' he mumbled behind his tight-lipped smile.

'You didn't manage . . . ?'

He was about to break the good news to her, when he thought better of it and shook his head contritely instead. Marroné had made of the prolonged barrenness of his belly an impregnable excuse to lock himself in the bathroom for extended periods of time whenever the manifold demands of married life or home became too much for him; especially since his study had been annexed as the little girl's bedroom and there was no other room in the house he could call his own. The bathroom had become the only place where he could enjoy some degree of peace and quiet, and devote some time to himself. Confessing to Mabel the success that had crowned his afternoon's efforts would be to deprive himself of that minimal but indispensable right to privacy.

Once the coffee cups had been cleared away, Doña Ema's working day was over and it was Marroné's turn to look after the children, while Mabel went upstairs to the bedroom to watch television for a bit. Much as he liked to picture himself as an exemplary father – the very phrase made him swell with pride – after a day of stress at the office the tasks it involved were capable of pushing him over the edge, for since the little girl's arrival, the demands of his children seemed irrationally to have multiplied not by two, but by ten. He would make a superhuman effort to remind himself that every opportunity for recreation was essential in the life of the executive, enabling him to return to his tasks with renewed vigour, but after a few minutes of lending them his undivided attention, he would start thinking about all the work he could be catching up on, or the books he could be reading, and which he did sometimes try to read while looking after them, with the regrettable result of neither being able to concentrate on reading nor enjoy the children, which meant he would end up losing his patience and yelling at them. Today he didn't last twenty minutes: while he was changing little Cynthia's dirty nappy, little Tommy in a fit of jealousy shook the changing stand and knocked the bottle of baby oil on the floor, which Marroné, of course, hadn't put the top back on; cursing, he leapt, cotton wool in hand, to wipe it up before it ruined the carpet and earned him another dressing-down from Mabel. His reprimand, not so much violent as tense with barely contained anger, set off little Tommy, who was a sensitive child at heart, and while tending to him, Marroné forgot about the girl, who, when he looked up, was teetering on the brink of the changing stand about to follow the bottle into the abyss. Once he had deposited her safely in the middle of her crib, he went back to consoling little Tommy and, by the time he noticed the fresh nappy, which should have been on little Cynthia, lying open and unused on the changing stand, her pee had drenched the sheets and soaked through to the mattress.

'I'm not cut out for this, I'm not cut out for this,' Marroné hiccuped, his throat closed by hysteria as he laid the little girl on the floor and stripped the sheets in order to pick up the mattress. He flirted for a moment with the temptation of sitting down on the floor next to her and starting to cry, but that would probably only trigger a sympathetic response in little Tommy, who, quieter now, had climbed up to the third shelf of the bookcase and was on the verge of falling backwards and breaking his neck on the edge of the crib. Having reached this point, he felt psychically and morally justified to go to his wife with the babe in his arms and the boy by the hand and guiltlessly say, 'Can you take them for a while? I'm going to try . . . '

'Are you going to be long?' Mabel asked him, and Marroné was tempted to scream 'Can't you see that, if you hurry me, I'll feel pressurised and end up taking twice as long?' when he remembered that he'd already undergone his daily ordeal and was only looking for somewhere quiet to get some reading done.

'I'll be as quick as I can,' he replied as usual and, before Mabel could answer back, he had left the room and was descending the stairs and heading for the bookcase, where he began running his index finger over the spines and titles in search of a book to keep him company. Drucker's *The Practice of Management*? No, too constipated. Edward de Bono's *The Use of Lateral Thinking*? Already knew it by heart. Schumacher's *Small is Beautiful*? It had been a gift from a hippie professor at Stanford and he hadn't been able to get past the opening pages. He needed something more reader-friendly, something from his favourite genre for example, a book that could draw ideas and principles of business philosophy from the great works of universal culture. He owned several, some very good, others so-so: *Jesus Means Business*, for example, was nothing but a rehash of Og Mandino's classic *The Greatest Salesman in the World*; but Konosuke Takamura's *Haikus for Managers* was a real oyster bank from which he had extracted such pearls as:

> A huge pyramid
> An elephant can't climb it
> A tiny ant can

But his undisputed favourite was *Shakespeare the Businessman* by R Theobald Johnson. Thanks to this volume he had been able to maximise the benefits derived from reading the Swan of Avon in the classrooms of St Andrew's, for *Shakespeare the Businessman* taught you to apply what you had learnt at school to the daily routine of the efficient executive, turning each play into a fountainhead of practical teachings: from *Hamlet*, for example, you could learn to avoid endless, fruitless procrastination in the decision-making process; from *The Merchant of Venice*, to pore over the small print of a contract, especially when dealing with venture capital; *Henry V* was a lesson in leadership, and *Timon of Athens* an appeal not to overspend on advertising and representation; *King Lear* alerted one to the dangers of dividing up a great family enterprise among the heirs, of rewarding the flatterer and punishing the critic and, above all, of putting off the appointment of a successor till the last moment and then naming them on a whim; *Romeo and Juliet* was about the sometimes tragic consequences of communication failures in companies, and *Richard III* about the destructive potential of the executive hell-bent on reaching the top by climbing a staircase of severed heads. *Macbeth* got it on the nose when it pointed to the wife who stays at home as the true power behind the unscrupulously ambitious husband, as did *Antony and Cleopatra* – but about the opposite risk: of losing in the voluptuous arms of a lover the Spartan virtues demanded by one's profession. *Othello* offered the most penetrating analysis of in-house intrigues – that daily hell unleashed by jealousy, envy and rumour – and of the unimaginable destructive potential of a mid-ranking executive who feels he has been unfairly overlooked in his promotion. *The Tempest*, on the other hand, was an object lesson in how to regain control of a company with minimum damage to the organisation; and Mark Antony's speech in *Julius Caesar* provided a master class in public speaking, combining the best classical oratory with the highly efficient use of the material props of a modern audiovisual presentation: the slashed cloak, the blood, the body of the assassinated leader. Bidding it farewell with a wistful caress of its well-worn spine, Marroné's finger moved on until it ran into Michael Eggplant's *Don Quixote: The Executive-Errant*, which his parents had recently brought him back from Spain. With a whoop of jubilation he grabbed it off the shelf and made straight for the bathroom, where, dropping his trousers out of mere habit, he sat down on the seat and began to read:

Hundreds of years ago western civilisation was about to perish under the onslaught of the armies of the night. There then emerged a special class of men, emissaries of light, pillars of society, defenders of justice and the true faith: the knights-errant. Thanks to them Christian Europe was able to defeat its enemies within and without, and prosper, sending out its light to all the peoples of the world. Today, as the darkness takes on new forms and once more lays siege to the citadel of civilisation, the future of the free world and the liberation of the iron-bound once again rests with a force of chosen men, the true heirs of the knights-errant of yore: the managerial classes – the executives-errant. Their castles are the dazzling crystal towers of corporations; instead of lances they bear fountain pens, and briefcases instead of shields; they travel not by horse but by plane, yet fundamentally nothing has changed. The emergence and development of the executive class is the crucial, defining event of our times, and one of the most significant in the history of mankind. More than presidents and statesmen, more than religious and military authorities, more indeed than the owners of businesses, it is executives who pave the way, who are in the front line on the battlefield as were the knights-errant of yore. Their appearance at the start of our century coincides with the most spectacular leap forward in the history of mankind: one that leads from a materialist civilisation, subject to the tyranny of existing resources, to an idealist one, in which the unlimited generation of resources ensures the true liberation of the human spirit. In this very spirit Cervantes' celebrated hero, Don Quixote of La Mancha, decides one fine day to turn his back on the meagreness of his material life and the shallowness of the world around him – gutless mediocre folk devoted to traditional ways of doing things, for whom the word creativity is anathema – and strikes out on the highways in search of adventure. Don Quixote's gesture encapsulates the adventurous spirit of today's businessmen: conquering new markets, daring to vie with the corporate giants, earning themselves a name and an image, and devoting their lives to it. Until this moment – his fiftieth year – he has done nothing with his life: a village squire, a poor squire, so obscure and retiring that we cannot be certain of his real name: Quesada, Quijana, Quejana . . . Sr Quejana has not lived, but merely vegetated in the shadows of others' adventures, like some small-time village tradesman who seeks consolation for the flatness of his life in the biographies of millionaires. Then, one fine day, he looks in the mirror and does not recognise himself. That dull, grey face, those lacklustre eyes, that look of defeat – the bitterest look of defeat, the look of someone who has never fought – cannot be his. Another expression is possible: that of his true self, that of his unexplored potential. And on that day he resolves to become Don Quixote of La Mancha.

Marroné closed the book for a moment. There's no such thing as chance, he thought. This book had been sitting patiently on the shelves of his bookcase for the right moment to awaken. And that night, of all nights, on the eve of his new life – a life of adventure, a life in which his dreams would begin to come true – it had called out to him, to pass on its message of encouragement, and his hand had reached for it. This was what he had been waiting for, he saw it clearly now. Tomorrow, when dawn broke, Ernesto Marroné would go out into the world. Who knows who would come back?

Anxious and enthusiastic, he skipped the rest of the introduction and, opening the book at random, began to read a section entitled:

SOME EPISODES ANALYSED

THE WINDMILLS

In this, perhaps the most famous of all his adventures, Don Quixote charges full tilt at some windmills he takes for fearsome giants, with predictable results: the great sails begin to turn in the wind snapping his lance into several pieces and bringing down horse and rider, who instead of recognising his error accuses some 'evil enchanters', who he claims are pursuing him, of having 'transformed these giants into mills, to deprive me of the glory of the victory'. Although the proverbial phrase 'tilting at windmills' has come to be associated with an attitude of heroic or, more properly, 'quixotic' idealism, the executive-errant would do well to avoid imitating our knight to the letter. The giants of the market do not surrender at the first charge, their weapons are many and far-reaching, and a small or medium enterprise willing to give battle must tread carefully if it does not want to bite the dust and wind up bankrupt. Windmills perform a useful function, like any big company; seeing them as enemies to be destroyed is another example of the aforementioned quixotic lack of proportion. The executive-errant must rather design better, cheaper, more efficient windmills, and offer them on the market, and the giants will soon become obsolete and collapse under their own weight without anyone having to be ground down to defeat them.

THE HELMET OF MAMBRINO

A barber comes down the road, wearing his shiny golden barber's bowl on his head to protect his hat from the rain. This bowl Don Quixote takes for the golden helmet of the legendary Moor, Mambrino, and after accosting him and tearing it away from him, he dons it himself, to ridiculous effect. The well-known saying 'all that glisters is not gold' would do very well to summarise the moral of this new adventure for the executive-errant: how many times on our journey does the oft-sought 'golden opportunity' seem to come our way, without us seeking it? That perfect deal whose brilliance blinds us at a distance, but once it is in our hands – and all our capital invested in it – turns out to be yellow brass that we have to 'wear on our heads' and we become the laughing stock of the business world.

THE FREEING OF THE GALLEY SLAVES

This episode is especially recommended for any general or personnel managers who might be tempted in these turbulent times to yield before the incessant demands of their employees. In this adventure our hero runs into a chain of galley slaves condemned by the king's justice, whom without further ado he decides to free, and sets about their guards. And in token of their gratitude he is rewarded with a hail of stones that knocks him to the ground. In this adventure our gentle knight, in the name of an ideal of justice as abstract as it is dogmatic, interferes with, of all things, state justice, setting free a band of dangerous criminals, whose guilt they have confessed to him themselves, thus becoming the first – but probably not the last – victim of their criminal actions. This is precisely the way trade unions or other workers' organisations proceed today: the workers, often 'chained' to them against their will, are led into action by resentful or opportunistic leaders, and shower us with stones where thanks are due. He who yields to the incessant and outrageous demands of strikers and expects those who benefit from his generosity to meet their obligations is not only guilty of quixotic naivety, but may have done his company serious, perhaps irreparable, harm.

An idyllic scene awaited him when he got back to his bedroom: his wife asleep with a child on either side; little Cynthia in the middle of the bed, her tiny, half-open mouth brushing the exposed nipple that peeped out from under the lip of Mabel's unfastened bra; Tommy at the edge with his mother's arm around him to stop him falling. Looking at them, he was overcome by a wave of tenderness that reached the depths of his being, where it stirred up a sediment of guilt that muddied the purity of his initial feeling. What kind of a man, he asked himself, extricating little Tommy from his mother's embrace and carrying him to his room, was incapable of spending some time with his children like any normal father? What kind of a man needed to lock himself in the bathroom to hide from . . . what? From a two-and-a-half-year-old boy, from a barely two-month-old baby? Was he, at twenty-nine, becoming one of those workaholics he knew so well, incapable of thinking about anything other than their jobs, who before long end up sleeping with the secretary and filing for divorce? ('In your case not even that,' his sly right brain whispered to him, 'she's sleeping with Cáceres Grey.') As of today he would do his best to be a better father, he promised himself as he carried the little girl to the bedroom that had until recently been his study, feeling her sweaty brow with the back of his hand to make sure she didn't have a temperature (he'd call the doctor, he'd save his little girl; reduced to tears, Mabel would say to him, 'If it hadn't been for you, I don't know what would have happened'), checking her nappy to see if it would last till morning – he could always change it, but with the shortage it was wiser to make it last as long as possible. Perhaps, he thought as he slid beneath the sheets and, trying not to make contact with his wife's body, rigidly lined up his own with the edge of the bed, the problem was that he had got married and had children too young: at an age when others could devote themselves fully to their studies and careers, he had had to divide his energies between work and home. Not that he'd had any choice: he and Mabel had met in the classrooms of the Faculty of Economic Sciences, where he gave classes as an assistant and she was finishing her last subjects, albeit embattled by endless assemblies and occupations and revolutionary trials of lecturers and tributes to Eva Perón and Che Guevara. Fleeing from the upheaval, they had met in the ground-floor bar and shared a complicit cup of coffee. At first, he had thought she looked quite nice, almost pretty if she'd known what to do with make-up, and through the layers of winter clothes her body had looked warm and desirable; but when at the start of the summer he finally managed to divest it of its last wrappings, her naked skin felt unpleasant, like one of those woollen mattresses that are soft on the eye but lumpy to the touch. 'She needs a good carding, not make-up,' his mind whispered to him as he caressed her mechanically and, thinking thoughts such as these, for once he didn't come too soon and, as he collapsed in tears into her arms, he must have made the easy mistake of taking relief for love. They went on seeing each other for two months, at the end of which Marroné was grateful for the respite provided by a trip Mabel and her parents made to Europe, which would give him a month to think about how best to end the relationship without causing her too much pain. But before the month was up, they were back and, by the time he'd recognised his future in-laws' Mercedes-Benz outside the front door of his parents' house, and the four progenitors had locked themselves in the living room for talks, and Mabel, her skin all red as if it had been pickled in brine, and wringing a little embroidered hanky between her bitten nails, had broken the joyous news to him, the future course of his life was all mapped out. The wedding took place two weeks later and they did without a honeymoon so that they could do up the house for the arrival of their firstborn, who stopped growing almost immediately and slipped away from them in a miscarriage, and had it not been for the need to put any small-mindedness aside and accompany Mabel through her subsequent depression, Marroné might have felt that to the indignities of blackmail had been added those of a confidence trick. Although over the years he had learnt to like her and appreciate her good qualities, there were times like this, while his sleepless eyes flicked across the shadows on the ceiling in time to the monotonous ticking of the clock, that he asked himself in bafflement if there wasn't a certain irony to the fact that Mabel had been the only woman he'd been able to have satisfactory or at least full sexual relations with precisely because he didn't find her attractive enough. Something similar, he told himself, often happened in the world of business: an efficient executive might chafe in the ignoble restraint of a job he considers below his abilities, but when he finally obtains the position he has longed for, next thing he knows his career, instead of being catapulted forwards, has ground to a standstill; he tried to shape this into a general rule that would in the fullness of time bear his name – 'Marroné's Law of Inverse Something or Other' – but sleep was already closing his eyes, and besides, he couldn't see himself using examples from his sex life in a business presentation . . .

3

THE BOSSES' BACCHANAL

'Eighty-nine busts of Eva Perón, standard model, plain plaster of Paris, at 2,000 pesos a unit, that's a subtotal of 178,000 pesos, plus three in white cement for outdoors, at 2,500 pesos a unit, that's a subtotal of 7,500 pesos, that makes 185,000 in total, a 10 per cent discount for . . . payment upfront, is it?'

Marroné nodded, avidly gulping in the refrigerated air: twenty-eight degrees in the shade at eight o'clock in the morning, the radio presenter had announced, not without a hint of malice, as Marroné drove down the freeway to the Sansimón Plasterworks, whose owner now took the cheque from his hands and, snapping it in the air a couple of times to test its elasticity, insisted on treating him yet again to the celebrated aerial tour of his impressive plasterworks, a proposal that Marroné, ever mindful of the demands of public relations, seconded with an enthusiasm as convincing as it was fake.

His guide had given his factory's shop floor the layout and even the dimensions of a cathedral ('190 metres long, three more than St Peter's,' he immodestly specified). It was organised over two levels: the Terrestrial, where the machines and their operators were located, and the Celestial, suspended in its entirety above the Terrestrial and comprising two large office wings situated over the arms ('Transepts,' specified Sansimón), the management's offices over the apse, and the overhead rails along which the foremen travelled the length and breadth of the central nave in their yellow chair-lifts.

He'd picked them up at junk prices in the tourist end of the Córdoba sierra, where the Sansimóns owned numerous quarries, and then had them dismantled, transported, reassembled and hung from the crossbeams and struts of the vaulted roof. They were boarded on the Celestial level, and each could comfortably accommodate two people, though the ones Marroné could see in motion were each occupied by just one black-helmeted foreman, whose job it was to keep an eye on the workers from on high and bark detailed instructions at them through a megaphone.

Sansimón led him to the first chair-lift in the line. After taking their seats, donning their executives' white helmets and lowering the safety bar, they set out on their trapeze artist's tour through the heights of the factory. Each chair was equipped with a personal console that let you move horizontally in all four directions and even descend to the shop floor via a simple pulley system, an option many of the foremen made use of to scrutinise the workers' labours at closer quarters. Combining the roles of driver and guide, Sansimón manipulated the controls at the same time as he gave a running commentary itemising the innovations and improvements introduced since his return from the United States.

'We brought in colour coding, as you might have noticed. Here in the Yellow Sector,' he said, pointing to the chrome yellow of the machines and the lemon of the workers' helmets, each with its black ID number clearly legible on the crown, 'we manufacture ceiling roses, mouldings, cornices, rosettes, friezes, balusters, corbels, columns and amphorae; in the Brown Sector stucco, gesso, plaster casts, floor treatments and insulation – oh, and chalk of all colours too, essential for educational purposes,' he rounded off, and Marroné thought he could see a delicate rainbow of fine dust at the heart of the uniform white cloud rising from all the general toiling beneath. 'In the Green Sector we make stuff for the medical industry: orthopaedic plaster, plaster bandages, plaster for death masks when all else fails,' he said, allowing himself the same joke he had cracked on all the other tours, and which Marroné laughed at with the same laugh. 'And now . . . ' he made a pause that had something majestic about it, as the chair switched rails and set off on its procession down the imposing central nave, 'for the Blue Sector, where we make partition walls, panels and plasterboards; maybe not the flashiest side of our extensive product range, but most definitely the backbone. But all this is just the beginning. Over there,' he said, pointing in the direction of the atrium, 'there's a revolution afoot in the construction industry, so watch this space: you can wave goodbye to bricks, forget concrete. The future is plaster! Just one hour after setting, Sansimón Super X is as hard and durable as Portland cement. You can combine it with fibreglass for high impact, with polystyrene for flexibility and – with sand and fuller's earth – it's both fire-proof and sound-proof. Gypsum is the *prima materia* the Ancients were searching for, the protean matter par excellence.' Sansimón waxed lyrical as he worked the chair's controls with one hand and Marroné's arm with the other, directing his attention here and there to the points he considered of most interest. And he had good reason to feel proud. The clouds of chalk dust rising like incense smoke, pierced by the shafts of light that streamed in through the high windows; the slow, elegant coordination of man and machine, moving in time through the stages of the liturgy; the exalted music composed by countless organs of steel, with their poundings and hummings, squelchings and whirrings, imparted its fullest meaning to what had seemed at first a mere architectural whim: the Sansimón Plasterworks was a true cathedral to human labour. Taken to these extremes, the efficiency of productive labour took on an aesthetic and – why not? – a spiritual dimension, and Marroné felt a tingling of pride well up through his core to his crimsoned cheeks: he too was part of all this, he was doing his bit, he was one of the numberless yet indispensable pillars of the faith. He was nothing less than an executive-errant.

A conspiratorial nudge from Sansimón drew his attention to a scene playing out a few metres behind them. From up above, in his slowly swinging chair, a foreman was lambasting a blue-helmeted operator through a megaphone.

'Blue Twenty-Seven, that plaque's cracked coz you was careless. Docked from your wages!' Blue Twenty-Seven looked up and said something that was drowned out by the altitude and noise from the machines. The foreman cupped his hand to his ear like a deaf old man and roared back through the megaphone.

'Can't hear you, Blue Twenty-Seven. You'll have to speak up,' he boomed, and winked at his boss, who shook his head as if to say, 'They're something else these boys of mine . . . '

Once the tour was over, Sansimón pulled the lever on the console and the chair began to descend vertically until it stopped half a metre from the shop floor. Taking his first steps on terra firma with legs of jelly – he wasn't what you'd call cut out for heights – Marroné followed the sprightly figure of Sansimón towards the workshop, plainly a far older structure housed in the armpit of the left transept. Within, a few sculptors and craftsmen in red helmets were working on long wooden tables, sculpting busts and figures that demanded a more craftsmanly approach: lovingly fashioning the latex and clay of the moulds, stirring the thin white paste in wide, shallow pans, applying the fresh plaster to make copies that, once cast, they smoothed and polished by hand. On either side, on old wooden shelves reaching up to the roof, were accumulated the spectral testimonies to five millennia of civilisation, perpetuated in this infinitely protean white stuff. As he walked, Marroné saw Chinese mandarins with conical hats, broad sleeves and long Fu Manchu whiskers; Buddhas in all postures and sizes, the smiles of the smallest – more cunning than enlightened – echoed by the broader-than-their-faces smiles of a choir of Carlos Gardels and those of a congregation of gluttonous friars rubbing their pot bellies; he took in the masks of tragedy and comedy, phalanxes of Michelangelo Davids flanked by Oscar statuettes, sphinxes, Tutankhamuns and Nefertitis, Egyptian cats, tablets and sarcophagi covered with hieroglyphs; shepherds and shepherdesses with crooks, panpipes and little lambs; he gazed upon repeated Nativity scenes (Herod's nightmare multiplied), a whole camp of nudes (kissing couples, sorceresses, girls with pitchers), Saint Georges and the Dragons, Aztec calendars, Myron Discoboli and lucky elephants; he came across a host of Venuses de Milo by a flock of Victories of Samothrace (the Venuses huddled together like skittles in a bowling alley, the Victories like doves taking wing); he spotted a whole row of Laurel and Hardy medallions jumbled between a pair of Einstein bookends; a Canova Pauline Bonaparte surrounded by coiled sausage-dog ashtrays; Don Quixotes and Sancho Panzas in a variety of poses: standing, on horse- and donkey-back, and even sitting on thrones; bas-reliefs of the Last Supper and an infinity of medals of Martín Fierro, with Sergeant Cruz, guitar, maté and horse; he saw Rodin Thinkers and Michelangelo Pietàs, wagonloads of Statues of Liberty, citadels of Eiffel Towers, tunnels of Arcs de Triomphes and bristling forests of Big Bens and Obelisks; massed ranks of Michelangelo Moseses directing their severe gazes at a chorus line of Marilyns with uplifted skirts; he spotted busts of Mozart, Beethoven, Schubert, Brahms and, with growing jubilation, those of the great figures of universal history: Socrates, Pericles, Alexander the Great, Julius Caesar, Napoleon, Lincoln, Lenin, Churchill, Franco, Hitler and Mussolini ('We sell those three under the counter, but they go like hot cakes,' Sansimón clarified) . . . Until he reached the pantheon of national heroes: enormous busts, life-size or larger, of San Martín the Liberator (young and sideburned, old and moustachioed), Belgrano, Sarmiento, Irigoyen and Perón (in two models: the general with furrowed brow, and in shirtsleeves wearing an avuncular smile), and finally – and at that moment Marroné really did feel like a knight-errant standing before the Holy Grail – four busts with the virile, classical, Spartan lines of the serene and peerless Eva Perón.

A voice stopped him before he could lay a finger on them. 'They're already spoken for, those are. We've been fair swamped with orders for her these last three years.'

It belonged to an old man in glasses, with a bushy, white moustache, wearing a cream-coloured cap rather than the regulation red helmet, whom Sansimón introduced as 'My old man, the founder of the company'.

'This young man is Tamerlán's head of procurement, Dad. He needs . . . how many was it? Ninety-two?'

Marroné nodded.

'Ninety-two busts of Eva, Dad.'

Sansimón Senior gave a low whistle.

'Sounds like you mean business. When do you need them by?' he asked Marroné.

'Today, Dad,' Sansimón answered. 'Matter of life or death.'

'Today? Are you serious? Tell me, do you see any automated machines here? Assembly lines? Mass-produced goods devoid of soul or beauty? Do you see men working like robots? No. And you know why? Because that's your way of doing things, out there in your big factory. In here men still work with their hands and take legitimate pride in the fruit of their labour.'

'Don't give me that old socialist crap again, Dad. I'm not a baby any more. Put them on sixteen-hour shifts with eight-hour breaks right away. Nobody's leaving till all ninety-four Evas are cast, dried and packed to go.'

'Ninety-two,' Marroné corrected him politely.

'What?' snapped Sansimón, who seemed to have forgotten all about him in the heat of the father–son tiff.

'It's ninety-two in total,' he reminded him. He was very pleased with the way things were going. Sansimón certainly knew how to inspire customer loyalty.

'Yeah, right. Whatever.' Then to his father, 'Are we agreed?'

'What? Overtime?'

'Half time and they can lump it. They still owe me from the last strike.'

'Perhaps you might consider,' ventured Sansimón Senior, appealing with exquisite delicacy to Marroné's understanding, 'taking a batch of busts of the General instead? This one, for example,' he said, pointing at the eternal smile of the tieless Perón, 'we have a considerable surplus of. We had a few returns because the clients said he'd come out looking like Vandor. You know Vandor,' he added, noticing Marroné's blank expression, 'the union leader who reckoned he could replace Perón in the workers' hearts.'

'Dad,' Sansimón tapped his foot impatiently.

'Yes, yes, I'm just a talkative old man with old-fashioned ideas. Well, in any case, you can see for yourself, he doesn't look a bit like him.'

Marroné pursed his lips in a non-committal smile.

'My . . . clients asked for Evas, specifically Evas. And your son isn't exaggerating when he says it's a matter of life or death.'

Sansimón Senior stood and stared at him for a few seconds, then, without another word, turned away to correct the work of a young sculptor, whose delicate hands and studiously hesitant speech gave him away as an artist or Fine Arts student. The son took the opportunity to bring the tour to an end.

'Come on, let's go to the office and shake on it,' he said, leading him away by the arm.

*   *   *

'I leave the little workshop to my old man, for sentimental reasons, you know,' Sansimón explained once they were back in his office. 'To be perfectly frank with you, it makes a loss, but what can you do? We're all ruled by our hearts, and it keeps him busy and leaves me to run the rest of the show. Sure you don't want them gilded? A few pesos extra and I can have her looking like royalty.'

'Look,' said Marroné, opening his palms on the table as if showing his hand, 'the minute it's all over, we'll be chucking the lot out of the eighth-floor window, I can assure you. They mean nothing to us, you understand. Peronist Party novelties. So if I have them gilded, the boss might not look too kindly on it. When they let him go, I mean.'

'I don't mean to put a jinx on him or anything, but that "when" of yours is a big "if". Look what they did to his partner.'

'We're making huge sacrifices to get the ransom money together. A cent saved is a cent nearer our target,' Marroné repeated a phrase from one of Govianus the accountant's listless harangues. 'All of us, from the managers to the lowliest operator, have been donating 15 per cent of our salaries to the ransom fund for the last six months.'

'Lucky bastard, that Tamerlán. If I was in his shoes, this lot of bloody leeches would as soon have me cut into little pieces as part with one red cent. Back again last week, they were. More demands. About falling wages this time. Tell me something I don't know. Here we are up to our necks in it like half the country, but instead of downsizing so the boat won't sink, their lordships punch more holes in it. Good job we got shot of the ringleaders before things spiralled out of control, otherwise . . . I've got a personnel manager worth his weight in gold, a godsend he is.'

'So they won't make a stink over the busts?'

'Who?' Sansimón had understood perfectly, but he was feeling cocky now and wanted to talk himself up.

'You know. The union.'

'Who with? *Me*? The *boss*? We play golf every weekend, me and the general secretary. Still holds his club like a mop, but what can you do? Pulled himself up by his bootstraps he did. They had a ballot recently and if the union wasn't nicked from him by them – what do you call 'em now, oh yeah – *hardliners*, it was with a little help from his friends – this friend. Had to sack qualified staff I did, 'cause the stupid bastards had joined the opposition. But you know how it is: you want to fuck in the grass, you have to fumigate for red ants. Commie infiltrators, that's the problem these days. Which is why . . . ' Sansimón broke off mid-sentence to flash the butt of a gun that could have been a Colt or a Smith & Wesson, Marroné couldn't tell, ' . . . I never leave the house without it. By the way, there was something I meant to ask you, just between you and me.' Sansimón leant forwards in treacherous confidence. 'Is it true they snatched Tamerlán in a poofters' sauna? That some Monto had to put his arse on the line for the Revolution?'

Marroné didn't really know what to say: not only did he have proof that the rumour was true, he even knew that the Montonero who'd acted as bait had received special training from a Chinese pederast to clamp his buttocks shut doggy-style and keep Sr Tamerlán there until his accomplices could take him away. The bodyguards had already been taken out by two sexy young guerrillas dressed as whores, who lured them into adjacent rooms where their comrades were waiting. Marroné tried to look suitably sorrowful, but in his heart of hearts he couldn't deny that his compunction coexisted with a certain gleeful vengefulness, a feeling shared by many in the company, though they would never admit it. Things had backfired on Tamerlán for once. Outwardly at least there was tacit agreement not to reveal more than strictly necessary, and indeed the official media reports were of the usual kidnapping in a car and bodyguards killed in the line of duty . . . Just then, Marroné found an opportunity to change the subject.

'The chair-lifts . . . They've stopped,' he said to Sansimón.

Sansimón turned to the inside window and saw that the chair-lifts had indeed stopped moving, save for a gentle swaying, and that the occupants, seated or standing, were yelling through their megaphones instructions that couldn't be made out through the thick glass panes.

'What the . . . ' Sansimón began to say, rising from his chair, when the door of his office imploded and six or seven workers in different-coloured helmets, wearing leather jackets over their work clothes, barged in en masse.

'This factory has been occupied by its workers, Sr Sansimón. From this moment on all the management shall remain on the premises as hostages,' reeled off a slim fifty-year-old wearing a white helmet. The white helmet on the head of a worker spoke for itself: power had quite obviously changed hands. Marroné had a sinking feeling in the pit of his stomach: a mute disappointment, tinged less with surprise than the confirmation of a basic unhinging between himself and the world. Things had been going too well.

Sansimón hit the red button on the intercom.

'Security!'

'Here they are.'

The wall of workers parted just enough to reveal the three security guards, from whose belts, relieved of their heavy burden of truncheons and guns, empty clips hung inert.

'They was too quick for us, boss,' said the oldest guard, a fat, moustachioed man who had every appearance of a retired policeman. 'There was nothing we could do.'

In a gesture more desperate than prudent, Sansimón's right hand scuttled crab-like towards his left armpit, and Marroné spun round in his chair to see all seven strikers, with almost tactful synchronisation, open their jackets to display an array of automatics and revolvers, some of which had no doubt been seized from the guards. In an instant – the one when it dawned on him he was sitting right in the line of fire – Marroné saw his whole life flash, film-like, before his eyes. He saw himself standing at the centre of a shameful pool of pee in the house of the little girl next door (his earliest memory?); he saw himself fleeing down dark corridors from the Paraguayan maid who was lashing him with a wet floor cloth; he saw the exasperated face of his kindergarten teacher telling him his mother would never come to pick him up if he didn't stop crying; he could feel the goosebumps on his shorts-clad legs during winter break-times at St Andrew's and in his chest the anguish of only winning the bronze medal for reciting a poem that opened *Up into the cherry tree, Who should climb but little me?*; he relived the humiliation of drowning in the school swimming pool and being saved by Mr Trollope, who had to dive in fully clothed; his father's exasperated reproach when his gun went off accidentally at the Federal Shooting Range rico-cheted again around his empty skull ('You're no use even at this'); again he felt his soul empty from his body with his first premature ejaculation, again he saw the whore's look of sadistic scorn as she made him wipe up the juvenile dribble that would soon be a river of humiliation, swollen by all the subsequent premature discharges until dammed up by a ministering angel, who immediately reappeared in a bridal dress, standing beside a wedding-cake figurine that bore his face; again he whirled through the vortex of blood and other substances he never imagined could issue from a wife, only to wake up on a stretcher, to the news that his son had been born with the correct number of fingers and chromosomes; he saw himself back in his apartment on the Stanford campus, trying to concentrate on Blake & Mouton, while through the wall came the exasperated cries of his child and through the window the moans of teenagers who appeared to attend college for the sole purpose of humping in the grounds night and day; he saw himself back in San Francisco for a brief visit that culminated in a panic-stricken stroll through the gayhippiepsychedelia terrors of Haight-Ashbury; and then straight down the rabbit hole, all the way to that first meeting with Tamerlán in Valhalla, a scene he knew – had always known – would be the last one his eyes would see before they sank into final darkness. All in all it was, he had to admit – and it made him rather sad to bid the world farewell on such a melancholy note – a rather dull movie. Then, just as his mind had begun to articulate the desire for a second chance, to try to live a better, fuller life, his wish was granted: realising the game was up before it began, Sansimón raised his hands and allowed a striker with a blue helmet and acromegalic chin to remove the Smith & Wesson from its holster and hand it to the man in the white helmet. No sooner was Sansimón allowed to put his hands on his desk than he was on the offensive again.

'You, and you, Trejo,' he said, 'have no business here. I'll report you to the union.'

'We're not in the union any more, Sr Sansimón. We were disaffiliated when you fired us,' retorted Trejo, adjusting his white helmet.

'For once we understand each other. To go on strike here, you have to work here. But as you don't *work* here any more, you can't go on *strike*.'

'The first of our demands is the reinstatement of our dismissed comrades,' croaked a fat man with a green helmet and several days' stubble, and with one eye veiled by a milky film.

'And what else do you want, eh? Executive salaries? A holiday camp with a golf course? Chauffeur-driven limousines to ferry you to work and back? Jacuzzis in the toilets?' Sansimón gulped in air with each item instead of releasing it; at this rate he was going to burst like a toad.

'The only thing we want for now, Sr Sansimón, is for you to come with us,' Trejo said to him.

Whether it was the man's intimidating laconic tone or because the invitation was accompanied by emphatic waving of the confiscated gun, Sansimón deflated like a fallen soufflé and, with the last wisp of air, his tiny voice wheezed, 'What . . . are you going to do to me?'

His fear was understandable. Workers might not have been in the habit of executing their bosses during occupations, but the way the reciprocal violence had been escalating it was only a matter of time before they started. Especially now there seemed to be more subversives infiltrating the factories than actual workers.

'Take it easy, boss. We're peace-lovers, we are. If we've come to this, it's only 'cause you gave us no choice. We're taking you with the others,' Trejo reassured him.

Meek as a lamb, Sansimón allowed himself to be led outside. He didn't even look at Marroné as he left. Nor did the strikers pay him any attention. Somewhat offended at everybody's indifference, Marroné decided to speak up.

'Errm, excuse me,' he ventured.

'Yeah?'

'What about me?'

The strikers consulted each other with a rapid exchange of glances, and most of them shrugged.

'You can leave when you like, chief. Only company managers to remain here as hostages,' the ringleader replied.

'Yes, but there's a slight problem,' said Marroné, smiling, searching for the words with utmost delicacy and tact, as if testing fruit in a supermarket. He remembered an anecdote from *How to Win Friends and Influence People* about Nelson Rockefeller emerging victorious from a tussle with strikers, but couldn't recall what tactic he had used or even which of the book's general principles the anecdote was supposed to illustrate. He'd have given a month's salary to have it handy. 'Look, mister striker, I can quite understand the justness of your claims, and I believe we should all fight for our rights, providing, of course, we don't violate the rights of others . . . '

'Get to the point, chief. We've an occupation on our hands in case you hadn't noticed.'

'That's exactly my point, because you see I've just closed a major deal with the company, I've even paid an advance, and if you're going to halt production, I think it's only fair that you respect any orders placed before the strike was called, such as mine, for the ninety-two busts of . . . '

'Oh, so *you're* the one who ordered the busts? You're the one who demanded our comrades in the workshop do piecework and forced us to bring the occupation forward!' the ringleader broke in, then immediately issued an order to his lieutenants, 'This one stays as well.'

Marroné flailed like a drowning man. 'Listen, co . . . comrades, these aren't just any busts. They're busts of Eva Perón no less: Evita, the Standard-Bearer of the Poor, the Lady of Hope, the Spiritual Leader of the Nation! Will you strike against Eva? What kind of Peronists are you?'

It was useless, they weren't listening. Tamely he let himself be led away by the heavy-jawed worker to a sector of the outer gallery where some office workers had gathered, several of whom were leaning on the banister watching the scenes playing out on the shop floor. Most of the foremen were still hanging in their chair-lifts like canaries on swings, some still hurling hoarse threats through their megaphones, others by now resigned to waiting for the strikers to get them down, using a system that had seemingly been adopted less out of efficiency than revenge: below one of the nearest chair-lifts several workers were holding a tarpaulin, stretched as tight as a drum-skin, and were urging the foreman to jump.

'Come on, mate, we ain't got all day, eh.'

'Jump, mate, jump! We'll be here for you.'

The foreman was doing his best to get to his feet, but his knocking knees wouldn't let him and he slumped back into his seat; he eventually made it up and, clinging on to one of the vertical bars with rigid, corpse-like hands, he gingerly put one leg, then the other, over the horizontal bar and, wobbling on legs that had started doing the Charleston of their own accord, readied himself for the big jump.

'Don't run off on me, lads, you could do me a serious injury,' he implored from his perch. 'Remember I always treated you decently.'

Marroné had never heard anyone beg through a megaphone before: it created a rather odd effect. Out of the corner of his eye he noticed the office workers beside him had started laying bets: 'A hundred says he jumps! Two hundred says he doesn't! Three hundred says he hits the deck!'

'Get a move on, will you! We got all the plaster in Paris if you break a leg.' The foreman leant forwards and they all ran off with the tarpaulin, shouting '*Olé!*' The poor sod above clung to his vertical bar like a stripper and then, whiter than any of the surrounding plaster, he wailed, 'Oy! Stop playing silly buggers will you, don't be so bloody daft!'

He was practically in tears and the workers were beneath him again, but the canvas rose and fell with their laughter like a cellophane sea, offering little in the way of safety.

At last the poor devil crossed himself swiftly, closed his eyes and leapt into the void. He landed bang in the middle of the tarpaulin, which gave almost all the way to the floor and then, answering the unanimous call of the six pairs of strong arms, bulged up and out, and launched him high into the air again. Then the blanketing began. During his first few pirouettes the foreman was still up to cursing the strikers and threatening them with reprisals, but as his somersaults got further and further from the ground, and his arms and legs flailed in the air more and more desperately, he went back to begging and pleading, and in the end just clenched his jaw and held on tight to his helmet in case it came off and he lost his teeth on it in one of the falls. Less out of mercy than weariness the workers finally deposited him on the ground and set off with their tarpaulin in search of another victim to rescue.

Later in the day one of the commissars came by and issued a directive to separate the management from the office staff; Marroné was herded with the execs into Sansimón's office, where, having recovered from the shock, the man himself ushered them in with a cheery 'Ah, Macramé, still here?' and introduced him to the members of his crisis cabinet: Aníbal Viale, the chief financial officer; Arsenio Espínola, the marketing manager; Garaguso, the personnel manager; and Cerbero, head of security, whose names Marroné jotted down in his notebook as soon as he had the chance. He asked for permission to use the phone and it was magnanimously granted by Sansimón, but no sooner did he reach for the receiver than an 'Oy, you! What you doing?' from one of the two commissars guarding them made him leap backwards as if the telephone had snarled at him. 'All communication with outside suspended till further notice,' the commissar told him, revelling in his bureaucratic tone, and Marroné was just able to make out the mocking grins exchanged by Sansimón and his men.

'Welcome to Socialist Argentina, Macramé,' Sansimón said to him tongue-in-cheek before returning to the dialogue of signs and whispers he and his management had been conducting.

Around midday two new workers came to relieve the guards and the personnel manager hailed them with a 'Baigorria, Saturnino, great to have you back with us, you don't know how much we missed you!' With the changing of the guard came some rolls and two litre-bottles of Fanta, which Sansimón and his management team shared out with an egalitarian disdain that duly included him. They had a radio on to catch the news, but there was no mention whatsoever of their plight, understandably so, since for some time now more factories, companies and government buildings were occupied than still in the hands of their rightful owners. What worried Marroné most was that the company might not have heard what had happened and attribute his inexplicable absence to negligence or – worse still – bad faith, and what annoyed him most was that he hadn't brought with him any of the management books he so enjoyed and which would have at least allowed him to extract some benefit from the bleak hours of waiting, which his comrades in captivity spent playing cards, sleeping in shifts on the white leather sofa or practising their putting with Sansimón's putter and a plastic cup. At one point he tried to interest Garaguso in the advantages of applying the techniques of *How to Win Friends and Influence People* to the settlement of union disputes. 'Yeah, yeah, I did that course too,' Garaguso interrupted him soon after he'd started, 'but I'd like to see Dale Carnegie take on these babes in arms with his sincere praises and friendly smiles. There are two and only two ways to influence a certain class of people: gold or lead. And as head of procurement you surely realise that lead's a lot cheaper than gold.' At about seven o'clock two workers in black helmets brought in the sales manager, who was sweating, dishevelled and sprinkled with white dust; he explained that, tipped off by a loyal worker about the start of the occupation, he'd hidden among the towering sacks of plaster and stayed put until he'd been captured making a break for the outside to bring back reinforcements. 'They're highly organised and synchronised,' he remarked

in a whisper to cap his account. 'This isn't just the workers – they're getting outside help.' 'You don't say!' sneered
Sansimón, belittling his revelation; then, turning to Garaguso,
he said, 'Remind me of your infallible infiltrator-detection
system again, will you? I didn't quite get it first time round.'
Garaguso shrugged off the jibe and immediately raised his
eyebrows inquisitively in the direction of the two commissars, who, in their boredom, were leafing through some
magazines, and Sansimón closed and opened his eyes with
all the deliberation of a prearranged signal. Garaguso eyed
the two of them the way a lion studies a herd of zebra to
pick out the weakest and, when his prey looked up from
the magazine and they made eye contact, he got up from
his seat and nonchalantly started closing in. From where he
was, Marroné caught the gist of their conversation.

'Listen, Baigorria. Us bosses wanted to organise one or
two things here – of a private nature, you understand, keep
it in the family, you know the sort of thing: nothing too
flashy, a box of whisky perhaps, some nibbles, quiet hand
of cards, couple of scags . . . Just to kill the time, right? Now
that we're here . . . And we got to thinking, you know, it's
true what you say about us having to learn to share and
that . . . Socialising, as you call it . . . '

Baigorria's mouth began to water in spite of himself.

'I mean, as we're all in this together, we should at least
have as good a time as possible, are you with me?' Baigorria nodded eagerly and Garaguso, knowing it was in the
bag, pointed almost tactfully to one of the disconnected
telephones.

'So . . . you don't mind if I make a couple of quick phone
calls?'

Saturnino came over to see what was going on, and Baigorria whispered the glad tidings in his ear. Standing beside Marroné, Sansimón explained the meaning of the ruse.

'At least now we know they're real workers.'

'How do we know?' asked Marroné.

'If they were undercover subversives, they'd never have gone for it. Revolutionary morality,' he elucidated.

Marroné seized the chance to raise his most pressing concern.

'So tell me . . . The little matter of the busts . . . What shall we do about them?'

Sansimón immediately went on the defensive.

'As you can see, *I* have no say in the matter any more. You'll have to discuss it with the boys,' he said, indicating the two guards with his chin.

'But in that case, the cheque I gave you . . . '

'Ah, no, that's another matter. They'll be delivered, you can be certain of that. Now, if there's a delay owing to circumstances beyond our control . . . '

'But you know we need the busts to expedite Sr Tamerlán's release. If you don't deliver them soon, they'll be no use to us at all.'

'Listen . . . Who are the ones holding him? If I'm not mistaken, it's the Montoneros, isn't it?'

Marroné nodded. Sansimón was leading him somewhere but he couldn't work out where. There was nothing for it but to go with the flow.

'And who do you think's behind all that's going on here?'

'The Montoneros?'

'Correct.'

'Not the union?'

'I've got the union in my pocket, sonny. The occupation's worse for them than it is for us. No, it's the Montos. So, if the ones asking you to have a bath take the sponge and the soap, it isn't my problem, or yours – it's theirs. Am I right or am I right?'

Marroné did his best to conceal his annoyance.

'The problem . . . '

'The problem,' Sansimón interrupted him gruffly, 'is that this occupation started because I had the bad idea – the very bad idea – of making the workforce do piecework just to save your boss's arse. Because I trust you've learnt something from your tour and don't expect some crummy little busts to make any difference to the yearly balance. But instead of apologies and gratitude you come to me with demands – worse still, with sly accusations. Next time someone goes down on bended knee asking me for a favour over a matter of life or death, I'll think with my head, not my heart.'

Marroné recalled one of the golden rules from *How to Win Friends and Influence People*: 'The only way to get the best of an argument is to avoid it' and he thought it inadvisable to contest such insidious reasoning. The occupation might be over in a matter of hours, as so often happened, and in that case it wasn't in his interests to get on the wrong side of Sansimón, who had clearly taken offence and treated him with manifest coldness thereafter; an attitude immediately picked up on and aped by his obsequious executives.

Lunch arrived an hour later. It consisted of a box of real Scotch whisky, another of local champagne, and cold cuts of sliced York ham and pineapple, turkey and glacé cherries, and king prawns and palm-hearts with thousand island dressing. The girls arrived half an hour later: one short and fleshy, the other tall and gangling with a husky voice, and the party got into full swing. Sansimón opened up his radiogram and put on some dance hits and then, while Cerbero and Garaguso strutted their stuff with the girls, began pouring the whisky into cardboard cups. Marroné approached the table, which the caterers had laid with a white tablecloth, and picked up a slice of turkey upon which a phosphorescent cherry sat impaled. Following his example, Baigorria and Saturnino sidled shyly over and stretched out their hands, Baigorria for a palm-heart, whose heart popped out under his rough grip, Saturnino for a king prawn, which he devoured shell and all with an audible crunching and pained expression; but by their third whisky they were wolfing down slices of turkey and ham as if to the manner born, and even allowing Garaguso to put his arms round their shoulders and press home his advantage. When he thought they were ready, he decided it was time to play his trump card and, beckoning them with his finger to watch, he began to pull down the taller prostitute's panties until, to the fanfare of her shrill, artificial laughter, out popped a limp member, as wrinkled as a prune.

She was a man! At first Marroné was as taken aback as the two commissars, but unlike him they soon recovered from the initial shock and, egged on by the drink, began to vie acrimoniously for the transvestite's company, while the woman, altogether forgotten, smoked a cigarette and watched the events play out with a seen-it-all-before expression. To stop her feeling left out Sansimón took her by the hips and manoeuvred her naked titties onto the glass top of his desk, pulled down her panties with a tug and entered her, while Espínola, pretending to hide underneath, licked her nipples through the glass and Viale diligently crammed rolls of ham into her mouth, which she could only chew and swallow; meanwhile, Garaguso and Cerbero had commandeered the tranny and, as the former inserted a prodigious erection into her mouth, the other, with a good deal of snorting, took her from behind. Yet there was something contrived and – why not? – even theatrical about the whole scene; something that suggested a live number performed by the company's executives for the benefit of their underlings, like in those progressive schools where the teachers dress up as children for the annual graduation party and play-act at behaving badly. Marroné had been to many a business convention and private party at which alcohol, sex workers and even drugs were freely available, but in this instance it was obvious that such histrionics were put on for the exclusive benefit of the two plebs, who were clearly having the worst time of it: the confirmation that all their fantasies about the dissipated and licentious lives led by their bosses at their expense were actually pretty accurate seemed to have robbed them of their capacity for reaction, or even righteous indignation, leaving instead two mere husks trembling with mute, affronted desire; so by the time the whore and the transvestite had gone from executive prick to executive prick and it was their turn, all that was left standing of their moral scaffolding was the requisite proletarian modesty to ask, after much tentative throat-clearing and shuffling of soles, if they could have their slice of the pie somewhere a bit more private, a mercy most graciously granted them by the conclave of executives.

No sooner had the two of them retired to Garaguso's office with their sexual partners (their objection apparently only went as far as doing it in the presence of their bosses, not in front of each other) than Sansimón pounced on one of the phones on his desk and Cerbero on the other one, any trace of befuddlement or intoxication evaporated as if by magic, and while the big boss phoned the general secretary of the union, the other got on to a trusted police chief of his acquaintance:

'Just a second, Babirusa, what do I stick in the envelope for you every month? Sugar-coated peanuts is it? Your people . . . a den of subversives, Turco, this strike thing's a smokescr . . . You've disaffiliated them? Ah, well, that makes me feel a lot better. Made them go without pudding too, did you? . . . The delegates are all from the Montoneros and the ERP, and the shop stewards are armed to the teeth . . . do *I* know who they are? Wasn't it you who said we'd sacked them all? Besides, the trouble started in the old workshop, Christ knows what those sonsofbitches have done with my poor old . . . I don't think the police will be enough, what we could do with here . . . '

Garaguso had been acting as look-out while they were on the phone and, when the hand that was tracing windmills in the air became a pair of urgently slicing scissors, they hung up in perfect unison and settled back into the pretence with their whisky glasses. Whether it was their uncontrollable excitement or because the conditioning of assembly-line production had affected their sexual behaviour too, the workers were done quicker than it would have taken Marroné, leaving their bosses little more than the absolute minimum to organise the factory's recovery with their allies on the outside. The problem now was that post-orgasmic relaxation, coupled with a misplaced egalitarian feeling

induced in all likelihood by the promiscuous cohabitation
of bourgeois and plebeian spermatozoa in the democratic
innards of the transvestite and the whore, had stirred a
geniality and over-familiarity in the two strikers, which their
bosses, now that the objective of making contact with the
outside world and setting the wheels of the rescue operation in motion had been achieved, treated with indifference
and at times even disdain. Baigorria in particular, who had
accompanied the whisky with an inadvisable mix of champagne, was going around hugging everyone, a situation
exploited by the ever-alert Garaguso, who stuck to him like
glue and continued his efforts at seduction: 'The rate you're
going, Baigorria, your blessed revolution's going to take
how long . . . ten, twenty years? And who'll pay your bills
in the meantime? Fidel Castro? Who'll buy your medicine
when the kids are ill? Che Guevara? Who'll pay for the iron
your missus saw in that ad on the TV, or the dress your
neighbour's daughter wears the day you finally get round
to banging her? Chairman Mao? They bang on to you about
our children this, our children that, future generations
the other . . . Life's for living now, Baigorrita. Think about
it, we're all after the same thing: a decent life. And what
do you need for a decent life? Money, Baigorrita, nothing
but money. The rest is fairy tales. Now, if it's money you
need . . . ' The party was by now approaching the moment
of maximum entropy: so drunk they could barely hold the
putter between them, Viale and Espínola giggled oafishly
as they tried to get a hole-in-one in the prostitute's vagina,
who, sitting on the floor with her legs spread, looked a lot
like one of those weird contraptions you find at crazy-golf
courses; meanwhile the sales manager, whose name Marroné

hadn't managed to jot down in his notebook, clocking the gawping mugs of Baigorria and Saturnino, shouted at them every thirty seconds 'You two can use her to practise your pool on when we're done!'; and the transvestite, who had swapped clothes with Sansimón and now looked like a lesbian from the 1920s, owned in a quite unprovoked fit of sincerity to being called Hugo and to doing all this to support his sick son, news that was received by all present – excepting Marroné and Saturnino – with gales of laughter, which, after a few seconds of puzzlement, Hugo himself joined in on, laughing most shrilly of all. Faring worst on the slippery slope was Sansimón himself: the combination of post-coital gloom, hangover and humiliating captivity at the hands of his own employees had wreaked havoc with his moral framework. Still got up in corset, stockings and suspenders, he fell prey to a bout of the drunken mopes and began to brood on his discontent:

'Everything, everything . . . Nothing's enough for them. They always want more. They start with the soap in the toilets and, when you agree, they want you to bend over and pick it up as well. You hold out your hand and they take your arm. Arm my foot! Shoulder. Neck. Head. And then they want more. More and more. So here you are. Yours for the taking. Eh? What are you waiting for?'

Finally cottoning on, Baigorria and Saturnino slowly turned their heads – Saturnino from gazing on his invisible member lost in the cavernous depths of the hooker's throat, Baigorria from the insidious drip of Garaguso's words in his ear.

Legs akimbo, grazing the carpet with the crown of his head, Sansimón pulled apart his hairy buttocks, separated by the narrow strip of panty fabric. In his inverted face his mouth opened and closed like the giant eye of a Cyclops:

'You want my arse? Here it is! Roll up! Roll up! First the union delegates, then the shop stewards, then health and safety, then hygiene! Then the union lawyer! And all the members! And while we're at it, everyone that's been fired for labour or political reasons since '55! Will you be happy then? Will you let me do my job in peace?'

He had dropped to his knees, head between his elbows, keeping his arse up high. To spare himself the rest of this sorry spectacle, Marroné grabbed his folded jacket and briefcase, and left the office without so much as a goodbye to those who wouldn't notice his absence anyway.

As he stepped into the corridor, he was enfolded by the hot, slightly gelatinous summer-night air and, in a matter of seconds, his face was moist with sweat. The windows were all open to let in the breeze (the air-conditioning had doubtless been turned off by the strikers on an egalitarian whim that for some reason excluded the management) and, rolling up his sleeves and undoing a couple of buttons on his shirt, Marroné went over to a window that overlooked the garden and the street beyond.

The front garden was coated in the plaster dust produced by the factory's round-the-clock schedule, and in the moonlight the talcum-powder paths, silver trees, wax flowers and flour-dusted lawn conjured what the landscape would look like if there were life on the Moon. Here and there, their light made all the brighter by the surrounding pallor, burnt the bonfires of the worker guards, and, as if riding the soft breeze, now and then there came the sound of voices, the occasional burst of laughter, the ham-fisted but resolute picking of a guitar against the rich chorus of frogs and crickets, which had surely turned albino to survive in this white-hued world. All of a sudden the pastoral calm was shattered by the sound of sirens, and the faint whiteness beyond the main gate was filled with a blinding blue haze. Half a dozen patrol cars, their headlights blazing, had pulled up en masse and, before taking up position, six or seven uniformed officers and another two or three in plain clothes had leapt out. For a second Marroné thought they would attack straightaway, but his hope soon died. Perfectly synchronised, black-helmeted strikers came running from all directions, the moonlight glinting on the metal of their drawn guns. Police and strikers spread out, facing each other in a precarious stand-off, with nothing between them but the flimsy wire fence – the police, for the time being, going through the motions with no other purpose than to show their faces and intimidate; the workers letting them know the factory wouldn't be retaken without a fight.

Marroné looked at his watch: it was quarter past four in the morning, and it occurred to him he might be able to find a phone and call his wife to reassure her and ask her to let the company know his whereabouts; but, anticipating just such an eventuality, as they had everything else, the strikers had locked all the offices except the main one, where the office workers captured at the start of the occupation were sleeping, guarded by two other commissars. After asking him where he'd come from and accepting his hushed explanation, one of the guards told him to find somewhere to lie down.

There were twenty odd people in the room and, despite the ample space available to them, they lay huddled on the carpet, the men in one group, the women in another, like sea lions on a beach, their heads resting on rolled-up jackets, imitation-leather cushions or even stacks of files. On several desks were scattered the leftovers of a frugal dinner: the ubiquitous ham and cheese rolls, many of them half-eaten, empty pop bottles, cellophane wrappers and bits of foil from biscuits and sweets, little plastic cups half-full of coffee and sodden dog-ends. The air-conditioning was off here as well, and as the windows looked inwards to the shop floor, the night breeze was even feebler than in the corridor, and the faces he could make out were sweating in their sleep. The more daring of the menfolk were sleeping in their vests, someone was snoring, a portable radio crackled into a slumbering ear and there was an acrid smell of cigarettes, sweat and sit-in.

Besides worrying about not telling the company his whereabouts, the mild displeasure caused by his colleagues' rebuff and the nuisance of not being able to brush his teeth, the situation wasn't as grave as it had first appeared. They'd probably let them all go tomorrow, except perhaps the senior management; and if they didn't, they'd at least let them make a phone call. Such events had become commonplace in recent years, and Tamerlán & Sons had had to deal with occupied construction sites on several occasions – and not just the sites of mere apartment blocks either, but mega-ventures like dams, freeways and airports. What worried him most was the possibility that the delay would put Sr Tamerlán in danger. What if the deadline expired while Marroné was locked away in here? If his boss died, he'd get the blame. Marroné's heart skipped a beat as it dawned on him that Sr Tamerlán's imprisonment was infinitely harsher than his own, and had lasted not just twenty-four hours, but more than six months. Only now that he was experiencing something similar first-hand did he feel close, not so much to this abstract person, the company's CEO, but to the fragile, frightened man nestling within, and he swore to himself that he would remain at his post for as long as necessary if it helped shorten such an inhuman captivity.

*   *   *

It was nine in the morning but the heat made it feel like noon, and Marroné lay sprawled in a chair surrounded by dejected office workers, waiting for the breakfast they'd been promised by the worker guard. He'd been awake for about an hour and, after a cursory glance at his fellow captives, had begun to toy with the idea of returning to his executive peers, to enjoy the air-conditioning and other creature comforts. But they wouldn't be released until it was all over, not to mention the possibility of all hell breaking loose and the worker commandos taking it into their heads to shoot the management: in that event the fact that he was from another company might be thought a subtlety worthy of little consideration. This lot, on the other hand, would be offloaded any time now and, concealed in their midst, he might be able to make his escape.

Breakfast arrived, borne by two workers in red helmets. It consisted of some stale bread rolls from the day before and a pan of weak, boiled coffee that every office worker worth his or her salt took as a slap in the face.

'This tar's a bit weak, lads and lasses.'

'Was it just the one bat they got to piss in the pot?'

'Hey, what have they been boiling? Shoes?'

'No, one of their own!'

Soon, after taking an incoming call, one of the commissars made an announcement that helped calm the general mood a little:

'You can use the phones!'

They had a minute each, but there was no need for the commissars to keep an eye on them: as soon as the second-hand had gone round once, the next in the queue would start chanting 'Time's up! Time's up!' and the receiver would change hands. So, despite being at the very back of the queue (a second's distraction and they'd beaten him to it), it took Marroné just fifteen minutes to reach the receiver and dial the number of the red telephone.

Govianus picked up at the fourth try.

'Marroné! Where the bloody hell are you? We thought you'd been kidnapped too! Have you got the busts?'

He gave Govianus a brief update.

'You'll have to look elsewhere,' he concluded. 'Ochoa has a list of suppliers . . . '

'What suppliers, Marroné? All the plasterworks in the country have come out in solidarity. I'd place the order abroad if I could, but imagine what they might send us. An Eva with Doris Day's face, or Faye Dunaway's,' said Govianus glumly.

'Production's at a standstill here. But I'll try and persuade them to make an exception for Evita,' he ventured without much conviction.

'Try, Marroné, try. It's our only hope.'

Marroné assured him he would do everything in his power and, before hanging up, asked Govianus to please ring his wife. The morning promised to be a tedious one, so he thought he'd make the most of it and have a quiet sit on the toilet, but when the cleaning staff had joined the strike, matters of hygiene had been left to individual users, who, unwilling to lower themselves to such a lowly task, had opted to let nature take its course. To make matters worse, Marroné had no reading matter with him, so to pass the time there was little else for it but to sit up in his chair and, notebook in hand, lend an ear to the chatterings of the office workers, who, with the artfulness of prestidigitators, had set about organising an alternative breakfast, whisking out of their drawers heaters, kettles, Thermos flasks, coffee pots, sugar bowls, mugs and spoons.

'Want me to whip yours?'

'Oh, go on then, I've got a bad wrist.'

'They aren't half dragging it out. Why won't they just let us go?'

'God, it ain't half funky in here!'

'If they don't put the air-conditioning on again for us, there'll be a right to-do here, matey.'

'Come on, Fernández, don't hog the biscuits. Food's for sharing, as the comrades downstairs say.'

Marroné jotted down his first name, 'Fernández', adding beside it the aide-mémoire, 'little old man, 70, 1950s fine-check suit, hogs biscuits'.

'Tsk, too much water. Pass the sugar, will you, Nidia.'

'Go easy on it boys and girls, we're running a bit short.'

Nidia was a secretary with lipstick stains on her teeth and one of those seen-it-all-before expressions only earned after thirty years working for the same company – observations that Marroné conscientiously jotted down beside her name in his notebook.

'Waiters in white gloves, caviar, lobster, champagne, god knows what else – the works. And here are we with pop, and ham and cheese rolls! And for dessert? Whores, five of 'em! Hostages? What hostages? They've got them up there living the life of Riley. And then they bang on to us about equality!'

'You're just miffed 'cause you weren't invited, Gómez.'

Marroné hastily wrote down the name of the man with long sideburns in the wash-and-wear shirt, grey and burgundy paisley tie, and blue bell-bottoms, who carried on railing at the joint iniquity of management and workers.

'And the lads got a slice of the pie too, don't you know? Get my drift, Ramírez?' he said to a young man, who went straight into Marroné's notebook, along with his moustache and long mane of hair, pink shirt and green-check tie. 'It's always the same old story in this country. It's either the sharks or the darkies that get the goodies, and we always end up looking on. We're piggy in the middle, the stick in the mud, take it from me,' clamoured Gómez. 'Now it's the lads are calling the shots. Have you heard what they're saying? They're going to turn the factory into a cooperative and bring in a standard wage. Managers to operators, everyone earns the same. Anyone doesn't like it . . . out on their ear.'

'What about seniority?' asked Fernández in concern.

'With all due respect, Fernández, they'll tell you to stick it up your jumper. Everyone's equal, so tough shit. And another thing that's out: pensions. From now on you work till you drop down dead like they do in Russia.'

Open-mouthed, the old man was shaking like a leaf.

'Don't listen to him, Fernández. He's just messing with you,' Nidia reassured him.

'What I reckon is that we should join the strike in support of our comrades in the Terrestrial Sector, who are sticking their necks out for us. Why do we always keep our mouths shut? Let's make our voices heard too. Or have we got nothing to say?' said Ramírez, working himself into a lather while unsticking the sweaty pink shirt from his torso.

'That Christmas box they owe us, for example,' chimed in a blue-eyed forty-something in a brown suit, who answered to the name of González.

'And the holidays,' added a bald man called Suárez, who, in spite of the heat that marbled his forehead with sweat, was still wearing his jacket and tie.

'And while we're at it,' the man in brown upped the ante, 'the coat-stand issue . . . Look at the state of my jacket . . . I still have two instalments to pay on it and it's already out of shape.'

Marroné stopped listening and devoted himself to studying these men and women whose company he had kept for barely an hour and whose souls held no further secrets for him: people with no horizons who had never taken a creativity course in their lives or ever heard of Dale Carnegie, R Theobald Johnson or Edward de Bono. His eyes alighted upon an easel on which sat a large pad of paper, of the type commonly used in business presentations. In that dust-covered lectern on which the inert pages had yellowed without ever bearing the fruit of gung-ho sloganeering, in the dry marker pens that would barely leave a mark, Marroné saw a symbol of all that wasted potential. Plenty of colour in the machines, plenty of chair-lifts, but the reality of the office was still the same uniform grey, a cesspool of routine, of disenchantment, resentment and envy, from which an office worker was released only in retirement or death. It was so easy to blame the system, the company, the bosses.

But what attitude did those very office workers adopt when offered the opportunity to change? Marroné had experienced first-hand how difficult it was to 'motivate the troops' in that kind of environment. Bent on putting into practice in his own procurement department what he had learnt in a work environment workshop he'd attended in the United States, called 'The Kindergarten Office', he had met with – instead of acceptance and enthusiasm – reactions that ranged from indifference to open or concealed boycott. His proposal that everyone undergo a few days' training (which he himself would coordinate for free) was greeted by his employees with a petition to the union, and he only managed to defuse the mood and persuade them to take part when he offered to hold it during working hours. He had even less luck with the workshop 'Buy While You Play', which would have consisted of a Sunday outing to the Tigre Fruit Market and a subsequent feedback session, but the mere idea of devoting part of their sacrosanct Sunday to work-related tasks unleashed an outright mutiny that included the sending of a delegation to Govianus the accountant and a week-long go-slow; not to mention Govianus's answer when Marroné asked him for permission to hold it on a weekday: 'A mini-bus, Marroné? To go to Tigre? To buy fruit? On a Monday?' ('Breaking Mondays' was another of the innovative ideas he'd disembarked with.) 'What a super idea! But tell me . . . will a minibus be big enough? Why don't we lay on a school bus instead, to make the journey more comfortable? Because I imagine you won't think of leaving the rest of us behind . . . And where shall we go on Tuesday? How about the zoo?' But Marroné wasn't disheartened by these remarks: abandoned by his superiors and distrusted by his subordinates, he was more determined than ever to forge ahead. First he tried to seduce them: he bought them all plants, but they were dead from lack of water before the month was out (save one plucky Pothos, which, after turning yellow and losing nearly all its leaves, stubbornly survived so as to remind him day after day of the futility of his efforts); he stayed behind after hours one Friday night to surprise them first thing Monday morning with a poster titled 'Choose Your Attitude For The Day', below which 'Option 1' depicted a face with knitted brow and 'Option 2' a smiley face, but not a week had gone by before someone had drawn an erect prick in the smiley's mouth and glasses on the frowning face with an arrow saying 'Govianus', and he'd had to take it down; his employees, of course, accused the other departments, though Marroné's own suspicions ran higher still, and he spent all that week studying the features of Cáceres Grey with ill-concealed suspicion. The brief maxims he wrote on different-coloured notelets posted around the office 'at random' were systematically sabotaged: if he wrote 'You can't always get what you want but you can want what you get', someone would add in pencil 'I got cancer'; and to his 'In spite of everything, the sun shines', some joker (probably the same) had added 'I got *skin* cancer'. When he instituted his policy of 'Catch your employee doing something right' and spent a week pouncing on them and shouting 'Aha! Gotcha! You're doing a good job!', the longest-serving member of the department, Ochoa, came on the others' behalf to ask him to desist from a practice that had them with their hearts in their mouths every hour of the working day ('We understand you're doing it with the best of intentions, Sr Marroné . . . '). In the end he'd just given up: the coloured balloons that, in one desperate, last-ditch attempt, he'd bought in a novelty shop, and blown and hung up with Mariana's help (that day he made the heart-stopping discovery that she didn't wear tights but stockings and suspenders) gradually deflated over the next few weeks until, depressed at the sight of them hanging shrivelled and dusty, looking for all the world like used condoms, he stayed behind one evening after hours to take them down so no one would see. The only tangible result of all his efforts had been to make himself the laughing stock of the other executives, who made him the butt of their jibes in their lunch breaks in the canteen: they would, for example, ask him with a sorry look for advice on how to motivate an unwilling member of staff and then, when Marroné had enthusiastically embarked on his spiel, sneeze and emerge from their handkerchief wearing a red nose and saying 'Will this do the trick?', which would then set the others off, and the procurement department came to be known as 'Circus Marroné' in allusion to a hideous TV clown whose surname, Marrone, was but an unaccented version of his own.

At that moment Marroné 'caught himself' succumbing to the toxic energy of discouragement and frustration, to the impotence of 'it's impossible to change a thing in this country with people like this'. 'No!' he told himself forcefully. 'No!' The risk of doing nothing is always greater than that of taking action: you don't lose faith in yourself when you fail, only when you stop trying. He looked around through different eyes, watchful and vibrant, and full of decision.

The mood was hotting up. The young, idealistic, pink-shirted Ramírez had apparently gone on haranguing them, and Gómez had finally had enough.

'Oh, so you don't understand us. Is that it? No, of course you don't. It must be hard for someone like you. Because you're different, aren't you, you can spot it a mile off . . . You used to be a student, didn't you? What of?'

'History . . . ' Ramírez replied, fighting off with a defiant gesture the slight stammer Gómez's sibylline haughtiness had started to cause him.

'History . . . ' Gómez said, repeating each syllable carefully as if savouring a fine wine. 'Yes, of course. That explains it. It must give you a different way of looking at things, a different . . . what do you lot call it? . . . perspective. Because all this is just temporary for you, isn't it. Whereas *we're* buried alive here . . . You probably pity us, don't you?'

'Leave him alone, Gómez, don't be cruel,' intervened Nidia maternally. But Gómez had tasted blood and liked it.

'Know how many of your sort I've seen since I've been in here? Want to know what comes next? For the next five years you'll keep telling yourself it's just till you get your degree; in ten, that you're going to pack it in and finish university, but all the while you'll feel it'd be a shame to give up the benefit of seniority; in twenty you'll start fantasising about getting yourself fired and setting up a newsagent's with the indemnity money; and so on, just ticking over till you've been here for thirty years and start crossing off how many to go before you retire. No one here gets out alive, sonny. If you had what it takes, you'd never have come here in the first place.'

'Don't worry about me,' said Ramírez defiantly when Gómez had finished. 'I'll shoot myself before I end up like you.' At that moment a young woman with ashen hair and a timid chin, who hadn't opened her mouth till then, began sobbing softly, and when Nidia gently asked her 'What's the matter, Dorita?', Marroné jotted down the missing name.

'I hate it when you fight,' she said, through her tears and sniffles. 'I find all that violence really upsetting.'

'Don't listen to them, silly. You know what men are like. If it isn't politics, it's football. They'll have made up by tomorrow, you'll see, as if nothing had happened,' Nidia consoled her. And then to Gómez and Ramírez, 'You're a right pair, you two are.'

'I want to go home,' Dorita insisted, laying it on thick.

Marroné decided the time had come to intervene. It was now or never.

'Have any of you ever done any visualisation?'

The seven pairs of eyes fixed on him. He had their attention now. Stage one was complete.

'Ernesto Marroné, Procurement, Tamerlán & Sons,' he introduced himself, shaking hands with each in turn and looking them in the eye with a smile to establish a more personal link through direct physical contact. 'Do you mind if I interrupt for a minute? Because we're ultimately all in the same boat and, if we all pull in the same direction, we may all go home safe and early. I've been following your conversation carefully and the words that kept coming to mind were *frustration . . . discouragement . . . helplessness . . . anger*. There's nothing worse than feeling trapped in an unpleasant situation and thinking we can do nothing about it, true? There are times when life feels like a life sentence, and our home or our office the prison we serve it in. Yes it's true this may not be the best job in the world: it's routine and boring, and the pay's never enough. And how do we react to all that? We grumble, we protest, we ask them to give us a raise, to change our job description, to change our boss. And when they don't, we feel helpless and frustrated. And now I ask you . . . What have *you* done to change things? Because if you can't change your job, you *can* change the attitude you bring to work. And if you can't change your boss, you *can* try and get the boss you've been landed with to change. You aren't happy with your boss . . . And what makes you think your boss is happy with you? Happy to see faces that reflect nothing day in day out but depression and discontent?'

He paused to gauge his audience's reaction. Apart from the predictable expression on Gómez's face, who was smoking a cigarette as much as to say 'I've heard this one before', he had the undivided attention of the rest of the group, whose ranks had swelled with the arrival of four more office workers – three men and a woman – who had homed in on the change of energy. Marroné was pleased. He had more than half the hostages on his side.

'Personally I tend to be an optimist. Some,' he cast a sidelong glance at Gómez, who smiled back politely, 'would say that being an "optimist" is synonymous with being a dreamer or naive. But "optimist" is derived from "optimise", which means securing the best conditions even under the most adverse of circumstances. We were talking about prisons just now. I hope that, after all that's been said, you'll agree with me that the real prisons are inside us: in our heads, our hearts, our souls . . . And to escape from them we've all been supplied at birth with a file, a hairpin, a skeleton key: creativity. It's commonly thought that some people are "born" creative,' Marroné's fingers notched the air with inverted commas, 'like inventors, artists, thinkers – and that others aren't. It's like saying people are born athletic, or muscular. Creativity is a universal potential, and as such it can be trained with specific exercises designed to trigger "boinks!" in the right side of our brains – the creative side. One of these exercises I was telling you about is visualisation. So . . . shall we give it a go?'

'I'll pass if you don't mind,' said Gómez, yawning conspicuously and getting up from his seat. 'Someone over there looks like they've found a newspaper. I'll see if I can borrow the classifieds. You can tell me about it later.' He waved goodbye to his colleagues, who, now that the source of toxic energy was at arm's length, looked more receptive and relaxed.

'All right then. Please make sure you're sitting comfortably. If any of your clothing feels too tight, please loosen it: ties, gentlemen; heels, ladies; belts if you're wearing one. Great. Now, close your eyes and try to relax. Breathe deeply, become aware of every breath you take. Veeery good. Breeeathe. Iiiin. Oooout. You can see blue skies. In the sky there are clouds. Each of the clouds is a negative thought, a source of anxiety. There are days when they all come together and overwhelm you, covering the sky till you can't see a single crack of blue. But not today. Today each one is a fluffy little white cloud, and you're just watching them float by overhead. And you feel mooore at ease and mooore relaxed. And every passing cloud is smaller than the one before. Until there are no more clouds at all and your eyes are lost in the immensity of the blue sky. No more anxiety. You're at peace. It's time to begin.'

He paused to gauge the participants' general state of mind and was pleased with what he saw.

'Darkness,' he said suddenly, and watched as a rictus of apprehension spread across their relaxed features. 'You're in a dark place, so dark you can't see your hands. You touch the walls: they're smooth and cold, and as you walk around them you can find no opening. You feel trapped. You want to get out. You can't breathe.' Suárez's forehead was once again marbled with sweat, and he was tugging at his shirt collar as if it were choking him. Time to ease up. 'Suddenly you see a crack of light at floor level. It's a door. You open it,' he said, and saw everyone untense their eyes and breathe with relief. 'There is some light, and it allows you to see a spiral staircase going down and down, round and round. I'm going to count as you descend. Ten, nine . . . you're going down . . . eight, seven . . . deeper . . . six, five, four . . . deeper and deeper . . . three . . . two . . . one. You're in a vast building that has the appearance of a cathedral. The light's pouring in through tall, stained-glass windows. You stroll around among different-coloured machines. You'd like to find out what they do and how they work. All in good time. Now, you come to a metal door. You open it. On the other side there's a large room with long wooden tables and shelves all the way up to the ceiling. They're packed with plaster figures. You look at them. You can touch them if you want to. Have you seen how smooth they are? Ever wondered how they're made? Want to find out? There's someone standing beside you now. Don't be alarmed,' he said, noticing several people start. 'He's a friend. He's wearing a white coat and a red helmet, and he wants you to take his hand. You take it. You let him lead you. In front of you there's a shallow pan full to the brim with liquid plaster. You sink your hands into it. Feel how cool it is? You stir it round and round, you feel like a child again.' They were becoming more and more involved in this exercise of the imagination and, in some cases, totally immersed in it: Dorita, for example, was kneading her skirt with clenched hands and rubbing together her thighs and knees while emitting little panting noises. 'Your friendly worker now leads you over to a series of casts. They all look the same on the outside: you can't guess what figures lie within. Want to find out? Pour some liquid plaster into the first one. Careful now! Don't spill any!' he said with mock severity, and several of them actually jumped, then relaxed again and smiled. 'One by one, you fill them all. By the time you've finished the last, the first one has set. Your friendly worker helps you open it: slowly now, carefully, you don't want it to break. And as you open it, little by little, you can see a nose, lips, eyes . . . Who could it be? The suspense! Now you've removed the cast and there she is for all the world to see. It's Eva Perón. Have you made just one bust of Eva? No, lots! For, when you open the next cast, there's another, and another, and another . . . All fresh and immaculate. Look at them . . . Aren't they beautiful? And *you* made them! Don't you feel proud? Now, you leave them to dry. You say goodbye. Goodbye to your friend too. You retrace your steps . . . no need to rush . . . you cross the cathedral, you reach the staircase. You start climbing. One . . . no need to hurry . . . two, three, four . . . you keep on climbing . . . five, six, seven . . . you're almost there . . . eight, nine and . . . ten. You open your eyes. You're awake. You're back in the room, but you're not the same as before . . . am I right?'

One by one the participants opened their eyes, rubbed them as if they'd just woken up, and looked about, puzzled, self-conscious, as if returning from a long journey. What exactly was it they'd just experienced? All of them except little old Fernández, that is, who'd fallen asleep during the exercise and was gently snoring, his head lolling over the back of the chair. A couple of shakes and he was awake.

'Well? How do you feel?' Marroné asked cheerily.

'Good, good,' some answered, while others nodded their approval.

'Did anyone see or feel anything they'd like to share with the rest of us?'

They exchanged the usual 'who's going first?' glances.

'Well, I . . . ' began the woman who had joined the group just before the exercise, a tanned thirty-something in a tailored blue suit and peach blouse. 'When I opened the cast, there was like this light coming out of Eva's eyes. And out of her mouth, and her ears as well. There was like this light streaming out of her. What does it mean?'

'Hold that image for now. It's important. We'll come back to it later,' he said, nimbly sidestepping the claptrap. 'Anyone else?'

'The worker had my father's face,' piped up González, his voice about to crack. 'He died two years ago,' he explained. Ramírez gave his shoulder a firm squeeze and González pressed his lips together and nodded several times in thanks.

'It was beautiful,' ventured Dorita, gazing at him with wide eyes, in which welled two deeply emotional tears, like spilt water reaching the table's edge. 'It had never occurred to me to actually go to the workshop and see what we make in this factory.'

'That's it!' Ramírez the rebel addressed his comrades, now highly motivated after the exercise. 'Let's go there right now! Let's join our brother workers!'

'How about this?' Marroné joined in, mentally rubbing his hands. 'What if I go down there now and have a word with them? If they agree to lift the restrictions on production in the interests of shop floor–office unity and to make an exception for Comrade Eva, we can get to work after lunch. Meanwhile, you can divide yourselves into two groups and suggest new ways to creatively and – why not? – entertainingly tackle the predicament we find ourselves in.'

'Like falling off a log,' Marroné thought to himself on his way down in the service lift, accompanied by one of the black-helmeted commissars, who gestured vaguely towards the gate and answered his question about who the leaders were with an 'Anyone in a white helmet'. On the way he came across three green-helmeted workers heading for the canteen and shouldering half a side of beef, a bulky sack of bread rolls and a crate of oranges; one worker in a red helmet and kitchen apron; and two in yellow helmets, twirling brushes and mops; the guards, he noticed, all wore black helmets. The strikers were clever: instead of doing away with the colour coding and letting everyone merge into chaotic egalitarianism, they had kept the coloured helmets but changed their meanings. A prime example of the efficient reallocation of existing resources.

Above the replicas of Michelangelo's Moses and David that guarded the entrance they had hung a white sheet with an inscription painted in broad red brushstrokes: 'Factory Occupation – Day 2'. The front gate and adjacent areas were a hub of feverish activity: the patrol cars of the night before had been joined by two assault vans and even a water cannon, and the uniformed police by another twenty-odd men, sporting the helmets and batons of riot police. A crowd milled about in the free space, brightening the work-day monochrome with holiday colours: the lorries and vans of the suppliers bringing in victuals for strikers and hostages were joined by paper-boys touting their newspapers at the tops of their voices; the strikers' wives and girlfriends had come, children in hand, with clean clothes and packed lunches, and exhorted their husbands not to give up the fight; street-hawkers wandered through the crowd peddling cigarettes, lighters, razors and razor blades, batteries, packs of cards and other trinkets; at one end of this seething human mass a *choripán* stall had begun to smoke and sizzle; a popcorn seller and an ice-cream seller were stationed at the other, and two Bolivian cholas had parked their stately anatomies on either side of the gate – one selling fruit and veg, the other ladies' underwear. There were also two press units – one from Canal 13, another from Radio Mitre – as well as a swarm of journalists, who tried to force their way inside every time one of the gates opened. After studying this colourful animated tapestry for a while, Marroné found what he was looking for: at the north corner of the factory a throng was gathering, in which the brightly coloured helmets stood out against the shade of the trees like Smarties on the icing of a cake. Marroné took a deep breath and set off to join it.

4

THE PROLETARIAN BOURGEOIS

In the ghostly shade of a plaster-shrouded ombú his old acquaintance Baigorria addressed his comrades from a wooden crate. Not a white helmet in sight.

'Comrades . . . We are living a historic moment here at the Sansimón Plasterworks . . . Our occupation has been a huge success . . . We've shown the bosses what we can do, and if we did it once we can do it again . . . But the fact is, comrades, if we keep this up we're playing straight into the management's hands. The storehouses are packed to the gunwales with goods going nowhere; you know that better than me. This strike's a godsend to them: they can stop production and not pay us a cent. I want to believe – want to believe – that those insisting on continuing this occupation are acting in good faith, thinking they're doing what's best, but it wouldn't be the first time they've pulled a fast one on us, comrades, that those who say they're our friends turn out to be at best useful idiots and at worst management spies, not to mention our old friends the infiltrators, those wolves in workers' clothing . . . '

Marroné was truly impressed. Garaguso the personnel manager wasn't just quick, he was subtle – Machiavellian even. In a matter of hours he had not only won over one of the strikers to his cause, but had turned Baigorria into a skilful orator capable of ensnaring his listeners unawares. Marroné felt like going up to him and giving him a few tips on making the most of body posture, auditorium layout and, above all, lighting, but some of his listeners had started speaking their minds.

'Shut it, scab! You blackleg bastard!'

'How much is Garaguso paying you, you fucking sell-out?'

'Go back to Babirusa, you turncoat!'

Imperturbable, Baigorria tried to go on with his speech.

'Comrades, comrades! Don't get me wrong. I'm not saying the occupation was a mistake, I'm not saying we should back down. I'm saying enough's enough, that we've got what we wanted. There's a time to sow and a time to reap, and if we don't gather it in time, what happens to the harvest, comrades? It rots! If we go on with this occupation, we'll gain nothing else and might lose all we've gained so far. The only thing we'll achieve is more wholesale firings and a small rise at most for those who stay on. So if you're willing to pay that price, then go ahead! You, Pampurro . . . Will you enjoy your match tickets knowing they've taken food from the mouths of Alfieri's hungry children? And you, Zenón, will you enjoy buying your wife that new dress knowing El Tuerto will be forced to work as a rag-and-bone man again?'

Out of reflex Marroné had already seized his notebook and quickly jotted down the names – 'Pampurro . . . Alfieri . . . Zenón . . . El Tuerto' – adding the essential aide-mémoires, and so bent on his task was he that he didn't react when a voice at his back exclaimed:

'Oy, you . . . What you writing?'

Before looking up, he instinctively tried to finish the sentence he was on, which turned into a black scrawl when a hand landed on his arm and gave it a violent tug.

'Comrades! I got a pig here! A grass!'

Giving him no time to explain, half a dozen strapping proletarian hands had pinned down his arms and shoulders, and a dark-complexioned man in a blue helmet and thick, black-framed glasses was scanning his notes with a calloused finger, spelling out each word with his lips.

'It's all here, comrades. We're all down here, one after another. Got ourselves an informer here we have, boys and girls.' Then, bringing his face to within centimetres of Marroné's, 'Who sent you, Cerbero or the pigs?'

'No, no,' stammered Marroné, overcome at the absurdity of the mistake. 'I read *How to Win Friends and Influence People*, I'm trying to please others . . . '

A hand closed over his face and he could no longer speak or see. It wasn't so much fear he felt as befuddled outrage. Had he been spared death in the crossfire yesterday only to get lynched over a ridiculous blunder?

'Now then, comrades, calm down, comrades . . . '

Marroné realised they had let go of him when his struggles met with no further resistance than gravel and air. He opened his eyes to see a worker in a white helmet – at last! – squatting studiously over him, his body blocking out the sunlight, his face encircled by a corona of flame-red locks. A second later Marroné's eyes had adjusted and taken in his features too.

'So, matey, what's all this the comrades are saying about a notebook?' the worker began, with quiet authority. If Marroné had had any doubts, the voice did away with them.

'Paddy? Paddy Donovan?'

The panic shifted, lodging itself for an instant in the newcomer's honey-coloured eyes as his milk-white skin reddened to rival his hair. He pulled himself together with a visible effort and gave him a jaunty smile, which he immediately bestowed on the rest of the audience.

'Must be mistaken there, chief.' Then, to the others, 'Hey, if this one's from the secret service, he should be sent back to spy school.'

Marroné had sat up and was mechanically dusting off the plaster that covered his jacket and trousers – and no doubt his face too – thinking it might be preventing Paddy from recognising him. All the anxiety of the situation had dissolved into stupefaction at such an improbable reunion.

'No, no, I'm certain,' he insisted with a smile. 'It's me, Ernesto, Ernesto Marroné, we were at St Andrew's together, remember? I used to sit at the desk behind you. We used to play rugby together; you were in Monteith and I was in Dodds.'

For a second he toyed with the idea that Paddy had lost his memory in a car crash and, having been rescued by a working-class family, now took himself for one of them. Perhaps he needed more basic sensory stimuli.

'Monteith, green shirts? Dodds, yellow shirts? The scrum? "Push, St Andrew's, push!"'

Fists pumping the air, Marroné froze in mid-war cry. Struck dumb, Paddy's eyes were on him, but the other workers, half-puzzled, half-wary, had fixed theirs on Paddy, who this time spoke with less conviction, almost tripping over his tongue.

'I . . . I . . . dunno what you're t . . . talking about, chief.'

Unable to tell if his friend's eyes were shining with confusion or entreaty and making the most of the fact that his exhortations, if failing to restore Paddy's memory, had at least led the others to suspect they were dealing with a harmless loon rather than a dangerous intelligence agent, he decided to beat a hasty retreat.

'I'm sorry. My mistake.'

Smiling insistently he backed away until he reached the statue of Moses at the entrance gate and sat down in its shade to study the man he had taken for his old schoolmate. The two were as similar as the replica now looming over him was to the original . . .

If Marroné had one hero in his youth, it was Paddy Donovan, whom the eye of memory always haloed with light in a sunny postcard of the rugby pitch; it was as if fate itself had made him captain of the green house of Monteith just to set off the blaze of red upon his head, and the games against Monteith were the ones Marroné always found hardest to win, at least until fourth year, when Paddy Donovan, to the despair of directors and trainers, abandoned rugby for the more plebeian football team, a symbolic gesture he would complete in fifth year by handing back the brown and turquoise prefects' tie in favour of the navy-blue and silver stripes of the regular school tie. Paddy, the first to smoke marijuana. Paddy, who wrote articles for the school magazine that the school authorities had invariably to censor. Paddy, who bedded the rector's daughter, a petite, liberated English blonde everyone wanted but nobody dared. They hadn't been friends, exactly, though less out of reticence on Paddy's part than timidity on Marroné's. The latter had never felt altogether worthy of such a friendship, a feeling that perhaps dated back to an episode in first grade, when, alone in the classroom, Marroné had amused himself by taking coloured chalk to the homework written on the blackboard – thinking it would please Miss – turning the drab white letters into pretty rainbows. But the scowling teacher demanded the culprit reveal his identity, and Marroné, paralysed and dumb on one of the desks at the back, found himself incapable of uttering the words of explanation. When she threatened to take away their trip to the cattle show at La Rural, Paddy Donovan, who had already cast two or three suspicious glances in his direction, raised his hand and confessed to the crime. The teacher thanked him for his honesty and gave him no other punishment than to clean the blackboard, which only further aggravated Marroné's sense of guilt: he'd behaved like a coward and let someone else pay, and all for the sake of an insignificant risk. He never admitted the truth to Paddy, so he could never thank him for stepping into the breach, and the suspicion that he knew and, out of delicacy, hadn't pressured him into speaking up, filled him with gratitude and bitterness in equal parts. On another occasion, when they were at seventh-grade summer camp, Marroné had been the victim of a case of quite gratuitous and unjustified bullying: he had accidentally set fire to a sixth-grader's tea towel and, just to annoy him, all the younger boy's companions, fired up by the impunity of the mob, had taken the side of the crybaby and set upon him – all except Paddy, who had sent them packing with a few choice words; and once again Marroné was unable to find the words to thank him. As soon as he had finished school, Paddy had gone away for a year to travel the world and Marroné had heard nothing more of him than the occasional rumour, which included all the forbidden words: hippies, drugs, communes and attempted suicide. They hadn't seen each other again, as Paddy never attended the annual old boys' dinners at the Claridge Hotel, but word reached them that on his return Paddy had settled down, studied law, carved out a career in his father's business and married a model who was on TV . . . No, Marroné concluded, he was seeing things, hearing things: this couldn't be his old classmate, not this red-headed proletarian striding towards him after sealing what looked like a challenge or a wager, exchanging a high-five with the blue-helmeted worker in glasses.

'Look,' Marroné began, 'I swear I didn't mean to . . . '

'It's me, you arsehole,' muttered Paddy out of the corner of his mouth, with his back to the group so his face wouldn't be visible. 'What are you trying to do? Are you trying to ruin me? I've told them I'm playing along with you to find out who you are.'

'But, Paddy, I swear I didn't know a thing. What's happened to you? You should have come to see me, there's always something at the company . . . '

All five of Paddy's fingers clamped shut on Marroné's hand to stop him reaching for his wallet.

'All I'm short of is them thinking you're trying to bribe me.'

'Forgive me, Paddy, but . . . Can you explain to me what you're doing here?'

'I'm prltrnsng myself,' he said through clenched teeth.

'What?' shouted Marroné. 'You're problematising yourself?'

'Proletarianising,' Paddy spluttered in exasperation. 'Making myself a proletarian.'

'But why? Has your family fallen on hard times?'

'No, no. We aren't on speaking terms. It's a personal decision, you understand, a renunciation. I've taken the vow of poverty.'

'You've become a priest?' Marroné asked with some relief. Paddy's family had always been devout Catholics.

'No. A Peronist.'

Paddy smiled. Now that the imminent danger of exposure had passed, he was beginning to sound like his old self again: warm, charismatic, the leader of the picket line, as once he was of the rugby team. He took Marroné by the arm.

'Let's walk.'

Skirting the car park, which rippled like jelly in the heat that radiated from the white gravel and the overheated bodywork of the cars, they reached the loading bay, where the drivers were relaxing over an *asado*, swigging wine from demijohns by their parked trucks. Gesturing to Marroné to follow him, Paddy went up to them and, after the usual round of friendly greetings, both men were offered a *choripán* and a glass of red.

'Are you still in touch with anyone?' asked Marroné, spraying crumbs, as they wandered off. 'I ran into Robert Ermekian with his wife and kid the other day at a performance by The Suburban Players, and what do you know, he only asked if I'd heard from you . . . '

Paddy gave him an oddly compassionate smile.

'What about you, Ernesto? Are you married? Have you got any children?'

'Yes,' he answered, beaming, 'two. A boy of two and a half and baby girl of a few months.'

He pulled the relevant photos from his wallet. The one of Cynthia was just after she'd been born: with her deformed head and lobster-red complexion, she looked more like Sr Tamerlán than ever, but he always forgot to change it for a more recent one.

'They look like you,' said Paddy, without a trace of irony, handing them back to him.

'What about you, Paddy?'

'There is no more Paddy. He's dead and gone. Call me Colorado, or Colo: everyone else does here. No, no I haven't got children, yet. My partner and I have discussed the issue and we've decided to wait till after the Revolution. That way they'll be raised differently.'

'Course,' nodded Marroné, who, beginning to get the picture, decided it was time to apply the rules of *How to Win Friends and Influence People*. 'There'll be plenty of day-care centres under socialism, won't there. It's a boon because it isn't always easy to find a decent nanny or a baby-sitt . . . '

Paddy was scowling at him. No, that wasn't it. He had nearly put his foot in it.

'I don't want them to be like us, Ernesto: raised to despise people with less money, less status or darker skin. Treating people like things and things like gods. Worshipping all things English and American, and despising all things Argentine and Latin American. "Command and obey",' he snorted in conclusion.

'Well, we were educated to be leaders, weren't we? And from what I can see they didn't do such a bad job on you,' added Marroné with a wink of complicity that ricocheted off Paddy's frown.

'No, Ernesto, that's where you're wrong. I'm respected here because I'm one of them. And learning to be one of them was the hardest thing I've done in my life.'

'Well . . . I mean . . . Couldn't you do more for them from a management post – or a political post? Even . . . I dunno, listen to me, even a union lawyer? You could be one, if you finish your training.'

'You're falling into the trap of bourgeois reformism,' Paddy shot back at him. 'Look, Ernesto, you may find it hard to believe, but the days of capitalism are numbered. There is no other future than the Revolution, and the Revolution can only be led by proletarians.'

'This lot?' asked Marroné incredulously, casting his eyes over the truck-drivers, who, having made short work of their first demijohn, had started cracking dirty jokes and were rolling about laughing. 'Are you sure? Have you asked them?'

'That's because it hasn't occurred to them yet. They want it but they don't know they want it. It's called alienation. Simple as that. Their class situation makes them proletarians who need to start the Revolution to end exploitation and thereby class society. Those are their objective conditions. But because of alienation their class consciousness is still bourgeois, so subjective conditions aren't fulfilled: they don't know they can and have to start the Revolution. This divorce between their objective and subjective conditions is what's holding back the Revolution for the time being. It's like saltpetre and sulphur: as long as they're separate, nothing happens; put them together and you get gunpowder. The communist old guard thought the solution was to educate the proletariat so that they would develop a revolution-ary consciousness. A huge effort with little to show for it. This solution is far simpler: Columbus' egg; the Copernican Revolution of the Revolution. If the mountain won't come to Muhammad, Muhammad must go to the mountain.'

'Wasn't it the other way round?'

'No. We're Muhammad. In them, the objective conditions have been met, but not the subjective ones; with us
it's the other way round. We *do* know it's necessary to make
the Revolution, but because we're bourgeois, if *we* wage it
on our own, it'll be a bourgeois revolution, like the French
Revolution.'

'Of course. And they cut lots of heads off, didn't they.'

'The heads are immaterial, Ernesto. Listen to me. If we
become proletarians, we're mixing saltpetre and sulphur.
We'll be proletarians with a revolutionary consciousness, and
when we've become true proletarians, the original proletarians – the masses – will follow us. Do you see how it works?'

Marroné nodded. Paddy had a talent for making himself
understood. A shame he didn't have the equipment to give
an audiovisual presentation.

'Ok . . . And does it work?'

'What?'

'This . . . proletarianisation thing.'

'Well . . . to stop living like a bourgeois is easy enough.
For better or worse we all did it as kids, right? When we got
into the hippie thing or backpacking.'

Marroné gave a non-committal nod.

'But we were just slumming it. The really difficult thing
is to stop thinking or seeing or feeling like a bourgeois.
Bourgeois consciousness is the most insidious thing going.
It's like an evil spirit that deceives you about everything,
everything . . . '

Marroné was about to mention the wise enchanters in
Don Quixote: The Executive-Errant, but Paddy was in full flow
and he couldn't get a word in edgeways.

'Becoming one of the people is like an exorcism, like purging the evil spirit from your body. But even so . . . Take me: my life's now impeccably proletarian . . . but at night I still have bourgeois dreams. Look, to give you an idea . . . the other day me and some comrades from the factory here went to the match, and afterwards to celebrate . . . you can guess where. Because I hesitated, I got the last girl in line, a young girl from the north who must have been under thirty but looked like she was going on fifty, with this double chin . . . Goitres are endemic in the Puna, you know. A drop of iodine in their diet and the problem's solved, but they're Collas of course, so who gives a damn about them . . . She was wearing this red PVC mini-skirt and laddered fish-net stockings and a blonde wig, and when she smiled at me the teeth that weren't gold were black and rotten . . . And I forced myself to think of her people, who've suffered nearly five centuries of oppression, and of the subhuman conditions of hunger and poverty she must have grown up in, the feudal exploitation she must have suffered in her land and the sexual exploitation here in the capital . . . And I reminded myself that physical beauty is a bourgeois privilege proletarians can't afford and that aesthetic norms are imposed on us by the First World and that a little chola, especially in traditional dress and not the synthetic garbage we sell them, can look prettier than a Swedish model . . . But I just couldn't get it up, see, nothing doing, and in the end to stop her giving me away to my comrades I shut my eyes and thought of Monique. I thought of Monique the whole time to get through it.' Paddy ended the story on a note of sadness, his eyes lost in the pale lunar lawn.

'Are you and Monique still together?'

Paddy let out a loud, sarcastic snort.

'Yeah, right! She works as a model by day and drops round my bedsit to rustle me up some spaghetti on the Primus at night. We separated the day I became an activist.'

'Oh. Sorry to hear that.'

'I'm not. Monique was a trap. You have to be awake, wide awake . . . So, tell me. What were you doing with the notebook when the comrades caught you?'

Marroné reeled off the spiel he had prepared.

'I was just jotting down their names because I think of the strikers as individuals, not an anonymous mass. I came down to look for one of the ringleaders to organise a joint activity, a kind of workshop, for office staff and workers, so the two sectors could get to know each other better and maybe find out that their ideas, their problems, their interests aren't that different after all . . . Actually, I'd thought they could spend an afternoon – today if you're on-board – making a series of plaster figures . . . ' he took a deep breath before the plunge, ' . . . of Eva Perón, as a token of fellow feeling between blue and white collar . . . But, as even the workers are "white" here, the first step's already been taken,' he concluded with affable acumen.

Paddy stared hard at him, without even blinking, then shook his head like a father about to reveal to his son the true identity of Father Christmas.

'It won't work, Ernesto. Like the typical petits bourgeois they are, office workers do their level best to live up to the bourgeoisie, which they aspire to, and to differentiate them-selves from the proletariat, which they're terrified of slipping into. They may occasionally form a tentative alliance with the proletariat if they think they have something to gain, but when it's their arses on the line, you just watch how fast they throw in the towel. That's why the only option, Ernesto, is to proletarianise yourself. If you like . . . I can give you a hand.'

'Well . . . thanks . . . ' said Marroné, trying to buy some time, 'I'd have to think about it.'

They'd reached the foot of the statues' cemetery, a towering mountain of broken or faulty pieces shining in the sun like a snow-capped peak. Marroné scoured the rubble in the vain hope of discovering a forgotten trove of chipped but still usable busts of Eva, but the nearest thing he found was a torso of Marilyn trying to push down her skirt to hide the fact that her legs were missing. Paddy rolled a battered Corinthian column over to him and, sitting astride an Ionic one, invited him to do the same.

'Look,' said Paddy after a second's pause, alluding to the mountain of smashed pieces with a wave of his hand. 'What do you see?'

Marroné ran his eyes over the jumbled heap: cracked mouldings, split columns, shattered amphorae, a legless David, a Discobolus whirling his stump, the masks of comedy and tragedy with missing jaws so you couldn't tell which was which, a ballerina tying the laces of a non-existent dance shoe, a Perón with a broken nose who resembled the Sphinx, an armless Botticelli Venus that looked like the Venus de Milo, a headless Venus de Milo that looked like a wingless Victory of Samothrace, the two halves of an Aztec calendar . . .

'There's a very high proportion of damaged pieces. The productivity index . . . '

'There you go again. You see everything from a business viewpoint. You don't think about the meaning of human labour. What does it mean to make these copies?'

'Errrr . . . ' Knowing that, however hard he thought, the evil spirit of the bourgeoisie would put the wrong answer in his mouth, he chose to gain time with an innocuous vowel sound.

'Exactly. Nothing. Ours is a culture of copies, imitations, replicas, and shoddy workmanship on top of that. Look at this,' he said, picking up a Pietà in which, rather than swooning his last, Christ melted like mozzarella over his mother's knees, who contemplated him more in disgust than in sorrow. 'Who could confuse this miscarriage with Michelangelo's original? We try to be like them and this is what we come up with,' he said, tossing it back on the mound. 'This mountain of ruins, of tack and broken replicas, is a monument to the borrowed culture we have tried to assemble out of our masters' leftovers. We content ourselves with fragments, with copies of copies, and, by fixing our eyes on them, we blinker ourselves to our own reality.'

Paddy had a point. Staring so hard at the broken pieces had dazzled him, and several little piles spun in a kaleidoscope of black residual images on his retinas.

'Europe's finished, like Fanon says. We have to leave it behind. You'd better start getting used to the idea. We have to travel light on this trip. And the day we arrive, we'll have to burn the boats.'

'What do you mean?'

Paddy pulled the two halves of the Aztec calendar from the immense pile and put them together so the break was invisible.

'When we're like this,' he said, holding together the solar disc, 'we'll have to forget all this.' His bright eyes cast a doleful glance over five millennia of useless western culture gathered in a sad heap of broken images at their feet. 'Paris. El Greco. Shakespeare,' he mused, with anticipated nostalgia.

Marroné decided to add a healthy dash of dissent.

'But you used to like Shakespeare.'

'True. Remember when we read *Julius Caesar*?'

'Yeees,' he began hopefully, thinking he could steer the conversation towards Mark Antony's speech, considered by both Dale Carnegie and R Theobald Johnson as the best Shakespeare had ever written.

'A play where the revolutionaries who want to save the republic are depicted as villains, and the dictator and his henchmen as heroes. And the people? They're either portrayed as idiots who let themselves be led by the nose or as a savage mob that goes around murdering people indiscriminately and torching everything in sight. If Shakespeare had been Argentinian, he'd have had Peronist mobs sticking their feet in the fountain and burning down the churches – the whole shooting match. I'm telling you, it couldn't be more anti-Peronist if it had been written by Borges rather than Shakespeare.'

Marroné gulped twice before answering. He was having trouble applying the principles of Dale Carnegie to Paddy's conversations. Very serious trouble.

'But we have a lot to learn from reading his plays,' implored Marroné. 'From *Hamlet*, for example . . . '

'Yeah, I'll give you that. A critical reading of *Hamlet* could help you make the leap from intellectual doubt to revolutionary certainty. If Hamlet would just stop navel-gazing, he'd realise there's a world outside the palace walls: beyond them the people of Denmark await him. If he'd taken the side of the people, all his doubts and hesitations would have evaporated as if by magic: he'd enter the winter palace with fire and sword, and wreak his revenge, because it would no longer be in the name of his father – who, let's face it, was just another oligarch – but in the name of the oppressed Danish masses,' he concluded. Then, after a barely perceptible pause: 'Ernesto, I want to ask you something, and I want you to answer me as honestly as you can. What does Eva Perón mean to you?'

The question took him completely by surprise. In despair he reached for a rule from *How to Win Friends and Influence People*, but his mind had gone blank.

'Errr … The Spiritual Mother of all Argentine Children … The Plenipotentiary Representative of the Workers … The First Argentinian Samaritan … ' He salvaged the phrases from his childhood memories, trying to wring from them the sarcastic tone his father used to give them as he spat them through clenched teeth. But he couldn't quite manage it. 'Perón's wife. I don't know. Nothing,' he eventually admitted.

'So,' said Paddy as if he'd been given the answer he was expecting, 'what do you want the busts for?'

'It's for an order,' said Marroné, trying to contain his growing exasperation. 'I'm head of procurement for a construction company, and they sent me to purchase them. My brief is to get quality, price and, above all in this case, fast delivery, which, incidentally, your blessed occupation is making rather difficult. I'm not after the Holy Grail, just a few mass-produced plaster busts. It isn't much to ask. Couldn't you just cut the crap and run them off for me, eh? Make my life a little easier? Some of us can't afford to just drop everything and devote ourselves to changing the world. We have responsibilities, a job, a family to keep . . . I'm sorry,' he said, wiping the sweat from his brow with the back of his hand. 'I don't know what came over me. Must be the heat.'

'It's all right, Ernesto, don't worry. It's a start.'

'The start of what?' Marroné asked with a trace of alarm.

'Cuba wasn't liberated in a day. I sent them packing the first time they came to talk to me too. But here I am,' came Paddy's oblique reply.

'Who talked to you? What about?'

'Look, I've got to go now. There are so many things we have to see to . . . It's extremely important that the strike goes well because it's a rehearsal for something bigger . . . If the workers see they can do this, they'll want more . . . We can't fail them.'

'Who are you? What do you want?'

'I'll bring you some reading matter tonight. And tomorrow, if you still want to know who we are, we can talk some more. I'm not saying we don't bite . . . The thing is *who*. Oh, and another thing,' he added with a knowing wink before leaving, 'I promise you that, if we start production again, I'll do everything in my power to give priority to your ninety-two busts.'

*   *   *

He realised something was amiss when he entered the cathedral and saw the hail of forms, receipts, invoices, carbon-paper, memos, chequebooks, letters, envelopes, folders, box-files, typewriter ribbons and other office equipment fluttering like confetti, hanging from the banisters in streamers and garlands, carpeting the floor and the machines, and lending the factory the general appearance of city streets at the start of the office workers' holidays. The area in front of the service lift was littered with aluminium food trays and disembowelled ham and cheese rolls, and when he looked up at the internal balcony, he caught sight of yet another tray, spinning as it fell, orbited by floating rolls, and had to leap aside to avoid it. As he climbed the spiral staircase, he could hear a confused buzz of hysterical shouting and laughter, and when he reached the platform, his suspicions were confirmed: the office workers had run riot, and were charging up and down the gangways and platforms with armloads of card-index boxes and box-files that they hurled over the banisters with whoops of jubilation. Led by Gómez and Ramírez, a picket line of administrative staff were attempting to storm the offices of the executives, who had set up barricades of filing cabinets and other office furniture, and were putting up resistance from within, the office workers shouting slogans like 'Down with privilege!', 'We won't eat rubbish!', 'Tarts for overtime!' and, from those within, a mixture of threats and entreaties: 'We can talk it over!', 'We'll sack the lot of you!', 'Calm down and we'll talk!' The two commissars had lost control of the situation and, leaning over the banisters, were shouting to their comrades.

Ramírez embraced Marroné exultantly when he saw him.

'You were right, Marroné! It was just a matter of daring! We can if we want to!'

Horrified, Marroné tried to explain to him that they hadn't grasped the gist of his proposal, but Ramírez was already off somewhere else and didn't hear him. Some of the men were lighting their ties as if they were the Stars and Stripes, while others had torn off their shirts and were jumping about in their vests, wheeling them over their heads and chorusing 'He cheats, he farts, he takes it up the arse! Sansimón, Sansimón!' and 'Garaguso is a wanker and he shags for Sansimón!'; the women, with Nidia and Dorita at their head, were hammering their shoes on the floor to break off their high heels, and two maniacs (one of whom was none other than the irreproachable González) were lugging the big pot of hot coffee brought to them by the workers in order to tip it over the railings; but, stumbling headlong into a fallen typewriter, they tripped and spilt its entire contents over the terrified Marroné, who for the third time in two days thought his final hour had come, until he realised the coffee was lukewarm and had succeeded only in ruining his James Smart suit and Italian shoes.

'What the hell do you think you're playing at, you bloody fools!' he blurted out.

González's blue eyes opened wide in genuine concern.

'Ernesto! My God! Are you all right? Let me help you!' he stammered, stretching out an inept pair of hands towards the sodden suit.

'Don't touch me! Don't touch me!' shrilled Marroné, on the brink of hysteria, slapping the hands away. He regretted it immediately when he saw the hurt expression in the two blue puddles looking back at him.

'It was an accident,' murmured González, about to blub.

'What's happened?! Didn't you carry on with the activity?'

'We were working in groups like you told us,' stuttered González, as if his boss had just shouted at him, 'and we kept smelling those mouth-watering *asados* they're making downstairs . . . We were sure this time it was for us too. As a token of us joining the struggle, see . . . But when we saw them coming in again with the same old rolls and burnt coffee . . . I dunno . . . we just lost it.'

Paddy was right, Marroné said to himself, grinding his teeth in an effort to restrain himself: it was impossible – im-poss-ib-le – to expect anything from people like this. You set up a visualisation for them and got them working in teams – one of the simplest, most elementary creativity exercises! – and they ended up behaving like schoolchildren on a graduation trip. He looked around in search of a culprit to vent his exasperation on. His eyes lit upon one of the commissars. Lugging the weight of his sodden clothes, coffee running in torrents between cloth and skin and overflowing out of his shoes, he plodded purposefully towards him.

'You lot,' he pointed at him with a stiff and trembling finger. 'You lot are responsible for this. That was my best suit! Made to measure! Just look at it!'

The guard, a young worker of twenty-five with Indian features, looked him up and down before replying.

'I've never had a suit to ruin.'

Marroné wasn't going to let him get away with that. Not this time. Not in a million years.

'Don't give me that. No. Just because you lot have always got social injustice on your side you think you can get away with murder. No way. You want to occupy the factories? Be my guest. You want to take over the country? Go right ahead. But this suit here, you'll have it cleaned or buy me a new one. We all have to take responsibility for our actions. I demand a solution.'

The worker shrugged.

'You can drop round the storeroom if you like. They're sure to have something to change into there.'

As the coffee cooled on Marroné's body, so did his irritation. There wasn't much else he could do under the circumstances.

'Where?' he asked with resignation.

'Go down in the service lift and turn right . . . '

Dorita emerged from the offices and ran to him.

'Sr Ernesto, are you all right? Did you scald yourself? Can I do anything to help?'

Though her presence right then was more a nuisance than anything, her concern helped to sweeten his mood. He'd been wrong to get annoyed. It wasn't an intelligent emotion, and stupid emotions were a luxury a man in his situation could ill afford.

'No, thank you, Dorita. This gentleman has just been kind enough to point me . . . '

The service lift guillotined Dorita into sections as it descended: first the head with its oddly bright eyes, which followed him down to the last moment, then the plucked-chicken neck, the flat chest, the boyish hips, the skinny thighs showing through the pencil skirt. Last came the bare feet, visible through the weft of her stockings, laddered in the riot. She didn't have ugly ankles, thought Marroné. Could it be that she had taken a fancy to him?

The storeroom manager, an old worker with blue eyes and white hair, gave him the once-over and grabbed some folded white overalls his size and handed them to him over the counter. He asked him if he wanted socks and shoes too, and Marroné accepted because he disliked the sensation of walking on wet sponges and, if he wanted to save his shoes, the best thing would be not to wear them until he could get them seen to by a decent cobbler.

'You can have a shower if you like; the changing room's right next door,' he said, handing him a towel.

The water was cold but Marroné didn't care, nor did he care about how rough and cheap the soap was, and he rubbed it with gusto over his stubbly cheeks, his arms, his hairy chest, back, buttocks and genitals, which he covered with a startled shriek when he saw her standing in the doorway, clutching her handbag – draped with a crocheted cotton cardy – in both hands, and watching him with her mouth half-open, her eyes wide. Only when Marroné doubled over and covered himself like a statue bereft of its fig leaf did she back out, mumbling apologies and dropping bag and jacket, which she came back in to retrieve just as Marroné, in an absurd reflex of courtesy, bent to pick them up. He quickly straightened to cover himself and backed away with thighs clamped tight, leaving the items on the floor. Gathering them up, Dorita beat a hasty retreat, while Marroné cast desperately around him as he finished rinsing off the soap: to cap it all he'd left the towel in the changing room and had nothing to cover himself with but a flimsy gold crucifix.

'Dorita?' he asked.

'Yes?' came her voice from the changing room. She was still there. Damn it.

'Could you . . . pass me the towel, please?'

'Yes, yes. Right away.'

The towel appeared around the tiled corner, floating in the air like a little ghost and, calling to him, shook itself a couple of times. Stretching out an arm, he took it, briskly towelled himself down and tied it around his waist. Dorita was sitting on one of the wooden benches, waiting for him, cheeks flushed, eyes lowered.

'I'm so sorry, Sr Marroné. I asked for you, and they told me I'd find you down here . . . '

'It's all right. Was there something you needed?'

'Just to tell you . . . that what you did for us . . . I wanted to thank you, nobody's ever made me feel . . . like I could contribute something of value . . . that I'm worth something, as much as the next woman . . . that I can be creative too, if I look inside myself . . . '

The towel on Marroné's lap started to rise like a circus tent, every word of Dorita's a tug from the dwarfs hoisting it skywards. He found nothing as stimulating as a dose of praise after a successful creativity exercise; there was no way to control it, and even if there had been, it was too late now: Dorita seemed incapable of taking her eyes off the hypnotic pulsing of the charmed cobra under the towel.

'Would you . . . mind if I had a shower too? It's so hot . . . You can stay, in case someone comes . . . I'm not embarrassed with you.'

Marroné could see it all before it happened: the scrawny, graceless body running with water under the shower; the fumbling foreplay; the dash to get in the tip if nothing else before his dignity drained away, along with his erection, in two or three brief spasms; and afterwards the concerned questions, the abject explanations, the sincere commiseration, so much more unbearable than outright derision. He took hold of the hand Dorita had tentatively raised to the top button of her blouse and, moving it as far away as possible from the throbbing centre of his being, he looked directly into her eyes and spoke to her.

'Dorita . . . I feel grateful for your words and also for . . . this . . . But I'm a married man, you know. I love my wife, I have a son of two and a half, and yesterday my dong . . . my darling daughter was two months old' . . . 'and you haven't had a bowel movement since you got here,' his meddling mind reminded him absurdly, as if that had anything to do with anything.

Dorita nodded contritely at every word he spoke, as if this was the story of her life. She fought back the tears.

'Now . . . If you wouldn't mind stepping outside for a minute . . . While I get dressed . . . Wait for me and we'll go up together if you like.'

Dorita nodded, chewing her bottom lip, and went to wait for him outside. Since not even his underpants had been spared the deluge of coffee, Marroné pulled his white overalls on, straight over his naked body (he didn't so much as put them on as climb into them, as if they were a diving suit or a spacesuit), and then the socks and heavy shoes. There was something exciting in his new outfit, especially in the way his still erect member brushed against the coarse cotton: he felt different, looser, bold . . . even . . . virile. Just then his eyes lit upon the bundle of sodden clothes and the shoes that, he now knew, would never be the same again, and he was seized by a sudden weariness. He pressed the shoes hard into the heap of clothes, wrapped them up in his suit trousers and tossed the bundle in the bin. 'Burn your boats,' he thought, and when he looked up he met in the mirror the reflection of a stubble-covered face topped with tousled hair and the rugged, set jaw of an explorer on the road to adventure. He undid the top two buttons on his overalls so that his pecs and the start of his clearly defined six-pack – which years of rugby had given him and two gym sessions a week had helped to preserve – were visible in the neckline. He frowned, raised one hand to his chest, clenched the other in a tight fist and smiled to himself: if they're after a model for the Monument to the Descamisado, they need look no further.

When he went out, Dorita was nowhere to be seen. On his way back to the service lift he ran into a worker in a white helmet who looked upset and came over to talk to him.

'Off upstairs, comrade?'

'Yes,' replied Marroné after a tiny, indiscernible pause.

'Tell Zenón and Aníbal just to let them go, tell them Trejo said so if they ask.'

'All of them?'

'No, no. The bosses stay. Just the administrative staff. The dickheads want to join the strike, they're cocking up all our organisation.'

When he got there, the office staff were still jumping up and down on the platform, hurling paper in the air and chorusing 'Jump, jump, jump, Sansimón's a chump!' Standing on a chair, his pink shirt drenched with sweat, Ramírez was doing his best to harangue them in a hoarse voice, but the general rejoicing drowned out his proclamations.

'Comrades. The time has come to shake off the labels of bootlickers, yes-men and wimps that we're always branded with. History is being rewritten, here, today, at the Sansimón Plasterworks, and this time us office staff are going to stand by the shop-floor workers to the bitter end. If we stick together over this, nobody can stop us, comrades . . . '

Once he had passed on the news to the two worker guards, calling them by their first names, Zenón and Aníbal (he'd learnt his lesson and decided to shelve the notebook and activate his memory), Marroné saw no reason to delay the good news.

'The order's come through from below! You can leave whenever you like!'

A jug of iced water poured into a pan of boiling water could not have been quicker-acting. The pandemonium ceased instantly and initial bemusement crept over the faces of the office staff, to be followed in quick succession, as they looked at those of their neighbours, by guilty relief, shame, embarrassment and, finally, ill-concealed satisfaction. Without saying a word, first one (Suárez), then another (unknown) began to make their way to the office to collect their things and leave. Ramírez tried to stem the flow with some feeble words of persuasion.

'Comrades . . . Where are you going? Are we going to miss the chance to show that they're wrong in what they say: that when the chips are down, we throw in the towel? That we're all talk? That we wouldn't say boo to a goose? Don't you want to stay, so that you can go back to your houses with your heads held high and say that we've earned some respect for once? If we leave, comrades . . . what will we come back to? The same old thing?'

Out of compassion Marroné went over to him.

'It's useless, pal. They aren't listening.'

Ramírez looked at him with blank eyes that showed no sign of understanding or recognition, and then, leaning on Marroné's shoulder, climbed down from the chair and headed for the office. His colleagues had started queuing up outside the service lift. In their midst, looking like butter wouldn't melt in his mouth, was Sansimón's sales manager, the one who had made a botched attempt to flee the day before.

'Oy! You! Papillon! Trying to pull a fast one, are we? Get back in there with the others,' Marroné said to him, tapping him twice on the shoulder.

The sales manager meekly obeyed without a word, merely casting a surprised look in Marroné's direction, as if his face were familiar but he couldn't say where from . . . Marroné rubbed his hands with pleasure. It was like a role play, and he was enjoying it enormously. It was a rule that always proved infallible: you never know your potential until you start exploring it. Just then the service lift arrived and Paddy, carrying a newspaper, stepped out, along with two others in black helmets. Paddy's jaw dropped when he saw him.

'Ernesto! What are you up to?' he said to him.

Marroné replied with a shrug and an expression of defiance.

'What? Are you the only one that can proletarianise yourself around here?'

The worker guards had started bringing the office workers down in two groups of ten. Dorita was in the second one, the service lift this time slicing her up the other way round, starting with her feet and finishing with her faintly moist eyes, which remained fixed on him until the last moment. Out of politeness he kept up his smile and raised hand until they vanished from sight, then turned to Paddy, who was still staring at him in astonishment.

'Well . . . that's the petit bourgeoisie off our backs. One less problem, right?'

'And you, Ernesto? What are you going to do?'

There was something he needed to know before he took a decision.

'What about the rest of the country? What's happening with the other plasterworks?'

Paddy smiled.

'All occupied. Nothing can stop us, Ernesto!'

'I'm sticking around then,' said Marroné without hesitation.

Paddy locked with him in fraternal embrace, and Marroné was awash with happiness. By what strange and crooked ways life made your wishes come true: Paddy and he were friends at last. As they parted, Paddy unfolded the magazine he'd been carrying and held it out to him.

'Here.'

'What is it?' Marroné asked.

'The reading matter I promised you. Give it a look and we'll discuss it tomorrow.'

Marroné glanced at the title page. On the cover a woman as taut and vibrant as a tensed string was haranguing a dark expanse that presumably harboured a multitude within, and above her tight bun, in red graffiti letters, streamed the caption 'EVITA MONTONERA'.

★   ★   ★

The cars pulled away one by one: Gómez's Peugeot, with González in the passenger seat; an impeccably preserved Auto Union with Fernández at the wheel; a Fiat 600 with Suárez, Ramírez, Nidia and Dorita squeezed inside it; and a Fiat 1500, a Citroën 3CV and a Renault 4L with all the others. Through the high window overlooking the car park,

Marroné watched them all as they clambered in, turned on their engines and headlights, and made for the entrance gate held open for them by the armed guards. It was getting dark but, far from letting up, the heat was mounting; heavy burgundy clouds, lit up by the recent passage of the sun, still burnt in the west, while others, the colour of lead and ash, gathered in the northern sky like an Indian raiding party.

What Marroné needed now was a quiet place to sit down and read the Eva Perón photonovel without interruption, so, after recovering his briefcase from the devastated main office, through which the rebellion had swept like a gale, one at a time he tried the doorknobs until he found one that turned, and crossed into a deserted office. After waiting for the few seconds the flickering fluorescent tube needed to provide a steady light, he made resolutely for the toilet, where he unbuckled his belt and sat down with the photonovel open on page one.

1919. Despite enjoying true democracy for the first time in its entire history, **the country toiled under the double yoke of Saxon imperialism and the land-owning oligarchy**, he read, reshuffling his buttocks on the toilet seat. *A nation divided into a civilised, white, European metropolis and a barbarian, American, mestizo hinterland.* **A wealthy country, rich in paupers. A country where patriots pay and traitors prosper**. *One 7th May, in a small town in this country – a town like so many other Pampas towns, founded on lands snatched from our Indian brothers by the military –* **was born one of the greatest revolutionaries America has ever seen: Eva Perón**, read the words above the photo, which showed an English-style train station, a cluster of silvery silos and the words 'LOS TOLDOS' in block letters on a shed wall. In the next photo was a woman in a little woollen jacket and headscarf, holding aloft a doll in the role of a newborn baby and exclaiming in an enthusiastic speech bubble: '*Look at her, Juan! Isn't she beautiful?*' The man these words full of hope were addressed to was older and smartly attired in a double-breasted pinstripe suit, with glossy hair and a finely pencilled moustache over his disdainful upper lip. His bubble was not one of dialogue, but of thought. It read: '*This one makes five. Time to get savvy.*'

True to his class values, Marroné went on reading, *Eva's father, Juan Duarte, left his wife (by devotion if not by law) and five children for his 'legitimate' family in Chivilcoy.*

Having experienced social rejection at first hand, **Eva knew from a very young age which side she stood on,** read the caption to the next photo, which showed her as a little girl in plaits and polka dots, shielding a frightened beggar boy from three brilliantined brats in short trousers and lace-up shoes, with rocks in their hands; and Eva's thought bubble bloomed with her first tentative childish judgement: '***Even as a little girl, every injustice was like a splinter in my soul.***'

On encountering this uncomfortable term, Marroné shuffled restlessly on his toilet seat as if fearing that some concealed peeping Tom could see not just his actions (he was in the bathroom after all) but the very contents of his mind, and that was, of course, absurd. He made the most of this pause to try a few strains, but to no avail. The next few boxes illustrated a string of soap-opera clichés: the selfless mother hunched over her Singer, pedalling into the small hours of the morning; the same mother in mourning, sheltering her five chicks under her wing like a black hen, and bowing before a lady in satin and mink who stood behind a closed wrought-iron gate, barking at her a bubble with the words '*How dare you? Get those bastards out of my sight, you shameless hussy!*' while the caption below explained that *Eva was just seven when Juan Duarte died in a car accident and she suffered the humiliation of not being able to attend her father's funeral*; then little Eva taking communion in a borrowed dress; Eva at school practising recitation and dreaming of being an actress; and the fifteen-year-old Eva evading the advances of a brilliantined beau who promised to take her to Buenos Aires and make her a star while his bubble revealed his wicked intentions, and hers, her precocious shrewdness: '*If this city slicker thinks he's going to pull a fast one on me, he's got another thing coming.*'

Marroné strained again, with no result save for the certainty of being far from his goal, then turned the page: the teenage Eva had now arrived in Buenos Aires *with her suitcase full of hope,* **like so many thousands of men and women from the marginalised and impoverished hinterland** *who migrate to the big city in search of a better life, and embarked on her career as an actress and model. But when the last footlight had gone out, away from the illusory reality of the stage,* **Eva encountered the same exploitation and the same injustices in the world of the theatre as she had in the outside world**. *She could do little about it for the moment. Whenever she demanded improvements, whenever she made herself heard to her bosses, she was invariably fired*, and the photo showed her with her back to the camera, sitting opposite a fat toad of an impresario puffing on an equally fat cigar as he tore a contract up in her face; another in a winter street, shivering in her threadbare summer coat, and, oblivious to her own distress, giving a coin to the same ragged urchin from Los Toldos (was Marroné supposed to believe the child had followed her all the way to Buenos Aires, or was this some kind of allegory?): '*I wanted not to admit, not to look, not to see the misfortune, the hardship, the destitution around me, so I plunged single-mindedly into my strange artistic vocation. **But the more I tried to lose myself in it, the more beleaguered I was by injustice**.*' The businessmen, the bankers, the rich **cannot hear the cry welling up from below, from the factories, from the shanties** . . . *Eva hears it and knows that she will one day speak for them. For she is no longer the same frightened little girl: Eva has changed.*

The change had been made clear by the choice of a different actress to portray her as an adult: it was visible from the first still, which showed her in a polka-dot bathing costume, her long legs bare, her feet crossed, her loose chestnut hair tumbling over her shoulders, her hands clasped behind her head to display the carefully shaven armpits. Her posture might be unnatural, uncomfortable, extremely 'camera-conscious', but in her forced smile and her eyes, which childishly solicited the photographer's approval, there was a genuine, uncontaminated joy.

Next came her radio days, where she seemed to be more at ease, for she wielded the fearsome corn-cob of a microphone like a gun, with all the decisiveness of *the great women of history – Elizabeth I, Catherine the Great, Isadora Duncan, Madame Chiang Kai-shek – whose lives she plays, unaware that one day she will be the greatest of them all*. This was followed by a still of Eva with her hair loose, staring directly into the camera and seeming to speak directly to him, to Marroné: '*There comes a point in every life when we feel we have to do the same things, over and over, for the rest of our days, and that our paths are fixed for all time. **But to all, or nearly all of us, there comes a day when everything changes, our "marvellous day". For me** . . .* '

The page ended and Marroné, more intrigued than he would have liked to admit, turned it and went on reading: '*For me it was the day my life came together with Perón's. That meeting marks the start of my one true life*.' The caption beneath read: *In January 1944 an earthquake destroys the city of San Juan, and Colonel Perón and Eva meet at a festival for the victims.* One image showed Eva atop a pile of rubble that purported to be the destroyed city, hugging the by-now ubiquitous ragged urchin from Los Toldos; another image showed her touching the epaulette of the uniformed man seated in front of her. Yet it was neither the images nor their captions, but Evita's words, that really made him stop and think. What, if he'd already had it ('*all, or nearly all of us*,' announced the bold print of Eva's admonition, with harsh sincerity), had been Marroné's 'marvellous day'? 'It could hardly have been the day his life had joined with his wife's,' one side of his mind whispered to him insidiously, while in a guilty reflex the other tried to conjure up images of domestic bliss: the house and garden in Olivos, the double bed, the two cots . . . Yet here he was in an occupied factory, disguised as a worker, reading a photonovel of the life of Eva Perón, and all of that seemed as far removed from the here and now as the abundant offspring of Gauguin and his stern Danish wife were from Tahiti. It was also possible that his 'marvellous day', he told himself with a shudder, had been the day of his interview with Sr Tamerlán. He found it painful to admit, but it was possible. Or perhaps it had been the day Govianus had set him his mission. It was hard to say for sure. Because the 'marvellous day' *might already have happened, or **might be happening now, this very instant*** (the bold type of the photonovel seemed to be shadowing his thoughts) and you might not realise until much later. Or the 'marvellous day' might arrive disguised as a catastrophe: the 'one true life' of Lester Luchessi, for example, had started the day he was unceremoniously fired from the Michigan Real Estate Co: without the goad of his outrage and panic he might never have become that providential man who saved the Great Lakes Building from rack and ruin, or the author of *Autobiography of a Winner*. So Marroné's 'marvellous day' could well be today and this apparent dead end. The change in Luchessi's life had come at fifty-something, the same age as Ray A Kroc or Alonso Quijano . . . or Juan Domingo Perón, he realised in amazement, swiftly flicking through the boxes introducing the newcomer to Eva's life.

Who was this handsome but obscure colonel that had become a household name overnight? asked the text, and proceeded to answer its own question with scant biographical details and a tedious list of Perón's achievements as head of the Secretariat of Labour, which Marroné skipped without compunction. He wasn't interested in this smiling, made-up Lugosi; he thirsted only for Eva. By the time he ran into her again, she had become Perón's mistress and was sitting at the far end of an unlikely but convivial café table, at which were gathered the motley adversaries of the now-famous couple: an indignant soldier in epaulettes wearing a cap with a visor and with a bubble saying '*He has the cheek to take that slut on parade with him!*'; a ranch-owner dressed like an English lord, who reminded him of his father ('*Before he filled their heads, labourers were meek and went about their work with a happy smile*'); a bespectacled man who wore a goatee and a French beret, which presumably marked him out as an intellectual of the left ('*Perón is a Nazi Fascist, no doubt about it*'); a snooty oligarch looking as if she could smell shit ('*You can't make a silk purse . . .* '); and a priest with an expression of infinite disapproval, who kept his counsel, having run out of space for a bubble. Beside them, shrugging off the inevitable criticism of the conservatives, there emerged from Eva's mouth the barbed words: '*Soon, along the wayside, our hypercritics began to shower us with threats and insults and slurs.* **"Ordinary men" are the eternal enemies of everything new, of every extraordinary idea and therefore of every revolution.**'

It had been the same with him, thought Marroné, when he'd brought back all those innovative ideas from the United States: he too had been held up as a madman and dreamer by 'ordinary men' like Cáceres Grey, who viewed him 'indulgently', 'pityingly', with that air of superiority adopted by the mediocre when faced by true men of genius. Don Quixote had also been thought mad by the 'mediocre men' of his village, but it was *his* name that was written in stone, while the hand of time had erased the names of the sane and the sensible, dissolved for ever in the half-baked wash of their inane vacuousness. '*I will not stop for barking dogs*,' added Evita proudly, in allusion to that famous saw from the Quixote, 'You know you're riding, Sancho, when you hear the dogs bark.'

But the dogs – the hypercritics – wouldn't give in and reappeared again and again over the next few boxes, this time in the form of four young women decked out in furs, hats and jewellery, waving little French and English flags, while among them strutted a blonde-haired, pot-bellied, Stetsoned Texan with an American flag emblazoned on his dickey. **The forces of the anti-people**, *from the oligarch traitors and the petit bourgeoisie to the socialist and communist intellectuals who had never seen a worker close up, led by the Yankee ambassador,*

Spruille Braden, **call for Perón's head and obtain his arrest**, read the text, and over the next few boxes a dignified if somewhat browbeaten Perón was shown being dragged away by police from the arms of a tousled Eva wearing a simple flowery dress, at first tearful and distressed ('*I had never felt so small or helpless as I did in those days . . .* '), then suddenly looking fiercely and resolutely into the camera ('*But then I took to the streets in search of friends who could still do something for him*'), then talking to the military, priests and politicians with their stony faces ('**Up at the top I met only with cold, calculating, "sensible" hearts, the hearts of "ordinary men"**, *hearts at whose contact I felt sick, afraid and ashamed*'); then with workers in helmets and berets under bubbles shouting '*Viva Perón! Viva Eva!*', housewives dropping their shopping to follow her, passionate shanty-dwellers with clenched fists raised aloft (*But as she descended from the neighbourhoods of the rich and proud to the poor and humble, people's doors began to open wide*). The sequence climaxed in an elongated box featuring an Evita who evoked Delacroix's Liberty (though with no breast on display), brandishing an Argentine flag and leading *the hopeful, swarthy crowd of* **workers, people, masses who first burst onto the Argentine political scene on that 17th October 1945 and made their voices heard**, and below: '**Ever since that day I have believed it cannot be hard to die for a cause you love.**'

Overleaf Marroné came across a double-page spread showing the Peronist tide filling Plaza de Mayo and clamouring for Perón's freedom in a variety of bubbles; a box with the *cabecitas* dangling their feet in the fountain (both apparently archive photos); and a roundel of the photonovel's two leading lights: an exultant Perón, with one arm raised aloft and the other around Eva's wasp-waist. *Like Venus from the sea*, read the pithily overinflated caption, *Eva Perón is born of those million mouths demanding the freedom of one man*.

So she too had known doubt and dejection, the dark night of the soul, thought Marroné, straining his abs again. Her acting career was over, fallen by the wayside along with the man who had raised her to the top; the enemy had won the day, all doors had closed, and she had even been beaten up in the street by a mob of extremists. Yet her spirit had won through, turning her darkest hour into victory. Bereft of everything, save her determination and courage, she had achieved it all: Perón's freedom, her marriage to him, a presidential candidacy for her husband and, for her, the title of First Lady at the ripe old age of twenty-six. She had had a clear sense of her mission: to save Perón and set him free, and she had stopped at nothing to fulfil it. What a woman, thought Marroné. Whether you shared her political views or not, it would be mean-minded – the stuff of 'ordinary men' – not to acknowledge her leadership qualities.

That was it, felt Marroné, as he gingerly detached his buttocks from the edge of the plastic toilet seat and rearranged them. He could see it clearly now: Evita had followed the Way of the Warrior, she was a samurai woman, and her lord was, of course, Perón: '*May it come as no surprise to those who seek my portrait in these pages but find Perón's instead. I have ceased to exist in myself, and it is he who lives in my soul, master of all my words and feelings, the overlord of my heart and life.*' As Marroné read, a maxim from *The Corporate Samurai* came to his mind: 'Your errors are yours; your successes, your lord's.' Or as Eva would have put it: '*I was not, nor am I, anything but a sparrow in a vast flock of sparrows . . . But he was and is a giant*

150

condor flying high and sure amidst the mountain tops. Were it not for him, he who came down to me and taught me a different way to fly, I would never have known what a condor was . . . '

And himself? Marroné too had a clear sense of his mission: he had to save Sr Tamerlán at all costs. The message was clear: all of us have our 17th October in our lives, and his was knocking on the door. He would follow Eva's example and save Sr Tamerlán, and, like that other 17th October, he would use the workers. He didn't yet know how, but he'd think of something. He wasn't the kind of man to stick to the beaten track or always drink from the same well. He would go on ploughing his own furrow while the hypercritics huffed and puffed, and the dogs barked till they were hoarse.

And there was another idea that had begun to nibble at the edges of his mind. If Eva Perón's exemplary demeanour on 17th October could be his lodestar in the current situation, why not write a book that would take her whole life and career as an example to be emulated? *Eva Perón in Enterprise Management*, for example, or perhaps something more metaphorical and less pedestrian, like *The Sparrow and the Condor*. A biography that would keep inessential ideology separate from the core issues: the mettle, the spirit, the will to self-mastery, the capacity for leadership. Had there ever been a better example in history of someone who could overcome the most adverse circumstances, create an image and a name for themselves and, with blind faith, reach the top against all the odds? Eva Perón was a born winner, a self-made woman who had created a product – herself – that millions in Argentina and around the world had bought and consumed. There were – it had to be admitted – powerful reasons why her example had not yet been taken up in the business world: one, the circumstantial anti-capitalist rhetoric and class resentment, which the age and experience that were denied her would no doubt have helped to assuage; two (it was painful to admit, but being economical with the truth would be worse), her being a woman in a still eminently male business environment, where few women could carve out niches for themselves.

Next he flicked through the pages that recounted Evita's initial faltering steps as First Lady, the gradual refinement of her tastes and the creation of a personal style, as reflected in her wardrobe and hairdos, culminating in her glittering journey to devastated post-war Europe, which, perhaps because of production limitations, the photonovel barely touched on, save to mention that on that tour *Eva indulged in rubbing the imperialist countries' noses in her regal show of wealth*. It was a crying shame, because the 'Rainbow Tour', as it was known, had wrought a sea change – a genuine metamorphosis – in the young woman from Los Toldos. Before that, Marroné reflected, Eva Duarte, later Eva Perón, had played only pre-existing roles: the young provincial girl who dreams of stardom, the influential lover of a powerful man, even the First Lady . . . And she had succeeded by making use of the tools of her trade: dresses, hairdos, make-up, studied gestures . . . But on her trip to Europe she began to enter virgin territory. Eva became Evita, and Evita was no longer an interpretation, but an entirely new creation. And this singular trait of Evita's manifested itself most fully in the Eva Perón Social Aid Foundation. One photo showed the Foundation's neoclassical façade; another, the torrent of letters that poured in to her daily, written by *mothers with ten or twelve children to look after, unemployed fathers, toothless*

152

old men, teenage prodigies with rag balls, the blind, the crippled, the syphilitic; **letters from the men, women and children of our people who were no longer alone,** *who had someone to listen to them and sort out their problems,* even asking her *from home or the workplace for footballs, clothes, shoes, furniture, false teeth, crutches and wheelchairs, bicycles, sewing machines, toys, cider and panettone for Christmas, or a trousseau for a wedding. These requests were not answered by faceless officials; instead everyone was given a personal audience with Evita*: and the photo showed her sitting at her desk, letter in hand, inviting incredulous descamisados to sit down, smiling as she listened to their dreams, their needs, sometimes their life stories; requests that were often nothing but pleas for attention, respect, someone to acknowledge their existence – in a word, love. Evita had set in motion one of the most innovative and truly revolutionary customer service departments in history: the Foundation was a well-oiled customer loyalty machine, once again testing the truth of the maxim learnt by Marroné on his marketing course: 'A company always makes the same product: happy customers.' And Evita knew how to promote consumption: rather than giving grudgingly to the people who turned to her, she would egg them on: '*Ask for more! The best, the most luxurious, the most expensive! Don't hold back! It's all yours now! Feel free and help yourselves!*' If you asked for a set of bed linen, you went away with a mattress; if a mattress, you got a bed; if a bed, a house. It was impossible not to be touched by the images in the next few pictures: Evita welcoming long queues of ragged paupers, handing out money from her own pocket when the coffers ran out; Evita kissing a leper; Evita sharing her cape with a beggar; Evita giving away her jewellery . . . '**For the love of my people**

I would sell everything I am and everything I own, and I think I would even lay down my life,' she said, and Marroné felt a knot in his throat: because that life, fanned by the breath from millions of mouths, was in fact consuming itself in a furious blaze. The queenly finery had long since been swapped for the republican simplicity of the grey or black tailored suit, and the unruly whorls and waves for the stony coiffure that would soon be made marble: as if refined and purified in that flame burning her inside and out, Evita had been hardening, her dress cleaving to her flesh and her flesh to her bones; her body tensing like a bow and her face sharpening to an arrowhead; her ever more prominent teeth sinking into the air with growing hunger. Perón, on the other hand, was the very picture of health, like a vampire feeding on Evita's energy, his piggy little eyes sinking like raisins into risen dough, the bloated tortoise face retracting deeper and deeper into the thick neck. And so the eternal couple – that work-team of the idealist and the realist (the very essence of Don Quixote and Sancho) – reached the day when, in front of more than a million faithful all screaming for her to accept, Evita was offered the candidacy for vice president. *'The time you have waited for for so long has come, Chinita,'* a tender, smiling Perón was saying to her on the balcony. *'Look, they've come from far and wide . . . Never before in the history of humankind has a woman been more loved by her people . . . '* And Eva, with pained countenance, *'No, Juan, I can't,'* prompting Perón's astonished reply: *'What do you mean you can't? Who deserves this post more than you?'* And Evita: **'I'm not cut out for posts and protocols . . . If I were in govern-ment, I'd no longer be of the people**, *I couldn't be what I am or do what I do . . . I've always lived in freedom.* **I was born for the**

154

Revolution. *Look at them. Do you see them? Do you hear them? There is no scene more beautiful, no music more wonderful. My place is among them* . . . **I am their bridge to you . . . I don't wish to be anything else. Promise me that if one day I am not there for them . . . you will go on listening** . . . ' And then, turning to the crowd who chorused her name: *'I am worthy not for what I have done, I am worthy not for what I have given up, I am worthy not for what I am or what I have. I have only one thing that is worthy and I keep it in my heart; it aches in my soul, it aches in my flesh and burns in my nerves. It is my love for the people and for Perón.* **If the people were to ask me for my life, I would give it to them gladly, because the happiness of a single descamisado is worth more than all my life.**'

What an orator, thought Marroné to himself, looking up for a minute at the closed cubicle door. It wasn't your run-of-the-mill campaign speech, a mere rhetorical exercise; it was *Public Speaking and Influencing Men in Business* by Dale Carnegie incarnate. Cold intelligence could make many a specific objection to Evita's words, but the heart was overpowered by them. That was the touchstone of a good speaker: when they managed to convey their passion even to those who didn't agree with their ideas. 'Touching people's hearts,' Marroné said to himself, 'is not the same as shaping their minds, but it's definitely a step in the right direction.' The formula sounded so apt that he vowed to jot it down in quotation marks, with his name at the side in brackets, in his notebook of famous quotes and phrases.

Allies of imperialism, the military and the oligarch traitors interpreted Perón's prudence and Evita's self-denial as weakness and launched their first coup, thwarted by the swift mobilisation of the people, who once again poured into the square to defend their leader. But Evita had understood that the presence of the people on the streets wasn't enough. She didn't want her descamisados to go like lambs to the slaughter. **As well as being mobilised, the people had to be armed**. And there she was again, in work clothes, hair loose, like a young guerrilla, examining a 9mm pistol that she had picked up from a table covered in an impressive array of hardware, remarking, *'With these in the hands of my descamisados, the oligarchs will shit their pants,'* while the box read: **5,000 automatic pistols and 1,500 machine guns bought with money from the Foundation, the first weapons of the Peronist People's Army, to be delivered to the workers to defend Perón and his government**. *Had these weapons reached their destination, Argentina's recent history would have been very different: Perón wouldn't have been overthrown by the Liberating Revolution, no exile or firing squads, no torture or murder of popular militants and workers' leaders . . . But, working tirelessly and frantically, sometimes sleeping no more than two or three hours a night, as if wanting in just a few short years to compensate the poor for more than a hundred of suffering, attending only to the needs of her descamisados, Evita has neglected her own, and the cancer prayed for by the oligarchy, and lamented so bitterly by her people, has now taken possession of her body . . .* Evita was now in her sickbed, receiving a group of five children, including the urchin from Los Toldos, and as she spoke you could see they drank in her every word: *'Just one thing I ask of you today, children: that you promise* **to defend Perón and fight for him to the death**. *When I am no longer here, you will have to take my place: you will be the bridge between Perón and the people, you will be the eternal watchmen of the Revolution,* **for you are my heirs**, and in the next picture, the five children, now grown up and with rifles in their hands, *never forgot Evita's message;*

*and today wherever there's a child crying for food, wherever there's a worker fighting against exploitation, wherever there are people fighting for their liberation, **there will always be a Montonero**.*

Once Evita was dead, the text proceeded rather more demurely, *she was handed over to the Spanish embalmer, Dr Pedro Ara, so that that she would live on in soul and body too; so that, **like Joan of Arc, she would be there to guide us in the struggle against foreign domination**.* The photo showed Evita in silhouette, covered by a shroud, while a bald Dr Frankenstein in white coat and glasses contemplated the maiden from Los Toldos – his masterpiece. *After the funeral, which lasted **a fortnight, during which the sky came out in sympathy with the dispossessed, accompanying their outpourings of grief with persistent drizzle**, the body was deposited in the General Confederation of Labour building, where it lay patiently awaiting the erection of the Monument to the Descamisado, which will be the tallest in the world at twice the height of the Statue of Liberty, and will contain a silver sarcophagus, the permanent resting place for her mortal remains.*

He smiled when he came across his old friend, the Descamisado of the Monument. His and Evita's paths crossed at every turn, in every box. The next few showed archive footage of the military's bombardment of Plaza de Mayo, of the coup that ousted Perón and of the iconoclastic fury unleashed by the anti-Peronists on effigies of Perón and Evita, and here again Marroné's and Evita's paths crossed. For, having been born at the height of the Perón administration, he well remembered the *pompier* portraits of the President and First Lady in the school entrance hall, by the dark wood panelling that listed in gold lettering the 'Dux Medallist Boys'; he effortlessly recalled the opening phrases of his first reading book ('Eva . . . Evita . . . Evita looks at the little girl . . . the boy looks at Evita . . . Perón loves children') and the bust of Evita that presided over the school's playground – an Evita with a plaited bun, mounted on a polished black marble pedestal, which they used as a base for tag or hide-and-seek. But suddenly one day – he must have been in third or perhaps fourth grade – he saw the mistresses, masters, headmaster and directors all kissing and hugging, and where the portraits of Perón and Evita had been, there now hung a portrait of the Queen, and they had new reading books, and there was no sign of the bust of Evita, not even of its pedestal: it had been removed, and the hole hastily filled with new flagstones, as if to erase every trace of her existence. And so it had been in every school, in every public office, in every hospital, police station and town square. Hundreds, perhaps thousands of busts of Perón and Evita delivered up to the fury of sledgehammers, pickaxes and iron bars: ears gone, noses gone, cloven in two, heads rolling with all the zeal of the French Revolution.

Just then a dull murmur reached his ears, muffled and powerful as the roar of the stadium on matchday. For a moment he thought his imagination had conjured up the roar of the people wailing for Eva's return, but after listening hard for a few seconds the sound had only increased, so, pulling up his overalls in resignation, he flushed the toilet and the water washed his weak pee away – the sole tangible result of all his straining – and poked his head out of the office's inner window. The sound came from the factory: it was the corrugated iron roof clattering and rattling in the falling rain. At that moment a bolt of lightning lit up windows and skylights, and a second later the first clap

158

of thunder shook the whole structure, which, like a huge metal drum, went on vibrating for some time. He went out into the main corridor and caught the first gust of fresh air full in the face as it came in through the open window; he thrust his hands and arms outside, and felt the icy water and the gentle pattering of a few small hailstones, which melted on his palms as he watched; then, lifting his hands to his face, he freshened his forehead, his neck, his ears, his tired eyes. The rain washed the snow-covered gardens, which appeared less white and more green by the lightning, their coat of plaster trickling away through the blades of grass, and flowing in milky streams down ditches and paths.

Watching the rain, Marroné lost himself the way others lose themselves in the immensity of the sea or the depths of a log-fire. Something had changed in him – something was still changing in him – after reading the photonovel of Evita's life. 'It's just another order,' he had snapped at Paddy, believing it to be true. 'They mean nothing to me; they're just mass-produced busts,' he had added, cursing his bad luck. But what if it wasn't just a question of luck, good or bad? What if there was a *reason* for him to get involved in the strike? At times his mind's eye caught flashes of a secret design, but for the moment all he could make out were a few loose ends. Could that be what Paddy had been trying to get across? He, Marroné, had marched in and ordered the busts like someone buying a dozen pastries – and from an oligarch exploiter no less. No, the busts of Eva couldn't come from the hands of dissatisfied, exploited workers: that was the lesson. They could only come from the hands of the satisfied, well-remunerated, well-treated working class . . . of happy descamisados. The busts of Eva couldn't be bought; they had to be earned. They would be his when he had learnt to be worthy of them.

But how? Whatever the answer, he knew that for the moment he had to watch and wait and listen. It – the answer – would come, as it had on so many other occasions, apparently out of nowhere, but a nowhere fertilised and cultivated with days or weeks of apparently fruitless effort. The bust of Eva was an oracle, a talking head that would give all the right answers when asked the right questions. And all Marroné's questions boiled down to one basic one: would he be a condor or a sparrow? A Don Quixote or a priest and barber? A 'man of genius' or an 'ordinary man'? Tomorrow maybe, or in the days to come, he was sure to find out, but he could already feel the answer incubating in the depths of his soul.

5

SEVEN DEBATING HATS

The day after the storm dawned crisp and sunny, with a brisk southerly breeze that had blown all the clouds from the sky. Its coating of plaster now removed by the rain, the skin of the landscape had emerged tender and soft as a newborn babe's, and the lawn, plants and trees gleamed with a green that hurt the eyes, as if every leaf and every bud were seeing the light for the very first time; the luxuriant ash trees cast green pools of shade for those in need of rest, the poplars flashed their silver coins and the plumes of pampas grass waved like sails straining for the open sea. The cloudless sky that sparkled radiant as sapphire, the clean air that filled his lungs, the singing of numerous birds whose whistling and trilling in the silence of the machines cheered the very air, and the happy faces of the workers diligently coming and going about their strikers' duties made Marroné believe at times that a new world had been born; that day and the ones to come might have been counted among the happiest he had ever known.

The work duties were rotated so that no one would feel bored or hard done by, the simplest tasks alternating with the hardest; that way, Paddy explained to him, they could also try out the order of the future society, where, as Marx had predicted, every man could develop in the area best suited to him: he could hunt in the morning, fish in the afternoon, rear cattle in the evening, and hone his critical faculties after dinner. Gradually Marroné settled into his new life. He threw himself with enthusiasm into the varied tasks, which he sometimes chose himself and sometimes was assigned, and each of which was designated by a different-coloured hard-hat: in his green hat he unloaded supplies from the delivery trucks, a task to which his rugby-player's physique was amply suited; in the red hat he introduced improvements in canteen management, varying the dishes on the menu and above all teaching the impromptu cooks the art of seasoning, about which they knew next to nothing; and, many a night he would don the black hat for guard duty, joining in with the songs around the bonfire, learning the words as he went, swapping dirty jokes and juicy anecdotes, which he often made up off the top of his head; he would talk football or politics, tweaking his language and views to his companions' abilities, which often turned out to be more sophisticated than he'd thought; and sometimes, his gaze lost in the crackling flames of the bonfire as it slowly collapsed into a heap of embers, he would ruminate on the turn his life seemed to be taking. A couple of times he sallied forth, sporting the blue hat of the propagandists, to hand out leaflets in the neighbourhood, always in groups of three or more, and escorted by an armed guard of black helmets; rather than fear the police, who were content for now merely to strain at the leash, their concern was that they would cross swords with the union thugs or the parapolice squads, both of which in the last few weeks had kidnapped and murdered several worker delegates. But all the same the people came out to hug them and slap them on the back as they went by, shouting things like 'Hang on in there, lads' or 'Don't let up, comrades'; housewives came out on the pavement with glasses of pop or jugs of fresh lemonade, handed out fruit or *alfajores* and packets of *milanesa* sandwiches 'For the lads on the inside', and Marroné now began to understand – because sometimes to understand something it isn't enough to read about it; you have to live and breathe it – what Eva must have felt daily in her office at the Foundation, constantly in the streets and roads of her country, and overwhelmingly from the balcony of the presidential palace: the soul of the people, the beat of its heart. It was a new reality, one that neither St Andrew's nor Stanford had prepared him for. So it was with redoubled enthusiasm that Marroné donned the yellow hat for cleaning duties, which he performed if not with gusto, then conscientiously and with dedication, and it was with an identical attitude that, donning the brown hat of the supply brigades, he spent many an afternoon collecting nuts and bolts as ammunition for catapults, or bringing office furniture down in the service lift to build barricades in anticipation of the police attack, which might come any minute. Only the leaders' white hats were off-limits to him for now: that office bore greater responsibility and was only renewed by assembly.

The permanent mood of cooperation, which turned every chore into a joy; the presence of Paddy Donovan, on the go around the clock, lending a hand in every activity ('The leaders wear white hats because white is the sum of all the colours: the white hat is a badge not of privilege but of duty'); the predominance of manual over mental labour – labour which, frequently taking place in the open air, gave him the freedom to go bare-chested – all of this made Marroné feel he was reliving the halcyon days of the summer camp on Mascardi Lake, of which he had so many good memories. His enthusiasm, his frank and open disposition and the smile that always played over his lips quickly earned him the recognition and soon the esteem of his new comrades. He could no longer cross the grounds without them greeting him as he went past: those who knew his name – whose numbers rose daily – would shout out 'Hey, Ernesto! Great stuff, Ernesto!', and those who didn't, 'Don't let up, comrade!' or 'Nice day, comrade!', to which he invariably replied: 'A Peronist day!' And for the first time in his life Marroné was grateful for the olive tone of his skin, the plumpish lips, the spiky black hair, which, coupled with his new overalls, the five-day stubble and the studied carelessness of his appearance, made it easier to pass himself off as one of them. Dale Carnegie's rules of conversation worked just as well in this world as the one they'd originally been written for, and for anything he couldn't hide – the educated accent, a certain bourgeois set to his body – there was always an alibi in all those middle-class youngsters that had been sent to the factories to be proletarianised and join the rank and file of the working class. The first day he had had to do guard duty at the entrance was a case in point: the Canal 13 mobile unit had approached and asked him a few questions for the daily news.

'Five days after the start of the occupation of the Sansimón Plasterworks, how do you view the situation?'

'Well like, the occupation 'ere and 'cross the 'ole country's still going strong, the lads 'ere are standing firm and morale's good and we are determined to pursue our struggle whatever the cost,' Marroné began, suddenly dropping all his aitches, and lowering the peak of his hard-hat so the camera wouldn't give him away.

'What news of the hostages? When do you intend to release them?'

'Well er . . . we already released everyone . . . 'cept the management . . . They's staying 'ere till they meets all our demands . . . Cleverer than a box of monkeys that lot are . . . Sr Sansimón wouldn't listen to our demands . . . ignored us didn't he . . . Laughed in our face he did . . . laughing on the other side of his now though inne eh?'

'They say there are infiltrators in your midst . . . professional agitators, communists, with links to guerrilla organisations . . . '

Marroné took belligerent offence, slid his hand inside his overalls and pulled out the crucifix he wore round his neck.

'You calling *me* a communist? What kind of communist wears a crucifix like this, pray tell? I'll bet you and that lot that's with you if you come in the factory and find a single brick that ain't Peronist I'll eat my hat.'

'What if the management don't give in? Are you going to stay here for ever?'

'If they don't back down that's their bad luck. They'll be left with nothing. We can run the factory on our own we can, if we puts our minds to it. We'll show 'em they's parasites living off the people and we'll all be a lot better off without 'em.'

'And what if the police try to retake the factory by force?'

'We'll be ready for them is what'll happen. Bring them on if they dare. They'll be in for a big surprise.'

The journalists' mistake was understandable in a way: their bourgeois consciousness made it hard for them to tell a false worker from a true one. But such an explanation didn't hold for the lady who wobbled up to him on two legs like flowerpots and handed him a trayful of empanadas, beaming at him through her remaining half-dozen teeth, 'For you and the lads, 'andsome. Don't let up, pet, we're all rooting for you 'ere we are. Keep going, got 'em by the balls you 'ave, don't let 'em off the 'ook now, that lot are more slippery than the devil himself, they'll stick the knife in when you ain't looking, mark my words. You just watch your backs. And make sure you get some proper food in you and a good night's sleep . . . Gotta stay fit and healthy, remember, case things get heavy like. Oooooh, I can tell you a thing or two about that. My late husband, God rest his soul, was just like you lot. Always giving them gorillas some, or anyone as 'ad a bad word to say about Perón.' And, if he was being absolutely honest with himself, these practical achievements of his filled him with satisfaction, but also with a nagging sense of unease. Were Dale Carnegie's tips, or Marroné's proven ductility, or his recently discovered thespian abilities enough to explain just how easy, how untraumatic his introduction to the world of the working class had proven? Or was there something else? From what he had gathered, Paddy himself had found it something of an uphill struggle, whereas he, Marroné . . . Because when it came to the executives and the office staff, he'd put all his efforts into fitting in, applying the rules of *How to Win Friends and Influence People* with equal zest, and it hadn't gone half as well as it had with this bunch. Perhaps the gene pool really was stronger than all else, and the fact of his adoption glared bright and clear through his upbringing in the bosom of a refined Anglo-Argentine family, his St Andrew's and Stanford education, the trips to Europe and the United States, the summers in Punta del Este; as did his hair, which, just days after escaping the hairdresser's practised hands, would already be verging on the mane-like, advertising his plebeian Indian blood for all to see. 'You can certainly tell you're the son of darkies!' His father's words, blurted out in a fit of exasperation, rang once again in his ears, as they did every time the subject came to mind. He had apologised immediately, but the ten- or eleven-year-old Ernestito had never forgotten or forgiven, sensing in those words a verdict that would brand him for ever. The stigma of his origins had dogged him with all the tenacity of a bloodhound at school too. Marooné! Maroon Monkey! Marron Crappé! were among his classmates' favourite insults when they ganged up on him, and thus his mixed feelings every time the strikers or slum-dwellers took him for one of them.

Another source of unease stemmed from the realisation of how little he missed home and work. True, he could use the phone as often as he liked, which he did at least once a day, to say hello to his little boy and his wife (who only through Govianus's timely intervention had finally renounced the belief that it was all a story Marroné had concocted to cheat on her), and to ring Govianus every morning to keep abreast of the latest developments. He could have climbed into his car and driven home or to work any time he liked: he was free to come and go as he pleased. Yet, as he had told the journalist who'd interviewed him for the television, the plasterworkers' strike was going strong across the country, and all attempts by the company to procure the busts of Eva through other channels had failed miserably. At least they had a man on the inside at Sansimón's: he was their only hope. Whenever he could – in conversation, at daily assembly – he would bring up the possibility of breaking the basic rule of every strike and producing at least just a few 'trial' busts, or would try to initiate the less headstrong in the virtues of the 'Japanese strike', where in true samurai fashion the workforce would work twice as hard to produce an unsellable surplus. And though the motion was never passed, he found out from subsequent conversations his ideas were not falling on stony ground. But these purely practical justifications weren't enough to hide Marroné's undeniable reluctance to return to the routine of his work and home life. Perhaps, he told himself to appease the misgivings of his bourgeois conscience, it all boiled down to a feeling that he was on holiday, without the usual timetables and chores: the occupied plasterworks had become a proletarian version of an all-inclusive holiday camp, complete with recreation activities and games. Only the several days without a bowel movement weighed a little heavy on him – that and almost as many without sex. There were times he regretted not having taken up Dorita's generous offer: her very lack of sex appeal could have worked – as it did with his wife – as an antidote for the malfunction in which his sexual timidity was rooted. By what sinister joke of nature, he sometimes asked himself, had his connections been switched? If his overeagerness were to move from his testicles to his intestines and their stubbornness make the reverse journey, all in his life would be well, he felt.

Meanwhile, there were crucial hours ahead, hours that could bring about that '17th October' he had read about in the photonovel. Though enthusiastically supported by the workers, their families and even the local residents, the occupation had begun to go flat, leaking air through a thousand little holes. The sheer number and variety of the tasks was overwhelming, and many were already beginning to mutter that when they worked for the management they at least had a timetable and a wage. The assemblies were held daily, sometimes at the rate of two or three a day, and were packed mainly by militants from leftist groups, who spent the time discussing the Chinese or Cuban Revolutions and calling for a minute's silence for Che Guevara or today's daily update of murdered militants. Most of the genuine workers had families to support and many of them missed sleeping in their beds, kissing their children in the mornings and banging the missus whenever they felt like it; also, Sansimón had gradually caved in to their demands, giving them pay rises, better working conditions, full payment of overtime, and the heads of Garaguso and Cerbero; but he had baulked at their demand to reinstate all those dismissed for union or political reasons since '55, and his outburst at their insistence ('Fine! And would you like me to suck their dicks one by one as well?') had rather dampened the negotiating climate.

Rumour had it that these concessions were no more than ruses – that Sansimón was only waiting for them to release him and vacate the factory before filing for bankruptcy and turfing them all out on the street – and many of them, their faith daily sapped by the sermons of Baigorria and his henchmen, had begun to believe it. Faced with this eventuality, the collaborationists were calling for the strike to be lifted before things got out of hand, the negotiators for consensus over a timetable of reinstatements, the moderates to pursue the strike but call off the occupation (which would allow them to stay at home all day watching TV, otherwise what in God's name were they striking for?), while the hardliners – now in a distinct minority – upped the ante: if Sansimón refused to play ball, they'd get to keep the factory and he could go cry into his soup. Everything seemed to be pointing to one big assembly that would decide once and for all whether to end the occupation or continue it.

It was held one cloudy morning, which again threatened stormy weather, inside the big empty factory, which, in the sepulchral silence where footsteps sounded like pounding hammers and cowed people to a whisper, looked now even more like a vast, abandoned cathedral. Its floor, machines, bags of plaster and the pieces that the announcement of the strike had left unfinished were all coated in a fine layer of dust. The air was strained and still, like an animal about to pounce, and, filtering in through clouds and skylights, the dead light made it hard to believe that just a week ago the whole factory had been clean and sparkling, and running like clockwork. He felt a little guilty for having caved in to the irresponsible delights of strike action: this was the result of the selfish satisfaction of his own desires; this was what happened when each part of the body worked for its own ends, with utter disregard for the health of the whole. What was happening at the Sansimón Plasterworks might well be a warning of what could happen across the whole country unless something were done to reverse the downward spiral into permanent chaos and conflict. Ah well, perhaps it wasn't too late to put things right. Because this time Marroné was determined to have his say. This time it was all or nothing. If he couldn't make his voice heard and make progress over the issue of the busts, he would take his mission at the

Sansimón Plasterworks to be over and continue the search elsewhere. He still had no clearly defined plan of action: first he'd observe, see how things were shaping up, then seize the slightest chance to bring up his proposal.

At the vague line dividing the blue zone of the nave from the brown zone of the apse, more or less where the altar would be in a real cathedral, they had erected a makeshift platform out of a truncated pyramid (more Aztec-like than Egyptian) of stacked wooden pallets, which had the additional advantage of providing natural ladders for the speakers to climb up and down. Virtually the whole workforce was there, including those officially on leave; they'd even invited the Sansimóns, Senior and Junior, as onlookers. The list of speakers was carried by Trejo, one of Paddy's lieutenants; Paddy himself – the whiteness of his hard-hat vying with the permanent smile that rose out of several days' growth of copper beard – was running the show.

The start was as predictable as it was disappointing, with the usual declarations of support from delegates of neighbouring factories, class-struggle unions, opportunistic politicians, student organisations, political youth movements and guerrilla organisations, regurgitating the obligatory quotes by Marx and Lenin, Ho Chi Minh and Mao, Brecht, El Che, Fidel and, of course, Eva Perón . . . By this stage several of the workers from the factory had started coughing, yawning and gathering in groups with their backs to the podium to talk amongst themselves. It was understandable, their lives and jobs were on the line, and they had to stand there listening to some shrill little pedant giving them the low-down on some worker's strike in Saint Petersburg. Marroné looked on with rising impatience at the received gestures and hackneyed phrases of the orators, who acted as if they hadn't even heard of Dale Carnegie, not to mention Demosthenes or Cicero. Not one of the speakers made any effort to put themselves in the other's place; they only listened to themselves: the art of persuasion had given way to loud-mouthed sloganeering. If only he could find the room to do some creativity exercise with them . . . But which one? He could forget brainstorming or brain-sailing: the dynamics of the assembly were already too turbulent, and the chances of entropic disorder grew exponentially with the number of people. A mind-mapping exercise would be ideal, but he lacked the basic materials: an overhead projector to write on, a blackboard . . . There was some coloured chalk, and the office easel was there to hand, but the felt-tips were dry, and anyway . . . No, it had to be something more dramatic that forced the participants to step outside their rigid, inflexible positions and put themselves in the other's place. In other words it had to be a role-play exercise. With the speed of a pocket calculator his mind reviewed all the known options, whether honed at meetings and workshops or studied in books on the subject. None of what he had done or learnt seemed to be any use to him, and there, he realised suddenly, lay the answer: creativity begins at home. The onus was on him to be creative; he would have to invent something new, something no one had ever done before. But what? What? He racked his brains, running his eyes over the motley crowd. How to captivate them? How to get through to them, these rookies? That was when his eyes fixed on the coloured helmets.

At that precise moment Ernesto Marroné had an inkling of what Moses might have felt on seeing the burning bush, or Archimedes on leaping naked from his bath, or Newton when the apple landed on his head. Rapt by the revelation taking shape effortlessly within him, it was with some effort that he managed to nudge Trejo on his right:

'Put my name down.'

His move didn't escape Paddy's notice.

'What are you up to?' he asked in surprise.

Without looking at him and with such assurance that his voice sounded as if it belonged to someone else, to the man he had become since feeling the magic wand, he replied:

'You leave it to me, I'll have this assembly on the right track for you in no time.'

He had to wait a while for those ahead of him on the list to speak and, although an impatience bordering on frenzy ate into his body with a furious tingling, he knew it was for the best, because it gave him time to work out the finer details of his original brilliant intuition and draw up a plan of action worthy of it. As at other key moments of his life his brain burnt white-hot, like a tungsten filament, and his whole environment was transfigured before his feverish eyes, as if what had changed were not just his gaze, but the very light itself. When it came to his turn, he mounted the steps of the platform with a steady purpose, and the tremulous note in his opening words was more an 'Oxford stammer' calculated to create sympathy in his audience than genuine nervousness.

'Comrades . . . ' He paused to make sure he had everyone's attention, then went on, 'I have been here for a while listening to one comrade after another telling us we have to pull together and that the workers have the final say and the workers wear the trousers. And in the end all they do is talk and talk, and tell the workers what they have to do' (*murmurs of approval*). 'Is it because they're afraid that, if they really and truly give the workers the final say, you'll say something they don't want to hear?' (*More murmurs, sporadic applause, someone shouts 'Nice one!'*) 'Comrades . . . We all know each other here, and we all know that at the end of the day it's always the same at these assemblies. Always the same ones who talk and talk and talk till people get tired and leave, and only then do they vote, and decide behind the workers' backs' (*more sustained applause, shouts of 'It's true!' and 'You tell 'em, comrade!'*).

Paddy watched him with a worried frown, and Marroné winked at him to reassure him.

'All right, all right, at the end of the day I'm yacking on too much too' (*laughter and applause*). He had everyone's absolute attention: the time had come.

'So let's get down to brass tacks – I mean the real facts. At Tamerlán Construction, where I'm from, we've invented a miles more efficient and entertaining way of doing assemblies. We use coloured hats; yes, just like the ones you're wearing,' he said, when several of his listeners instinctively raised their hands to their heads. 'Seven comrades, seven volunteers: come up here onto the platform, each wearing a different-coloured hat. Well? What are you waiting for?'

The workers looked at each other doubtfully, but their eyes sparkled and half-smiles crept over the corners of their mouths; their hesitation wasn't a sign of rejection or distrust, but the initial reticence of children before the party entertainer summoning them to a game: a mixture of desire, a little embarrassment and bags I go first.

A worker in a green helmet – the one with a jutting acromegalic chin like tango singer Edmundo Rivero's, and one of the party that had burst into Sansimón's office that far-off morning when all this began – raised a large, heavy hand, like an asbestos glove filled with steel. Marroné invited him up onto the platform. He was followed by: the black-helmeted Saturnino, Baigorria's grim companion the night of the bosses' Bacchanal; Baigorria himself, wearing a yellow hat; a young Indian-looking man called Zenón wearing a red helmet, who had helped Marroné replace his ruined suit; and the fat man in the brown helmet and milky-white eye that everyone called El Tuerto. Marroné was wearing the blue hat of the propagandists, having spent the day before phoning in to various radio programmes to outline the rationale and progress of the occupation. All they needed now was a white helmet, and the group would be complete. But the last one up there – Pampurro by name – wore green.

'Ok, we have a problem. We've got two green hats up here, but we're still missing a white hat. Looks like our good leaders have had a fit of embarrassment (*laughter*). Well, Pa . . . Colorado? Can you lend us yours? Come on, don't be shy. Lend us it a bit, will you? We'll give it back afterwards. Promise.'

With a fixed smile, Paddy swapped helmets with Pampurro and donned the green one, and Marroné smiled: a sudden picture from their schooldays – Paddy's red hair and the green Monteith shirt – flashed before his eyes.

'Right, now comes the interesting bit. Pay attention. When the factory belonged to Sr Sansimón here (*general laughter, jeers, face like thunder of said Sansimón, who had been scrutinising him for some time as if trying to work out where they'd met. Marroné thanked his stubble which, though sparse, had altered his appearance considerably*), each colour stood for a section: white for the bosses, red for the workshop, black for maintenance . . . With the occupation we've turned things around: now it's the leaders who wear the white hats (*only one person laughed – the young sculptor from the workshop – the irony being lost on the rest*), the blue hats who do the propaganda and the yellow hats who do the cleaning; except that the hats are rotated periodically and therefo . . . and that's why the tasks are, too. What I'm proposing to you is closer to the second way than the first. In this debate each colour has a task: white is neutral, and the one wearing it has to present the facts as they stand, the way things are, not the way we want them to be, as objectively as they can. Red is the colour of passion, of high temperatures, so the one wearing the red hat has to speak from his feelings – anger, exasperation, fear – whatever they may be . . . ' He was improvising, thinking on his feet, but each idea immediately found its proper place and expression, the words following one another effortlessly. His brow seemed to have been touched by some divine inspiration – just like Eva Perón whenever she spoke to the people. 'Yellow is the colour of the sun, comrades, and the one wearing it . . .' he touched Baigorria's head for a second, ' . . . has to give a positive, optimistic appraisal of the situation. The one wearing the black hat, however . . . ' he looked at Saturnino, who, with his permanently gloomy expression, was tailor-made for the part, ' . . . always has to imagine the worst, warn us of the possible consequences – the most serious he can imagine – of our actions and decisions. Green is the colour . . . '

' . . . of hope!' shouted an enthusiastic voice in the crowd. They were behind him now, no doubt about it.

'Of course,' Marroné conceded with a TV presenter's smile, 'and of nature too, of all new things that grow . . . The one wearing the green hat has a very tough, a very special mission.' He paused until Edmundo Rivero's face had taken on the required gravitas. 'He has to be *creative*. He has to contribute new ideas. Even if they're absurd, even if they sound ridiculous, even if they seem to go against reason and experience.' It would have been quicker and simpler to say that the one in the green hat had to apply lateral thinking, but he doubted whether a single one of his audience was familiar with the concept. 'That leaves us the brown hat.' He hadn't the slightest idea what to do with the brown one; he had one colour left over and he'd run out of ideas. Why not let them be a bit creative too huh? 'Let's see now . . . What can the brown hat do, comrades?'

'Spread the shit!' shouted another voice in the crowd, and they all celebrated the witticism with laughter and raspberries.

'Exactly! At every meeti . . . at every assembly there's always a trouble-maker, a party-pooper, a shit-spreader. That, comrade,' he said, slapping El Tuerto on the back, who was laughing in anticipation, making his bombastic pot-belly ripple with delight, 'will be your task. But mind you don't mess it up. There's a difference between spreading bad blood – sowing doubt and discord – and alerting us to risks or keeping an eye out for all that can go wrong as we draw up our plans for the struggle ahead. That's the job of our friend in the black hat,' he said, turning to Saturnino, the corner of whose mouth barely twitched in acknowledgement. 'Right. I think we're all set, aren't we?' he asked, and paused to see if they noticed his mistake.

Several hands went up and waved at him insistently.

'The blue hat! The blue hat, Ernesto!'

'Huh? You what?' Marroné played stupid, eventually rolling both eyes upwards to 'discover' with pretend embarrassment the blue hat sitting atop his own head. He took it off and slapped his forehead with the palm of his hand.

'Blue. The colour of the sky, which is all-seeing because it's above and beyond us. The one wearing the blue hat – in this case, me – is the conductor of the orchestra, the organiser. And also the one who sums up and draws conclusions. But we've still a way to go before we get to that. Like any other game, the best way to learn is by playing. So I suggest we get cracking and just see as we go along. So, let's kick off with the white hat. How are things going, Pampurro, my friend?'

'Eeeh . . . Well . . . Errr . . . The occupation's been on for a week now, and most of our demands have been met. The morale of the comrades is still high, though a few of us are getting a bit tired, actually . . . ' began Pampurro, rubbing the sole of his work-shoes on the rough boards of the stage.

'Hold on a second,' Marroné interrupted him politely. 'I think we're encroaching on red hat territory here. Zenón?'

'I reckon we've been too soft . . . Sr Sansimón here's been exploiting the workers for years . . . If we set him to work in the Blue Sector eight hours a day, with the noise those machines make so you can't hear yourself think, breathing in that dust all day long so you can't sleep at night for coughing, with that lot shouting at the workers through their megaphones to work harder and charging them for every piece they break . . . I reckon he'd give us everything we're asking for before the day's out, comrades.'

'A wonderful green-hat type of proposal!' Marroné inter-vened. 'See? We've only just started and we already have a new idea. Get the bosses to do our jobs, so they can experience what the workers have to put up with first-hand. Anything to add, comrade?' he said, turning to Edmundo Rivero, who stared back at him in asinine bewilderment. He clearly wasn't the most suitable candidate for the green hat; Marroné would have to find a way to get it to change owners asap.

'We're getting there, we're getting there. We're getting some positive energy now. Well then, yellow hat: what do you say? Shall we give it a go?'

The question was a loaded one: up until now Baigorria had been the staunchest opponent of the occupation. Would he be capable of playing along and seeing things from the other side?'

'Well, if you ask me, comrades,' began Baigorria, all nonchalance, 'I reckon things are going brilliantly. Get a load of old Sr Sansimón there, how contented he looks. Lean over the wire fence and give our old friend Plod a wave. They're so busy looking after us they wouldn't leave their post, not for hot pizza. What I reckon, comrades, is that they won't just grant us all our demands, but a whole lot more, so let's get asking: a twenty-hour week, three months' paid holidays, four meals and a siesta with an optional slag thrown in for anyone who isn't feeling sleepy . . . '

Some celebrated his wit; others booed him. But the fact was that, irony apart, Baigorria had understood perfectly how the game worked. Garaguso's influence had awoken in this once apathetic and unimaginative man latent qualities of leadership. He could be an adversary to be reckoned with if you got on the wrong side of him.

'Now,' said Marroné, rubbing his hands contentedly, 'let's hear the other side. The black hat.'

Saturnino contemplated his former partying companion with a wicked look in his eye.

'All I've got to say is that, if we don't lift the occupation soon, they'll blow us to kingdom come and we'll lose everything we've gained so far. The government was listening to us at first: sent us a representative and two big mouths from the Ministry of Labour they did, and now they won't even answer the phone. They're calling us anarchists and communists on the radio, and saying we're full of infiltrators and subversives. Any night now they're going to throw everything they've got at us, and if the police don't succeed, the army will. At best we'll all be sacked; at worst we'll all get whacked.'

The audience's response was instantaneous. 'Coward! Traitor! Sell-out!' And that wasn't all they said.

'Just a moment, just a moment!' mediated Marroné. 'Sounds like you're all doing the job of our comrade in the brown hat.'

'The fact is that you've sold out to the management,' El Tuerto lashed out at Saturnino without warning. 'You and that one,' he said, roping in Baigorria with a flick of his finger, 'are traitors to the workers' movement.'

'Me? A traitor? Say that again if you've got it in you!' said Saturnino, working himself into a lather and advancing, fists clenched, on his colleague, who puffed out his chest (or rather his belly); had the others not restrained them, the fists would have flown. Far from daunted, Marroné decided the time had come to up the ante.

'All right, all right. Now you'll really see what this game's about. Change hats.'

The two of them stood and gaped at him.

'You heard me: Saturnino, you take the brown one, and El Tuerto, you put on the black one.'

This time they complied. But they went no further.

'And?'

'Fucking arsehole,' the now brown-hatted Saturnino spat at El Tuerto.

'You'll come to a bad end you will, sonny,' reacted El Tuerto, after donning the black hat, then, including the audience with an arc of his finger, 'so'll you lot.'

Even El Tuerto and Saturnino ended up joining in with the general cackling that ensued, then they both shook hands, and everyone cheered. They'd got the idea: the exercise was turning out to be a triumph. The positions were nothing more than that – positions; their identities weren't involved; they could change them as easily as putting on and taking off a hat. And this was just the start. Leaving behind their fixed roles and seeing things from the other's point of view were steps that led up to the game's ultimate goal: opening the doors to the green-hat proposals; finding new, creative solutions to old problems. Even Paddy now looked at him differently. Marroné felt a secret warmth run through him.

'Well, now it's time to open the game up a bit. Anyone who wants to say something can come up, or speak from where they're standing. But before you speak, just make quite sure you've thought about what you're going to say and that you've got the right hat on.'

Several hands in the audience went up. One of them belonged to Sansimón Senior, who had been whispering throughout with the young sculptor from his workshop. Marroné decided to risk it and invited him up.

'Which hat, comrade?'

'White,' said the old man.

The workers regarded him with curiosity, though without hostility; his son's face, however, was contorted with suspicion. The old man studied the array of coloured helmets at his feet like a seabed covered with coloured snails. Then he spoke:

'I've chosen the white one because it's the information hat, and I've got something new to tell you. You all know that, when I founded the Sansimón Plasterworks, I was just like you. It was just a little workshop in a house in Constitución: there were three assistants and myself, and the four of us did everything. Then, thanks to God and the hard work of the people, we started growing, until we became what we are today. The current CEO, who is here with us today, claims he was the one who built this great company from its humble origins, but that's his way of looking at things. I know that the reality is very different. I know that the ones who made the Sansimón Plasterworks what it is today are you – all of you.'

His first pause was filled with a general ovation. The old man could certainly deliver a speech, that was for sure.

'The CEO's chair isn't a throne,' he went on once there was silence again, 'and a factory isn't a kingdom handed down automatically from father to son. When I saw that the time had come to step aside and leave the leadership in more capable hands, I had a very different idea of how the company should be run. In my youth I read Proudhon, Bakunin, Kropotkin – and this hand shook the right hand of the Spanish Civil War hero, Buenaventura Durruti . . . I learnt a lot of things back then . . . That man must not be a wolf to man, that dignity is worth more than a full stomach . . . '

Marroné was beginning to get impatient: if the old man started banging on about his socialist past, all that he'd accomplished so far would fly out of the window. Just then he spotted the young sculptor wading through the sea of comrades waving a sheaf of papers over his head, and when he noticed old Sansimón Senior's smile, Marroné understood it had all been just a ruse to buy some time.

'Most of all I learnt that the land has to belong to the peasant who works it and the factory to the worker!' declared the old man, stretching out a hand to take the papers his assistant held out to him. 'And here's the proof!' he exclaimed, bearing them aloft and letting them flutter in the breeze. 'These documents prove that I'd decided to hand the factory over to all of you! And this exploiter – this fruit of my loins! – who only the virtue of his poor mother prevents me from calling something else, had me legally declared mentally unsound, presenting these papers here as proof! Only a madman, argued his lawyers to a judge he'd bought off, would want to give his factory away to his workers.'

Marroné couldn't believe his ears. It was as if the will scene from *Julius Caesar* were playing out before his eyes. But then again, in the world of applied creativity, stranger things than this happened every day. Once the floodgates were open, it was impossible to predict what might pour out of them.

'So he took the lot!' the old man went on, unable to contain himself. 'But it's time to tear off the mask! *You* are my true sons! *You* are my heirs! What you're doing here is nothing more than taking back what belongs to you!'

There was pandemonium: hard-hats flying up in the air, effusive hugging and kissing, and in the midst of it all, unnoticed or almost unnoticed, came the brief, disconsolate remark addressed by a glassy-eyed Sansimón Junior to his father, who, arms folded, loomed giant-like high up on the stage.

'You too, Dad?'

Marroné felt a hand on his shoulder. It was Paddy, who had climbed up. For a few seconds they looked on in silence.

'It's like I said, see?' said Paddy eventually. 'There you have a perfect example of revolutionary consciousness. Old Sansimón is breaking the family ties and class conditioning, and making a stand with the vanguard of the proletariat and the working class.'

'You reckon?' Marroné answered him with more sadness than he would have wished. 'I thought he was just doing it to humiliate his son.'

'You don't have to go on pretending, Ernesto. I'm onto you. You aren't what you seemed either. You never cease to amaze me. Did you have this all worked out with the old man?'

Marroné shook his head. His eyes were on the patriarchal, almost prophet-like posture that Sansimón Senior had struck, and he was too busy with his new idea to answer his friend.

'Fetch me the Moses.'

'What?'

'The big one, at the gate. Oh, and a sledgehammer, too.'

'What are you going to do?'

'It's green-hat time for me.'

As he waited for the statue, Marroné gestured for silence. It didn't take long: by now he had all these fierce strikers eating out of the palm of his hand. Mark Antony himself couldn't have done better.

'Comrades!' he said, and the effect of his voice on the crowd was like oil on troubled waters. 'We have all of us, here at the Sansimón Plasterworks, just been very privileged: we have been shown a glimpse of a new society, a new Argentina, where capital and work can march not in conflict, but hand in hand as General Perón and Comrade Eva wanted them to. What Sr Sansimón Senior has done here today is a landmark, and an example to us all, including his son, although right now he doesn't look too happy about it.' They all cheered except the butt of the joke, who had been studying Marroné's face with a frown and redoubled attention ever since he'd taken the floor again. Was he about to recognise him? Well, there wasn't much he could do about it: the die was cast. 'This, comrades, is the real, deep meaning of the word revolution: when those who only yesterday were enemies meet today in brotherhood. And now, comrades, the factory is ours. And not because it's been given to us, even if we are grateful to Sr Sansimón Senior for his gesture; they have merely given back to us what was ours in the first place: this is not an act of charity, but of justice, as Comrade Eva would have wished. The question now is what to do with it? A factory in the hands of its workers . . . Can it be the same factory as before? A new world has opened up before us. What do we want to do with it? The same old thing . . . or something new? Time to get creative, comrades. Let's all put the green hat on for a minute.'

The workers all looked at each other, or rather at their different-coloured helmets with mounting puzzlement.

'Metaphorically speaking,' Marroné clarified. '*Imagine* you're wearing it.'

And that was when Sansimón pounced.

'I know you! You're Macramé you are! Tamerlán's head of procurement!' Then to the others, 'Don't listen to him! This man's deceiving you for his own wicked ends!'

A spectral silence fell. The eyes of the crowd went from Sansimón to Marroné and back to Sansimón, as if they were watching a game of tennis. The spell was broken by a timid voice, which, preceded by a raised hand, rose from the heart of the expectant throng.

'That's not a green-hat proposal.'

There were murmurs of approval for the keenness of the observation, and a ripple of faint applause. The thin-boned, timid-looking young man who had made it smiled with pleasure and even blushed slightly. Again the note of discord came from Sansimón.

'Green hat my arse! This man's an executive from a rival company! Now I get the picture! They want to put me out of business and then buy us for peanuts! They're using you! Can't you see?'

'Brown hat, brown hat!' several of those present demanded. 'If he's going to spread the shit, he should be wearing the right hat!'

An obliging hand landed the right hat on Sansimón's head with such force that the peak came down to the bridge of his nose. Like some circus clown act, they had to help him wrestle it off and put it on again properly.

Still a little befuddled, he began to rant and rave again, but Marroné milked the pause provided by the gag for all it was worth. He spread his arms wide and opened his fingers to call for silence. A couple of elbows to the ribs got the message across to Sansimón.

'White hat reply,' enunciated Marroné, and traded his blue hat for the white of Pampurro, who was still on the platform. 'White, the colour of facts. What Sr Sansimón says, comrades, is all true.'

A sigh of dismay rippled through the congregation. It was exactly what he was looking for. Like stealing candy from a baby, he thought to himself.

'It's true, comrades, because, like all good manipulators, Sr Sansimón deals in half-truths. It's true that I was born with a silver spoon in my mouth . . . But it's also true that I'm adopted and came from a home more humble than many of you. It's true that I came here as an executive of Tamerlán & Sons . . . Who have I kept it from? But taking part in this occupation has changed me, and today I feel like one of you! Just look at me . . . Is this the face of a boss, an oligarch, an exploiter of the working class?' ('No, no,' several people shouted back.) 'It's true that I was posh . . . a little bourgeois . . . a . . . All right, let's hear it, brown hats!'

'A nob! A ponce! A toffee-nosed git!' they supplied enthusiastically, with broad grins.

'Thank you, comrades . . . I expected no less. As I was saying, every word is true . . . But it's also true that Perón was a soldier and Evita was an actress, and if it's rich kids we're talking about, Che Guevara knocks me into a cocked hat!' he concluded just in time, as a fork-lift truck came trundling through the crowd in the direction of the stage, with the imposing bulk of Michelangelo's Moses wobbling in its metal maw.

The Sansimón incident had been a godsend: it had allowed him to inject a little excitement into what otherwise would have been idle time. All those who were with him on the stage, including an increasingly dumbstruck Paddy, helped unload the plaster colossus with the utmost care so that it wouldn't topple over and end up in smithereens on the floor. 'If they only knew what I had in store for them,' thought Marroné, smiling inwardly. After thanking everyone, he asked them all to climb down, as he needed as much space as possible for the next stage. At his request an obliging comrade had laid the sledgehammer at his feet for when he needed it. All eyes were fixed on him; the green helmet was back on his head. Rolling up the sleeves of his overalls, Marroné took a step forwards. The time had come to show these amateurs what a decent audiovisual presentation was all about. If only Sr Tamerlán were there to see it, he thought, before launching into his speech.

'You're all familiar with this gent aren't you, comrades? You've been seeing him day in day out – some of you for years on end – every morning when you come in to work and every evening when you leave. Some of you may know that this is an exact replica of Michelangelo's Moses, the original of which is in Rome. Moses, gentlemen, was a prophet who led his people out of slavery and guided them to the Promised Land, though he himself never set foot in it. Some of you – I can see it in your eyes – think you've already guessed why I've had it brought here. You think I'm going use it to draw an analogy between Sr Sansimón and Pharaoh, between the liberation of the people of Israel and the liberation of the workers of this plasterworks. Well, you're right. And wrong. Just as this Moses is and isn't the real thing. You know what the difference is between this Moses and the one in Rome, comrades?'

Seizing the opportunity of Marroné's pause for effect, the young sculptor raised his hand.

'The other one's made of marble.'

'Exactly!' exclaimed Marroné, pointing at him. 'Our comrade here knows what he's talking about. Our comrade here couldn't be more right. The other one is made of Carrara marble, and Michelangelo – the great Michelangelo – climbed the mountain himself to select a flawless block. But this thing . . . ' He spat on his palms, rubbed them together and, picking up the sledgehammer by the end of its long handle, swung it in a wide arc that ended with a sickening thud full in the great patriarch's stomach. When the cloud of dust had cleared, through the dented mesh and fragments of plaster that hung precariously from their twisted wire threads, all could see the gaping hole Marroné had opened: the left forearm, and much of the chest and abdomen had spilt into the hollow innards of the imposing monument.

'See? See? It's hollow! Hollow like everything we've been landed with from outside. Over there they may be great works of art, comrades; here they're nothing but empty shells. I ask you, comrades, is this the Promised Land that foreign capital is trying to sell us? A beautiful façade, yes . . . But what's inside? Nothing! That's why the General said "Neither Yankees nor Marxists – Peronists", comrades. We don't want anything to do with foreign ideas that later turn out to be as hollow as this dummy. You can stuff your Moseses, your Davids, your Venuses de Milo, your Eiffel Towers! They want to sell us a French pig in an Argentinian poke, comrades! Let's stick with what's ours for once! But what *is* ours, comrades? You don't need me to tell you; even little children know that, comrades! The *Martín Fierro*, the Obelisk, Gardel, Perón and the Difunta Correa! And most of all Evita, the First Worker of our Argentina and the Eternal Guardian of the Revolution, comrades!' The last few phrases he had to yell till he was hoarse to make himself heard above the noise of two hundred roaring mouths. He'd done it. He'd won. The day was his.

'Smash 'em to bits! Destroy the foreign casts!' shouted several enthusiasts, as if they were carrying lighted torches.

Time to channel all that energy.

'Comrades! Comrades! Where are you going? Can't you see the green hat? I haven't told you about my new idea yet.'

Several people laughed. It's true! The idea! The green-hat idea!

'I propose that this new plasterworks – this liberated plasterworks – should be renamed the "Eva Perón Plaster-works" in honour of our Queen of Labour. And to celebrate, the first thing that should come out of its workshop today, yes, today is a consignment of ninety-two busts of Eva Perón. So, just like the days of the Foundation, when our Good Fairy was with us, the first profits will go straight into the pockets of the workers as a gift from Eva Perón. The days when the bloodsuckers kept the biggest slice of the pie are over. On behalf of Tamerlán & Sons I guarantee immediate payment here and now.'

After the lap of honour, with the workers carrying Marroné on their shoulders round the whole perimeter of the factory, they set him back on the stage, beside the battered Moses, and marched in orderly fashion towards the work-shop to finish their task. Hands on hips, Marroné looked on with satisfaction. And Paddy, who had climbed up onto the platform after the celebrations, looking from him to the gaping Moses, and back, was almost lost for words:

'Forgive me, Ernesto. I thought . . . Never in my life have I seen an assembly turned around like that. You're a born cadre,' he said with an embarrassed grin. 'And there's me explaining the difference to you between subjective and objective conditions, and you looking like butter wouldn't melt in your mouth . . . ' No one was close enough to overhear, yet Paddy lowered his voice to a whisper. 'You're a mole, aren't you? Who are you with? The ERP or us?'

'Look . . . ' began Marroné reluctantly.

'I know, I know, don't say a word,' he said, zipping his lips. 'There's just one thing I'd like you to tell me, as long as it doesn't get you into trouble. Where did you get your training? Have you been to Cuba?'

'Eh? No, no,' answered Marroné, whose attention had suddenly detached itself from what was going on around him, as if obeying some inner call.

'Something the matter?' asked Paddy, seeing him so rapt in thought.

'No. Yes,' he answered as a faint smile crept across his face in response to the rare miracle about to repeat itself for the second time in a week. Something in his life was changing, no doubt about it. And, as if to himself, though not so softly that his friend couldn't hear, he said, 'How odd. I have this sudden urge to visit the toilet.'

6

THE SANSIMONAZO

News of the expropriation of the Eva Perón Plasterworks (formerly the Sansimón Plasterworks) by its workers spread through the neighbourhood and local factories like wildfire, and very soon went nationwide on radio and television, which pitched the story under the sensationalist banner 'ARGENTINE SOVIET ERA DAWNS'. So no one was surprised when the number of men and vehicles in the police guard surrounding the premises doubled, and any workers not on Eva production were consigned by their white-helmeted comrades – which now, of course, included 'El Negro' Ernesto – to beef up the military supplies and defence divisions. When he wasn't lingering in dewy-eyed contemplation over the moist Evas accumulating on the drying racks, he would don the brown helmet and assist in the gathering or production of items for the defences: filling bottles with ball bearings and marbles, learning to manufacture caltrops and Molotov cocktails, rolling barrels of fuel or paint stripper to the factory's entrances, confiscating all the pepper supplies from the kitchen or scrounging reserves from neighbouring grocers, inspecting the fire-extinguishers and fire-hoses, which one very hot day he and his comrades ended up turning on themselves, knocking each other over in rowdy cowboy duels, tripping each other up with jets of water as hard as iron bars, in an impromptu carnival romp from which they emerged grinning and drenched.

The episode perfectly encapsulated the general atmosphere that reigned in the liberated factory: they all knew an attempt to take back the Eva Perón Plasterworks was on the cards, but no one believed it was imminent. There were too many of them for one thing, and to a man they were ready to fight to the bitter end in order to defend it. The barrels of fuel and paint stripper stockpiled at the four entrances had been put on display as a gesture for the benefit of the presiding judge, just to let him know that, were the police to attack, they would at best recapture a pile of smoking ruins. And then there were the hostages. It wasn't that the workers meant them any harm, but in the event of an attack they might be tempted to use them as human shields – and who would thank the government for recovering the factory if the owner and its chief executives had to attend the reopening in body bags? The strikers also had the people behind them, as demonstrated by the support of the locals, who cheered them every time they set foot in the neighbourhood, often lavishing provisions on them and waving the strikers away when they offered to pay with what little money they had, and generally egging them on (it was a humble neighbourhood, practically a shanty town in parts). Statements of support kept pouring in from neighbouring factories; student associations and political parties; improvising orators, of whom there was never a shortage at the gate, spoke of the Eva Perón Plasterworks as the vanguard of the proletariat and the spearhead of the Revolution. And as if that weren't enough, Marroné had been going with unprecedented regularity since the day of the assembly. Something of the reigning euphoria must have infected him when he spoke with Govianus the accountant on the phone.

'Is something the matter with you, Marroné? You sound different . . . '

'It's the joy of knowing I'll soon have those ninety-two busts for you, Sr Govianus,' he answered exultantly.

And to some extent it was true. At this rate they'd be packed and loaded by the 24th, a day late, true, and cutting it pretty fine, because, being Christmas Eve, they only worked a half-day; but the assembly had voted to celebrate the recovery of the factory by throwing a big *asado*, open to all – except, of course, police and bureaucrats – and Marroné felt it wasn't the right time to spoil their fun and blow his credit with them by being a stick-in-the-mud and insisting they finish the job first.

The day of the *asado* dawned bright and sunny, albeit on the warm side, and the workers were up early to get everything ready for the big bash. They set up tables from the canteen and workshop in the front gardens, watched over by the now companionless David and, realising there weren't enough, supplemented them with trestles and planks, desks from the offices and even with doors they'd taken off their hinges, draping them with tablecloths of various patterns and colours, contributed by local women, many of them strikers' wives. Makeshift *parrillas* cobbled together from gratings, railings and chicken-wire had to be added to the existing ones, and the vast horseshoe of grills was lined below with beds of glowing coals and above with a lorry load of meat – a gift from the workers at a nearby meat-packing plant – which in no time at all was hissing and crackling over the coals, enveloped in the clouds that rose from the sizzling fat, and emitting the most mouth-watering smells in the world: whole sides of beef trimmed with garlands of black puddings, pork sausages and chitterlings; armies of chickens whose skins crisped and goldened; whole sucking pigs, butterflied and gleaming like polished leather, smiling at the thought of how delicious they'd taste; and there, wielding the long knife and fork of the *asador*, stood El Tuerto, presiding like a grinning Cyclops over this general holocaust of roasting animal flesh. Under a stand of willows, to keep the morning sun off them, stood two tall pyramids of demijohns – one of white, one of red – which had either been donated or sold by local shopkeepers at cost price. There, too, sat heavy wicker baskets lugged by two men apiece and heaped with bread rolls, which, bisected by a brigade of slicers, gaped in anticipation of the sausages and black puddings that would soon fill their jaws. The salad committee were hosing down tubs of lettuces, and slicing tomatoes and onions, then chucking everything into enormous troughs into which others poured bottle after bottle of corn oil and wine vinegar, and tossed it with trowels and wooden spatulas. The blue hats had spent the day before handing out leaflets and sticking up posters, and the news had been spread through a double megaphone atop a Fiat 500, which drove round and round the station square; and all this, coupled with word of mouth and especially the smell that wafted over the brick-and-mortar shacks and corrugated-iron-roofed hovels, and drifted maddeningly in through windows and chinks – passengers were even said to have jumped the train at the station to try their luck – meant that a throng of neighbours and gatecrashers joined the contingents of worker delegates, students and sympathisers, all of whom began milling about among the smoking grills, sitting at the tables or on the lawn, and cadging the first swigs of wine in wax-paper cups. Dozens of children played among the trees, most of them the sons and daughters of workers from the factory, hugging the legs of parents who in some cases hadn't seen them for days, and Marroné looked on at them with a touch of healthy envy. He had called Mabel the night before, suggesting she should drop in with the children to enjoy a day in the country with his new-found friends, an invitation she had not only most emphatically declined but had followed through with a flurry of recriminations and tears for all the time he'd been away, which segued seamlessly into the subject of the seasonal festivities: 'Mum and Dad are expecting us on Christmas Eve like every year, and I've already made arrangements with yours for . . . ' Marroné had been non-committal, and Mabel took a breath before launching into a second tirade, 'I knew it! I knew it! I knew this was all an excuse for you to snub them! I know you, Ernesto Marroné!' 'No, you don't,' he said to her, after he'd hung up, 'and if you think things are going to be the same when I come back – if I do come back – you've got another thing coming.' Still, all in good time; for the moment he could just wander and gaze at the kites overhead, listening to the crackle of their paper and the snap of their tails every time the hovering police helicopter flew off, watching any of three football games taking place in the unwooded parts of the grounds, listening to the music from the bands playing on the podium that had been Marroné's stairway to glory, now reassembled under the shade of the pines. A four-piece was onstage; *siku, quena, charango* and *bombo*, played by swarthy young men in ponchos with vicuña and cactus motifs: it was The Atahualpas.

> *'Through the jungles of Bolivia*
> *Always watchful, never trivial,*
> *On a mule called Rocinante*
> *Rides this new knight-comandante.*
> *He's the Revolution's tiara*
> *And his name is Che . . . ?'*

. . . they asked, pausing and pointing at the audience of wised-up youths, most with long hair and haversacks, who chorused back 'Guevara!', and yelled *'Presente!'* and *'Viva!'* Another coincidence, or rather sign, mused Marroné, who hadn't missed the unmistakeable reference to his colleague from La Mancha.

But most of the time he simply strolled about, enjoying the transformation of the factory's green lawn into a public park, now and then issuing directives or dealing with workers' queries: the comrades standing guard in the factory were asking to be relieved ('Time up,' he answered); should we take the hostages something to eat ('What hostages?'), or invite them to join in? ('Screw them, the exploiting scum!'); the people wanted to cool down with the fire-hoses, could they? ('Water to the people!'), and every query concluded with the invariable 'What should we do, Ernesto?', which became the badge and catchphrase associated with the new Marroné. At one point in this constant toing and froing he ran into Paddy, who had also been rushing back and forth, fielding people's questions. They stood together for a moment, looking on at the spectacle unfolding before their eyes.

'Now you see why I became a proletarian?' his friend exclaimed exultantly. 'Just look at this. Where else do you find fervour like this?'

Marroné recalled the stands back in St Andrew's celebrating Paddy's try against St George's, but for some reason he felt it would be unwise to bring it up.

Out of sheer contentment Paddy put his arm around Marroné's shoulder, shaking him, then squeezing him tight. Marroné felt a lump rise to his throat and for a moment he was on the verge of confessing to his part in the coloured-chalk episode, but then he thought it might ruin the moment and let it pass.

'We'll beat those sonsofbitches with sheer people power! This is what our Revolution's all about, Ernesto! Look at their faces! Who's going to stop us now, for Christ's sake!'

'Comrade . . . '

They both turned round at the same time. The man in mirrored sunglasses who had spoken was dressed in a light leather jacket, zipped up to the collar in spite of the heat, his hair slicked behind his ears into an astrakhan of tight curls at the nape.

'Miguel!' Paddy said with pleasant surprise. 'How's it going?'

He made to embrace him, but Miguel held out his hand coldly, ignoring the one Marroné had politely extended in his direction.

'What's all this, Colorado?' he said to Paddy.

'This? It's the people in power!'

'But Colorado . . . I waltzed in through the front gate like I owned the place. No one to stop me. Your security . . . it's a mess! Haven't you seen the pigs outside?'

Paddy gestured at the factory gardens, which looked like a public promenade on a bank holiday. The thunderous thudding of the helicopter overhead again drowned out part of his reply, ' . . . enough people power!'

Marroné still stood beside them, biding his time. Only then did the newcomer seem to notice his presence.

'And who's this?'

'I thought *you* people had sent him,' answered Paddy, looking at Marroné with dawning perplexity.

The time had come to seize the initiative.

'Ernesto,' was all he said, having been aware for some time now that guerrilla leaders never gave their surnames, and, with his best *How-to-Win-Friends* smile, held out his right hand again, this time right in the face of the ill-mannered Miguel, who had no option but to shake it. He even responded by cracking a tense smile.

'Ah, yes. A pleasure, comrade. Heard a lot about you. You saved the occupation in injury time. You're from the North Column, aren't you?'

Marroné's own house being in Olivos and his parents' in Vicente López, he felt authorised to answer in the affirmative. Ah well, in for a penny . . . Miguel turned back to Paddy, his tone and facial expression hardening perceptibly.

'Well, Colorado, for a start you can tell your happy people to up and leave right now. The party's over.'

'But . . . '

'Are you questioning a direct order?'

Marroné watched the colour rise to Paddy's neck and cheeks. He had seen him like this at school when some master or other was giving him a mouthful. The newcomer's high-handedness made Marroné smile to himself. At school no one could keep Paddy down. How much less now that he had the whole of the people behind him.

'No,' said Paddy, bowing his head.

Marroné was dumbfounded. He was in the presence of something unheard of, or at least beyond his ken. Paddy taking orders, meekly and obediently.

'Maybe I'm wrong, you tell me. You reckon there's a lot to celebrate? You liberated a factory, true . . . but 99.9 per cent are still in the hands of the capitalists and the bureaucracy. And by making the workers owners of the company, you're actually deproletarianising them . . . giving them a taste for capitalism. A typical liberal, petit bourgeois deviation, and proof that the proletarianisation process in you is only skin-deep . . . Scratch your surface a bit and all that good old English education shines through. You've been fraternising with the unions too long, Colorado. Our organisation does not pander to trade unions: it dictates to them. We can't afford to fight for the workers' creature comforts in this one and then let them go all bourgeois on us: they have to be toughened up and made ready to seize power. We're not asking for soap for the toilets any more; we're making the Revolution not just for the happy few,' he said, taking in the motley throng with a sweep of his hand, 'but for everyone. So now, if you haven't got the balls for the Revolution, just let us know and we'll sort it out no sweat, because there are hundreds of comrades willing to lay down their lives in your place. A strike's no laughing matter, Colorado. As long as there's a single Argentine that suffers, it's our duty to suffer with them. What are you celebrating here? The fact that, while you're stuffing your faces, the underfed minors working in the Tucumán sugar mills are starving to death?

Or that you're getting pissed here while our comrades fighting in the mountains are drinking their own, just like they had to in Che's column?'

Paddy made the most of the pause to collect his scattered thoughts.

'The strike, the occupation, the recovery . . . it was decided by all of us, in assembly. We should hold another one if we're going to suspend the celebrations. And I don't think the vote will go in our favour . . . ' he countered. 'Me, I don't give orders to anyone here.'

'I know, Colorado. *I* do. Look,' he said, resting one hand on Paddy's shoulder, who tensed visibly as if someone had just jabbed him with an awl. 'I know that at the end of the day you've done important work here. Even your deviations weren't the product of bad intentions. So I'll make an exception and let you in on a couple of things. If Ernesto agrees, that is.'

Marroné nodded and acknowledged the courtesy with a curt smile.

'The leadership has something big up its sleeve . . . First, we're going to get the union back . . . You know what I'm talking about. Babirusa's one block we can't afford to stumble over again, you know that better than me . . . Meanwhile, mingling with all these lovely citizens strolling in through the gates you so generously left open, the big cheeses from the union are wandering around taking notes on the means of access, the cracks in the defence and the folk they're going to whack – with you top of the list. That's one reason to wrap this carnival up: it's a serious breach of security. Easily fixed though. I've sent for our people; they'll be here before nightfall. But your liberal antics have called for a stronger remedy. I'm relieving you of your duties, Colorado. You're being moved to the military front. That way you'll still be fighting for all of . . . them.' He gestured vaguely towards the factory building. 'Just in a different arena. Look on it as a promotion if you like. We have to move forward, Colorado, take the leap to the next stage. The days of the specialist cadre are over; what we're looking for now are all-rounders who'll tackle anything we throw at them. Every militant has to be a soldier prepared to lay down his or her life.'

Marroné was about to chip in with a helpful quote from *The Corporate Samurai*, but thought better of it, as it might give him away. Paddy frowned, more concerned now than annoyed, until in the end he ventured to ask:

'You're going to whack Babirusa. And you want me in on it.'

'Is that a problem?'

'No . . . But . . . Is it necessary? We'll wipe the floor with them at the elections. Just look at all this.'

'I have. You said the same thing last time. And two days before the election Babirusa got into bed with the management and they fired all the comrades on the rival list. Babirusa's a traitor to the workers' cause. And he has the blood of several of your comrades on his hands, in case you'd forgotten.'

Paddy had starting to fume again.

'Course I haven't forgotten. Are you suggesting . . . '

'I never suggest; I say. So? You're scared?'

'No, Miguel. It's just that your way we erase all differences. Even if that traitor Babirusa bags the elections with fraud – or with blood – he'll still be branded a traitor. But if we whack him, what does that prove? You can whack anyone, makes no difference if it's Tosco or Vandor.'

'See what a petty petit bourgeois you are? All we need now is for you to start carrying on about the sacred value of human life. Know what, Colorado? In case you hadn't heard, our objective here isn't to end up moral champions, but to make the Revolution. The Revolution isn't for the faint-hearted, in case you didn't know. Now, let's get the job done because I'm starting to get a bit pissed off. We'll have tea and scones together another day if you want to go on talking. Right, you've a five-o'clock appointment on the last bench at the station, downtown platform. Meanwhile we'll pull the plug on this little shindig. Coming, Ernesto? People still don't know me around here, so I'll leave the talking to you.'

Marroné nodded because he was in no position to refuse, though he'd rather have stayed with his dejected friend. He grabbed him firmly by one arm all the same and gave him a hearty slap of encouragement on the other, but then turned round out of reflex to make sure he hadn't stained Paddy's white overalls with coloured chalk.

'I like El Colorado,' Miguel said to Marroné as they walked away. 'Give him time and I think he'll make a helluva cadre. Trouble is, he was a bit old when we got hold of him. Certain vices are very deep-rooted after a certain age . . . You can't wash the stigma of English school away with a bit of elbow grease. Training a real worker cadre takes years, as you well know. Ah well . . . A bit of the old hand-to-hand won't hurt him. So there's no need for you people to worry because, as you can see for yourself, everything here's right on track . . . '

At these words Marroné almost slapped his forehead. So that was it! Miguel had taken him for an observer sent by the upper echelons, and he'd gone to town on Paddy's reprimand in order to ingratiate himself. It had felt familiar from the start, a paranoia, commonplace enough in the world of business, that became attached to every newcomer to the office. Oh, well. Miguel's misunderstanding could work to his advantage if he was careful not to put his foot in it.

'You work at Tamerlán, don't you?'

Had Miguel rumbled him? Marroné's heart skipped a beat.

'Keep your friends close . . . ' he mumbled.

'Brilliant,' concluded Miguel. 'Always need somebody on the inside. Impeccable operation from start to finish . . . ran like clockwork. Did you come up with the plan?'

'I just sent in the intelligence,' answered Marroné with a false modesty that Miguel took as a yes, as Marroné had expected him to.

Joined by Miguel, who followed him everywhere like his shadow, Marroné went about waking up the workers sleeping it off under the trees, ordering them to down some coffee and don the right hat; he had the entrance gate closed and gave the gatekeeper strict instructions to open it only for those who were leaving; he had the embers doused, the unopened demijohns stored in the warehouse, the footballs rounded up, the tails of the kites rolled up, and the general shower of paper cups and plates, serviettes, plastic bottles and butt-ends that had fallen on the green lawn raked into piles and swept into binbags. It wasn't a pleasant task but it had to be done, and a sign of the new-found discipline and influence among the workers was that, although a few grumbled and others answered him with a reluctant 'Now, Ernesto?', not one argued or shirked when it came to doing their jobs. His companion was more impressed by the minute, and Marroné, who was bursting with pride, could see himself in the not-too-distant future sharing his rich experience with a spellbound audience in a leadership seminar. 'A born leader will lead no matter what,' was the byword that formed magically in his mind, and he made a mental note to jot it down in his notebook as soon as he found time for a breather.

The people Miguel had promised arrived in a minibus that same night. There were six of them: four men and two women, all young, thought Marroné, though he never got to see them up close. They wore jeans or work trousers, training shoes and t-shirts or open-necked work shirts, and carried long bags so heavy they seemed to stretch their arms; their load clunked with hardware when they set it down. Miguel spent five minutes whispering to them, after which they melted into the shadows.

'If you agree,' Miguel said to Marroné as soon as they'd gone, 'I'll take over the military command, so we don't get under each others' feet. But we'll plan the overall strategy together.'

They decided to set up the command post in Sansimón's office, which had been vacated at Marroné's suggestion 'to put an end to unfair privileges'. The moment they set foot in it, they reeled from the stink of confinement: the sweat, the fags, the spilt beer, the stale food and yes . . . even rancid semen. In the space of just a few days the top brass had shed their veneer of civilisation, which apparently included basic hygiene. Marroné gave the cleaning committee a stern telling-off: just because they were bosses and exploiters of the working class didn't justify their having been kept in degrading conditions. We don't want to come down to their level, he told the committee, taking inward delight in the squalid scene; and, quick as a flash, they opened the windows to let some fresh air in, took out the rubbish, sprayed the place with deodorant and vacuumed the floor. He and Miguel stuck around sipping maté until dinner-time, with lights off to be on the safe side as the broad window looked onto the street, making them sitting ducks for any crack snipers posted out there. Bringing all his business acumen to bear, Marroné said little and listened hard, asking precise questions and giving open-ended answers, constantly reminding himself it was Miguel not him who was under examination, which his counterpart did indeed seem absolutely convinced of and talked a blue streak in his efforts to ingratiate himself with the superiors who had sent Marroné in to spy.

'The idea is that each occupied factory acts as a trap for the union's bully boys, the Triple A and the police. We plant a platoon of fighters in each, under heavy cover. Then we whack some union bureaucrat, see, to provoke them. When they waltz in thinking all they're up against is workers with small arms and no target practice, they'll cop the surprise of their lives. They won't catch us napping again; this'll be *their* Ezeiza massacre, you can be sure of that. And when the people see them running out, they'll realise we're the only ones who'll stand by them.'

Marroné nodded at everything in agreement and even permitted himself the luxury of implying that none of this would be overlooked when the comrade came up for promotion. But that night, after taking a shower and donning clean overalls – a garment he now felt as comfortable in as if he'd been wearing it all his life – and lying down on the sofa bed in what had once been Garaguso's office, he found it impossible to get to sleep: every little noise made him jump, imagining as he did that it might be the crunch of a boot, the hammering of a semi-automatic rifle, the sound of a grenade rolling across the floor; so he decided to get up and do the rounds of the pickets on guard duty to make sure they were all alert and at their posts. The night was as cool and clear as the day had been hot and radiant and, remembering that tomorrow would be Christmas Eve (or rather today, as it had just struck midnight), he looked up at the sky, as if searching for a new Star of Bethlehem to announce the birth of . . . who? The new Ernesto Marroné?

The armed guards at the main gate were clearly visible, silhouetted against the police floodlights; low voices could be heard at the sentry posts on the eastern perimeter and at the northern corner, and the night fires burnt brightly; only at the southern corner did darkness and silence reign: there lay El Tuerto and Pampurro, fast asleep, having been at the bottle throughout. Pampurro was leaning against a tree trunk with a certain decorum, and El Tuerto was sprawled on the damp grass, snoring, saliva dribbling from his open maw. Marroné stooped to pick up the fallen weapon, which turned out to be Sansimón's Smith & Wesson, and cocked it by El Tuerto's ear, but got no more response out of him than a resounding grunt. Pushing him with the tip of his shoe, he rocked him back and forth until one sleepy eye opened.

'I think you dropped this, comrade,' he said, swinging the gun on one finger by the trigger guard.

Hauling himself upright, El Tuerto gave him a roguish grin and held out his upturned wrists as much as to say 'It's a fair cop', while Marroné slowly uncocked the gun and laid it on El Tuerto's open palms. He gave him a quick two-fingered salute and walked away whistling, making a V for victory at the whispered 'Thanks, Ernesto!' behind him. They were good men after all, just a bit short of training.

He hadn't run into any of the Montoneros Miguel had sent for, but that came as no surprise: professionals of their standing wouldn't let themselves be spotted that easily. But the exception proves the rule, Marroné confirmed yet again as he crossed the entrance to the right transept and made out a figure beyond the green machines, sitting with its back to him under one of the many lights that hung from the roof, orbited by insects. It was one of the two girls, he found out as he approached stealthily and saw her long, chestnut hair tumbling loose down her back. As he walked around her, he discovered what it was that had her so engrossed: on her lap lay an open book. In his surprise – she was the first reader he'd come across since he'd arrived – he must have made a noise, for a second later the girl had dropped the book with a startled shout and was pointing her FAL straight at his head. But this wasn't what left Marroné paralysed and open-mouthed; it was the face of the young woman now staring into his, her eyes bulging with fright. Marroné had recognised her immediately. It was Eva. She too seemed to recognise him, because she instantly lowered her gun and saluted.

'Forgive me.'

Marroné said the first thing that came into his head.

'At ease, comrade.' He pointed to the fallen book. 'Reading, are we?'

Impulsively Eva made to grab it, but Marroné stopped her with a chivalrous palm and crouched to pick it up. It was a paperback with a fuchsia-pink cover, from the base of which rose a forest of raised hands, two or three with open palms, but most with index fingers pointing upwards; Marroné's almost physical sensation of discomfort was so intense that he couldn't help glancing at Eva's face to see if she had noticed. But she only seemed concerned about the book, whose predictable title, *The Wretched of the Earth*, meant nothing to him, even though the name of its author, Frantz Fanon, was vaguely familiar. Out of sheer curiosity he opened it at random.

'Please can I have it back?' begged Eva, holding out her hand. 'I swear it won't happen again . . . '

'Don't worry,' Marroné said, all condescension and bonhomie. 'Guard duty can get pretty tedious, I know. But I don't need to tell you what could have happened if it had been the enemy instead of me.'

She nodded contritely, brushing the hair from her face. There was no doubt about it: she was the Eva in the photonovel and, with her light-brown hair down like that, she reminded him especially of the young woman posing cheerfully in her polka-dot bathing costume: he would have liked to make her laugh, see her smile again, this time in the flesh.

'What's your name?' he asked her.

'María Eva,' she answered, after a slight hesitation.

Of course, thought Marroné. It was her *nom de guerre*,

obviously, and it would have to do, because a guerrilla leader would never ask for her real one.

'So María Eva's a reader, is she?' he said in a tone that was trying to be pleasant but, he realised too late, made him sound like a secondary-school teacher ticking her off. 'Don't worry,' he hastened to correct it. 'We'll keep it just between you and me this time. I'm an avid reader too, I read whenever I can, even on the . . . er . . . the bus,' he said, nimbly negotiating the hurdle he had inadvertently set himself. 'May I?' he said, opening up the book at random and starting to read:

To begin with, the impossibility of going up to a woman, the risk of never seeing her again another day, suddenly lend her the same charm as illness or poverty will to a place they prevent us from visiting, or the fray in which we shall surely die to the dull days we have still to live. So that, were it not for habit, life should seem delicious to those people who may at every hour be in danger of dying – all mankind, that is. Then, though the imagination is carried away by the desire for something we cannot possess, its flight is not held back by a reality fully perceived, in these chance meetings in which the charm of the passer-by generally stands in direct proportion to their briskness. The night may fall and the coach go fast, in the country, in a town, but there is no female torso, mutilated like an ancient marble by the speed which draws us on and the dusk which shrouds it, that, at every corner of the road, in the depths of every lighted shop, does not fire Beauty's arrows at our heart – Beauty, which tempts one to wonder at times if it is anything in this world but a makeweight added by our imagination, overwrought as it is by regret, to the fleeting and fragmentary shadow of a woman passing by.

In his astonishment Marroné checked the top of the page: *In the Shadow of Young Girls in Bloom*. Intrigued, he looked at the first page: 127. Then he clicked: what he was holding was a fragment of a larger work, torn from the original and stuck inside another book's cover.

'Please, don't tell my superior,' he heard María Eva's voice say. 'Last time he caught me reading Proust, he made me write a self-criticism. If he finds out I've lapsed again . . . '

'So that's why you hid it inside the Fanon, is it?' he asked with a smile.

María Eva flashed him a smile, at once shy and impish. The first. She was definitely the Eva in the photonovel. But he decided to wait until they were on closer terms, before he asked her.

'So, do you like him?'

'Fanon? Well, sure, he's right about everything he says, of course: the culture of the coloniser and the colonised, right? Of course, the situation in Africa's a bit different from ours . . . I mean, when he wrote it, they really were colonies . . . '

'No, Proust,' he cut her short.

She spoke quickly, almost apologetically, as if ashamed of her own enthusiasm.

'Aaaah. Sure! Well, I mean, he's a real bourgeois; no, if only, not even a bourgeois; he's an out-and-out oligarch: all

those princesses and marquises, and their residences . . .
They're all such snobs . . . It's almost embarrassing at times.
You'd think there'd never been a revolution in France. And
he's sooo European . . . I know the comrades gave me funny
looks when they found out, but I dunno, it's kind of like a
vice . . . And there are other things about him . . . his relationship with his mother – wanting her to tuck him in and
all that, and Swann's love for Odette, and the walks around
Méséglise and Guermantes . . . You're reading and suddenly
you're there, in the countryside . . . Oh, I'm sorry . . . I'm
talking as if everyone had read him. That's so rude of me,
I'm always doing that. Comrade, have you ever . . . ?'

'Please, call me Ernesto,' he reassured her, desperately
scrabbling in his memory for scraps of information about
Proust: he'd written *In Search of Lost Time*; there were several
volumes; and it had something to do with memories . . . But,
as far as he knew, there wasn't a single business title along
the lines of *In Search of Lost Profits* or *In the Shadow of Young
Markets in Bloom*.

'No, I can never find the time for things like that,' he
quipped. 'As you know, being an officer isn't a part-time . . .
er . . . But you have to take a break occasionally, don't you.
You can't be reading Marx and Lenin and Mao all the time,
now, can you. At the moment, for example, I'm reading . . . '
He took a breath before saying, '*Don Quixote*.'

This time he was rewarded with the full, radiant, eternal
smile of the photo.

'I don't believe it. I finished it a couple of months ago.
I can still remember the day. Oh, when he died all huddled
up and shrivelled like that, it made me feel so sad . . . I wept
like a little girl.'

Marroné looked at her sternly.

'Now you've told me how it ends.'

María Eva clapped her hand over her mouth and opened her eyes wide in horror.

'Only joking. I know how it ends,' he lied to reassure her.

María Eva suddenly seemed to recall where she was and looked anxiously around her.

'I should be getting back to my post, shouldn't I? If Miguel were to see me . . . '

'I'll take the rap,' said Marroné, squaring his shoulders and puffing out his chest to assert his rank.

'Thanks.' That smile again. 'It's just that . . . Miguel isn't just my superior . . . he's my partner, you see?'

Marroné did see, and intercepted the downward rictus of his mouth just in time.

'Right,' he said, trying not to let his disappointment show. 'Maybe we'll find more time to talk tomorrow. I just wanted to ask you one thing: are you the Eva in the photonovel?'

This time she reacted differently: she blushed in shame, like her biblical namesake, but covered her face rather than her sex.

'Don't tell me you've read it,' she said through her fingers.

'Yes. You're the one who plays Eva, aren't you?'

María Eva took her hand from her face and gave a tight-lipped nod.

'Why are you embarrassed about it? You look great.'

María Eva stared at him for a second, as if trying to guess the reply expected of her.

'Yes, I know. I really admire Eva, and I loved playing her; I took it really seriously. Course, I had to go on a diet for the part about her illness . . . *The Reason for My Life* can be a bit daft in places, like this little fairy tale, but then we all know it was ghosted for her when she was ill . . . We tried to bring out the real Eva. The original script was really good, I don't know if you've read it . . . It was by a comrade, Marcos, you know. They rewrote bits of it later, to make it more militant, beef up the slogans.' It suddenly seemed to dawn on her that, as a leader, Marroné may well have been the one who'd ordered the changes in the first place, because she abruptly interrupted herself. 'It isn't a criticism, eh. I know what we need isn't armchair literature, but books for the trenches. Still, I dunno, I find the whole idea of these militant photo-novels a bit hard to swallow. They're bourgeois prejudices of mine, aren't they. As a girl I was taught they were just pulp for the pig-ignorant, because they were read by proles. But why shouldn't a well-made photonovel ultimately be as valuable as a film, or a comic? I'm not talking about *El Tony* or *Intervalo*; I'm talking Oesterheld, right?'

Marroné nodded, though he hadn't the faintest idea what she was talking about. He was overwhelmed by the strangeness of it all: a beautiful young woman dressed in worker's clothes, packing an FAL and discussing Proust was nothing his previous life had prepared him for.

'So, you aren't going to ask a worker to read this,' she said, holding up the copy of Fanon, although she may also have been referring to the Proust within. 'But there's one thing I don't get . . . I mean, I'm told not to read Proust because he's bourgeois, because he's European, because the people won't understand him . . . Yet everyone in Cuba reads Lezama Lima, or Carpentier, and neither of them have a trace of the worker about them . . . And that's ultimately why we're leading the Revolution, isn't it? The Russians

214

didn't burn the Hermitage. They opened it up to the people. I don't know . . . I suppose you have to renounce Proust at this stage . . . and reclaim him after the Revolution, when we can read him properly – all of us, not just a select clique. I felt the same when I used to act.'

'You're an actress?'

'Couldn't you tell, from the photonovel?' she said with a coy laugh.

'Film or television?'

'No, just the theatre.'

'So what made you give it up?'

'Well, you guys don't leave us much spare time, actually. Don't take it the wrong way, I'm only kidding. Let's see . . . how can I put it? One day . . . I saw the face of the audience. I was playing Nora, and I slammed the door and rattled the wings night after night just so that all those good married ladies could go home happy. Antigone too: I buried my brother to keep the spectators from being alarmed by all those corpses they were reading about in the papers. Then I read Brecht and realised I was falling into the trap of cathartic theatre. I realised I was acting to soothe the guilty consciences of the bourgeoisie. I took my act to the shanties, but the feeling just wouldn't go away . . . What I was doing wasn't getting through because my acting was still bourgeois. That was when I realised that, much as I loved it, I had to give up the stage . . . But then, everything we renounce now the triumph of the Revolution will give us back a thousandfold, won't it? So that's how I went from acting to action. Just like Evita. Goodness! Now I really do have to get back to my post. I've really enjoyed talking to you . . . er . . . '

'Ernesto,' repeated Marroné, who, if truth be told, had barely said a word, this time not because he was applying the sixth rule of *How to Win Friends and Influence People*, but out of dumbstruck devotion.

He bade her goodbye with a vaguely military salute, but gave it a nonchalant air as if to say 'We're bigger than all this', and began to climb the spiral staircase to avoid the service lift, which was too noisy. He spent a while leafing through the photonovel, looking for photos of María Eva, tenderly caressing the polka dots on her bathing costume and the breasts beneath her uniform, then switched off the light and lay there turning over their conversation in his mind; only when bars of dawn began to filter in through the shutters did he manage to catch a couple of hours' sleep.

First thing in the morning he found himself in the canteen, sharing the breakfast of rolls and *maté cocido* with his comrades, when Zenón, his transistor radio glued to his ear, raised his voice over the general hubbub to announce:

'Babirusa! They've taken him out!'

Instantly, like a goal celebration at the Sunday match, a deafening victory roar shook the canteen windows and helmets flew into the air, landing on heads and feet, smashing plates and cups. The workers hugged and kissed, or pinched each others' cheeks, and some even climbed onto the benches, jumping up and down as if they were on the terraces, and singing:

> *'Babirusa, you brass whore,*
> *Say Hello to old Vandor!'*

Zenón, who still had his ear glued like a plunger to the radio, interrupted the revelling to relay the devil in the detail.

'Mown down outside his house. Got one of his body-guards too. Hasn't checked out yet, but they're saying he won't make it.'

But Zenón's running commentary didn't seem to make any difference to the mood of the diners, who gave another raucous cheer and carried on regardless with the old chants. At least, thought Marroné, the workers didn't pull their punches when it came to expressing themselves. He thought it unlikely that, if anything similar happened to Sr Tamerlán, the office staff would dare to be so open about their feelings, even if many in private wished him the worst that fate could throw at him. How very petit bourgeois!

Amidst occasional laughter, jokes like 'Heard the new song about Babirusa? Which song? The one that goes "And though the holes were rather small . . . "' and the odd little sing-song, the workers slowly dispersed to their respective posts. As soon as the Evas were finished, they'd be off to their homes to get ready for Christmas Eve; and after Christmas – a working-class Christmas at last – they'd be back to full production: no more exploitation, no more capital gain, no more alienated labour; the Eva Perón Plasterworks was liberated territory and in it the socialist utopia was very much a fait accompli, Marroné told the workers as he bid them goodbye with a pat on the back or – the more trusted ones – a slap on the buttocks. They were still leaving and he was about to join them, when he came face to face with a ghost. It was Paddy. All expression had drained from his face and his eyes were dead.

'Pa . . . Colo! Come here, sit down. Have you had any breakfast? Fancy a bite to eat?'

'Not hungry. Gimme something to drink.'

Marroné clicked his fingers for Pampurro, who was in charge of the kitchen today, to bring him a *maté cocido*. Paddy gulped it down thirstily, his throat bulging at every swig.

'Everything all right?'

Paddy shook his head.

'Want to talk about it?'

Paddy repeated the gesture.

Marroné sat beside him for a few minutes, watching him, keeping him company. It pained him to see his friend in this state, although, if he were being truly honest with himself, part of him envied him too. He'd been in a shoot-out; he'd fired at other people – maybe he'd even *killed someone* too. Would *he* have the guts if he found himself in Paddy's shoes? He didn't think so, but life sometimes had surprises up its sleeve. If someone had told him the morning he'd left his house, as he did every day, on his way to what was then the Sansimón Plasterworks, that in little over a week he would have become a strike leader and be taken for part of the top brass in a guerrilla army . . . what would he have replied? That they be locked up without delay, no doubt. It was one of the lessons he'd learnt from reading about the life of Eva Perón. Who are we really? Who really knows what they're capable of under certain circumstances and what they aren't? Perhaps his friend was asking himself the same questions right now. Or perhaps, he corrected himself, looking again at the expression on Paddy's face, he'd found some answers. Which didn't seem to be to his liking.

'All right . . . I'm going to see how production's going,' he said eventually, slapping his knees.

Paddy barely looked at him as, in a broken voice, he said:

'They saw me, Ernesto. Babirusa's people are looking for me right now. Look at me.' A flap of his hand took in the flaming beacon of his hair and beard. 'You can spot me a mile off. I'll have to go underground for a while.'

'You're safe here,' Marroné reassured him in all confidence. 'The comrades and I will look after you. Miguel's brought in six specialists . . . '

'Yeah, I know. But I never wanted to go underground. I'm a born front man, me. My thing is to be among the people. But if I stick around here I'm fucked.'

'Now you're being melodramatic,' said Marroné jovially. 'If you ask me, it sounds like they're the ones whose days are numbered. Just like the whole capitalist system, right?' he said, thumping him on the back.

When he stepped outside, he came across a bizarre sight, even by recent standards. A vast cloud of butterflies was crossing the factory gardens; it must have been some kind of migration, for they were all flying in the same direction, approximately due west: they were coming from behind the workers' quarter, beyond the entrance gate, pouring through the gaps in the ever-tighter cordon of police cars and policemen, or flying straight over their heads and then crossing the wire fence, in which some got caught and fluttered for a few seconds. The ones that made it through crossed the entire premises of the factory and, after negotiating the wire on the other side, disappeared into the first outcrops of the shanty town beyond the black waters of the stream. As far as he could tell, they were all the same size and pattern, but wore a variety of colours: rust-tinted orange, lemon yellow, greeny yellow, immaculate white and sky blue, and when he managed to catch one in his fingers – it wasn't hard, all he had to do was put his hand in the air and they would fly into it – he could see at closer quarters the hairy body, the iridescent eyes, the bright-green buttons of the antennae and the grey rim at the apex of the wings. He let it flutter off and gazed with curiosity at the coloured dust it left on his fingertips, and it was as if a distant memory were trying to come back to him. Rubbing his hands on his overalls, he set off back to the workshop. On his way, he ran into two workers swatting butterflies like houseflies as they walked, but a third – the man he had christened Edmundo Rivero – had stopped whatever it was he'd been doing and was gazing at them transfixed, his mouth half-open under the weight of his jaw, his great hands hanging motionless at his sides.

In the workshop everything was running like a dream. The workers greeted him without looking up from their tasks, which they tackled with renewed glee and determination now that everything was theirs; and Sansimón Senior, who was still directing operations, came over to welcome him in person and, taking him by the arm, steered him in the direction of the workbenches. The last of the Evas had just come out of the drier and was waiting alongside nineteen companions to be packed away in its nest of tow and wood, and loaded onto the van with the seventy-two others. He ran his fingertip over the delicate, slender neck and rounded chin, slowly traced the outline of the enigmatic smile, ascended the slight curvature of the nose, the open forehead, the hair pasted to the skull and the intricate, tightly tied bun that would reveal the fate of the country to the hero who could unravel it. They were his. He'd done it. In a couple of hours at most he'd be back at the office, Govianus would congratulate him, Sr Tamerlán would be released, Cáceres Grey would be sacked, and Marroné would be handed his job or any other he asked for.

It was all too good to last, he realised a second later when he heard the first dull bang and knew without needing to be told that things had returned to their usual state of catastrophe. The first shot set off a string of others, and several smoke grenades came crashing in through the windows in a hailstorm of broken glass, and ricocheted into two busts of Eva, splitting one of them open on the table and sending the other crashing to the floor. The men in the workshop ran back and forth willy-nilly, the way ants do when their nest has been kicked; some had tied handkerchiefs over their noses against the smoke, but most were just groping their way towards the exit, pushing and shoving and trampling everything in their way, including of course the odd bust that had fallen from the rocking shelves. Wearing the black hat of the defenders, El Tuerto climbed onto the table in a heroic attempt to stem the pandemonium, but managed only to play Godzilla to the few Evas still left intact on the table.

'Remain calm, comrades! Fall back in orderly fashion! The factory is yours! Defend it!' he shouted in between the coughing fits that tore through his throat. A single idea was hammering on the anvil of Marroné's brain: the van. Save the van! Get in the driver's seat, put your foot down, drive through the hail of bullets, hunched over the wheel, straight through the wire if necessary and don't stop till you've reached 300 Paseo Colón and delivered the seventy-two busts, packed and parcelled, and later, in some other life, worry about the twenty that were missing. As soon as he put his head round the door, he knew that not even that grace would be his: hit by some projectile or set alight by the workers as a barricade, the van was now an orb of fire, its precious cargo aflame on its pyre of tow and wood. The heat forced Marroné to back away.

'They've sent in the Air Force! We're being bombed!' a boy running past shouted to him, his eyes bulging with fright. But it wasn't true; at least, when he looked up at the sky, Marroné could see no aircraft raking across it, hear no roar of jet engines; all he made out were a few lost butterflies, straggling and directionless, which, smothered by the fumes and smoke, fell to the ground as if gassed.

Coughing up his lungs and groping blind and swollen-eyed, Marroné made his way back to the now empty workshop. If he was quick, he kept repeating, there was still time to save a few; he could charge back and forth from workshop to car with an Eva under each arm, through the crossfire and explosions, until he'd saved the last remaining bust, but no sooner had the thought taken shape in his brain than a tank came crashing through the brick wall, knocking all the Evas off their shelves, its caterpillars proceeding to grind the few unbroken by the fall to dust.

'Back to the factory! Back to the factory!' shouted a distant voice in the fog, and Marroné, whose brain was too battered to think for itself, followed the order, dragging himself out of the workshop on all fours.

On his way to the factory he came across the young rebel office worker, Ramírez, running along the outer wall of the transept clutching a machine gun. They took cover at what had been the inner corner of the left transept of the building and crouched down together for a moment.

'What are you doing here?' Marroné asked him in amazement.

'To Die in Madrid!' came back the cryptic reply and, planting one knee squarely on the ground, he started firing on the tank, which was pivoting in search of a target. Two bottles came from nowhere and smashed over its skin of iron, bathing it in fuel but failing to burst into flame. 'What are they trying to do? *Clean* it? The bloody incompetents spout World Revolution and don't even know how to mix a bloody Molotov,' spat his mind in contempt. To avoid being blown to pieces together with Ramírez, Marroné staggered off, his arms wheeling like a drunk. What was all this? What was Ramírez, the paper-pusher who'd been wearing a pink shirt and green tartan tie when they'd met, doing firing on an armoured car with a machine gun? Who was in charge of the casting in this ridiculous film?

No sooner had he emerged from the smoke and the entrance was in sight than a giant's hand slammed into his chest, sending him flying backwards, skidding wildly on his backside. As he flailed to free himself from its grip, he realised he was soaking wet.

'Whoa, hey! It's Ernesto!'

His own men had hit him with the fire-hose. 'At least we didn't plug you one,' said the arms that picked him up off the floor and dragged him inside by the armpits. Before he could even attempt to regain his senses, he was surrounded by half a dozen workers asking for all sorts of instructions and, as he peered over the ring of heads, he caught sight of the face of María Eva, her FAL slung over her shoulder; she saluted gravely when their eyes met. She had tied her hair back for combat, making her look even more like the Eva in the photonovel.

'Comrade María Eva is in charge of defence operations,' he said off the top of his head to wriggle out of it. 'I want you to obey her every command as if it were my own,' he said, with more composure, and headed into the factory to find a safe place to hide until all this madness had blown over.

Grenades came through the skylights and windows with monotonous regularity and, if you looked up or weren't wearing your helmet, the vicious rain of glass could leave you badly cut, or worse still, quite blind. But no sooner had they landed than they were picked up and launched back by the ever-vigilant workers, usually with unerring aim, and controlled fires were dotted about, their smoke neutralising the gas and making the air still just about breathable.

His first idea had been to take refuge under a desk or sofa bed in one of the offices, but then he called to mind the fuel barrels and garlands of grenades, as well as Miguel's promise to blow the factory sky high if it was attacked, and it no longer seemed like such a good idea. He was in the grip of these deliberations, crossing the central nave in the direction of the apse, when a hand deposited a jar of marbles and ball bearings in his, and a voice yelled in his ear:

'It's the Cossacks! The Cossacks are coming!'

His sense of reality was so badly shaken by now that he wouldn't have been at all surprised when he turned round to find himself face to face with a host of fierce, bearded faces wielding sabres and wearing fur caps; but as usual the reality was even worse: in through the entrance to the atrium, whose barricades of furniture and beams had been swept aside by the personnel carrier, charged a troop of mounted police on monstrous brown steeds, galloping at full tilt and wielding what might have been truncheons or whips. Again the sense of unreality trumped common sense, and Marroné just stood there in the middle of the nave, as if, by staring hard at them, these figments of the enchanters who were pursuing him would pop and vanish like bubbles into the air. What was wrong with all these people? How on earth could a fucking cavalry charge be bearing down on *him*, a St Andrew's graduate and head of procurement at Tamerlán & Sons, as if they were back in the Middle Ages? Luckily for him, someone else, of a more practical, less metaphysical turn of mind, hurled a paper grenade at the wall of jostling steeds, whereupon it promptly burst, sending clouds of pepper into the air and making the horses rear and prance, forcing their riders to halt the charge to bring them under control.

He was running for the apse when the voice of command reached his ears once again.

'The marbles! Throw the marbles!'

Blindly, he obeyed. Maybe too blindly, for instead of throwing the jar backwards between himself and the horses, Marroné flung it *forwards*, and when the jar shattered on the floor and the coloured marbles scattered in all directions, it was Marroné that went skating uncontrollably and fell flat on his face. The pain as he hit the floor was unspeakable and for a moment he thought he'd swallowed some of the marbles, which now floated in his mouth in some kind of thick soup, and it was only after taking cover behind one of the brown machines and spitting a spurt of blood into his palms that he understood he'd split his lip, bitten his tongue and broken God knows how many teeth. 'With everything I've got on, and I have to make a dental appointment!' grumbled the old part of his mind indignantly, still obstinately running about bumping into the walls of his skull like a headless chicken.

Still, there must have been enough marbles rolling about to have come between him and the horses, for they had gone into a stiff-legged *Holiday on Ice* routine, bumping into and falling over each other with great thuds, squashing at least two riders against the cement floor or the machines.

'Nice one! Way to go, Ernesto!' he heard someone shout. He poked his head out of his hiding place; an iron hand closed over his arm like a mantrap and hauled him to his feet.

'Don't hurt me! I'm a hostage!' he was about to scream, but he recognised Saturnino's features just in time and saved the disclaimer for the right occasion.

'Ernesto! You been hit?' he asked him in concern, and then, in reply to the burbling sounds coming from Marroné, who discovered he could barely talk for the blood pouring from his mouth, he shouted, 'Come on! We're falling back!'

Saturnino led Marroné towards the barricade, which followed the line of blue machines. They crouched low as they ran, because shots could now be heard inside the factory too. Manning the barricade were a couple of workers with small-arms, and a guerrilla with a light machine gun, while most of the others had only catapults and bolts; three men lay on the ground, their white overalls stained with blood. Two weren't moving: one, unrecognisable for the burns to his face, giving off the pestilential stench of charred flesh; another, fists clenched, as if someone had been trying to prise something away out of them, and teeth bared, as if they too had been summoned in defence of it. It took Marroné a couple of seconds to realise that what he was looking at was a corpse; and another to notice that this was – or had been – the young worker called Zenón. The third, eyes half-closed, was fat and very tall, and was frothing at the mouth, his forearms flapping back and forth, like one of those wind-up bath toys; him too Marroné recognised, for he had got to know all of them by now: he was a River Plate supporter like himself, and they'd spent a morning chatting about the championship they might win after eighteen years without a trophy. 'We won't let it slip away this time,' the young, fair-haired giant had assured him with a slap on the back that almost broke his spine. Kneeling beside them, Edmundo Rivero hid his heavy face in his great hands and wept.

'Let's go, comrade. We don't cry over dead combatants, we step in for them!' the guerrilla shouted to him, and Marroné was tempted to pull rank and tell him to shut his mouth. Something had quickened inside him when he saw those bodies lying there. He'd also noticed the looks his men had been casting in his direction as much as to say 'Do something!' Absurdly, and quite inappropriately, the indifferent features of Tamerlán as he donned the finger-stall appeared before his eyes. All this was for that sonofabitch? No sooner had the thought crossed his mind than the jumble of emotions distilled to a clear, burning rush that rose through his chest and throat, and flooded into his tingling arms. Marroné was suddenly *very* angry.

'Gimme a fucking gun!' he shouted.

He'd barely got the words out before he had one in his outstretched palm. He recognised it immediately: a Browning 9mm. Once he reached puberty, his father would regularly take him to the Federal Firing Range, so he knew how to handle a gun and didn't think twice as, quick as a lizard, he took a peep over the barricade, pinpointed the advancing forces taking cover behind the machines and emptied the remaining contents of the clip at them. Back on the floor, while – his hands barely trembling – he banged in a fresh clip a guerrilla had tossed to him, he realised what had happened: 'I can do it too. I am brave after all!' He'd tell Paddy the moment he saw him.

But for now he had other fish to fry. The man at his side gave a cry and rolled away, tiny objects were bouncing all around him as if being hurled with great force from above.

'Snipers! Up in the roof! Let's get out of here!'

Marroné looked up and saw what was going on. The aggressors had set the yellow chair-lifts going again and were zooming about, gunning them down like fish in a barrel. Only the enveloping smoke, especially thick up in the roof, prevented them from being picked off one by one, like olives stabbed with toothpicks. He fired a few shots upwards, but no joy as far as he could see, then dragged himself under a heavy machine to shield himself from the death raining down from the sky.

From his hiding place he watched a patrol led – or at least headed, because the real leader, a fifty-something with a face as red and meaty as raw steak and hair as white as fat, had him firmly by the arm – by a terrified Baigorria and made up of heavies carrying clubs or chains, as well as several revolvers and at least one sawn-off shotgun. 'That one,' Baigorria pointed suddenly with a trembling arm, and the men behind him leapt on a wounded striker dragging himself across the floor and, when they hauled him up by his hair, Marroné recognised Trejo, who was no longer wearing his white helmet, perhaps to escape detection; a ruse that, thanks to Baigorria's untimely intervention, hadn't worked.

'Where's El Colorado, the sonofabitch? Where's El Colorado!' they screamed at him in unison, and his reply – if he gave one – apparently didn't satisfy them, because without asking twice they'd let go of his hair and, before he even hit the ground, they'd laid into him with sticks, chains, lengths of lead-filled hose, and knuckle-dusters, which glinted with every raised fist. One even wielded a spade.

'This is for Babirusa, you lefty cunt!' said the man with the white hair when they were done, and Marroné shut his eyes and covered his ears to drown out the shotgun's thunder that finished the sentence off.

When they were at a safe distance, Marroné felt a wetness between his legs and wondered if he'd been hit. He touched it, looked at it, smelt it. It wasn't blood; it was urine. Feeling not so much shame as detached surprise, as if it had happened to someone else, he began to drag himself towards the exit that led to the service lifts, which would allow him to get up to the offices and hide until the worst was over; he now regretted binning his James Smart suit and Italian shoes, for even in that state they would have served to identify him as one of the hostages (wasn't he, after all?) and minimise the risk of being gunned down before getting a word in edgeways, should he have to give himself up.

But the assailants seemed to have chosen this as their meeting point, and the apse was swarming with riot police looking like armoured beetles, union thugs and security personnel. Like a praetorian guard, they rallied round the recently freed Sansimón, who, dishevelled and bald (he must have been wearing a toupee), with blackened face, torn shirt and sporting only one shoe, was screaming wildly at the top of his voice:

'Get me Macramé! I want him dead! No! I want him alive. I want to torture him!'

There was only one thing for it. In his flight from the workshop he'd caught a glimpse of one of the huge vats brimful of fresh plaster, ready for use in the first batch of products from the newly liberated plasterworks. A team of fire-fighters was patrolling the corridors, dousing the fires with their extinguishers, and under cover of their white clouds he managed to dodge from one machine to the next and finally reached the edge of the vast pool of white. A thin crust had formed, like a crème brûlée, which Marroné broke with his boot and the thick watery paste folded itself coolly around him as he slid silently into it. He had picked up a piece of half-inch tubing on the way and, gripping it firmly in his teeth like a snorkel, he sank back in the thin gruel until he was lying flat. His plan was to stay submerged in this white mire until night fell, though exactly how he would check the light with his eyes closed under all this plaster was a riddle he hadn't yet solved. Maybe if he counted the seconds, he could get an approximate idea of the passing of time. But he soon lost count, as keeping track of the seconds on the one hand and the minutes on the other sent his brain into a tailspin, and it was getting harder and harder to breathe too, either because the density of the liquid, far greater than water, was compressing his lungs, or because . . . the plaster was setting! Panic welled within him at the thought. What if, by the time he decided to get out, it was too late, and he wound up buried prematurely in a sarcophagus of calcium sulphate? The claustrophobia flooded through him in wave after wave of sheer, breathless panic, and, by raising his knees and levering himself up onto his elbows, he pressed with his forehead until he felt the fresh crust give, and, with the gingerliness of an old man extricating himself from a slippery bathtub, he lowered himself down from the vat and took two faltering steps, dripping like a pat of butter in the summer sun. Before he could take a third, he heard voices approaching. He couldn't run in this state: he was a target with arrows pointing at him and a big sign saying 'PLEASE SHOOT ME'. Utterly at the end of his wits he froze where he stood. He gazed blankly around the jungle of corbels, amphorae and columns, looking for anywhere to hide – and then inspiration struck. He puffed out his chest, put his hand to it, clenched the other into a fist, and raised his forehead proud and high to the future. Then he shut his eyes: if he could resist the urge to open them, there was an outside chance they would take him for a model of the Monument to the Descamisado and walk straight past.

It worked like a dream: the patrol or whoever it was he'd heard approaching walked straight past without noticing him, one of them panting the mantra 'Motherfuckincunt! Motherfuckincunt!', which gave Marroné no clue as to whatever or whoever it was they were looking for. He opened his eyes a crack: the coast was clear. The plaster must have set on contact with the air, which no doubt improved his camouflage; all he had to do was remain perfectly still, like one of those living statues you see in squares or in the street. Luckily, the blood had stopped dripping from his lips.

That was when he saw them coming back, led by the white-haired man whose face looked like an Arcimboldo of raw steaks, and Marroné shut his eyes tight so they wouldn't see him as they passed. They didn't, but stopped right in front of him, puffing and panting and all talking at once, muttering, 'Take that, you sonofabitch, motherfuckincunt, fucking lefty scumbag, Happy Christmas,' and with every phrase came a whish of air – dull and muffled from the clubs, dizzying and sibilant from the chains – invariably climaxing in a thud and a moan, a cry, sometimes a crunch. 'Come on, come on, finish him off!' urged a hoarse voice full of hatred or maybe just weariness, and then came another: 'Whoa, don't be in such a hurry, I want to enjoy this.'

Unable to stop himself, Marroné began first to loosen his eyelids without actually unsticking them, then separated them very slightly until a filigree of pale light filtered through the crack, the way you loosen a closed shutter in the morning with the first tug. He kept his breathing shallow – very shallow and very slow; inside he shook with every blow, but outside – he hoped, he prayed – there was nothing to see. By the light now coming in through his eyelids he could distinguish shapes and colours through a faint mist. To see more clearly he had to open his eyes still further, but he remembered having heard or read that the eye of a predator is hard-wired for movement; but no predator – not even *these* – would spot the stop-motion of his eyelids. He could now make out the thugs' faces: they were red and sweaty, and they huffed and wheezed from the effort; they spat as they swore but, lucky for Marroné, they were intent on their victim, who he couldn't make out, because his forehead was still tilted upwards. Stage by stage, his eyes abandoned faces for shoulders, shoulders for chests, chests for bellies and bellies for knees, until his gaze reached their feet and the thing that lay between them.

It was face down, and the blood made the white overalls looked like a slaughterman's; he wouldn't have recognised him if it hadn't been for the unmistakeable copper tone of his hair. The instant he did, his legs nearly gave way. He heard a gasp of horror escape his lips, but the thugs mustn't have heard it above their hoarse wheezing. Or had he only gasped to himself? Paddy was still moving, his arms and legs bending and stretching as if trying to carry him away from the pain, but his body wouldn't budge. His friend was being murdered before his eyes and he was powerless to do anything.

They went about it with a methodical slowness, like a long, physically demanding job for which you have to save your strength, and every so often one of them would stand up, arch his back with his hands on his kidneys and, after wiping his forehead with his forearm or a handkerchief, return to the task in hand. Arcimboldo didn't take part, but merely supervised, hands on hips, and every now and then gave curt instructions or checked his heavy Rolex. A police officer came over to see how they were getting along.

'Gonna be long?'

'Nah. Five minutes tops.'

It felt like five hundred years to Marroné. He had to keep his eyes half-open now, for if he closed them the tears would roll down his cheeks, carving broad, skin-coloured furrows through the white plaster, and his disguise would be blown. But if he kept his eyes like this and concentrated every ounce of his being on fighting back the tears, he could just about swallow them. His greatest fear was that he might start sweating from the heat and the effort of keeping still, and it occurred to his mind – not to him – that every minute Paddy took to die increased his chances of being caught.

Arcimboldo checked his watch again and, true to his word, though the policeman had walked off by now, he called a stop to it and bent down to check Paddy, now face up from the kicking, for a pulse. Attempting to stand again, his downturned palms charlestoned in the air two or three times before he held them out to be pulled to his feet. They walked off in silence, pulling the knuckle-dusters off their swollen fingers, rubbing their red-raw knuckles and looking around for something to wipe them on.

Cracking with every step and flaking like old plaster, Marroné began to move: he went over to his friend and touched his face with one outstretched finger. The one remaining eye suddenly popped open, and Marroné leapt backwards, barely able to contain his scream. The eye cast desperately about itself in all directions: there was no way to get him out of here or ask for help, and he was next on their list. But there was something he owed his friend, and it was now or never.

'Paddy . . . ' He crouched down and whispered in his ear. 'That time with the coloured chalk . . . remember? It was me. I did it.'

Staring into his two, Paddy's one good eye widened visibly, as if he were trying to absorb the enormity of what he'd just heard. Then it closed for ever.

*   *   *

Darting between the smoking ruins and freezing statue-like every now and then, Marroné made it to the right transept.

The door was just a stone's throw from the perimeter fence, which had been breached in places by the attackers. Moving cautiously through the scattered barricades, he ran into El Tuerto, who took one look at Marroné and crossed himself.

'I'm still alive, you idiot,' he whispered to him, when he understood.

'Jesus Christ, Ernesto. I thought you was a ghost,' said El Tuerto with one hand on his chest.

'They've killed Paddy.'

'Who?'

'El Colorado,' he corrected himself.

'Yeah, I know. And Trejo. And Zenón. And at least two others.'

'Hey . . . What about the lads from the . . . Montos?'

'Ah. Dead meat the lot of 'em.'

Marroné's heart skipped a beat.

'The girls too?'

'Them first.'

'Both of them?'

'I 'ope so, coz them as they take alive . . . You know. They took the lot of 'em. It's just you and me left.'

'Shouldn't we turn ourselves in?' asked Marroné.

'Are you shitting me? They'll fucking murder us. You first.'

Marroné swallowed. It was exactly what he feared he'd hear.

'So what do we do?'

'It'll be dark in a bit. My house is on the other side of the stream. If we make it across without 'em seeing us, we can hole down there for a bit.'

By heaving the sacks around, they managed to make a tiny cubbyhole in the wall and, after dragging themselves inside, they blocked up the entrance with another sack and crouched there, not daring to say a word until the crack of light darkened from yellow to mauve to purple and black. Then they moved the sacks again and stuck out their snouts like a couple of armadillos in their burrow. A strong wind had picked up, whipping handfuls of plaster dust into the air, which blinded them and made them cough, but at the same time veiled their movements. The gardens had returned to the ghostly whiteness of the early days and, in the radiant light of the police spotlights, once again resembled a snow-covered landscape. Fortunately for Marroné and El Tuerto, the factory wall cast a long shadow that reached all the way to the wire fence and, groping their way along it for some distance, amidst the blinding dust clouds, they eventually came to a hole just large enough to crawl through. El Tuerto went first, getting stuck because of his girth, and Marroné had to find a firm foothold and push him through by the arse.

They forded the stream – more of an industrial sewer flowing with oil – from whose swampy depths, with every squelch they took, came protracted gurgles of foul-smelling gas. With difficulty they made their way up the steep slope of the opposite bank, composed entirely, Marroné discovered, of layer upon layer of garbage, which crumbled under their feet as they climbed. A little further on they could make out twinkling lights from what appeared to be not electric bulbs, but flickering candles, and clutching El Tuerto's hand so that he wouldn't get lost, Marroné set off towards them.

7

A PERONIST CHILDHOOD

No sooner did the first gloom of dawn creep through his sleep-encrusted eyelids than the man woke up and wondered who he was. The two words that came into his mind – 'Ernesto Marroné' – though not quite enough, did at least allow him to move on to the next question: where exactly, and in what, was he? He was sitting, his knees forced into his chest by the cramped circular walls; these were rough and fluted and, when he rapped on them with his knuckles, they gave a metallic boom. In the roof, which was flat, there was a round hole about the diameter of a teacup, through which dribbled the meagre light and air; stretching up his arm, he could just about manage to poke his fingers through, which, from the outside, he imagined – in a spasm of spliced consciousness – must have looked like worms wriggling their way out of a tin can. The bottom, on the other hand, was little more than a soggy mass of flakes that crumbled in his fingers like wet choux pastry, leaving his feet resting on the spongy surface of the ground, which, when trodden underfoot, exhaled a nauseating stench that made the air quite unbreathable. He couldn't lift it, whatever it was he was in, but, by pushing the walls with his hands, he discovered it was possible to move it from side to side and, by rocking in ever-widening arcs, he eventually managed to tip it over, and he backed out to find himself on another planet. Neither the lunar landscape, riddled with potholes and craters full of iridescent water that reflected nothing but itself, nor the mountains that fumed relentlessly despite the swirling drizzle, seemed to belong to any natural geography. They did to human geography, though: the vast marches of polythene bags, grizzly newspaper, plastic containers and broken bottles, the snowdrifts of flaking polystyrene, helped him grasp the fact that he must be in a garbage tip. He cast about him in all directions: as far as the misty drizzle revealed any shapes, there wasn't a single house, not a single tree – nothing but the sheer spurs of the tip, made ever hazier by the distance and the rain. He made for a steep bank along which muddy waterfalls cascaded softly over inflated cliffs of polythene. His whole body ached, as if he had been in a rugby game after which the other team, not content with whipping them on the field, had barged into the changing rooms and beaten them with sticks; and incapable of remembering what had happened, he tried to imagine how he might, in one of the possible worlds his mind was capable of grasping, have come to such a sorry pass. He didn't even recognise as his own the clothes he stood up in: the buttonless, double-breasted serge jacket, which he could barely fasten over the bleached-out t-shirt; the elasticated tracksuit bottoms with foot straps, so short they left his ankles exposed; the fraying espadrilles, whose rope soles softened by the water had begun to unravel and dragged behind him like dead snakes. Didn't he use to wear suits of the finest cashmere, ties of silk and Italian shoes? No, that had been in another life. White overalls, boots, hard hat? Not any more, it seemed. The images dissolved in the pools of his memory as soon as he tried to grasp them, and in like manner his feet, as he attempted to scale the bank, churned the crumbling rubbish without going anywhere. It was as if, in the relentlessly repeated act of climbing, his muscles were in pursuit of a memory rather than a physical spot, and they found it when he reached the top: he had already been here, not long ago; but it had been darkest night and he hadn't been able to see, as he could now, the winding palisade of dilapidated shacks, huddled together like cattle in a flooded field, between the grey drizzle and the vast mirror of water; and it was only now, when his crusted eyes met the crusted landscape, that it all came flooding back to him.

Paddy was dead, the busts were gone and his own life had been saved by a miracle. Dragging him by the hand like a rag doll – the battered knight-errant assisted by his faithful squire – El Tuerto had led him down the indistinguishable alleyways of the rickety maze: dogs barked as they passed, children scattered before them, *chamamé* and *cumbia* duelled on rival radio sets. 'This way, Ernesto . . . mind yer head . . . Geroudofit, yer mutt!' El Tuerto shredded his sentences between gasps. On yet another anonymous corner he gave Marroné a shove without warning and they crashed as one through a swing door on tyre hinges.

The house was part airbrick, part corrugated iron, part wood. Lit by a couple of candles, the front room contained: a chest of drawers upon which stood a black-and-white TV set, whose light, he would later discover, came from a kerosene lamp set in its hollow innards; a half-open

Siam fridge; a Gilera motorbike, whose back wheel and various parts were dotted about the floor (El Tuerto was a mechanic at the factory); a stout woman in a mousey, floral-print dressing gown that enveloped her like a badly wrapped parcel; and two girls of six and ten, playing with dead babies on the dirt floor (upon closer inspection they turned out to be bald dolls with missing arms or legs). The woman was in the process of making *milanesas* in a frying pan that wobbled precariously atop a Primus stove on the floor and barely turned round when the two quivering lumps burst in.

'Oh. So you're back, are you? Well? How did you get on with the strike?' she asked, her feigned innocence dripping with malice as she slapped a raw cutlet in egg and breadcrumbs. 'Over is it? Get everything you bargained for, did you?'

'Shut your face, Pipota, and stick your 'ead out to see if we've been followed,' barked El Tuerto at her, unbuttoning his overalls; it was an order she chose blithely to ignore, returning instead to the hypnotic sputterings of her *milanesa*. 'Oy! Ernesto! What you waiting for?' yelled El Tuerto, making Marroné leap into the air with alarm.

El Tuerto was already down to his underpants, which peeked out red from beneath the thick fold of hairy belly, and was trying to extricate his boots from his overalls spread on the floor.

'Get out of those things, will you. If the pigs show up, or the union goons, you're dead meat.'

Marroné hastily complied, but when he reached the fourth button (he was having difficulty undoing them, as they were now welded with hard plaster to their buttonholes), he realised there was a problem. He called El Tuerto to one side and whispered in his ear:

'Errb. I dot dothig odd udderdeath,' he said, gesturing at the three ladies present.

'Eh?' answered El Tuerto. 'I didn't get a bloody word of that.'

'I dot wedding eddy udderdads,' he rephrased, pointing insistently at his crotch. His thick tongue and tumid lips could barely form words.

El Tuerto was now jumping about the room as if in a sack race, pulling on skin-tight jeans below his Huracán shirt.

'Naaaah. Don't worry about those two, won't be the first cock they've seen. Just as long as it *stays* visible . . . And the other one must have lost count by now. Right, Pipota?' he chuckled as he rummaged in the chest of drawers and tossed Marroné some light-blue Lycra underpants and the drainpipe tracksuit bottoms, a buttonless double-breasted jacket, and a bleached-out t-shirt in quick succession. 'Try these on. I got better threads than these, but you can't be going around the place all got up like a dog's dinner, now, can you? You'll stick out like a sore thumb. Alright, Ernesto, go on; you can use the bedroom if you're that fussed about it.'

The room he had entered lay on the other side of a cotton counterpane, attached to the door frame with drawing pins, and every square inch was taken up by a double bed covered with a brand-new Afghan blanket, a three-piece wardrobe whose veneer was chipped at the corners of the doors, a night table, a lighted candle in a candlestick and, asleep on a camp bed, a tiny little old man who looked so still and worn by life that he might actually have been dead.

Through the curtain, as he undressed – no mean feat, for the fabric of his overalls was by then as hard and unyielding as plasterboard and, rather than a man disrobing, he felt like a chick hatching from an egg – Marroné had eavesdropped on the conversation.

'So you're out of a job again, are you?'

'But I wasn't fired this time, Pipota. I was on strike.'

'How long d'you last this time? Twenty days? What did I tell you? Bet you don't see the end of the month out.'

'Listen 'ere, old girl . . . we was fucked. Several of the comrades pegged out. I got out of there by a sheer fluke.'

'All right, keep your shirt on. We'll get by on the *milanesa* butties. I'll make another batch straight off, now you're back to lug the basket around. What about me laddo in there, who's he? Got to put grub on his plate, too, have I?'

At this point El Tuerto's voice had fallen to a whisper, and his wife must have been suitably impressed because she had answered in the same hushed tones. Marroné also remembered feeling a rather mean-minded relief at overhearing his hosts' conversation. All the women he had met during the strike were self-sacrificing proletarians who put their shoulders to the wheel, took whatever came their way and supported, not to say encouraged, their husbands' bravery – and all without a word of complaint. Of course, he'd only met the ones who had visited the factory. There were also, he now realised, women who stayed at home, cursing and muttering as they fried their poisoned *milanesas*.

Moving delicately and feeling as fragile as a limb just out of a cast, he'd sat down to get changed on the bed, which was so high (each leg stood on three bricks) that his feet didn't reach the floor; the next thing he remembered was a hand slapping him gently to bring him round from his comatose slumber.

'Ernesto . . . Ernesto . . . There's some people 'ere as wants to see you,' El Tuerto told him.

There were three of them. The first, between forty and forty-five, was tall, dark-skinned, mono-browed, sunken-eyed; he wore bell-bottoms – from under which peeped the toes of moccasins – and a short-sleeved safari shirt, and smoked super-king-size, which he pulled out of one or other countless pockets weighed down with buckles; he was backed up by a hulk with long hair and a moustache, wearing a tight-fitting, flesh-coloured polo neck and towelling wrist- and head-bands, as if he'd just dropped in after a game of tennis; and a lad who couldn't have been more than twenty, in a shimmering brown velvet jacket, the crease in his immaculate white trousers ironed sharp as a knife, and whose unruly quiff had been slicked back into a roof of corrugated iron. They shook hands very formally: Sr Gareca, Malito and El Bebe. El Tuerto had brought them all chairs, but had parked himself on an upended orange crate; he poured them a glass of unchilled white wine from a bottle without a label and sent the girls into the other room; La Pipota, meanwhile, went on with her *milanesas*, filling the scant breathing space with a choking fog of burnt oil and kerosene.

Sr Gareca had opened by acknowledging their achievements in the shanties and had thanked them for their contributions of cider and panettone on Christmas Eve, then gone on to explain how they'd do their best to pay them back ('You scratch our backs . . . '), even if they did lack the wherewithal. But then, the mutual return of favours aside, one thing was clear: they all had the same interests at heart, like dragging the poor out of their poverty (here La Pipota, who, with snorts of disbelief and exaggerated gesticulations, provided a running commentary on all she heard, had said – as if to herself, but out loud for all to hear – 'Yeah, right, just as long as *them*'s the poor,' and her husband flashed her a withering glare with his white eye, which, like one of those purple rings you buy at the seaside, seemed to change colour with his mood). They shared the same enemy, Sr Gareca had continued, not letting on he'd heard a thing, and then, after all, they were all Peronists, weren't they. At this point Malito had whispered something in his ear, and Sr Gareca had muttered back through clenched teeth, 'Not now, wait a bit.' Up till now, Sr Gareca resumed his introduction, they'd been getting along famously, 'All for one and one for all' as they say; whenever the need had arisen, they'd helped each other out, and if there had ever been any friction, or the odd misunderstanding, they had worked things out with goodwill 'and above all respect'. He spoke carefully, choosing his words and using them painstakingly to construct his sentences, which he invariably ended with an 'Am I making sense?', to which Marroné would invariably reply with bouts of vehement nodding, though he understood less and less of what was said. Satisfied, Sr Gareca had paused, lit up another super-king-size, let out the smoke and set off again with a 'The fact is . . . ' that had sounded promising but he soon lapsed back into his circuitous progress through the chaff without ever reaching the wheat: things, it seemed, had changed; now they could no longer each tend to their own little patch; the time had come to join forces and think big. 'He wants to do business with the company,' Marroné had told himself, beginning to join the dots: since Sr Tamerlán's kidnapping they'd been dishing out food in the shanties like there was no tomorrow; in fact, he himself as head of procurement had been responsible for finding the cheapest fare, and it made perfect sense for the panettone and cider he'd ordered to end up here in this shanty town; what made no sense at all was that the very same shanty housed a company that wanted to do business with Tamerlán & Sons, and that someone like Sr Gareca was its owner or CEO. Unless, of course, it was all about sanitary landfill, which made quite a lot of sense, especially if it involved buying the land for a song and bulldozing the shanties to push its value up; Sr Tamerlán had made many such an investment. 'The fact is we've got the people, we've got the territory and we've got the experience; I won't bore you with all the details, but right here in the area we've done two factories, a hospital and a lumberyard . . . ' Oh, so this was another construction company then, and what Sr Gareca was proposing was a merger. So the rumours going round were true: far from being kennels for slumdogs, dark shores where the jetsam from the city's churning wake washed up, the shanties were miniature republics, underdeveloped versions of those European principalities that flourish away from the asphyxiating regulations that hold back the economies of the big republics. As rumour had it, the shanties were a vast black market, an archipelago of miniature duty-free zones, like the tax havens of the Caribbean, amidst an ocean of asphalt and cement. They had everything; everything was bought and everything was sold: what you couldn't find elsewhere you could buy here, and Marroné made a mental note to ask about those disposable nappies. These true clandestine industrial parks were home to textile firms, furniture factories, bottling plants that filled brand-name bottles with foul substances, slaughterhouses for contaminated animals and travel agents that organised package holidays back home for illegal immigrants. He'd heard all this before but had dismissed it more often than not as fantasy and exaggeration. And now he had the tangible proof before his very eyes: one of these entrepreneurs, who had, by dodging the taxman, entered the fray with the lowest prices and made an astronomical killing, was daring to speak with one of the giants of the field as an equal.

'Don't forget the pharmacy,' the young man in the velvet jacket had chipped in at one point, and Sr Gareca included it forthwith in his oral curriculum. The ever-obliging El Tuerto went around attentively refilling their glasses, while his wife went on frying her *milanesas*, and every one she tossed on the growing stack was accompanied by a barbed sideswipe: 'Oh. Right. The lefties gang up with the pimps and we're saved!'

'In drincidle id sounds like an inderesdig drodosal,' said Marroné at one point, and he felt the tension in the atmosphere ease immediately, while the three visitors exchanged half-smiles and satisfied glances, and El Tuerto blurted out an exultant 'I told you? Didn't I tell you?' Sr Gareca lit the first cigarette of a new pack (he seemed to have one in every pocket – even his sleeves had pockets) and, exhaling, he got right down to brass tacks. 'Here in the shanties we're in a position to offer you free transit and lodging, and outside, contacts in the other settlements. Men: no less than fifty. We can count on you, can't we Tuerto?' El Tuerto nodded, and Pipota muttered, 'Yeah, right. When they scarper at the first shot, he'll be the one leading the pack.' The three men no longer looked at the wife but at the husband, as if urging him to take matters in hand, and El Tuerto, realising he'd have to deal with a sharper weapon than his wife's tongue if he didn't oblige, covered the two metres between them in two strides and stood beside her, this time without a word.

'Something the matter? What are you stood there looking at me for?' brazened Pipota, in the same flat tone as before. Without answering the question her husband grabbed her right hand, which was running with egg, and thrust it, palm down, into the breadcrumbs. But only when he twisted her wrist to coat the back of her hand with breadcrumbs did the penny drop, too late to prevent the mechanic's sinewy mitt from plunging her breaded right hand into the boiling oil. It can't have been more than a second, and it was by no means burnt to a crisp – just a light goldening; more the egg and breadcrumbs than the underlying flesh – but it was still pretty shocking: Pipota emitted a string of fearsome shrieks and, when her husband let go of her, she fled the house, knocking over oil and Primus as she went. Sr Gareca and his men exchanged approving glances, Malito even going so far as to give El Tuerto, who was tidying up the mess, a pat on the back. Picking up where he left off, Sr Gareca went on with his business proposal. 'We 'ave the will, we 'ave the grit, we 'ave the people. What we 'aven't got is the infrastructure, see. The kit.'

He handed Marroné a folded piece of graph paper torn from a spiral-bound exercise book, on which there was a typewritten list:

GEAR REQUIRED

- 10 11.25mm Ballester-Molina automatics; 20 magazines each.
- 10 9mm Browning automatics; 20 magazines each.
- 10 Ithaca pump-action shotguns, plus cartridges.
- 5 Halcón machine guns; 10 magazines each.
- 5 PAM machine guns; 10 magazines each.
- 20 FAL rifles; 10 magazines each.
- '3 Uzi sub-machine guns; 1,000 rounds.
- 1 MAG general-purpose machine gun; 2,000 rounds.
- 500kg gelignite; 20 electric detonators.
- 50 grenades.
- 1 anti-aircraft battery (model to be decided).
- 20 anti-personnel mines.
- 10 anti-tank mines.
- 1 bazooka.

While Marroné's widening eyes read through the list, Sr Gareca felt the need to go on with his explanation. 'We reckon that under the current circumstances we are ready to take the leap from isolated, individual actions to a full-scale, coordinated attack on simultaneous fronts. We're getting nowhere offing the odd pig in the street: we have to take the police station, seize the arsenal and blow the place sky high. We're not hurting them by holding up grocers or kiosk-owners, who at the end of the day are all our brothers. We have to hit them where it really hurts: supermarkets, banks, multinationals . . . Because that way it ain't stealing any more; it's taking back what they took from us, just the way you lot taught us. I mean, what's the robbing of a bank compared to the founding of a bank . . . ' he went on. 'That's why we've decided to join the armed struggle. What we *will* need is a couple of trained instructors too, coz it's not like we're about to stick heavy artillery into the hands of any silly prat.' Malito whispered in his ear a couple more times until, in exasperation, Sr Gareca finally caved in: 'Comrade Malito here wants to know if the campaign of police executions is still ongoing, coz he wants to join it, and can you notch two up for him: one from the hospital and another from the raid on the armoured truck last September?' Marroné looked up from the piece of quivering paper in his hands into the eyes of a Malito beaming at him with a broad, friendly grin. He went back to the list after croaking out a 'No droblem'.

'Whaddaya wad de dazooka and de bines for?' asked Marroné out of professional reflex. He was after all head of procurement and accustomed to considering any order exorbitant on principle.

Sr Gareca, Malito and El Bebe looked at each other rather taken aback, as if their confidence in him was suddenly wavering. 'To defend the settlement, in case they send in the tanks. The idea – I mean, if you agree, of course – is to declare this a liberated zone. Us and the other neighbourhoods can form a cordon street by street and cut off the capital.'

'And the andi-airdraft?' Marroné insisted. 'Don't you dink id's a bid ober de dop?'

Once again the triple exchange of looks, only this time there was a faint note of reproach in Sr Gareca's tone:

'Every time you lot pull a big one, comrade, they let the local neighbourhoods have it. It ain't just the pigs we're up against now, it's the bleeding army. Only two days ago – two days – they razed the Iapi and the 25 de Mayo settlements to the ground with fighters and helicopter gunships. That's the whole point, comrade. You do what you have to, but then don't go and leave us up the creek.'

After that the discussion relaxed and took a more predict-able turn: Marroné, nodding and numb with tiredness, ticking off the items on the shopping list, asking for unnecessary details and coming out with the occasional reservation for the sake of verisimilitude; at one point Pipota returned, her hand wrapped in a rag, and disappeared into the bedroom, where the two girls were asleep on the bed; at another point an insistent drumming began overhead, and, looking up at the corrugated-iron roof, Sr Gareca remarked that it was good news, because the rain and its consequences – the poor visibility, the mires, the floods – meant that the police were less likely to move into the neighbourhood. He had barely finished the sentence when the barking of dogs, the shouts, the gunfire and the raking white-hot beams of spotlights that tigered their shapes through the walls announced the start of the raid.

Guns drawn, the three men bundled Marroné over the bed and over Pipota and her two daughters, who lay hud-dled and bawling beside her, then kicked down one of the bedroom's plywood walls and burst into the alley winding off through the shacks. Drenched in seconds and half-blind from the water pouring from the corrugated-iron roofs, he let himself be dragged along identical, criss-crossing alleys, switching course abruptly and forced to dive whenever they ran into the spotlights and gunshots (Malito threw himself on top of him every time, using his body to shield him from the bullets). Down dizzying tunnels of black-ness that seemed to swing up and down as they went, one moment up slippery slopes, the next down liquid slides that plunged into deep vertical wells, Sr Gareca guiding the way, El Bebe firing to cover them as they retreated and Malito flying Marroné behind him like a kite, they finally came out into the open at the edge of a bank, whereupon Sr Gareca grabbed him by the arm and shouted in his ear over the din of the rain, the barking and the shots, 'Now hide, we'll throw them off the scent,' then gave him a shove that sent him rolling downhill. Bouncing like a ball, sometimes on inflated bags that cushioned his fall, at others on jagged edges and sharp corners, he eventually reached the foot of the mountain, whereupon the kindly flash from a bolt of lightning silhouetted the squat outline of a bottomless barrel, where he curled up inside, trembling with cold and fright; but then, realising the meanest searchlight would still pick him out like a rabbit on the road, he tilted and tipped it till it stood upright, the narrow orifice in the top doubling as breathing- and spy-hole. Through it, if the rain that found its way inside didn't sting his eyes, he would have been able to spend the entire night gazing at a small disc of blood-red sky. Abandoning the upright, he hugged his knees and slid down, like melting ice cream into its cone, awakening several hours later, in the same position, to the small, white circle of dawn overhead.

He had been wandering about among the hunched and shapeless shacks for some time now, up to his knees in mud and water, shivering in his soaking clothes, without spotting a single other human form. He plucked up the courage outside one brick house to clap hands and shout '*Ave María Purísima!*', the way they do in the countryside. But no one answered his call, not even when he banged on the metal

door with his open palm and shouted 'Please, open up!'
Then, from a neighbouring shack, someone did appear: a
boy in shorts of a nondescript shade, a t-shirt so short it left
his distended belly exposed like some uninhibited pregnant
woman's, and blondish hair blanched more by malnutri-
tion than by race, his legs sticking out of wellington boots
so large the edges dug into his groin, but even then barely
rose above the water.

'Sweedie . . . is bubby in?' Marroné asked him, and his
own voice frightened him: it sounded like a toad venturing
out to croak in the rain.

The boy shook his head. He was staring oddly at Marroné.

Swatting away a couple of flies that insisted on clamber-
ing over his eyelashes and lips, he tried again:

'Aren'd dere eddy growd-ups wid you?'

As if summoned by some magic spell and preceded by
the swell displaced by her body, a toothless Indian crone
in a Pepsi t-shirt and men's jeans several sizes too large
appeared in the cave-mouth. She sized up Marroné with a
single glance.

'Out of here, you bum! Go and do your begging somewhere else!' she yelled at him, before grabbing the child by
the hand and disappearing into her riverside grotto.

A little further on, however, from a coloured barge
beached in the mud for the rest of time, someone did answer
his call.

'Psst! Young 'un!'

A Bolivian woman in bowler hat and plaits peeked out
of a porthole, shooing him away.

'Hide yourself, young 'un,' whished the chola. 'They're
still snooping around.'

'Excuse me,' he said, without understanding properly. 'I'm looking for El Duerdo's house. Do you dnow hib?'

The chola shook her head, so hard her plaits cracked like whips.

'Bibota?'

Nope.

'Señó Gadeca? Malito? El Bebe?'

This time she switched to an emphatic nodding that left her hat tilted to one side, and a smile that revealed a gold-sheathed incisor, which for one sorry second Marroné envied, lit up her face.

'Where cad I find deb?'

The chola's finger pointed upwards, and Marroné's gaze followed it, as if he hoped to see the three of them winging their way across the overcast sky. When the penny dropped, his stomach turned and he struggled to get out the question:

'Wad happened?'

The chola made a gun of her hand and her finger pulled the trigger.

'All thdee of dem?'

'Señó Gareca were still a-moving. Like dis,' she said, imitating a mermaid dancing in the waves. 'El Bebe were me hubbie's nephew, dead as a doorknob he was, his body tossed at de wayside. Dey was defending some big gun commandant from de guerrilla. Dey done took dem all away.'

Marroné thanked her, as a calf might thank the slaughterman that has just dealt it the hammer-blow, and staggered off through the current as best he could, past floating bits of wood, drowned rats, islands of excrement and even, face down, the corpse of a man. He had to get out of this water maze as fast as he could, away from this mock Venice of cardboard and tin. 'I'm not from this place, this isn't my country, there's been a terrible mistake, help me get home,' his head implored powerful imaginary intercessors. As in fairy tales, the babe had been stolen from his cradle and whisked through the air to a faraway land of monsters, a world that was the precisely detailed denial of all he knew and loved; he had to escape by his own native wit or he would drown and his corpse float off face down after the other one to join the rest of the trash at the foot of the steep embankment. It wasn't so much the dying that bothered him as dying here, in this place, amidst the rubbish and the mud. He yearned to return to the golden rugby fields of his youth, feel the sun on his face, the scent of trampled clover in his lungs; if his blood had to be spilt, would that it were in a brand-new Dodds shirt, flowing red on yellow like a blazing sunset, rather than sucked from him by these sticky rags or mingling with the eddies of sewage that hemmed him in on all sides. If he could just sit down and rest for a minute, get out of the rain and his feet out of the water, regain a shred of human form, just maybe he'd be able to come up with something.

A rusty Fanta sign nailed to a wall of planks; a sheet of blue polythene propped up by two sticks that, buckling under the weight of the accumulated rainwater, formed an elegant baldachin; and a wooden bench moored with a piece of rope to prevent the current carrying it off, which came into view on peeking round the corner of one of the main channels, told him that, for once, his prayers had been answered. Relieved, he straightened the floating bench and sat down on it, his rear sinking below the waterline, and no sooner had he negotiated some kind of balance than he noticed the slant-eyed face of a man watching him from behind the bars of the window.

'I wad somedig to drink. Somedig strog,' ordered Marroné, stifling the urge to kiss his hands.

The man vanished into the gloom and came back with a glass of colourless liquid, but when Marroné reached out, he withdrew it into the depths. Marroné rummaged in his pocket and pulled out a huge, white, roughly square-shaped piece of limestone. Bashing it several times on one of the bars, he eventually managed to crack it and prise it open like an oyster: inside was his money, which the plaster had preserved from the ravages of the water. He daintily extracted a wad of whitish notes, still damp and stuck together, peeled one off and handed it to the man, who in return handed him the glass, the contents of which Marroné downed in one. It was cheap gut-rot, which might have been nothing more than rubbing alcohol diluted in water but, together with the tears in his eyes and the burning in his throat, he felt the warmth return to his frozen limbs, the blood to his heart and his soul to his body. He chased it down with another, which he paid for with a few coppers from the change, then, at fainting pitch, ordered a meat pasty, which promptly popped out through the bars. It was as cold and wet as a frog's belly, but he wolfed it down without noticing. No doubt thanks to the alcohol that had burnt out his taste buds, it didn't taste as bad as it looked, and he ordered two more, paying up front as before. He felt better with some food inside him – more upbeat, less defeated. He'd wait until nightfall and get out of there; it would be easier under cover of darkness to elude his pursuers. He told the wordless man he needed somewhere to rest for a few hours.

A gesture was all it took to tell Marroné he had to enter by the back door; a few more pesos to buy him the privilege of a high bed that looked as if it was floating like a boat on the water (now he understood why they put bricks under the legs); and two minutes to undress and fall asleep under the dry blanket. He dreamt that his team had just won the rugby championship final: the captain of the rival team came up to congratulate him with a smile, his hair flaming like a beacon in the afternoon sunshine, and Marroné awoke, his eyes bathed in tears, to the sound of weeping.

The tears were his, but the weeping was coming from the next room, or maybe the next house (like dogs' territory, boundaries here were invisible to the naked eye). He put on his barely dry clothes and, noticing with relief that the flood had retreated and left behind a memento of sedimental slime, like a lake bed, he squelched through it in his espadrilles – first inside then outside the house – in search of the source of the weeping, which seemed to coincide with a faint flickering light in a nearby window. A cool breeze was blowing and, high above, amidst the blue-grey clouds, twinkled a paltry scattering of urban stars. He pushed open a wooden door a good deal smaller than its frame, and made for a cradle improvised from a cardboard box, with tea towels for sheets, dimly lit by a lone candle set beside a picture of Eva Perón, before which stood a bunch of fresh flowers: humble daisies and honeysuckles. So their paths had crossed again; here he was, still fluttering round her flame and, for all he tried to get away, he always ended up coming back. 'What is it now?' he ventured to ask her. 'What do you want from me? Why have you brought me here?' He picked up the paint-pot-lid candlestick and brought the flame close to the face of the child within: a boy, just a few days old, a couple of weeks at most, his little almond eyes almost closed, his mouth and cheeks sticky with grime, and atop his head a crest of spiky, jet-black hair. What was such a tiny infant doing alone? What kind of people were these, how far had ignorance and poverty dehumanised them, that they could abandon such a small babe in arms? Another possibility occurred to him, and he clapped his hand to his mouth in horror. Perhaps the parents had been gunned down too. He felt, if not guilty, at least implicated, and recalled the late Sr Gareca's lucid words, about taking responsibility for his actions, and decided to honour his last wish: he picked up the baby, cradling it to stop it crying, the way he used to with little Cynthia (only, she slept in a white wicker cradle with frills and flounces, holland sheets and satin bedspread), feeling its soft warmth against his chest. Marroné's eyes filled with tears a second before his mind understood: the child was him; he was gazing at himself in a mirror of the past. This was how he had come into the world, this was how his life had started out: the same life in store for this child would have been his, had fate or chance not snatched him from the shack and carried him off to the palace. Not the same, he corrected himself; this child's would be far worse, for the life of Ernesto Marroné (though, obviously, he wouldn't have been called by that name) would have played itself out under the protection of a real-life Eva, not a mere icon like this. A series of imaginary flashbacks screened an alternative past – what his Peronist childhood would have been like under the constant care of Eva: a safe, hygienic birth in one of the brand-new hospitals that bore her name, his early years spent with his mother (his father was for now a hazy figure in this retrospective fantasy) in the spacious halls of the Maid's Home, sleeping under satin quilts, playing with other children like himself – a Peronist child was never lonely – and drinking his milk on Louis XIV chairs upholstered in light brocade beneath chandeliers with crystal teardrops, until that 'marvellous day' in his mother's life. 'We're going to see her, Ernestito!' she said to him, picking him up and dancing with him (had his foster parents adopted him with that name or had they given it to him?). When the day finally came, his mother dressed him in a short-sleeved shirt, tie, short trousers and lace-up shoes, giving his slicked-down black hair a neat parting and wavy quiff; they took the tram on Avenida de Mayo and got off at Paseo Colón and Independencia, outside the imposing columns of the Foundation. Ernestito would be four or five years old. No, he couldn't be, he realised, doing the sums; Eva would already have been dead by then. Three then, the age at which bourgeois or proletarian consciousness is born: the visit to Eva would be his earliest memory and brand his class consciousness for the rest of his days. Smiling, helpful uniformed men and women – her secretaries and assistants – would give them directions. 'You have an audience with the Señora? This way please.' They would walk past a long line of men in uniforms, cassocks and suits, and elegant, bejewelled women, and his mother would murmur, 'I think these ladies and gentlemen were here first.' 'Them?' Eva's private secretary would say with a disparaging wave. 'They are nothing but ambassadors, generals, businessmen, high-society ladies and church dignitaries. For decades they've gone first while the people waited. Now it's their turn to wait. With Eva the last shall be first, and the first last,' she concluded, pushing open the swing doors to Eva's office.

She was seated behind her desk, legs crossed, dressed in an impeccably tailored suit with velvet lapels, hair gathered in a tight bun, and she was radiant: light poured from her eyes, her brow, her mouth and her ears, encircling her like a halo. His mother made to kneel and kiss her hands, telling Ernestito with a tug to do the same, but Eva stopped her with a gesture, and it was she who stood up, walked around her desk and came over to kiss her. 'Your name's Eulalia, isn't it?' said Eva, without checking her notes (Eulalia? Where on earth had he got that name from?). 'I've seen you at the Maid's Home on several occasions. So you're looking for a house. What is it? Don't you like it where you are? Do they treat you badly? Are you short of anything?' Stammering, his mother would explain her reasons: the boy's father worked in the sugar-cane plantations in Tucumán and had nowhere to stay when he came to visit; if she had somewhere of her own, maybe . . . Eva Perón listened and nodded and smiled; then, half-turning, all briskness and efficiency, to her court of ministers and trade unionists that, only now they were needed, Marroné's fantasy had summoned: 'House, furniture, kitchen equipment and refrigerator, and a job in Buenos Aires for her husband. Are you married?' she asked as an afterthought, and Marroné's mother shook her bowed head in shame. 'Make that a bridal gown too.' And by the following day they were installed in Ciudad Evita, in a smart little Californian bungalow with a front garden, two fully furnished rooms and a refrigerator in the living room; not one of those modern ones with angular, aggressive edges, but a Siam with rounded feminine forms, overflowing with food like a maternal breast, and atop it a little shrine with the portraits of Perón and Eva. His parents' wedding – she all in white, he uncomfortable but happy in his first dark suit, smoothing his pencil moustache, the pair of them hand in hand in a long line of couples, all dressed the same, like a line of toppers on a wedding cake, a mass proletarian wedding officiated by Eva in the flesh, acting as everyone's godmother; then the carefree childhood in a modest, but clean and comfortable, home, the games with other children of his kind in the community park (never lonely, with no one for company but the television or the maid in the gloomy Belgrano flat, never the endless Sundays, never children at St Andrew's, whiter than him, shouting 'Marron Crappé'). There was more: school, where the teachers read them *The Reason for My Life* without a twitch of sarcasm; the visits to the Children's Republic, with its little scale houses, shops, churches and swimming pools; the Children's Football Championships, where Eva always kicked off and handed out the medals afterwards, and Ernestito, who had scored the winning goal for his team – for in this other life he was a star of the national sport of football, not foreignising rugby – would always cherish the gold medallion with her profile on it, received from her very own hands; the Peronist Christmases with toys from the Foundation at the foot of the tree, and the inevitable cider and panettone on the chequered tablecloth; the Children's Tourism Plans, the journey on the train where first class was working class; the stay in Chapadmalal, at one of the eight hotel complexes perched atop the cliffs as if standing guard over the people's happiness, together with other children like Marroné, who, thanks to Evita, were seeing the sea for the first time. Yes, yes, that childhood might have been his had he not been robbed of it by the oligarchy, had he not been torn from his mother's arms by an elderly couple, incapable, out of selfishness or laziness, of having children of their own until it was too late, then deciding on a whim to get themselves one, like someone buying a puppy in a pet shop.

And at that point Marroné was at last granted the vision of the face of his true mother: not the face of that vaguely affectionate, always distant lady that popped up now and then to keep an eye on the maids and lecture them on how to bathe him, dress him and feed him, but the brave, obscure woman who had borne him in her belly for nine months, perhaps trekking long distances on her journey from the countryside to the city (he'd got it into his head they were from Tucumán and was surer of it with every passing minute), supporting him with one hand and stroking him with the other while she talked to him. But the dream was shattered no sooner had it begun: she hadn't the wherewithal to keep him, she was alone in the monstrous, indifferent city. Why hadn't she turned to Evita? Why hadn't she taken her helping hand? There was no way of knowing. Yes, there was, he told himself, transforming his despondency into decisiveness. The time had come to ask the questions he never had: he would confront his parents, and if they didn't talk, there would be birth certificates, adoption records . . . If she was still alive, he'd find her, go to see her and ask her. Because, while he was ignorant of the motives, there was no doubting the sentiment: he could see her clearly, torn apart by tears after signing, without having looked at the papers they handed to her (perhaps she couldn't read), then regretting it, trying to go back for him and being held back, first by the strong arm of a head nurse, then ushered out into the street by another younger, pleasanter one, repeating to her 'It's better this way'. Marroné's eyes filled with tears at the imaginary scene. Cradled in the warmth of his lap, the baby had fallen asleep and, all emotion, Marroné swore to him he'd never put him through his own terrible ordeal of orphancy: if Evita wasn't there, he'd take charge and adopt him – if not as a son, at least as a godson. He'd look after him, watch over him, make sure he wanted for nothing. Because, for all he'd been brought up a bourgeois, his soul was anything but. He was, he realised at last, a Peronist born if not bred. The time had come for him to adopt his true identity. It suddenly became clear, crystal-clear, the reason for his presence in this incredible place, which had at first seemed to him the most foreign and alien of places, and now turned out to be the country of his lost childhood. If his steps had guided him to this shanty town and this house, it wasn't because he was the victim of circumstances, but because he was following a path. All of this had happened – all of it: Sr Tamerlán's severed finger, his captivity in the occupied factory, becoming a workers' leader, the struggle against the forces of the anti-people, the death, or sacrifice as he could see it now, of Paddy, María Eva, El Bebe and so many others, his flight through the mud and water, the very existence of his genteel neighbourhood and this slum, of Montoneros and Sr Tamerlán – so that Marroné could find Marroné. Because he would only find out who he really was when he uncovered the obscure past that had been denied to him, the roots that reached deep into the garbage and the mire. He now also understood the deeper meaning of his mission (which might also be his life's mission): it was nothing less than to carry the spirit of Eva, embodied in her busts, to the very heart of the corporation. For, being neither *us* nor *them*, he was the chosen one, predestined, belonging to both worlds. Like Eva, he was a bridge. Carrying Eva to the corporation, opening the corporation up to Eva: this way capital and labour would march hand in hand rather than be at loggerheads, and this senseless war that had claimed so many victims would come to an end. And, as if blessed by a vision underwriting the truth of his revelation, at that very moment he saw Eva Perón walk past the window of the shack.

8

THE FOUNDATION

Marroné dropped the baby unceremoniously into its card-board box and sped out of the shack, oblivious to its cries, to pursue her down the pitch-black streets. Her dress was embroidered with rhinestones and sequins, her wrists, neck and ears shone with blinding white stones, her platinum hair was tied back in a severe bun and her violet halo banished the impenetrable darkness as she went: it was impossible to lose sight of her. She crossed the mud – furrowed with tyre tracks and pitted with fetid puddles – without so much as staining her lace hem, her feet barely touching the ground. It was definitely her and, more out of an urge to share his astonishment than to corroborate the obvious, Marroné said to a boy of around twelve, the only mortal within earshot out there on the edge of the shanties:

'It's Eva!'

'Course it is. Who do you expect?' the boy answered phlegmatically.

He thought at first it might be the ghost of his own María Eva, killed in combat and returning to earth in all her pomp and glory to lead the oppressed in the last battle against the forces of the anti-people; but when she looked about her at a particularly complex intersection of alleyways, and her glowing profile was silhouetted against the surrounding darkness, the difference in features became apparent; if this floating, glow-in-the-dark Eva wasn't his very own, she could only be the real one. Dazzled, he followed her light like a moth, leaving behind the squalid shanties and crossing a dark wasteland, then climbing a long embankment – Eva with no apparent effort, Marroné slipping and sliding on the trails of muddy clay and the long water-combed grass. For a while now the chorus of frogs and crickets and the occasional barking of a dog had been joined by a continuous, monotonous hum, which he knew to be the high-speed contact of tyres on tarmac: he couldn't be far from the freeway.

He saw her silhouette crest the embankment and nimbly vault the guard rail, pausing for a moment at the hard shoulder as if, more than the risk itself, she feared the shock her spectral apparition might cause the unsuspecting motorists; then one of her diamond-dusted shoes stepped boldly out onto the asphalt, and she strode decisively across. Haloed in the strobes of frantically flashing headlights, she shone like a comet, and, as they swerved to avoid her and the lurid red eyes of their tail lights vanished into the vaporous fog, the echoes of their horns hung in the air like ships' sirens over water. As he followed her, meticulously treading in her footprints, he could see himself – his consciousness split like two halves of an apple – behind the wheel of one of those cars, knuckles white, eyes bulging, heart thudding in his throat. What was that? Did you see it? Was it a woman or a ghost?

Once he had negotiated the last guard rail, and before skittering down the slope of wet grass, Marroné saw where it was she was headed: about fifty metres away, brilliant white against an arc of dark cypresses that cupped them like a hand, gleamed the monumental forms of a neoclassical temple, complete with a ghostly array of statuary. Avoiding the freeway exit and the car entrance, Eva made resolutely for what turned out to be a door concealed in the privet fence surrounding the premises, and shut it behind her. Upon opening it, Marroné discovered that it led to a path laid with white gravel, which crunched softly beneath the soles of his espadrilles, and was lined with privets too tall to see over. The faint light from the waning moon gave the path a satiny sheen, and every dozen steps or so glaring Martian-green spotlights lit the bushes from below. Afraid he would lose first Eva and then himself amid this intricate maze, he quickened his pace; sometimes she would disappear for a few moments around a sharp corner or unexpected bend, but if he didn't let her get too far ahead, her halo still shone above the privet to guide him on his way. But as luck would have it, just as he had felt confident enough to let her get a few steps ahead, a clump of grey clouds scudded across the sickle moon like a drawn curtain, and Eva's faint phospho-rescence was blown out like a candle flame. Marroné began running to catch up with her, taking the right-hand path at a fork and then, in the irrational certainty of having taken the wrong turning, retraced his steps and plunged headlong down the left-hand one, sprinting now and scratching his arms on the briars; he was still running when the maze came to an abrupt end, and he emerged onto an open lawn dotted with topiary, across which Eva glided, borne up on the dome of her skirt like a woman in a Monet painting, in the direction of the Greek temple, so close now that its imposing Doric columns seemed to lurch out at them. At this distance the resemblance, which had been clear from afar, was all the more striking: the place they were making for was a simplified scale reproduction of the Foundation named after the woman whose ghost was now climbing the broad steps to a solid bronze door. Just as she reached it, the moon reappeared, allowing Marroné to take in the topiary of privet, elaborately pruned into motifs from Peronist iconography: medallion profiles of Perón and Eva, a Peronist Party badge, a pair of hands raised skywards as if waiting to embrace all visitors. He looked away only for a few seconds but, when he turned back, he could see no trace of Eva. She had vanished, along with her halo. Marroné's steps rang hollow among the bare columns, which turned out to be not marble, but plaster; the whole façade – including, high above, a Venus de Milo with arms, a Botticelli Venus with clothes, a Victory of Samothrace with smiling head and a Virgin Mary – bore all the familiar hallmarks of the Sansimón Plasterworks. Descending a couple of steps to get a better view of their faces, he instantly recognised in each and every one the unmistakeable features of Eva Perón. This discovery fanned a hesitant, almost extinct flame of hope: if Eva had appeared to him just when he'd thought all was lost, it was to act as his guide. But why him? Had she, too, been fooled by his current proletarian looks? Or was it precisely the opposite: that being not of this world, she could see into his soul – the soul of the Peronist child he should have been?

Fortified by these thoughts, he gave two or three firm knocks on the solid door, on which Perón's head was sculpted in bas-relief. A peephole in the General's face promptly opened, and when two suspicious, beady eyes peered out at him, he felt as if the General himself were inspecting him.

'What you want?' asked the voice within.

'I'm looking for Eva,' replied Marroné, without hesitation.

As if he'd hit upon the password, he heard the sliding of heavy bolts, and the door squealed open.

'Step inside, please. Eva is expecting you. Please join the line.'

The doorman was wearing the livery of a footman in Peronist colours: light-blue Tyrolean suit embroidered with gold thread, frilly white open-necked shirt with the Party badge on the chest pocket, silk stockings and black patent-leather slippers. Marroné took his place at the end of the line. Two things surprised him. The first was the ragged appearance of his companions: there were plebs like himself, beggars and slumdogs; peasants and farmhands too, even a gaucho in full regalia; a few workers in overalls and helmets; a fat man in a leather jacket who looked like a trade unionist; and, last, a couple of toffs in impeccably tailored suits – each of them clutching a letter. The second thing he noticed was that they were all men, and adults: no women or children in sight. Oh, they must have shown in the women and children first, thought Marroné. Like the Peronist slogan went. Did it? Or was he getting it mixed up with the safety procedures for evacuating a ship? The queue wound round the corner of a corridor, then climbed a few stairs, at the top of which Eva's office surely awaited. At first the queue hardly budged, which didn't surprise him because Eva, as he well knew, had only just arrived; but after a few minutes she must have settled in because they started to shuffle steadily forwards.

So it was true, thought Marroné to himself. All those rumours, all those legends. Evita is among us, Evita is back. *Evita is alive*, just as the graffiti he'd always found so absurd claimed. She hadn't died in '52 – her cancer had somehow been cured; or maybe it was all a ruse to trick her enemies into *believing* her dead, and so the much-trumpeted corpse that had been paraded everywhere had been nothing but a simulacrum. But if that were so, Eva should be over fifty by now, and the woman he had followed down the narrow alleyways of the shanty town looked not a year older than Eva when she died – or even several years younger – but then again, many people claimed her illness had shrivelled her to the likeness of a doll. Might she have been frozen? Perhaps that had been the job of the famous Doctor Ara: to keep her dormant until a cure for her illness was found. Or what if she had actually died but her impeccably preserved body had been reanimated intact by the Umbanda rituals of Minister José López Rega, much given to dabbling in the occult, and the sleepwalking Eva he had been following was in fact a zombie? He was only too aware of how deranged these thoughts were (though in fact they were less outrageous than the tangible reality they scrabbled to explain).

He had reached the top of the stairs now and was through the doors to Eva's office, and there she sat, in her Louis Quinze chair, behind an imposing mahogany desk, legs crossed, bun bunched, answering the requests whispered in her ear by each petitioner and reading their letters with radiant smiles, every inch the Eva he had followed. Save for one detail: instead of wearing her white dress, dripping with jewels, this Eva was nude.

Marroné looked ahead, at the line of men standing between them, then behind, at the newcomers. No one else seemed to have noticed the anomaly, or they were all turning a blind eye out of politeness or embarrassment. Or was this a case of the Empress's new clothes? He looked again at those ahead to see how the procedure worked. Like fettered galley slaves, the men shuffled forward in single file, heads bowed, hats in hands (those wearing them, at least), their postures and contrite expressions redolent of the faithful taking communion. On reaching her desk, they would each hand her their letter and she would open it, read it, write something on a card, hand it to them with a smile and let them in. Only with those in authentic English or Italian suits did the procedure vary somewhat: she responded to their letters not with a fresh smile, but with an indignant scowl, pointing a compelling arm to a corner, where others of their ilk stood and waited. The man in front of him, a tramp with dishevelled hair and grubby, foul-smelling clothes, prostrated himself before her and asked to kiss her hand, to which Eva graciously consented. And finally it was Marroné's turn, and such were his embarrassment and her composure that he was the one who felt naked and exposed.

'Welcome to the Eva Perón Sexual Aid Foundation. All your desires will be satisfied. Did you bring your letter?'

Marroné tried to keep his eyes on her face, but they kept slipping downwards to the violet nipples and the dark bush peeping out from between her crossed thighs. There was another reason, apart from the ones on view, for his bewilderment: this Eva was not the same one he'd followed through the alleyways of the shanty town. The darkening of her complexion could at least be blamed on the change from moonlight to electric light, but her ears stuck out like a chimpanzee's and were made doubly prominent by the severely tied hair, whose style was different again: rather than the usual high bun, this one, as befitting her attire, wore an altogether less austere, more bouffant chignon.

'Well?' said Eva encouragingly.

'No . . . er . . . the letter no . . . '

'Not to worry,' said Eva nonchalantly. 'You can ask me for whatever you want, don't be afraid. Whisper it in my ear if you're embarrassed,' she concluded, aligning one of her radio dishes in his direction.

'Busts,' blurted Marroné in the end. 'I want busts of Eva.'

Eva jotted something down on a card with the letterhead of the Foundation and handed it to him with a smile. Marroné made for the door through which those ahead of him had exited.

More surprises awaited on the other side. The door led to a vast lounge decorated in the official Peronist style: a soft blend of Soviet Constructivism and Californian Provençal, with touches of neoclassical stucco; around this fantastic décor strolled as many as a dozen and a half Evas. There were Evas with chignons and Prince of Wales-check suits; Evas in veils and hats; Evas in summer dresses with their hair down; a Dior queen bejewelled from head to toe; another wrapped in sumptuous furs; another encased entirely in black vinyl; one wearing nothing but stockings and suspenders, and another not even that, both with stern-looking buns. Upon closer inspection the variety of builds and features became apparent: they were unified in a general 'Evita' look by the high or low heels to even up their differences in height, the make-up to lighten their skin tones, the clothing to flatten the bustier ones and, above all, the dyed hair: it wasn't for nothing that the naked ones with no distinguishing features wore the obligatory bun. A crowd of men swarmed about each, like drones about a queen bee and, try as he might, nowhere could Marroné spot the Eva who had led him there.

His nostrils filled with the scent of cheap eau de cologne and his ears with a shrill voice before his eyes located the source of both.

'First time, am I right?'

Slick as butter in a hot pan, a footman had slid up to him wearing an embroidered jacket that barely covered his backside, tight torero trousers and bright satin slippers, all in light blue and white and gold. Marroné nodded, still speechless.

'Well? What do you think?'

He groped in the recesses of his stunned mind for something to say.

'Well . . . At long last . . . the happiness of the people.'

One particularly insistent worker kept sticking his nose under the bell-shaped Dior skirt, trying to crawl under it on all fours, while Eva waltzed around him with amused giggles, tapping him with her fan in mock discouragement.

Marroné's companion gave a brief forced laugh, followed by a hirsute handshake:

'Aníbal Vitelo at your service. As is everyone here at the Foundation. What can I do for you?'

'I'd like to . . . look around.'

'Allow me then. I shall be your cicerone.'

One of the three waitresses swept by, serving cider from a bottle with the profiles of the presidential couple on its label: she was wearing high heels and a sober tailleur that, when she turned round, he saw was held together by nothing more than two satin cross-straps, leaving her back, buttocks and legs totally exposed. Marroné's guide took two glasses and handed one to him to toast Eva.

'Cheers . . . Here's to all of this . . . What have you ordered? Can you show me your card?'

Marroné held it out to him in a daze, only now noticing what it said. The naked Eva had scrawled 'Busty Evita' in an illiterate hand. Aníbal clapped his palms in the air. The three nearest Evas turned around as one.

'Let's see, girls . . . '

One was wrapped from head to foot in a sumptuous sable coat that rippled over her in superb folds like the skin of an animal too big for its body; Marroné's eyes took in the marbled pallor of her complexion, the purplish lips, the dainty feet shod in still daintier shoes. Another, the tallest, floated over in a gold lamé dress, like someone out of a Metro-Goldwyn-Mayer film: train fanning out behind her, wasp-waisted sleeveless corsage pushing up her breasts, gold sandals with pearls, and banana curls. The third wore a simple floral-print summer dress, flat-soled sandals and loose chestnut hair and, for one hopeful moment, Marroné thought his own María Eva had come back to life. But when he looked more closely, he realised it wasn't her.

'This poor little greaseball wants to see Eva's bust.'

The Eva in furs had only to open her sable coat wide, as she hadn't a stitch on beneath; her large, marmoreal breasts were pear-shaped and stretch-marked, lined with faint little sky-blue veins. The Eva in the floral dress first helped the Hollywood Eva unfasten the hooks that girded the corsage to her body, then, while her companion levered first one then the other white breast from her bra cups, she had only to loosen one shoulder strap then the other to pull the dress down to her navel and display her small, round breasts.

'So, comrade? What do you think? Does Eva deliver or doesn't she?'

In his infinite tiredness and confusion Marroné felt he was slowly coming apart, separating into his component parts: while his mind waved its legs in the air like an upturned beetle, searching for words to clarify the ridiculous misunderstanding, his nether regions responded to the display of female flesh with a pulsing erection and waves of sexual obfuscation that rose to his cheeks and clouded his sight. He clung to his sense of duty as to a mountain ledge.

'No. I . . . I meant a bust . . . like a statue . . . in stone . . . or plaster . . . ' he concluded, his voice growing smaller with each word.

Puzzled, his chaperone stared at him, but only for a moment. Then, with a knowing look, he gestured to the three Evas to cover up.

'Oh. Busts. As in . . . busts . . . Like the ones they have in schools you mean, don't you? We haven't any . . . no demand for them. We do have a statue, though. Would you like to see it?'

Marroné nodded in relief, though he wasn't sure why. Maybe because a statue was something graspable in all the confusion.

The fountain was round and lined with coloured tiles. At its centre stood the statue of Eva, naked: her long hair loose in the breeze, one slack, cupped hand barely covering her sex, the other raised above her head, innocently holding out an apple, from the core of which flowed the water that enfolded her arm like a transparent fabric; her small, not-too-pert breasts; her belly with its taut roundness; her exquisite buttocks and dreamy thighs. All this enthralled him with its beauty. But it was on her features, her smile that belied the stiffness of the marble, that his gaze dwelt. Because he had recognised her: it was his very own María Eva.

'It's . . . it's her,' he stammered.

'Yes, it's a pretty good likeness, isn't it? We're all very proud of her here. And she has her admirers. There are those who come just to see her. A number of people have wanted to buy her. But she isn't for sale. Real Carrara marble, mark you,' he clarified, making her right buttock ring with a flick of his nail. 'Go on, feel her.'

Marroné stretched out a trembling hand, which his companion caught in mid-flight.

'Marble dolls it is then. Come with me. I think I have just the thing for you.' He'd started getting pushy as soon as he thought Marroné had a weakness for kink. 'You sound like you're looking for something really special.'

Marroné took another sip of cider and nodded. It must have been either fatigue or confusion that made the bubbles go to his head like champagne, and he felt the onset of a wild euphoria that was no less pleasant for being quite out of place.

'This, for example,' said his guide, pointing to a large red brocade sofa on which a few perfumed toffs were sniffing panties and evening shoes, stroking silk stockings and plunging their noses into thick mink coats, 'is Fetishists' Corner. We provide only the very best. See that sable coat? It's the one Eva was wearing when she received her decoration from the hands of the Generalísimo. Franco, I mean. And that salmon pink and blue feather cape is a Dior exclusive.'

'Are they all the real thing?'

'The ones that aren't, are perfect replicas. Not even Dior himself could tell the difference. The blokes in suits,' he said, taking in the throng of punters with a gesture, 'are masochists. More than anything they like spending hours in the waiting room, seeing her minister to the needs of the darkies and the workers first, right under their noses. They'd stay there for ever if it was up to them; when morning comes, the cleaning staff have to shoo a lot of them out with their brooms. They love that too.'

A hairy bald man in a light-blue tutu was dancing on tiptoe, holding a magic wand with which he would, now and again, daintily tap his companions, who would lift their snouts from Eva's undergarments in reply, give a low growl and then go back to their ferretings.

'Dior again. Some aren't content just to touch them. The Good Fairy costume was so popular we had to make five replicas. So, if that's your thing, you'll have a ball. Now, if you ask me, I'd recommend the ones of flesh and bone. We cater for all tastes, as you'll see. I'll give you the price list: lady with whip, ten thousand pesos, yes, the one in boots and black leather; Eva in furs, the one you've just seen, twelve thousand; horsewoman in white pleated shirt, riding crop and riding boots with spurs, ten thou – doesn't that bun look deliciously tight?; governess with cherry lips, stiletto heels and pointer, also ten thou – she comes with a class in Peronist Party doctrine; Admiral Evita, that one, no, the one in the tailleur with the gold buttons, braid and epaulettes, eight grand, and that's pretty much it in our disciplinary line. Next up are the princesses and Hollywood stars: The Prodigal Woman, that one over there in velvet, with dark ringlets, twelve thousand – the dress is authentic, isn't she a dead ringer for Hedy Lamarr?; the one over there . . . no, no, the one in the peasant costume, with the plaits behind her ears . . . she's the one from *The Circus Ride* – a little on the dull side, she's on special offer at seven, but I wouldn't recommend her. The one in gold lamé, twelve thousand – get a load of the tits on her . . . '

'And . . . the one in the flowery dress?'

'Ahh . . . You fancy her, do you? Delicious little pair of funbags as well. That one's Perón's lover, Tigre island model, ten thousand – good enough to eat. In the Evita Duarte line – which won't burn a hole in your pocket – there's the little rising star, the one rolling her eyes like Betty Boop, very twenties, eight grand; that little chick in the Boca shirt and hot pants is doing good business, eight again – a real bargain; and last there's the country wench, able and willing to keep the old boss happy, four thousand five hundred. What else? Oh. The Santa Evita line: there's the Madonna of the Poor, complete with halo, twelve thou – hasn't a stitch on under that cloak; the one with the hair-weaves in the mantilla and the black silk dress, with the Order of Isabella the Catholic Cross over her bosom, thirteen thou – had her audience with the Pope in that habit she did . . . And I think that's it, apart from the specials.'

'The specials?'

His companion's voice dropped several decibels:

'Cancer victim. Twenty thou. Thirty-three kilos.'

Marroné gave a low whistle.

'Gosh!' He was slightly tipsy from the cider and gradually getting into the spirit of the proceedings.

'She really does have cancer. Pays for her treatment with whatever she pulls in here.'

'They're still pretty pricey though, aren't they? They're not exactly tailored to a worker's pocket, shall we say.'

His guide looked at him for a few seconds with a sort of a halfway smile, unsure whether to take him seriously or not; in the end he decided not to.

'You really do get into character, don't you? I admire the realism,' he said, holding Marroné's filthy rags between thumb and forefinger, smelling them and wrinkling his nose in disgust. 'Don't get me wrong . . . it isn't a criticism, you understand,' he said, pointing floorwards with his eyes. 'Still, those espadrilles . . . a bit old hat if you ask me. Adidas trainers are way more "shanty" these days. Which company are you from?'

'The game's up,' thought Marroné with an inward sigh, he'd been found out. Perhaps it was his English-school accent that had given him away.

'Tamerlán & Sons.'

'Ohhh . . . You should have said so in the first place. Old customers . . . If your dear President had stuck with us, we wouldn't be lamenting his sad plight. The guards here are top drawer. A lot of punters bring their own, of course, the neighbourhood being what it is. Look, over there, that's a colleague of yours if I'm not mistaken.'

Marroné followed his pointing finger, and could barely contain his surprise when he saw, nuzzling the equestrian Eva's riding boots and trying to lick their soles, the irreproachable Aldo Cáceres Grey on all fours, dressed as a beggar except for his exposed arse, the crack of which the rider was languidly caressing with her crop.

'Ah . . . Marroné . . . ' he stammered in embarrassment when he saw him loom over him. 'What are you doing here?'

Cáceres Grey's expression was that of a life member of the Jockey Club, in his favourite easy chair in the library, on seeing the butcher from the corner shop, who has just been admitted for a look round. Marroné knew that expression all too well; too often had he been on the receiving end of it at school, and a fierce smile of triumph spread inwardly across his lips.

'Same as you, I suppose. First time?'

'Errm . . . No, well, actually . . . ' he began, but at that moment, still seated in her armchair, his Eva caught the back of his neck between sole and heel and thrust his face to the floor.

'I told you not to talk to strangers, slave!'

'Ooow . . . Now just hold on a second. He's a colleague from the company.'

'All the better. He can have a good look at what I do to you and tell everyone about it at work tomorrow.'

'Well, you look busy. See you around . . . ' said Marroné, turning to go.

Cáceres Grey attempted to extricate himself from under her sole and got a thwack across the buttocks from her riding crop.

'Ooow! You filthy black slum bitch!'

'Down, boy! And don't speak unless you're spoken to.'

Marroné rejoined his guide, more and more composed by the second now he'd begun to understand.

'We're all businessmen, here.'

'No, not everyone. That one over there, the one dressed as a farmhand, he's a rancher. The docker in the gym vest with a handkerchief round his neck owns several shipping companies and the conscript being drilled by Admiral Eva is a colonel in the artillery.'

'All anti-Peronists. Gorillas,' mused Marroné. 'Now I get it. And that one?' he said, pointing at a football hooligan with a curly mop and hairy white belly protruding from beneath his San Lorenzo shirt.

'Him? No, he actually works here. We lay on the real thing for the punters who like being buggered in drag. There's an entire wardrobe at your disposal if you're that way inclined. '

Marroné declined the invitation with a flick of the wrist:

'Thanks. And the ones that look like trade unionists?'

Two fat men – one olive-skinned with a centre parting, the other with slicked-back curls and several days' stubble, neither older than forty – were receiving a football and a bicycle from the hands of the Good Fairy.

'Trade unionists. They come here quite a lot, as you'll see – nostalgic steelworkers mostly. Loaded with cash they are, but they still hanker after the golden years of their humble childhoods, when they used to get presents from Eva,' he said, with a puff of scorn, which Marroné seconded to conceal any hint of embarrassment, the memory of his own shanty-town epiphany still fresh in his mind. 'But they're in the minority. The ones that truly love her – worship her, I mean. Two classes of people come here as a rule: those who come to humiliate her and those who come to be humiliated by her. Or, not to put too fine a point on it, to fuck or be fucked.'

'Literally?'

'Those ones over there. The three tall ones? The Three Graces we call them.'

The Three Graces consisted of the lady in gold lamé, the governess with the angular jaw and sharp nose, and one he hadn't noticed before, wearing an ermine-trimmed silk suit as white as daylight and a diamond tiara. All three had large feet and prominent Adam's apples.

'As well as being distinguished, our clients can be very specific at times. "I want my Eva to come with a dick. And one that works." So we ask them to go easy on the hormones.'

Marroné was genuinely impressed, not only by what was on view, but by the lesson in business lore: they had found a niche in the market and had made it flourish with an almost infinite product range that exhausted all possible combinations. No, not all, he suddenly realised:

'What about . . . the Montonero Evita?'

His guide let out a shush and fanned the air with his fingers to tell him to keep his voice down.

'Shhh. Don't even mention her. What are you trying to do? Make them shit themselves? Some things just aren't funny. So, are you ready for the pièce de résistance?'

They went up some stairs and through a door. By now, Marroné had the impression that the world held no more surprises for him. But he was wrong. They were in a quadrangular room upholstered entirely in black velvet: portraits of Perón and Eva covered one of the walls, and hundreds of coloured votive ribbons, most with gold lettering, were pinned to the upholstery: 'YOU LIVE ON ETERNAL IN THE SOUL OF YOUR PEOPLE – TRAMWORKERS UNION – NATIONAL ATOMIC ENERGY COMMISSION.' The centrepiece was a couch surrounded by fresh flowers and covered with a silk sheet. And there, on the sheet, lay Eva.

She looked like Sleeping Beauty, and her skin had the pallor of marble and the sheen of wax. A snippet of schoolboy Shakespeare flashed across his mind: 'Nor scar that whiter skin of hers than snow / And smooth as monumental alabaster.' Her hair was combed back towards the nape in two thick Greek braids, and an ivory coloured tunic covered the rest of her body, save her hands – which clasped a rosary over her belly – and her naked feet with their slender toes, which Marroné could barely prevent himself from kissing.

'So? What do you say?' The procurer's voice rang stridently in his ears.

'She's . . . perfect,' he said in a whisper, incapable of taking his eyes off her.

'Thirty grand.'

'She's . . . the real one?'

'Of course.'

'I thought she'd been returned to Perón.'

'Perón got screwed. He got one of the three original replicas. You know, modelled in wax directly from the body.'

'And does anyone ask for her?'

'She's our top earner. The military really get off on her.'

Marroné contemplated her head and the line of her shoulders with keen professionalism. Give him a saw and he might just be able to separate them from the rest of her body; that would make one bust – ninety-one short – but it would be a start. He immediately decided he was losing his mind.

'So . . . Which one'll it be?'

Marroné's brain groped for the contents of the calcareous bivalve that had once served him as a wallet. He couldn't leave without consuming something, not after being treated to such a display.

'Errr . . . How much did you say the country girl was?'

He recognised the look at once. It was the kind a Dior salesman would give a customer who, after being shown around the entire season's collection, abjectly asks to be reminded of the price of the ankle socks.

'This way.'

He had to shove the wooden door, which danced on its hinges. The room had peeling walls, a cheap print of the Virgin Mary, a sagging iron bed, a chair and a night table with a bedside lamp and red lampshade.

'It's an exact replica of the rooms in the brothel run by Eva's mother, Doña Juana, in Junín. It was where Eva, aged twelve, auctioned off her virginity at a party for the local ranch-owners; not out of need, but out of a sheer taste for vice,' he recited in the monotone of a tour guide reeling off the same old spiel day in, day out.

'I thought that whole brothel thing was a load of bull.'

This time Aníbal's expression was openly hostile.

'What do you think this is?' he said, embracing the surroundings with raised open arms. 'The National History Museum? If so, it's news to me. So. Do you want her or not? Alright. Wait here.'

'Errrr . . . ' began Marroné.

'You can have her for four. Enjoy.'

Marroné sat on the bed, which sagged even lower, the metal springs groaning as if injured. The room had no windows or openings of any kind, and smelt like a damp kennel. Beside the bedside lamp was an ashtray overflowing with cigarette butts; had he had a lighter, Marroné would gladly have lit one. He opened the drawer: no lighter, no matches; just a candle end and a copy of *The Reason for My Life* in the perennial Peuser edition he remembered from his schooldays.

She entered without knocking. He'd barely noticed her in the lounge, and it was plain to see why: she was a tiny, transparent slip of a thing, slight and flat-chested, with legs like a lapwing's; she was wearing a cheap, printed cotton dress, smoke-coloured stockings and Basque espadrilles laced up her calves. She can't have been more than fourteen and, rather than bed her, Marroné felt like fixing her some cookies and milk.

'Were you looking for me, sir?'

Marroné's eyes welled with tears. What in God's name was a child like this doing here? Perhaps, the thought suddenly occurred to him, this was why he was here today; perhaps his true mission was to save her and, by doing so, the busts would magically be his. He immediately decided he was raving again: he was willing to believe in anything if it looked like offering him a way out of this maze.

'Come here, don't be afraid, sit down here, beside me,' he eventually managed to say. 'What's your name?'

'Eva, sir.'

'No, I'm asking you your real name.'

The girl looked at him for a moment with her dark, unfathomable eyes, then said:

'Eva María.'

'Where do you come from, Eva María?' he said, following her drift.

'Los Toldos, sir,' she said, without hesitation; she'd learnt her lines well. 'Shall I take my dress off?'

Before Marroné could do anything to stop her, she'd whipped it over her head and was standing naked, save for a pair of turquoise suspenders, which, together with her smoke-coloured stockings, suggested not so much bad taste but only poverty. The bastards think of everything, Marroné said to himself. Her breasts would have fitted snugly into English teacups, and her pubic hair was dark but sparse, leaving her narrow slit exposed when she stretched out on the bed: she looked as if malnourishment had stopped her from developing fully. It was the last snatch of social conscience his mind was capable of before his spring-loaded erection toppled what little of his moral scaffolding was left standing, and he decided he'd had enough: enough of trying to understand what was going on, enough of being nice to everyone, enough of doing the company's bidding and Sr Tamerlán's especially, enough of winning friends only for them to get killed in the blink of an eye, enough of the stinking clothes he was wearing . . . 'I'm going to screw her, I'm going to screw her and you can all fuck off,' he said to himself, slipping his t-shirt over his head and tugging his pants and underpants down so fast his member bounced up and down like a springboard. Gripping his glans in his palm, like someone stopping a shaken bottle of beer, and muttering through clenched teeth 'you whore, you little whore, you black slum bitch', he launched himself on top of her in an attempt to get a hole-in-one, but missed, and all his virility dribbled away through his fingers in two or three miserable spasms. Eva must have felt it, because she sat up with a start.

'Sorry, sir!' she exclaimed, as if it had been her fault. 'Don't worry, I'll clean you up.'

She disappeared into the little bathroom, while Marroné sat on the bed, holding up his cupped palm to stop the dripping, and was soon back with a damp cloth.

'No, no, don't,' mumbled Marroné, stricken with shame, but Eva wouldn't have any of it.

'Let's see, hand first . . . This little piggy, then this one, till they're nice and clean . . . Don't worry about the bed, the maids'll change it . . . Ooh, look, it got on me too, it's all over my muffin.'

She looked a lot more comfortable in her new role, more self-assured: she had clearly been in domestic service. She reminded him of a maid his parents had had – somewhat older than Eva María it's true, and darker-skinned and bustier – who'd turned him on as a teenager; he used to follow her around the house with his tongue hanging out and a couple of times tried to spy on her naked through the keyhole, but to no avail; he had hoped he would lose his virginity to her and told all his classmates he had, but in the end he had never actually dared, and his father had had to take him to a brothel. That was his first premature ejaculation, and the woman had made him wipe it up, standing over him making sarcastic remarks while he got down on his hands and knees: this early humiliation could well have been the stigma that turned into a trauma what would otherwise have been no more than a mishap. And perhaps now this sweet little girl had come to redeem the unnecessary cruelty of that callous whore, and somehow bring the cycle to a close; perhaps this was the dawn of a new era, though he didn't actually care much because all he wanted to do was die on the spot and be done with it all.

Eva María had returned to the bathroom with her cloth, and Marroné heard the water running, then the squeak of the tap. This time she'd soaked it in warm water and put a little soap on too.

'Lie back, please, sir,' he heard her say.

Without opening his eyes he obeyed. She ran the cloth first over his forehead, ears, eyes and cheeks; when she got to his neck, she got up and rinsed it again. Wetting it whenever it cooled, she bathed his chest, arms, abdomen, thighs and shins; then she whispered in his ear for him to turn over and repeated the procedure on the other side. Marroné hadn't bathed since his days in the factory, and Eva María washed him clean of all he had been through since: the crust of plaster, the urine, the blood, the oil-slick stream, his intimate contact with the garbage and mud of the shanties. She lingered long and tender over his feet, devoting a warm cloth to each, and she must have brought alcohol because he felt a sharp stinging at several points, from sores or cuts. When he turned over he saw her standing at the bedside, alcohol in one hand, cotton wool in the other. She was smiling shyly.

'There's still another half an hour to go. Would you like me to stay?'

She didn't wait for Marroné's nod. She lay down beside him, nestling into the hollow at his side, with her head on his shoulder and one leg wrapped over both of his. Marroné slid an arm under her neck to caress her hair and back, and, after two or three strokes, fell sound asleep.

She wasn't there when he awoke with a start and a moan. Regaining his sense of the present, he put his shabby clothes back on and checked his wallet to see if she'd emptied it. He took out the four notes and slipped them into *The Reason for My Life*.

He stepped out into a corridor of identical symmetrical doors; he couldn't remember coming this way on his way up, though he might have forgotten. The doors were so thin that he could hear everything going on behind them: the familiar moans, a recording of Eva's hoarse voice tirelessly repeating 'I offer you all my energies so that my body can be a bridge to the happiness of all. Walk over it . . . ' One stood ajar, and Marroné spied the lady with the whip riding a naked fat man dripping with gold and chains, and shouting, 'What kind of an oligarch are you? You don't even have the balls to exploit Bolivian workers!' Then, spying Marroné, she cracked the whip on the wooden floor and beckoned to him to come in. 'Look,' she said to her steed, 'here's a slumdog come to stick his filthy cock in you. Now you'll see what's good for you.'

Reeling, Marroné backed away and stumbled down the stairs. In spite of the music still playing (wan tango Muzak), the artificial light and the welded-shut blinds, he felt, in his stinging eyes and jaded blood, the end of the party and the closeness of dawn. It was also being heralded by the dynamics of the sexual encounters, which had now spilled out from the reserve of the bedroom and across the half-deserted lounge. The governess was disciplining one of the trade unionists with her cane, forcing him to recite the Twenty Truths of the Peronist Creed and whacking him every time he got one wrong; The Prodigal Woman leapt from one side of the red brocade sofa to the other, hitching up her heavy velvet skirt to reveal an outsized, flesh-coloured strap-on dildo swinging from its harness, just out of reach of the costumed tramp drunkenly grabbing at it; and, last of all, the radiant Eva, whom Marroné had followed through the alleys of the shanties – his Divine Beatrice who had led him from the dark forest, his luminous Tinkerbell – was being served simultaneously by the colonel, the businessman and the rancher, striving to hump her back to what in their eyes she had never ceased to be: the whore of Babylon, a peroxide blonde harlot, a black slumdog. Her bun – which was mostly hairpiece – had come undone and was now being batted about on the floor by a tortoise-shell cat.

Dragged down by his cider hangover – a first far worse than he had ever imagined – and racked by an exhaustion that had escalated from the physical to the metaphysical, Marroné cast about in all directions to see if he could find something to cling on to in the midst of the wreck. Then he saw the statue of Eva, standing tall and proud and unscathed in the general corruption scattered at her feet, and she was the most beautiful woman he'd ever seen. Rapt by her loveliness, he knelt down in the fountain and kissed her small, frozen feet, resting his cheek against her fine ankles, not knowing whether it was the water flowing from her hands or his own tears running down his cheeks. Prostrate before her, he confessed his boundless contrition and remorse.

'Radiant Eva, immaculate Eva, Eva most beauteous, I beseech thee . . . I don't love my wife, I can't stand my children, I try to influence people, I left my best friend for dead, I've been . . . fingered . . . I don't know what to do. I'm lost, I can't go on, I can't go back . . . If you know, my lady, I beg you, show me the way . . . '

And, when he raised his eyes to her face, Eva seemed to answer him. Not in words, but with an eternally even, eternally quiet smile – a smile of stone. The tilt of her neck and face, the half-open eyelids, the slight curve of her nose, all seemed to be pointing to one spot, which was hidden by Marroné's hands and face. He drew them back hurriedly:

on one side of the pedestal, carved in Roman characters, there was a name, which must have been the sculptor's: Rogelio García.

Marroné clasped her cold and lovely body and, standing on tiptoe, stretched up to her lips to leave his offering of a kiss.

'Thank you, Evita . . . Thank you . . . '

On his way out he ran into Aníbal, who, yawning profusely, was locking up.

'Would you like them to bring your car?'

'No, I'll walk, thanks.' Marroné groped for a plausible lie. 'I came . . . by train.'

'You amaze me. What a passion for the authentic.'

Outside, a pale dawn had taken the heavens by storm. He didn't need to ask for directions: he had only to join the blurred V of hazy figures converging on a single point with the defeated, trudging gait of those who rise in darkness every working day. Near the train station was a bar, whose tables and windows were thick with dust, turned to velvet by the early morning sun, and right next to the door, a public telephone, so orange it glowed. He ordered a milky coffee and croissants, and asked for the telephone directory; he found the man he was looking for with his third call.

9

EVITA CITY

A train so covered in graffiti that it looked like a mural on wheels pulled up in eerie silence at the deserted platform. Marroné curled up like a dog at the far end of the last carriage and noticed that, like himself, the inside was broken in a variety of ways: the green imitation leather of the seats was cracked or slashed; the rings of the handrails had been wrenched from their leather straps; the windows were jammed shut or had panes missing, and bore the scorch marks of flames that, after bursting them, had licked their innards. The train got under way with a series of choking rattles; it was like travelling in a snake with a broken spine. Two stations further on and his carriage had filled with early birds on their way to work, the odd old man, hawkers peddling their wares – and with a certain curiosity he noticed that no one had wanted to occupy the three free seats around him. He must have looked and smelt worse than he had supposed. But he didn't feel like company anyway and, turning back to his jammed window, he devoted himself to contemplating the landscape through the dusty glass filigreed by old rain: unplastered, flat-roofed brick or cement houses, building sites suspended in eternal construction as if a magic spell had been cast over them, mechanics' workshops overflowing with cars, front gardens, builders' yards, sheds, fields, churches, shops, cars at level-crossings, main roads bristling with intrusive perpendicular billboards. The rhythmical impetus of the train drew a forgotten childhood prayer from his lips: 'Good Fairy who laughs with the angels, I promise to be good as you wish, respecting the Lord, loving my country, loving General Perón, studying and being for everyone the child you dreamt: healthy, happy, polite and pure of heart.' At the moments of greatest acceleration between stations, the contours and boundaries of the visible world began to merge and give: a cart morphed into a gate, a low wall into some waste ground, the sky blue of a house into the blue sky. When the train slowed down again, with a clatter like a captive Titan rattling his chains at regular intervals, things would return to their original, separate selves; but there came a point when the crazed engine driver just kept accelerating and they zoomed through first one station, then another, then another, each platform shorter than the last; the eye became incapable of taking in anything more than a single long broad brushstroke sweeping across trees, houses, gardens and signs, and soaking up their colours to paint a face so huge Marroné feared that, when complete, it would be too vast for his eyes to take in.

He opened them to a disc of sky bordered with heads, and in its outline he could make out the profile of her face. Disappointed to find that what they'd taken for a fatality had been no more than a fainting fit, the ring of people around him immediately opened and the beloved features melted away like a cloud into the sky. But that instant had been enough to make Marroné smile in recognition: it was Eva, of course; she was still with him, she was everywhere, she would never abandon him. Before the crowd had dispersed, two men hauled him up by the armpits, supporting him until they were certain he wouldn't fall again and break his neck on the platform, and sending him on his way with an 'Alright, pal, get yourself back home now and sleep it off', and other such trifles. After doing his incoherent drunk impression and muttering his unintelligible thanks with a faraway smile (he'd decided to role-play the character; if he had lost the ability to win friends and influence people – and everything suggested he had – he could still at least play along with them), he looked up at a sign to discover that by some miracle they'd got him off the train at the right station – the one the man had mentioned on the phone – and decided to take it as a good omen, being in great need of one: if the evil enchanters had not given up their pursuit, they may at least have taken the day off.

The tracks in these parts ran along a deep, narrow gully, along which he could see no more than a patch of blue sky, the ubiquitous English station, another train whose great solar eye approached as silently as the one that had brought him, and the riotous summer foliage of the chinaberry trees, whose merciful shade shielded him from the unforgiving sun. With some difficulty he climbed the uneven steps of a cement staircase and, nearing the top, looked around him. Beyond the mandatory park of eucalyptuses that lined the tracks, stretched an ordered landscape of little bungalows shaped like pats of butter, with Spanish roofs, columns and wooden shutters with diamond fretwork, gardens with flower beds, the odd parked car and occasional garden gnome. He ventured along leafy streets that looked straight but curved imperceptibly as he walked, passing several children riding bikes in the middle of the road, an old woman wheeling a shopping bag and a soda-siphon delivery truck, before plucking up the courage to ask a passing resident out walking his dog.

'Oh, yes. That's in the First District, over towards the bun. Let's see . . . Keep still, boy!' he told the cocker tugging at its lead. 'You go straight on . . . '

'Along this one?'

'No, you're heading for the nose that way. No, if you want the bun, you go straight on down here, and then . . . You'll see a big square, somewhere around the cheek . . . Turn left and keep going . . . There's a big tall building right in the middle of the bun – a five-storey tower block. The house you're looking for is right opposite. Can't miss it.'

And indeed he couldn't, but it was more than ten blocks in the blazing sun and more than once he felt like throwing in the towel. He couldn't have said what kept him going: it didn't feel as though it was him but the houses that were moving, filing past him on either side like a procession, displaying all the personal touches that the inhabitants' instinctive sense of difference had added to the basic Peronist bungalow: spear-headed railings, slate or wood cladding, porches, bay windows and quaint colonial streetlamps. The house he was looking for turned out to be on a corner, one with a rounded chamfer rather than the usual angled one, and a lawn that sloped to a low, trim privet fence, beyond which a rich array of statues and fountains was spread across the kempt front garden. This was the house. Outside the front gate, in the shade of an old red pick-up with a wooden box, a girl and a boy in swimming costumes were playing with watering cans, toy buckets and a hose-pipe.

'Hello, lamb. I'm looking for Sr Rogelio,' said Marroné, addressing the boy in as friendly a tone as he could, but when the girl started to wail and the boy to shout 'Grandpa! Grandpa!' with barely contained alarm, he decided he hadn't hit the right note.

The man didn't emerge from the house but from an adjoining shed, evidently an extension of the original bungalow. He must have been somewhere between sixty and seventy, with white hair and dark skin, and his eyes were black and bright, like pebbles in a basket of wrinkles. He could, Marroné felt, have been his own grandfather – the original, not the fake. He was wearing a canvas apron over his loose-fitting clothes and clutched a hammer and chisel in his strong sculptor's hands. His grandchildren had clung to his legs and peeked out from behind them.

'Yes?' he asked tentatively, putting away the chisel in an apron pocket but still gripping the hammer. 'Are you looking for someone?'

'We spoke on the telephone. It's about the busts.'

★   ★   ★

He had leant on the gate to steady himself, and the grandfather had helped him to the kitchen, where he recovered sufficiently over biscuits and maté to explain what he'd come for.

'My name's Ernesto and I'm . . . well, you know, with the special forc . . . no, I mean the revolutionary . . . You must have come across our . . . ' he said hopefully, but seeing the man's growing confusion, he was forced to be specific: 'In the Montoneros. So, as part of the programme for deprived areas, we want every shanty town to have its very own bust of Eva . . . '

Don Rogelio listened to him carefully, his calm, kind eyes fixed on him, and, feeling uncomfortable with the baldness of his flagrant lies, Marroné decided to season them with a pinch of truth.

'I'm on the run, Don Rogelio. At this moment I'm being pursued by the union mob, the Triple A and the police. I look like this because I've been hiding away in a garbage tip. If they get their hands on me . . . '

Rogelio put one of his hands on his, covering it completely.

'Don't you worry now, Ernesto. They can't get to you here. You're inside Eva now.'

He pointed to a picture on the wall; it was just a page torn from a Filcar street guide, coloured in and covered with notes and numbers; a map whose blocks, squares, streets, train tracks and freeways formed, sharp and clear against the background of empty lots that encircled it, the unmistake-able outline of a bust of Eva. Marroné's first reaction was to think he was hallucinating again, but as he began to find his way round the fantastic cartography, he remembered he was in Ciudad Evita, the model village whose outline had indelibly stamped the profile of Eva Perón on the surface of the pampas. Don Rogelio, meanwhile, had started to outline his theory about the inviolability of this Peronist Jerusalem.

'Don't forget that the figures of the General and Eva came in for some pretty brutal treatment after the coup against Perón – what *they* called "the Liberating Revolution", but what *we* knew was our return to bondage. Rampant iconoclasm it was: pictures, posters, busts – no image was spared . . . Except this one, the biggest of all: maybe because it is so vast that, like the Nazca Lines in Peru, it can only be seen from the sky. Ironic, isn't it? At one time there were rumours about them bringing in bulldozers and teams of conscripts, or radical and socialist volunteers, to alter the street plan and change her profile to Sarmiento's or Yrigoyen's; so we took turns on guard duty for several nights, all set to make a stand, even prepared to lay ourselves down in front of the machines as a last resort; but in the end they never came. One possibility that occurred to us later was that they could just as easily obliterate her features by building new neighbourhoods around them: but, besides being expensive, it wouldn't have been any use, because Eva's profile would still have been there, hidden yet visible at the same time, like those figures you sometimes discover hiding within a picture of another subject. So we eventually came up with the theory that Eva's outline is like a magic circle, a stockade against the gorillas lying in wait in the jungle beyond. In here at least there's still an island of the Argentina she dreamt up for us, the Argentina they stole from us after she died.'

Don Rogelio's serene, unhurried voice soothed him like a lullaby: Eva's protecting you – You're inside her – Eva's Island – Eva loves you – Eva will look after you.

He awoke with a start from his nodding, his head nearly on his knees.

'So everything in our power we can do . . . ' Don Rogelio had carried on. 'The doors of this house are never closed to a comrade on the run. Do you have any idea of the times I've had to hide? And been spared the nick by the help of a neighbour or a stranger? Actually, if you need houses, or families to hide your people in . . . I'm kind of in charge of neighbourhood business. We stick together in this place,

Peronists through thick and thin; not the kind who go around shouting "Viva Perón" on 17th October and keep their mouths shut on 16th June. Alright, come on, I'll show you the workshop before you drop off in that chair.'

In his short walk through the garden he'd already had the opportunity to see that Don Rogelio's work married a pure and delicate love of matter with a dubious taste for the plebeian. Proof of the former lay in his onyxes, marbles and granites, which seemed to be shaped more by the caresses of a loving hand than by the blows of a hammer, and in his polished woodcarvings, which seemed to have been moulded in some previous liquid state; proof of the latter, in the proliferation of shepherds, shepherdesses and naked nymphs, of gauchos with rugged, whittled features, and indomitable Indians with tensed throats and prominent teeth. Marroné, however, only took this in fleetingly and obliquely, for his eyes had locked like traps onto a shell-like forehead, a delicate swan neck and a cascade of loose hair pouring over translucent alabaster shoulders.

'It's her, isn't it?' he asked in hushed reverence.

Don Rogelio nodded, silent and smiling. At that moment his two grandchildren came in – still regarding the shabby, bug-eyed Marroné with suspicion – and sat down, one on each of their grandfather's knees. He waited until they'd made themselves comfortable before beginning his story.

'I only saw her up close once. She came to visit us for the opening of the union building, and she dazzled us all, even the communists and socialists who'd sworn they weren't going to greet her. She was wearing a wasp-waisted dress,' he said, looking at the little girl, 'in crimson brocade with gold thread and long sleeves, and a silk skirt embroidered with silver, and her hair was loose – just like spun gold it looked – all the way down to her waist.'

'Was she like a princess, Granpa?' she asked him.

'Yes, but a princess of the people. Anyway, what stunned us most was her whiteness . . . I've heard her compared with magnolias and jasmines and snow, but she was different. White, translucent, yet with an inner fire. Like a flame burning in an alabaster lamp. Look, to give you some idea . . . When she arrived, we'd just finished lunch, so we offered her some red wine. She took the glass with a smile and drank it right down. You could see she had a thirst on her. And her whiteness was so pure we could all see the wine run down her throat, and we stood there and marvelled. Perón was opaque, always had been. The time I sculpted him, I did him in black granite. But Eva was so transparent . . . Through her skin . . . shone the people,' he concluded, looking straight at Marroné with his kind, dark eyes. 'I tried to put all that into this sculpture,' he said, turning to the swan-necked Eva. 'But it's only a partial success.'

'How much?' asked Marroné, cutting him short lest the whole story be a ruse to bump up the price.

'I wasn't thinking of selling it, Ernesto. Not for now.'

Marroné's eyes were as hard and bright as the obsidian of an Aztec priest's dagger. Tethered for days, the Tamerlán & Sons head of procurement roared inside him like a caged tiger with an empty stomach.

'Just name your price. And for ninety-one others too,' he said, sweating and trembling from head to toe as if he had the fever.

Don Rogelio showed him a wicker chair, and Marroné sat down gratefully.

'They're very important to you, aren't they?'

Marroné nodded with imploring eyes, his Adam's apple pumping like a piston with every gulp.

'The poor children of the shanties . . . ' he began.

'But I don't see how I can help you. I'm a carver, I make one-offs, originals. What you need is someone who can mass-produce them.'

He would have grabbed him by the lapels and shaken him if he'd had any.

'I need those busts! I don't care how! I don't care if they're made of papier mâché, tin foil or plasticine!'

The two children had taken refuge behind their grandfather again. Marroné slumped back in his chair, his every limb trembling.

'Forgive me.'

Don Rogelio kept his benevolent eyes fixed on Marroné's.

'Right, children, off you go, I think I can hear your mummy.' He sent his grandchildren away with a pat on each of their bottoms, then turned to Marroné. 'Ernesto . . . you aren't a Montonero, are you? You aren't even a Peronist. Do you want to tell me about it?'

Marroné fought an irresistible urge to fall to his knees and kiss his hands.

'I'm a top executive with a leading construction company,' he said, beginning his harrowed confession. 'I realise that, seeing me like this, you may find it hard to believe, but look,' he fished the bivalve out of his pocket, rummaged in it and pulled out his driver's licence, his medical insurance card, his San Isidro Athletics Club membership, and spread them out on the workbench to arouse, if not the credulity, then at least the compassion of the man in front of him, but Don Rogelio stopped him with an outstretched hand.

'It's alright, Ernesto. I have no reason to doubt your word. If you say so, I believe you.'

Marroné felt his eyes flood with tears.

'It's just that I lied to you before.'

'Well, I suppose you had your reasons.'

He nodded dumbly, gulping back the snot.

'The Montoneros have kidnapped the president of the company. He's a good man, but he's had some . . . er . . . bad press lately. One of the conditions for his release is that we put a bust of Eva in every office. That makes ninety-two busts in all. I've been hunting for them for weeks, but powerful forces have been moving against me,' he babbled, because it was no longer the old Marroné talking, but the paranoid bag of shredded nerves the events of the last few days had turned him into. 'Help me, please, Don Rogelio. I don't know who else to turn to. Even if you just made me one or two little sample busts, it would buy us some time . . . '

Don Rogelio had pulled a half-smoked cigar out of his shirt pocket and lit it with an old petrol lighter; it was a cheap, foul-smelling cheroot and he chewed on it with manifest delight.

'Here's what I suggest. You get yourself bathed, changed and have a lie-down for a while till lunchtime. And after something to eat, when you've got your strength back, we'll carry on talking. What do you say?'

Marroné nodded, still more disbelieving than frankly grateful, and followed Don Rogelio through the garden, the multicoloured strip curtain and the kitchen to the master bedroom, which contained a double bed, a wardrobe, a crucifix and olive branch, and a photo of Don Rogelio as a young man embracing a smiling, even younger woman in a floral dress. From the wardrobe his host produced a pair of trousers, clean and pressed, and a freshly ironed shirt, some thick cotton underpants and a pair of flip-flops.

'I'm giving you the flip-flops because all of my shoes will be too big for you. Let's see, what else . . . ' He reached up to the top shelf for a clean towel. 'I think that'll do for now,' he said, laying it on the pile on the bed.

Marroné looked on with the wariness of a little boy accustomed to each display of affection being the prelude to a slap; but after his shower with hot water and lots of soap, and the clean clothes, he felt his optimism and his faith in his fellow man rise in him again like the dawn of a new age. He felt even better when, after a deep, refreshing sleep, Don Rogelio's two grandchildren burst into the room giggling and shook him awake without showing the slightest sign of fear.

Saturday was family lunch day at Don Rogelio's. He had so many children (nine, only counting the ones still living) that they came in two contingents: one on Saturday, another on Sunday, depending on work and commitments. The children's mother had put a giant pan of water on to boil and was slicing tomatoes for the sauce; then one of her sisters arrived, with her numerous offspring in tow and a husband staggering under a tower of boxes of ravioli that reached his nose. Marroné was introduced to everyone as they arrived and helped set up, under the combined shade of the fig tree and the vine, the table of trestles and planks, which the women laid with vinyl tablecloths. Grim as the conversation was, ranging from the repression in the factories to the growing daily death toll or the recent botched coup attempt by the military, the atmosphere was generally festive and light-hearted: seated at the head of the table and flecked with dancing flashes of green and gold, Don Rogelio was a sun around which his children orbited like planets and his grandchildren like moons. For a moment the memory of the cheerless Sunday barbecues with his in-laws in the back garden of the house in Olivos came flooding back to Marroné, every one of them an instalment in the unpayable debt he'd incurred by accepting their contribution to the purchase of the house and swimming pool: the puckered face of his father-in-law every time he tried the meat his son-in-law had cooked, his wife and mother-in-law's endless confabs, withdrawing as soon as they'd finished eating to discuss matters of child-rearing, and abandoning him to the interminable postprandial prattle of his gorilla father-in-law.

At that moment Don Rogelio had clinked his glass with a coffee spoon to call for silence for the toast.

'To all of this,' said Don Rogelio, taking in the throng with an ecumenical gesture. 'We don't ask for much, do we? This will do. But we'll not be content with less.'

It was true, so true, thought Marroné, as if the words had been meant specially for him. Wasn't this what life was all about? Was there anything else one could ask for? And at that moment, he had a vision of himself in thirty or forty years' time, in another life: a Peronist patriarch in a house like this, surrounded by children and grandchildren, reaching a serene and ripe old age, eating the secure fruit of his harvest in peace beneath his vine. Could proletarianising be the way forward, after all? Had Paddy been right all along? Had this scene been conjured by his friend for his edification from beyond the grave? The cherished syllables came back to him: 'If you like . . . I can give you a hand.' But he'd taken no notice and slapped the hand away, he thought, flagellating himself to the verge of tears once again. He was becoming a crybaby. 'And a proletarian crybaby at that!' the sly side of his mind whispered in his ear. He mentally shooed it away with a 'But it isn't too late'. His friend wouldn't have died in vain. Yes, that was exactly what he'd do: give up this senseless, monomaniacal search for the busts, abandon the rat race of the business world and leave everything behind. Everything: Sr Tamerlán, his wife, his in-laws, the house in Olivos. Then he'd sort out his bourgeois children's visiting regime – because in his new life, naturally, he planned on having others – and come and live in Ciudad Evita. It couldn't be as hard for him as it had for Paddy, after all. In the space of a few days he'd almost unwittingly made as much – or more – progress than his late friend had in months. 'Or rather regress,' his mind took to whispering again, for in his case it wasn't so much a matter of taking the plunge into a new world as of rediscovering his roots; not of wrenching his fate out of joint, but of straightening out the kink others had inflicted on it . . . of going back to his origins, of listening to the call coursing through his veins . . .

Don Rogelio had seated him on his right-hand side and, with a fresh cheroot fuming away in his hand, engaged him in conversation, which Marroné, revived by the ravioli and red wine, listened to with the utmost reverence, for he had decided this man would be his guide and role model in the new life he was about to embark on. Sitting on at the table after lunch, the bees buzzing about the green grapes that hung from the vine above, the newborn cicadas singing, and beetles with metallic-green wing cases and antennae with black pompoms drowning in the wine at the bottom of their glasses, Marroné felt he had found his way at last, especially when Don Rogelio leant over to him and, in the tone of a grandfather who has prepared his grandson a surprise, said into his ear:

'I'd like to introduce you to a friend of mine.'

They had only to cross the road, which shimmered like a piece of corrugated iron under the mid-afternoon sun, and walk through the pillars and the few cars parked in the shade of the tower block, to reach the entrance. They went up by the only lift in working order (the other two weren't only not in working order, but their doors were welded shut); it was an open lift shaft and, as they ascended, Marroné was treated to a series of extended panoramic views of Ciudad Evita through the double-grille doors: a succession of red-tile roofs and bright-green treetops stretching out to the perimeter that etched her profile into the land. The building grew slummier the higher they got, and the small green-grey tiles grew thinner on the walls: where the flats of the ground floor had seemed fairly decent, the top floor was a succession of dilapidated lairs, and there was no further sign of any tiling. From the corridor on the right his nostrils were flooded by the combined aroma of grilled meat, woodsmoke and pitch – and a snippet of his father-in-law's after-dinner wisdom came back to him, 'These Peronists! They give the darkies proper apartments to live in and first thing you know they've gone and ripped up the floors for their *asados*!' – and, still hungry despite all the ravioli, he was on the verge of grabbing Don Rogelio by the arm and suggesting they gatecrash the gathering; but the sculptor had already taken the left corridor, at the end of which was a glass-brick wall. In the blinding back-lighting his guide was reduced to a supernatural silhouette, and Marroné felt as if he were following him, not into one particular apartment or another, but into the light itself. They passed doors secured with padlocks, doors repaired with planks, doors sealed with barricade tape saying 'POLICE LINE – DO NOT CROSS', and knocked twice on the last one on the right.

'Alright! Alright! Keep your shirt on!' answered a gruff voice from inside, and soon enough they heard the drawing back of bolts, and the door opened as far as the chain would allow. 'Oh, it's you,' said the voice, recognising Don Rogelio. 'Why don't you let me know beforehand?' He closed the door and opened it again, this time wide.

The shutters were down and the room was dingy; fortunately enough as it turned out, because seeing it in the clear light of day could have been a very depressing experience. General disorder vied with the dirt and the bizarre layout: a television on the bed, a bicycle serving as a clothes horse for underwear, a stiff and dusty suit on a coat-hanger hanging on a nail on the wall, like an installation in a gallery. It was the kind of habitat a single man can only achieve after long years of dreary celibacy. The man must have been Don Rogelio's age, but the same years seemed to have passed over him not once but several times, like a car reversing over roadkill again and again to finish it off. He was taller than Don Rogelio but his hunched shoulders made him look more or less the same height, his skin was the colour of the ash overflowing from his ashtrays, and he coughed continuously. After introducing them and giving his friend a light-hearted ticking-off for not accepting the services of a cleaning lady he'd recommended, and after Rodolfo – for that was the name of the owner of the apartment – retorted with a growl and a 'She's after something else that one is', Don Rogelio came to the point, still all mystery.

'The comrade here wants to see them.'

To Rodolfo's raised eyebrows Don Rogelio responded by taking hold of Marroné's shoulder and resting his arm on it as if on a firm and reliable support.

'It's ok. He's with me.'

Rodolfo ushered them to another door in the same corridor, next to the lifts. After a brief tug of war Rodolfo managed to extract the padlock from the two rings it gripped and gave the door a shove. Marroné was expecting more or less the same kind of dingy hovel as the first, but was hit by a blinding light that poured in torrents through the wide windows of a vast room, which in some earlier day and age must have been a tea room with a panoramic view of Ciudad Evita. A second later his eyes managed to focus on its contents and he knew what Ali Baba must have felt when he stumbled upon the treasures of his cave. Overflowing from shelves, counters, niches, tables, packing cases and chairs, and spilling out over the floor, were more busts of Perón and Evita than he had ever seen or could even imagine. They came in all sizes and materials: white plaster or cement, painted gold, silver or black, cast in bronze, some gleaming, others weathered and green; carved in marble, granite, onyx or wood; modelled in clay or terracotta; some the size of a fist, others twice life-size; most with neoclassical, but some with romantic or even pre-Colombian features. Mass-produced pieces featured more abundantly, but there was no shortage of original works of artistic merit. But that was the least of it: the main thing was that there were enough Evas in this room to fill three office buildings like his, and as he gazed at them, Marroné felt his pupils narrow to two vertical slits; his tail, had he had one, would have rhythmically lashed his sides. Like the cat that won't take its eyes off the canary but keeps purring to demur its intent, he asked in a voice that was barely more than a hiss:

'Where did you get them?'

'Soon as news got out that Perón had thrown in the towel, Rodolfo and I grabbed our old banger of a pick-up – the same one parked out there – and started doing the rounds. Because it wasn't just the government; the civilian commandos didn't hang around: wherever they saw a portrait, a statue or a bust that bore even the slightest resemblance to Eva or Perón, they'd hack it down, knock it over, send it rolling across the floor. That day, right here in Ciudad Evita, we saved every one we could: the one in the school, the one in the square, the one in the sports centre. Then we started getting tip-offs: the girls from a textile factory had been hiding one for months . . . another one at a cold-storage plant, a library, the baggage handlers at Ezeiza . . . Each and every one of these Evas and Juans you can see has a history; feats of heroism great and small were needed for them to get as far as this; as you well know, you could spend months in jail if you were caught – just for having a photo or a picture of them in your house.

Marroné had started roaming around the improvised gallery: not even in the Louvre or the Uffizi had he felt anything remotely similar. The busts were all cleaned and shined and polished: clearly any devotion to cleanliness and order that Rodolfo might have had in him he lavished on his cherished collection, and had nothing left for his own life. He had them all facing the window so that they could entertain themselves day and night with contemplating the beauties of the Peronist citadel. And there they had been all along, waiting for him to collect the codes and solve the riddle. Where else could they have been? Here, right at the heart of the bun. He should have known. But of course, you can't reach the heart of the maze without roaming its passageways first.

'Nineteen years they've been waiting for the General to return. Almost all of them have their provenance noted down,' said Rodolfo proudly.

He turned over a small black Eva for Marroné to read the yellowing piece of paper stuck on the base: WOMEN'S PP BASIC UNIT – P PERÓN DISTRICT. Then – with both hands – a larger one, in cement: BERAZATEGUI WORKERS' DISTRICT – SQUARE. And another, in bronze: GAS WORKERS' UNION – BA PROVINCE. And another: AVELLANEDA HOSPITAL – ENTRANCE.

'The idea was to put each one back in its original place,' Don Rogelio explained.

'Still is,' declared Rodolfo categorically.

'We can talk about that later,' said Don Rogelio, with a wink at Marroné.

But Rodolfo seemed determined to take a stand:

'When he did eventually come back, I wrote him a letter. Then another, in case the first had got lost. Then another, and another. I gave up in the end.'

'I told you, Rodolfo, the General never got them. All his correspondence was being screened.'

Rodolfo stared at his friend through black orbs of bitterness.

'He read them and used them to wipe his arse on is what I reckon. The Perón that came back wasn't our Perón any more. They did something to him, López Rega and that whore of a wife of his. Anyway, makes no difference now. He's dead and gone. Who are we going to give them to now? There's nobody left as deserves them.'

He finished speaking and gave Marroné a flinty glance – the first. It was but an instant, yet it spoke volumes. He had caught in Rodolfo's eyes the fiery glint of fanaticism and the insane possessiveness of the collector; and if Rodolfo had seen something similar in his – if he had read how he felt, that is – they stood as much chance of coming to an agreement over Eva's busts as Paris and Menelaus over Helen.

They arranged a little *asado* for the same night, at Don Rogelio's – just the three of them. In the violet twilight, with the first star hanging motionless in the sky and the first moth throwing itself headlong at the naked light bulb that hung over the grill, Don Rogelio told him his friend's story while building the pyre of screwed-up newspaper, kindling and charcoal to start the fire. Marroné found it hard to follow, as he was busy making a mental inventory of the busts he'd seen, classifying them by colour, material, style and size – he had to choose them carefully: he didn't want the office turning into a junk shop, after all – and only caught the odd word here and there.

'Action in the square . . . the military . . . Perón . . . angry at the Church . . . to defend . . . several were armed . . . '

'Huh? To defend the churches?'

'It was us as torched the churches, Ernesto.'

'Oh. Sorry.'

'But that was later. I was telling you about the bombardment of Plaza de Mayo. Most went along like any other day . . . in ten years we'd gone soft and let our guards down. They sent the planes in early. Rodolfo had gone with his wife, and they spent the time walking round and round the city centre, which was chaos, not knowing what to do. By the afternoon, when the leaders of the uprising had surrendered, they approached the square, to see if they could do anything to help. They got there just as the last wave came in – the worst. Rodolfo had a bit of luck, good or bad depending on how you look at it: he was only wounded in the leg. But his wife . . . She was six months pregnant at the time. He was very bitter. Wouldn't come to our house while my wife was alive. We used to meet up outside, in the houses we'd hole up in, or when we pulled off the occasional act of sabotage together . . . '

Marroné was outwardly calm, making the appropriate signs of dismay or distress whenever the springs of the story seemed to require it; but inwardly he was a ferret, incapable of keeping still for a moment, sniffing about for the entrance to the rabbit warren. While providing him with some useful information on his rival and his potential weaknesses, Don Rogelio's account only confirmed his initial fears about Rodolfo: the man was obsessed, a madman shackled to a trauma for life; it was going to be very tough, not to say downright impossible, to tear the Evas from his clutches. His evaluation was confirmed in the first phase of the *asado*, when, between mouthfuls of sausage and black pudding, Don Rogelio invited him to tell his friend the truth of the matter. Marroné gave his table companions a watered-down version they could swallow, highlighting the involvement of 'the company' (he'd decided not to name it just in case) in the building of new schools, hospitals, union hotels, the Children's Republic (a tactical strike) and the plans for the Monument to the Descamisado during the first Peronist government.

'So your boss is a Peronist, is he?' asked Rodolfo, still frowning suspiciously.

'Of the first water,' Marroné asserted categorically. 'Believe it or not, he arrived in the country on 17th October 1945 and was the first to dip his feet in the fountain. His father was a frequent guest of Eva and the General's, and he met them himself as a very young man at the Residence.'

'So why's he been kidnapped by the Montoneros?'

'That one's too easy,' thought Marroné, 'he's handed it to me on a plate.'

'Correct me if I'm wrong, but . . . I was under the impression that the hallmark of all true Peronists was the way they go around bumping each other off.'

Rodolfo and Don Rogelio exchanged glances of *truco* partners facing the ace of swords.

'What did you say his name was?'

He hadn't, of course, deliberately.

'Fa . . . Fausto Tamerlán,' he said, bracing himself for the shock wave.

'Tamerlán? The one from the construction company?' spluttered Rodolfo in outrage. 'He's a bigger gorilla than King Kong that one is. My nephew was a union delegate on a building site and the security guards beat the crap out of them.'

'Er . . . No . . . ' He decided to try a weak line of defence. 'That must have been his father . . . Or his partner . . . They're both dead,' he added with a winning grin.

'Rodolfo . . . ' Don Rogelio intervened.

'What?'

'Let him have them. They'll at least be used to save a life that way.'

'Yes, the life of one of the sonsofbitches that sent in the planes, and the gangs to hunt us down one by one.'

'Ernesto says not, and I for one believe him. Besides, who are we to decide who lives and dies?'

'*They* decide.'

'Yes. But we want to be better than them, don't we? Listen to me. Everything we lost . . . Everything you lost . . . you won't bring it back by clinging onto idols. They're just figurines of wood and stone. They aren't Perón and Eva. Let him have them.'

'What do you know about loss?' Rodolfo retorted, resentfully. 'Rolling in children and grandchildren the way you are?'

'Everything that's mine is yours. The doors of my house are open to you day and night.'

'I don't want your family's charity,' he blurted out, regretting it immediately. 'Forgive me. I didn't mean that.' And then, obliquely, to Marroné, as if he'd offended him too: 'I apologise. I'll have to think about it.'

'Go ahead and think about it, take your time,' thought Marroné to himself, refilling Rodolfo's wine glass.

By the second bottle they were getting all nostalgic about the days of the Resistance.

'Remember that time we graffitied the glassworks and were nabbed by that sergeant . . . ? What was his name?'

313

'Merlo?'

'That's him! Comes at us blowing his whistle he does, and this lunatic,' said Don Rogelio, slapping Rodolfo on the shoulder, 'only goes and throws the bucket of paint over him.'

'I can just see him standing there with his little whistle, blowing bubbles,' Rodolfo added as soon as the guffaws allowed him to breathe. 'Ffff! Ffff!'

'Took them two or three days to catch up with us,' Don Rogelio rounded off the story. 'What a going-over we got! Submarines: dry, wet, semi-liquid.'

'In shit,' Rodolfo elucidated. 'How many months was it that time?'

'Dunno. Must have been about five.'

Marroné listened with a painted smile, hands clasped beneath the table, slowly windmilling his thumbs. When they'd finished up the wine, he offered to go out and get some more from the general stores in the tower block.

'Blimey, Ernesto!' they exclaimed when they saw him come in with two bottles of Château Vieux. 'You didn't half push the boat out! What do you take us for? A couple of gorilla toffs?'

He'd actually bought the most expensive label the meagre store had to offer in an attempt to placate – or rather suborn – the evil enchanters pursuing him with all the savagery of bull-dogs in a dog-fight, but he concealed the fact with a magnanimous gesture of 'It's the least I can do for my new friends' and filled their glasses as fast as they could down them – except his own, of course, from which, after each toast, he would wet his lips without drinking.

' . . . coal, potassium and sulphuric acid. And it doesn't let out a wisp of smoke and then before we can leg it . . . Phut!'

'Were there many casualties?' asked Marroné thoughtfully.

'What! It was the work of this loon. Everywhere filled with black smoke, you could see it twenty blocks away. That was how we got caught again. And back to the clink we went.'

'And what about Teresa? Did you tell him about Teresa?'

'Teresa! What's she up to now I wonder.'

'Dead probably. There aren't many of us left any more.'

'Once at the Party offices we were arguing about Manger, see . . . '

'Tell him about Manger, he doesn't know who he was.'

'Oh, you're right. What an idiot. It's just that I think of old Ernesto here as one of us,' Rodolfo said to him, with a grin of drunken camaraderie which Marroné returned, with compound interest. 'He was a foreman at the textile factory, always trying it on with the girls he was, made the women delegates' lives not worth living. So we've been discussing what to do about him for two hours and this, that and the other, and then Teresa, fed up to the back teeth, whistles to us and when we all turn and look at her, she lifts up her skirt – she was famous for wearing no knickers – and goes, "This is for whoever beats the crap out of that fucker."'

'So we all piled round to his place to give him a good seeing-to. The lads were lining up to hit him. Took Teresa a whole month to pay us back.'

'Woman of her word that Teresa.'

'And tough as nails to boot. A true comrade.'

They sailed on into the past down a river of wine.

'And who was going to take us on after that? Workshops, a bit of manual work, odd jobs . . . '

'We stuck a gas cylinder in there . . . Boom! Sarmiento got to the moon before the Yanks did.'

'Eight months!'

'"There's a man at the door," my youngest shouts when I show up on the doorstep.'

'After eight months' porridge beggars can't be choosers.'

'You must mean . . . The old pork sausage!'

'Yes, but good old Peronist pork!'

'And watching it burn away, I thought to myself . . . if only the General could see me now!'

Marroné proceeded with premeditated stealth as soon as the two men's snores fired the starting gun. Cautiously, he unhooked a bunch of keys from Rodolfo's belt and grabbed those to the pick-up off the kitchen worktop; then, before opening the gate, he oiled the hinges with olive oil from the glass cruet. As the driveway sloped slightly, all he had to do was take the pick-up out of gear and release the brake, and the old banger slid back towards the road, where he got out and pushed for about fifty metres, busting several guts and sweating buckets all the way to the tower-block entrance. When he saw that the third lift – the one they'd taken that afternoon – was out of order and locked, he almost gave in to the urge to sit down on the kerb and weep, but he pulled himself together and set off on the five-floor ascent with fierce determination, muttering over and over again, 'Fucking darkie Peronists, they don't deserve what they've got. Give them a model city and all they do is wreck it.'

On his first trip he grabbed two of the largest busts, one under each arm; he had to stop three times on his way down to catch his breath and, by the time he'd finished securing them at the back of the pick-up, he was out of breath and his knees were wobbling; a speedy bit of mental arithmetic told him that at this rate it would take him another forty-six trips; he had neither the strength nor the time before sun-rise, so on his next trip he chose only the smallest busts and filled one of the wooden crates, but he barely got as far as the landing before collapsing from exhaustion. Emptying out half the pieces, he could just about manage it, and, now that he'd established the limits of his endurance, he adjusted the number with each round trip; he was also in two minds whether to carry less and make more trips, which would sap the energy from his legs, or to make fewer trips laden like a mule; in the end he put aside all calculations and aban-doned himself to a mindless doggedness that bordered on insanity. At one point he tripped on his way down, and the busts rolled downstairs in fragments that got smaller and smaller as he watched; at another, an early bird – the kind of old biddie there's never a shortage of when you least need one – opened the door as he was making his way down with a granite Inca Eva and a Quebracho Toba Eva (all the smaller or lighter pieces were already in the box of the pick-up) and demanded to know what he was up to.

'Haven't you heard? There's a military coup on the way, Señora,' he said, as quick to the draw as a sheriff in a spaghetti western. 'And Ciudad Evita's top of their list. If they catch us with this lot, there'll be nothing left of this building but rubble.'

But he realised he'd laid it on too thick when the petri-fied woman wanted to wake up the whole building to lend him a hand. He stopped her by arguing that the old pick-up was full and told her he'd take up her offer when he got back. He'd decided to load up more than the ninety-two in case any got broken on the journey, but, drained of every last drop of strength, had stopped somewhere around the hundred mark. It was starting to get light, and the building would soon be a hive of busy Peronists, all wide awake.

The clapped-out old pick-up responded to the ignition with a series of intermittent, hoarse coughs; only at the fifth try, after Marroné had prayed as never before to God and all the saints he could remember, did it judder into life with a series of grudging jolts. Making a beeline for the base of the bun, he came out at the Ricchieri Freeway, which flung him like a stone from a slingshot out and away from Ciudad Evita. He hadn't slept properly for days, he was dehydrated and exhausted to a degree he'd never imagined possible, but he had the busts, he thought, as he aimed the clunking red pick-up like a ballistic missile straight at the doors of 300 Paseo Colón. No Soviet tank in World War II, nor even Castro in the Cuban Revolution, had advanced on Berlin or Havana with such devastating momentum as did Ernesto Marroné on the city of Buenos Aires.

10

THE OTHER NINE FINGERS

He drove like the wind, his fingers locked on the wheel like the teeth of a dog on a bone, shielding it with his body, glancing with lightning speed through windscreen and mirrors, and windows left and right; had it been possible he would have looked upwards through the roof at the sky, whence calamity might also rain in the form of fire and brimstone. On the plus side, the traffic was unusually light even for this early hour, something which had at first filled him with grim forebodings, as if the deserted streets were a stage for the evil enchanters to burst upon, leading the armies of the Apocalypse; but as the minutes passed and all remained quiet, the tense rictus of his sphincter against the wood-bead massage cover slowly eased and, keeping a judicious distance from the traffic around him, he drove towards a green spot slowly growing in the blue-black east. When he swung onto the General Paz Freeway and saw the first row of houses in the capital filing silently past on the right, his eyes welled with tears. You're home and dry, he told himself, sobbing and hiccuping with gratitude; nothing bad can happen to you now.

A first pothole on the Alberdi approach road, and the real or imagined sound of dozens of unpacked busts crashing into each other and shattering, reminded him that he'd better slow down, and he kept tight to the kerb for those first blocks, like a nervous swimmer who stays close to shore. Before his bleary eyes the city slowly stretched, yawned and shook itself awake: the odd bus starting out on its route, the bakery opening, the concierge sluicing down the pavement, the newspaper seller at the lights offering him a paper he refused so as to focus on the task in hand. On his right, a merry band of revellers in evening dress were leaving a reception room and hanging around on the pavement; after staring at them for several seconds he came up with the solution to the conundrum: a wedding. When, after broadening invitingly, the avenue wickedly reversed direction without warning, he had to take a diversion to the right and endure a few blocks of anxiety before coming out onto Avenida Directorio, whose one-way lanes downtown and slight (possibly imaginary) slope would now lead him straight as an arrow to his target, signposted by a brace of pink clouds floating in the distant azure like two flocks of flamingos in flight. He nodded off once or twice at the wheel, but it was ok: his little pick-up was like a faithful horse that knew which way to go, eating up the green lights as it went. Avenida Directorio, which at one point became Avenida San Juan, billowed up and down like a magic-carpet ride at the fair; the city, Marroné realised, was in fact not as flat as a billiard table, as was always claimed, but gently undulating. Unless it had changed in his absence.

He was no longer dazzled by the streetlights and traffic lights, or the headlights in the mirrors: daylight had spread to all corners of the sky. The piece of sky that loomed ahead of him now burnt an angry orange against bright blue: he was driving straight into the rising sun.

The last set of green lights beckoned to him welcomingly as he swung onto Paseo Colón in a broad curve; he drove past the Doric columns of the Engineering Faculty, smiling to himself, and hung a right onto Avenida Belgrano to take Moreno and park, at last, half a block from 300 Paseo Colón, right outside the entrance to the company's building. He switched off the ignition and said a short prayer of thanks. He'd done it. Mission accomplished.

It was almost seven-thirty in the morning by his watch, but the city centre was inexplicably deserted. A bus went by, then a taxi, then nothing; even the kiosk on the corner where he used to buy the paper was all locked up and bolted. The door to the garage should have been open since seven, as it wasn't unusual for executives to make an early start in order to get on top of their workload, but even when he knocked several times on the heavy brass ring, and then rang the janitor's bell on the entryphone, he got no answer. Something strange was going on, not just at Tamerlán & Sons, but right across the city. Where had everyone gone? Was there something going on that everyone but him was in on? He crossed the four lanes of the avenue to the square opposite to scan the windows of the building for a revealing light. Nothing. The first rays of the sun had just clawed their way above the two battlements of the Customs House, catching the domes of the neighbouring office buildings like a flame lighting a row of candles. The bells of a nearby church – probably San Roque – struck the half-hour; he couldn't remember ever having heard them before. He was thirsty and hungry and found a kiosk open on the other side of Belgrano, where he bought himself a packet of crackers and a bottle of chocolate milk with a straw in it, and dragged from the still-sleepy kiosk owner the answer to the riddle:

'It's Sunday, chief.'

'Just my fucking luck,' muttered Marroné and, adding two tokens to his order, asked for the nearest phone.

It was on the corner of Venezuela and, loath as he was to let the old pick-up out of his sight, there was nothing else for it. He dialled the number of Govianus's house – the only one he knew by heart.

'Ah, Marroné,' a thick voice at the other end eventually answered. 'It's you. We'd given you up for dead. So you got the news that . . . What was that?'

'The busts, Sr Govianus,' he interrupted him eagerly. 'I have the busts. I'm standing by the truck outside the door of the company right now. But I can't find anyone to open up for me.'

'Well . . . difficult, you know? On a Sunday at . . . ' he paused to pretend he was looking at the time on his alarm clock, just to make Marroné feel bad, 'twenty to eight in the morning. Lucky for you I was in, wasn't it? Waiting by the phone.'

Marroné started to get irritated: after all he'd been through, he'd hoped for a warmer reception, and he was also worried about the pick-up and its contents. What if they'd followed him and were taking advantage of his absence to make off with the lot?

'Sr Govianus, I don't think you heard me. I have the ninety-two busts of Eva Perón, the ones we need to free Sr Tamerlán. I got them, I finally got them. But I can't leave them in the street for long. Can you hear me, Sr Govianus?'

'Yes, Marroné, perfectly,' the accountant answered, in the same insipid tone. Perhaps what had happened was so huge, so unexpected, after all hope of good news had been lost, that he couldn't take in the news. Marroné heard a prolonged sigh at the other end of the line. 'All right, Marroné. Stay put while I get dressed and drive over.'

The accountant lived in Caballito: if he got his skates on, the light traffic would mean he'd be there soon, so Marroné decided to hunker down in the car and have breakfast, and not budge an inch until Govianus arrived; but a brand-new surprise awaited him back at the kerbside, which was empty of all other vehicles save the patrol car now parked behind his pick-up. Inside the car sat an overheated policeman, while the other sniffed around the pick-up, tugging at the ropes that fastened the tarpaulin to the box, trying to peek inside. Striding over to him, Marroné tried to contain the washing machine now churning in his empty stomach: they were under an administration that was Peronist in name at least, and there was nothing wrong, in principle, with transporting a cargo of busts of Eva Perón; but he had an educated accent and was dressed as a worker, which, until proven otherwise, made him a potential guerrilla. There was also the possibility that he was on the wanted list, his photo or identikit plastered all over the streets, and in newspapers, and on television; and as if that weren't enough, he'd just parked a clapped-out pick-up truck with dodgy contents in a sensitive area of town containing, in a two-block radius, the Ministry of the Interior and the Central Police Headquarters, the Ministry of the Economy, the Libertador Building, which housed the Ministry of Defence and the General Staff, and last but not least, the Pink House.

'Morning,' said the policeman at large, with that curt urbanity they often affect once they've zeroed in on their prey.

'Morning, Constable ... er ... Officer ... Any problem?' Marroné answered with an ingratiating, brown-nose grin.

'This yours?' he replied, pointing to the truck with pursed lips.

'Errrr ... yes. But I was just on my way, eh. I had to make a quick phone call,' he said, with gestures that invoked a vaguely telephonic distance.

'Hands on the bonnet if you don't mind.'

He frisked him quickly, not forgetting armpits and crotch, then said:

'Papers.'

Braced for the worst, he fished the white clam out of his pocket, extracted his identity card and handed it to the policeman, who gave it a couple of perfunctory flips, then froze at the photo of an immaculate Marroné in jacket, tie and slicked-back hair. Working hard to square it with the black-nailed, tangle-haired, stubbly creature that stood before him in flip-flops, he said flatly:

'Car papers ... '

It was just as he feared. He had forgotten, or rather been too preoccupied to dig out the papers for the pick-up. His only hope was that Don Rogelio was in the habit of leaving them in the glove compartment.

'Excuse me.'

The policeman stayed the hand that Marroné had slipped into his pocket, felt it and helped him remove it, daintily, with a bunch of keys between thumb and forefinger. Marroné gave the officer in the patrol car a sidelong look. He was wearing mirrored shades, smoking a cigarette and swatting a fly that was trying to sip the sweat from his forehead. In the angle of his arm, resting on the open window, lolled the barrel of a shotgun. After rummaging in the glove compartment to make sure there were no lethal weapons or pamphlets for guerrilla organisations, his partner emerged with a cracked leather wallet that turned out to contain – blessed be the Mercy of the Lord – the papers for the pick-up. The policeman held it open in Marroné's face, confronting him with the photo of a Don Rogelio a good ten years younger. Marroné knew the time had come to talk up a storm.

'Errrr . . . He's one of our suppliers. He had to make an urgent delivery to us and . . . found himself prevented from doing so due to this wee health problem he's got . . . hernia. So I had to take charge myself. Which is why I'm dressed like . . . Oh, this is where I work,' he said, pointing at the building. 'I'm head of procurement here, if you'll allow me.' He pulled out his wallet again and took out his business card. Cracked and crumpled as it was, it looked like a leftover from a job he'd been fired from years ago.

The policeman didn't so much as look at it, handing both sets of papers straight to his partner, who flicked his fag onto the street and got hold of the radio. Marroné took a discreet look at his watch: it had been twenty minutes since he'd called Govianus; as things were, his only hope was to keep the policemen busy until the accountant got there. His officer had gone back to tugging at the ropes and tarpaulin.

'Would you mind?'

With a sigh, Marroné began to struggle with the knots, taking as long as he dared without arousing suspicion. When he pulled the tarpaulin to one side, a big fat beam from the still-rising sun fell on the first row of Evas like a spotlight. At least two were broken.

'And what's all this?'

'Eva Perón,' he said, for want of a better answer.

His partner called him over from the car. They whispered to each other for a few seconds, then his cop came over, the holster of his gun now conspicuously unfastened.

'You'll have to come with us.'

'Listen, Cunstable . . . Officer . . . ' Then he remembered that one's own name was always the sweetest in any language and, after glancing at his badge, added: 'Duquesa . . . ' The surname was bizarre, and now it sounded like he was taking the mickey. 'It's taken me two weeks – the worst two weeks of my life – to get hold of these fu . . . busts, and if I don't deliver them today, right now, the life of a very important person could be in jeopardy, and when they find out that you, Officer . . . The president will be here in just a few minutes – he's the one I just phoned – so I'd ask you to be a little patient and kind . . . '

Marroné had again dug the bivalve out of the depths of his pocket and now, opening it, he tugged at the tip of a note; but, being all stuck together, they came out in a single wad, which it would have been rude to hold on to once proffered. The policeman took it between thumb and forefinger, then slid in a fingernail to divide it into two equal halves, like someone opening a sandwich to get rid of the filling, and handed one to his partner. He opened the back door of the Ford Falcon and ushered Marroné inside.

'Five minutes.'

They felt like the longest five minutes of his life. The sun beat down on the tin roof and the sweat ran down his forehead in thick beads. The two cops had confiscated his crackers and milk, which they sampled without a word; he was desperate for a sip but didn't dare to ask: he had to appear friendly and relaxed to avoid their suspicions.

'Looks like it's going to turn out hot, eh?'

They didn't even bother to look at him in the mirror. The second hand ticked implacably on its course – only one and a half turns to go. His whole being was concentrated on the narrow rectangle of the rear-view mirror, which reflected nothing but the broad avenue, now a barren moor void of cars and pedestrians.

But Govianus arrived in the nick of time. Marroné, expecting a car to pull up behind him, at first didn't recognise the accountant when he saw him sauntering down the embankment of Avenida Belgrano, whistling, rolled-up newspaper under one arm, hands in the pockets of his white-striped tracksuit bottoms, which, added to the matching top, the cream-coloured Adidas sneakers and the sunglasses, gave him the air of a football coach, while the two men on either side of him – a blond man with an American-style buzz cut and a swarthy one with a moustache, both also in sportswear – looked more like wrestlers or boxers. Completely ignoring the officers, who did get salutes from his bodyguards and responded in kind, Govianus inhaled deeply as if in the mountains, and looked around him.

'Actually this is rather nice on a Sunday morning, eh? Almost . . . ' he checked his surroundings again to see if they would supply him with the word he was looking for, ' . . . bucolic. I'll have to come more often.' Then he leant into Marroné's window and, with a confidential nod, gestured towards the front seat: 'Friends of yours?'

Brushing the crumbs off his uniform, the first policeman got out of the passenger seat and gave him a stiff two-
fingered salute.

'Sir?'

'Sir, in this case, is the president of the company, and
this gentleman you have been entertaining so kindly until I
arrived is, believe it or not, one of my top executives.'

The policeman's attitude changed radically. Despite his
joviality and informal appearance, the accountant radiated
so imperious an air of authority you could almost touch it.
And if any doubts remained, his bodyguards were there to
clear them up.

'And if I wanted to corroborate . . . '

'You have only to call Commissioner Major Aníbal Ribete
on your radio, or better still Commissioner General Eduardo
Verdina. Oh, but how foolish of me. They'll probably still
be at home at this time of day. Luckily, I have their private
numbers memorised. I suppose that, being a question of such
extreme importance as this, they won't mind if we get them
out of bed on a Sunday morning.'

The rest of the time was spent on formalities; Marroné
would have liked his money back, but felt that, all in all, he'd
got off fairly lightly, and left it to Govianus, whose sangfroid
and calm, almost blasé, composure he'd found truly impressive, to finish getting rid of the police, get the concierge out of
bed (he was holed up with a tart and Govianus asked for her
number, for future reference, before sending her away), slap
the keys to the pick-up into his open palm for him to put it
in the car park and post his bodyguards at the door. Stressed
and drained as he was, Marroné felt relief that someone else
should be taking charge at last, and took no further initiative

beyond warning the concierge of the fragile nature of the cargo, underlining the fact that they were 'Busts, in assorted media; some are works of art', for Govianus's benefit, who, so far, no doubt owing to the need to tackle more immediate matters, hadn't so much as bothered to glance at them.

'So, Marroné. Here we are again,' said Govianus, adjusting his glasses and resting his elbows on the arms of his chrome chair.

They were back in the bunker, on either side of the armoured desk, but not all was the same as before. The vault seemed to have shrunk, along with its furnishings; or perhaps, paradoxically, it was just that in his sportswear the accountant looked much more imposing than in his usual poorly cut suits. Or, thought Marroné, drawing in air before starting on the tale of his adventures, it was he who had grown. Before allowing him to begin, Govianus conjured from a bar concealed behind sliding panels a bottle of nice, cold mineral water, together with a glass, in what Marroné chose to think of as a first token of recognition for successfully completing his mission. As he spoke, Marroné downed glass after glass, feeling better with every gulp; the slight phosphorescence of the submarine twilight was a balm to his tired eyes and, though the air-conditioning was off, the air felt as cool and fresh as a wine cellar.

When he'd finished his account – which didn't take too long, for, while there was much to tell, there was also much that was beside the point, and he left out many details – Govianus sat there staring at him for a few seconds without saying a word, as if trying to take in the new image of a man he may have underestimated (it was understandable; not even Marroné himself had, in his wildest dreams, imagined himself capable of so much), then held out the newspaper, now unrolled, across the desk. As he read the headline Govianus was tapping, Marroné's soul slumped floorwards; had the blood clotted in his veins and all his remaining teeth fallen out simultaneously, he couldn't have been more stunned.

KIDNAPPED BUSINESSMAN MURDERED

Well-known construction magnate Fausto Tamerlán, who was being held by an extremist left-wing group, was found murdered today. After an unsuccessful rescue attempt, in which at least four people lost their lives and the same number were injured, the body of the 40-year-old businessman was found last night in the Lomas de Zamora area. Tamerlán had been kidnapped by the outlawed subversive organisation in June this year. His charred remains were found inside the premises where he was being held captive. The premises were set on fire by the extremists when surrounded by members of the armed forces and police taking part in the operation.

THE OPERATION

The intervention by the joint forces began with a police surveillance operation after reports from neighbours alerted the authorities to unusual movements in a bungalow at the junction of Catamarca and Monseñor Chimento, 500 metres from the Municipal Park and the same distance from the Arroyo del Rey. After the arrest order for the property's inhabitants had been duly served and several warning shots fired into the air, the occupants opened fire on the forces of law and order, who successfully repelled the aggression. A cordon was set up and the ensuing exchange of shots was intense and prolonged. After nearly an hour of gunfire, a series of loud explosions was heard from within the premises, which were almost immediately engulfed in flames. The rebels are thought to have doused the interior with fuel before detonating their grenades. They then took advantage of the ensuing chaos to attempt to break through the cordon, at which point they were brought down by the regular forces. Due to the quantities of fuel used and the violence of the explosions, the property was no more than a heap of smoking ruins by the time fire-fighters arrived at the scene.

ON THE INSIDE

Amongst the rubble were found the lifeless bodies of Sr Fausto Tamerlán, apparently executed by the outlaws on finding themselves surrounded, and a person of male sex, whose identity had not been ascertained at the time of going to press. Sr Tamerlán's body was swiftly identified by the missing index finger from the right hand, severed previously by his captors as a way of exerting pressure in the hostage negotiations. Police Sergeant Alberto Cabeza and two conscript soldiers, who have not been named, were injured in the shoot-out and the explosions.

'No . . . no . . . no . . . no . . . no . . . no . . . no . . . ' he heard a voice repeating as he read, which, of course, turned out to be his own.

And then it dawned on him: it was punishment for stealing the busts! The evil enchanters were sending him a premonition of the consequences of his actions! Fortunately, it wasn't too late to put things right! He would go up to his office, grab a fresh chequebook, drive the clapped-out old pick-up all the way back to Ciudad Evita – but only after unloading it – and pay those two fine old gents triple their asking price! And when he got back he would no longer be met by the contrite face of Govianus, but by Sr Tamerlán's, smiling and safe at last! 'Couldn't he somehow turn back time?' he whimpered inwardly, restraining himself from grabbing the newspaper and tearing it to pieces.

'I'm sorry, Marroné,' said Govianus, stretching out to pat the forearm into which he had sunk his face. 'I know you did all you could, but in times like these it's rarely enough. I would like to have told you last night as soon as the news reached us, but I had no way of contacting you. Let's just say we lost track of you there for a few days. Anyway, if it's any consolation, I don't believe getting the busts here a couple of days sooner would have changed anything. Because, between you and me, it's better not to believe all you read in the papers. You know what those warning shots were? Mortar shells. The subversives couldn't have surrendered even if they'd wanted to; not even the cockroaches were spared. Looks like it's all part of a novel way to discourage further kidnappings: they take out the hostage along with the goons.'

332

As Govianus spoke, Marroné looked up every now and then to glance at the headline in case the bad news had turned to good, or the newspaper to an albatross taking flight on paper wings.

'And we did everything we could not to let either the army or the police find out, believe you me. They must have followed Ochoa.'

Marroné looked up again from the hollow of his forearm.

'Ochoa? Was he there?'

Govianus tapped with one index finger on the part of the article where it said 'person of male sex, whose identity'.

'He was carrying the cash for the first payment. Procurement is your field, after all, so we felt it was only right for your department to handle things, Marroné. And as you weren't around . . . '

He refrained from completing the phrase out of courtesy, but he couldn't have made it clearer to Marroné: Ochoa had died in his place. Govianus took out a packet of Benson & Hedges, muttered 'I had given up', offered him one and lit it after his refusal.

'What about the money?' asked Marroné, trying desperately to cling on to something.

Govianus blew a series of smoke rings in reply.

'All of it?'

'Well, if we're keeping track, we've come out on top: had he made it, there'd still be two more payments to go. Anyway, for better or worse, it all seems to be over now.'

'What do we do then?'

'We all go home, Marroné. Better get some rest, we've a busy week ahead of us. Want me to call you a car?'

'No, I meant with the busts . . . the ones I brought.'

'Oh, yes, right. I'd forgotten. We'll put them up anyway, so now if they kidnap me, we'll have saved a bit of time. Is there anything else?'

'Errr . . . ' The accountant's previous remark had reminded him he had no way of getting home. 'My car . . . I left it at Sansimón's, and I . . . I'd prefer not to have to go back and get it. Can we have it sent over? Maybe not today, but tomorrow?'

'No can do, Marroné. It was burnt.'

'What do you mean it was burnt?'

'Sansimón set fire to it personally.'

'But he can't do that. It's a company car!'

'And I needn't tell you what he wanted to do to you. It's understandable: the man was upset. He told me you incited the workers to mutiny personally. Luckily, he remembered you by another name, and I didn't take the trouble to correct him. But I advise you to let someone else deal with any plasterwork orders for a time. Oh, and some well-dressed men came snooping around asking for a certain Macramé. I told them no one by that name worked at the company, of course. By the way, Marroné, the overalls suited you, eh? You looked very comfortable in them.'

Marroné's eyes opened wide in two panic-stricken Os.

'We saw you on the news. People in the company talked of nothing else all week.' Govianus leant over the table slightly and lowered his voice to ask him, 'Tell me something, Marroné. Just between you and me . . . You wouldn't be an infiltrator by any chance?'

Marroné got up from his chair and, sensing that his legs might not be strong enough to bear his weight, rested his palms on the desk. He had to make a supreme effort of will to master the quavering of outraged honour in his voice.

'Sr Govianus, in the past I think I have demonstrated my unswerving loyalty to the company and to the person of Sr Tamerlán.' Hysteria fought for control of his throat. 'There are people who gave their lives for those busts to be here today,' he said, on the brink of tears. 'I nearly lost my own on several occasions.'

'Everyone's giving their life for something these days,' remarked Govianus, with measured scepticism. 'I don't know what's going on. It must be something in the water. I mean, if they do it willingly, to my mind . . . But you know how it is. Afterwards they always want something in return.'

'You do not know . . . you do not know . . . ' Marroné hiccuped, 'what I have been through these last few days. Look. I gave my teeth for the company!' he said, lifting his upper lip with two fingers to display his broken incisors. Only after freezing with gums bared and upper lip curled like a dog's, did he realise the gesture might have come over as rather melodramatic, for, though Govianus had recoiled and clapped his hands over his mouth in shock, he could also have been trying to disguise his laughter.

'All right, Marroné, I'll take your word for it. This time we'll put it down in the debit column as an excess of zeal. But do try to act with caution from now on. Just in case your efforts to save the company end up bringing down the capitalist system.'

Marroné sat back down in his chair in a series of stop-motion poses like some articulated dummy. He left his hands resting on the metal surface so that Govianus wouldn't notice how badly they were shaking.

'What now?'

'What do you mean?'

'What happens to the company? Will you go on as president?'

'Ah. Until the Family decides otherwise . . . But just between you and me . . . I'm a little tired. These are not good times for the company man. We seem to be to blame for all the world's ills. Besides . . . being an accountant, I don't want to be reduced to counting up to nine one day, then eight the next, then seven . . . ' He wiggled his fingers in the air and bent them one by one to illustrate. 'And that's the best-case scenario. I'm not cut out to be a hero, Marroné, never mind a martyr. But you . . . You've demonstrated truly incomparable loyalty and efficiency . . . So I was thinking . . . of offering you the . . . '

Marroné opened his mouth as if to speak but could manage no more sound than a gaping fish. A spasm had seized his throat like a hand and squeezed it tight. Him?

'I have no doubts that, when the Family find out all you've done, they'll be keen to second my proposal. I know I'm asking a great deal. You, a young man with a wife and small children, your whole life ahead of you . . . So I'd ask you not to answer me immediately, to think it over, see what your nearest and dearest have to say . . . But before that, I suggest you try it for size, see how you feel . . . '

Govianus rose from his throne of black leather and chrome and offered it to Marroné with a studiously courteous bow. So it was true. The presidency of the company was his for the taking. Not even in his wildest dreams . . .

As if in a trance, he got up from his chair, took two steps, stumbled, realised one of his feet had gone to sleep and was bare on the thick carpet, found the missing flip-flop and, playing pat-a-cake with the reflection of his palms, edged around the desk until he stood on the other side. Then he took a firm grip of both the arms lined with soft leather, softer than he'd ever touched before, and eased himself slowly back in the armchair, while Govianus chivalrously held the back for him. With faint squeaks and sighs, the joints of the chair adjusted themselves to his body as if they had been expecting him. The leather seemed to stretch and swell at his caress like a cat.

'Well, Marroné, I'll leave you two to get acquainted. We'll talk tomorrow.'

Alone, Marroné ran his eyes over the helm of the company that he had just been placed in command of. Everything looked different now he was the captain of the ship. So this was how you reached the top? By following these long and winding roads where calamity lurked round every corner? Were they right then, Dale Carnegie, Lester Luchessi and R Theobald Johnson, whose teachings he hadn't been following so assiduously of late, but who, even now, had gone on watching over him and guiding his steps? Was it true that the executive-errant who kept the flame of his faith burning was always rewarded in the end with a crown and a throne like the one he now sat in? Ah, if only his St Andrew's classmates could see him now. Marooné, Marron Crappé, President of Tamerlán & Sons (he'd keep the name for now) before the age of thirty. And his father . . . and his in-laws . . . When they were face to face, he would let his wife talk and rant and rave and shout herself hoarse till she was blue in the face, and then, in a single sentence – 'I'm the new CEO of Tamerlán & Sons' – he would shut her mouth for ever. And put his house in order; he'd start by sending Doña Ema packing. And at work . . . Cáceres Grey was the

Señora's nephew, so he couldn't very well fire him. But perhaps it was better that way . . . inventing inconceivable fates for the arrogant snob, like sending him to supervise the works on the dam in Catamarca, followed by the mines in Salta . . . 'You like it dirty, don't you?' he'd snipe . . . Yes, a new day was dawning. All the dangers and obstacles, all the trials and tribulations had meant something: a test of his mettle, a baptism of fire before the great task ahead. So this was the anvil on which the CEO's character was forged: the sword of the samurai executive (a shogun executive in his case) was made of tempered steel. Well, here he was. The condor had reached its nest in the heights. His 17th October, his 'marvellous day' had come at last.

Just then the accountant popped the feathery ostrich egg of his head back round the open door.

'Ah, Marroné, one little thing I was forgetting. Happy Innocents' Day! You *were* born yesterday. See you tomorrow.'

For one puzzled second Marroné sat there with his mouth open, his eyes fixed on the point of the door frame where the laughing gnome's bald pate had been. Then, with feverish fingers, he grabbed the newspaper to check the date, which could only be . . . 28th December: the Feast of the Holy Innocents. Sonofabitch.

*   *   *

Back on the sun-drenched pavement, Marroné realised he had no money on him, not even for bus fare, never mind a taxi: the bent copper had taken his last peso. He could always take a taxi and pay when he reached home, but his house keys were in his briefcase, which was still in the pulverised plasterworks, and, faced with the eventuality of finding no one there and having to deal with a furious taxi-driver – or the far worse one of his wife being in, refusing him entry and money, and having to deal with her *and* the taxi-driver – he decided to have a look round the now-bustling square in search of someone who would be moved by his appearance and could spare some change. He eventually settled on a young blonde girl in jeans, Flecha trainers and open Chairman Mao shirt over her gym-vest, who was out walking her collie under the old *palo borracho* that stood at the centre of the square and stretched the umbrella of its foliage over all. She not only agreed to give him the money he needed without pulling the usual face of disgust or annoyance, but gave him a smile and a 'Good luck, comrade' before following the shaggy dog tugging at its lead. He watched her walk away, mottled with green and gold sunlight and shade: give her a neatly tied bun and she'd make a nice Evita, he caught himself thinking.

The journey on the 152 bus didn't feel too long, as he fell asleep after a few blocks; and had it not been for an opportune police roadblock at the Presidential Residence in Olivos, where the bus was stopped to check the passengers' papers, he would have ended up going all the way to the terminus. It was around noon and, as he wandered the leafy pavements, the plumes of smoke from countless Sunday *asados*, climbing over walls and fences and into his nostrils, reminded him that he hadn't had a bite to eat in over twelve hours. If he was lucky – if they weren't at his in-laws' – he'd find lunch ready and waiting when he arrived. It hadn't occurred to him to ring and tell them to expect him. What a surprise they had in store!

Little Tommy was first out to greet him, slipping through the thick legs of Doña Ema, who had opened the door, and hugging his legs tight, repeating 'Papi! Papi! Papi! Papi! Papi!' as Doña Ema piped over her shoulder 'Here he is at last, Señora!', and when Marroné looked up from his son's little head with tear-filled eyes, it was to see his wife roaring down the steep staircase like a Valkyrie on her heavenly steed. As ideas go, dropping in on Mabel unannounced after a fortnight's absence, in the state he was in, had been about as good as poking a wasp's nest with a stick.

'Have you gone stark raving mad, Ernesto Marroné, or are you trying to drive *me* mad, or what? It's been five days since we heard from you, then suddenly you turn up like this, out of the blue? We thought you'd died in that factory, do you understand? We thought you were dead! Five days we've been wandering the morgues and hospitals with Mummy and Daddy! Morgues, Ernesto! Do you understand what I'm telling you? I had to look at corpses! Corpses, Ernesto! And you didn't even have the decency, the thought, the *heart* to pick up a phone? To let us know you were alive at least? You even ruined Christmas for us, made it the worst Christmas of my life! And Daddy calling all his judge friends and military friends and police friends, making a fool of himself, wasting his valuable time because I thought they'd killed you or taken you in! We're cancelling your parents' for New Year's Eve and spending it with mine; it's the least they deserve after all they've done! Where were you? What are you doing in those clothes, Ernesto? What have you got yourself into? Everyone saw you on the news, talking like a darkie, and I had to pretend it wasn't you, that you were with me that day! The phone never stopped ringing! Ernesto, if they got you mixed up in anything funny, if they threatened you, we have to go to the police right away and straighten it all out.

You're different, Ernesto. What have they done to you? Did they kidnap you? Did they drug you? Did they brainwash you? Why won't you say anything? What are you showing me your teeth for? How did you do that to yourself? Did you get into a fight too? Over a woman, over some dark tart? You got into a punch-up over a darkie? Don't you lie to me, eh, don't you go taking me for a fool, I know it was all a front so you could run off and go whoring. You've got some dirty black slumdog bit of fluff on the side, haven't you? Have you had children with her too? Have you been leading a double life? Explain it to me, Ernesto, because if you don't explain it to me I can't understand. I can't understand how a married man with a tiny, months-old baby is capable of abandoning his family and not even bothering to let them know he's still alive. You know that what you've done is grounds for divorce? Daddy's already spoken to the lawyer: she told me I could shut the door in your face if I wanted to. What *has* happened to you? Have you had an identity crisis? You went looking for your original family? Go and live with them then, go and live in some tin-pot neighbourhood and leave us all in peace! You'd be capable of that, just to get me off your back, wouldn't you? You think I don't see how your face twists with disgust when you introduce me as your wife? How you're always comparing me to other people's wives? When have you ever said an affectionate word to me in public? When? And when you do say something at home, it sounds as if you've memorised it from one of those books you lock yourself in the bathroom to read! Sir is ashamed of his wife, Sir could have done better. Do me a favour! Have you looked at yourself in the mirror lately? In those clothes with no teeth you can tell a mile off just what you are! Or do you think you're the only one here who was forced to get hitched at gunpoint? You think I set you a trap, you think I was dying for it? Mummy and Daddy took me on that trip to forget you, and guess what? It was easy! Until I did the pregnancy test! The night of the wedding, after you fell asleep, you know what I did? Of course you don't, because you don't give a monkey's about anyone but yourself. I spent the whole night up, crying. Crying because I'd married a man I didn't love and who didn't love me. A man who brings me the withered flowers they sell at traffic lights, so he won't have to stop at a proper florist's! A man who's never given me a single orgasm in my life!' At this Marroné covered the ears of little Tommy, who went on chanting his litany of 'Papi! Papi! Papi!', then pointed with his eyes at the doorway, which was filled by the chuckling bulk of Doña Ema, who seemed to find the scene as enormously entertaining as her afternoon soap. 'What? You're worried about Doña Ema hearing? You think we haven't discussed any of this before? If I'm still on my feet and not in a mental asylum, it's thanks to her, not you, I can assure you!'

Marroné would have liked to say about himself all the derogatory things he knew the other person was thinking or wanted to say or intended to say, but Mabel had beaten him to it, and as he was still a little dazed and couldn't quite remember if the rule was about pleasing others, or getting others to think like you, he said instead, solemnly, to sober her up, 'Sr Tamerlán is dead.'

'Of course he's dead! He was killed in cold blood because you weren't capable of getting together a few shitty little busts! What good are you? And what'll happen to the company now? Are they going to close? Will you get the sack for being a waste of space? All we need now is for you to lose your job. So I'm telling you, Ernesto Marroné, if you're thinking of playing the race card to worm out of your family obligations you've got another thing coming. You'll pay alimony and maintenance on the dot or I'll have you thrown in jail.'

All of this Marroné listened to in such silence and with such patience that he appeared not to be a man of flesh and bone but a statue of stone. With stones such as these was the path of the executive-errant strewn. On wicked ears fall deaf words, as the saying goes; those blinded by their bourgeois consciousness would never understand, just like sparrows when the condor squawks. In short, honey is not made for the ass's mouth.

'Are you listening to anything I'm saying, Ernesto Marroné? Haven't you anything to say for yourself?'

'I need a minute to . . . er . . . you know.'

'Now? Do you take me for a complete idiot? Are you having me on?'

'Señora, the baby's crying,' the voice of Doña Ema intervened angelically from the floor above them, whither she'd departed minutes earlier.

'You haven't heard the last of this, Ernesto Marroné; this is just the beginning,' threatened Mabel as he climbed the stairs, holding the boy by the hand.

This was his window of opportunity. Making a whistle-stop raid on his shelves, he grabbed his copy of *Don Quixote: The Executive-Errant*, whose spine jutted out a little further than the rest, dived into the downstairs guest *toilette* and bolted the door. They'd have to send in the tanks if they wanted to get him out now; his empire may not have been vast, but it was at least his, and in it he was the lord and

343

master of himself; with that and a stimulating book in his hands, he thought, as he adjusted his buttocks in the familiar hollows, he wanted for nothing more, and with a deep sigh his whole body relaxed into the seat. He looked forward to a short transaction, followed by some reading to crown the satisfaction of the successful mission, but, after a couple of tries, he realised it wasn't going to be as easy as he'd thought. Perhaps his body needed some time to absorb the news that the finger that had tormented him for so long (in the company of its nine fellows) was gone for ever. He was in no hurry, in any case; not now that he was finally home. He opened the book at a random page and it turned out to be exactly the one he was looking for. 'Things are getting better already, see?' he said to his imaginary audience before starting to read:

END OF PART ONE

It is not all roses in the life of the executive-errant, explains Sancho to his wife in the tender speeches they exchange once he is at home again; it is very true that most adventures do not turn out to a man's satisfaction so much as he would desire, for, of every hundred encountered, ninety-nine are likely to be troublesome and untoward. So our Don Quixote has been returned to his village against his will, locked away like a lion or a bear in the cramped confines of a cage, not able even to relieve himself. It would all seem to suggest that the evil enchanters, who delight in thwarting his triumphs and in stirring up bad blood between him and his jealous Dulcinea,

Lady of the Market, have been victorious yet again,
delivering him defenceless into the hands of mediocre men who are envious of his fame and genius; and
it is true that both he and his faithful squire have
yet to see their hopes fulfilled: the long-awaited vice
presidency continues to elude Sancho (though his
sack runs over with jingling gold coins), while Don
Quixote is still far from his CEO's throne, and the
tangible and abiding love of Dulcinea, Lady of the
Market. But it is not for nothing that our hero has
travelled the ways of business, breaking down obstacles to free enterprise, tilting at challenges from the
competition and confronting market giants, removing bureaucratic hurdles and, above all, applying
creative solutions to our ever-changing reality. No,
the ingenious Don Quixote shall not sit quietly by;
yes, the executive-errant shall wander on. Just like
the modern manager returning from a business
trip in his plane, Don Quixote in his cage looks
into his accounts: the results may not have been
what he expected, but no matter. For he has tested
his strength and discovered he can be the man he
has dreamt of being; he has realised another life is
possible; and, above all, he has tasted the forbidden
fruit of adventure. And as he returns to hearth and
home to recoup his strength in the warmth of his
family's bosom, he looks forward to the time when
he will make a second sally and depart in search of
adventures new.*

---

* To be continued in: *A Yuppie in Che Guevara's Column.*

Dear readers,

We rely on subscriptions from people like you to tell these other stories – the types of stories most publishers consider too risky to take on.

Our subscribers don't just make the books physically happen. They also help us approach booksellers, because we can demonstrate that our books already have readers and fans. And they give us the security to publish in line with our values, which are collaborative, imaginative and 'shamelessly literary'.

All of our subscribers:

- receive a first-edition copy of each of the books they subscribe to
- are thanked by name at the end of these books
- are warmly invited to contribute to our plans and choice of future books

BECOME A SUBSCRIBER, OR GIVE A SUBSCRIPTION TO A FRIEND

Visit andotherstories.org/subscribe to become part of an alternative approach to publishing.

Subscriptions are:

£20 for two books per year
£35 for four books per year
£50 for six books per year

OTHER WAYS TO GET INVOLVED

If you'd like to know about upcoming events and reading groups (our foreign-language reading groups help us choose books to publish, for example) you can:

- join the mailing list at: andotherstories.org/join-us
- follow us on Twitter: @andothertweets
- join us on Facebook: facebook.com/AndOtherStoriesBooks
- follow our blog: andotherstoriespublishing.tumblr.com

Current & Upcoming Books

Title: *The Adventure of the Busts of Eva Perón*
Author: Carlos Gamerro
Translator: Ian Barnett
Editor: Ana Fletcher
Copy-editor: Bella Whittington
Proofreader: Alexander Middleton
Typesetter: Tetragon, London
Typeface: Linotype Swift Neue / Verlag
Cover Design: Hannah Naughton
Format: Trade paperback with French flaps
Paper: Munken LP Opaque 70/15 FSC
Printer: TJ International Ltd, Padstow, Cornwall, UK